John Osborne was born in Fulham on 12 December 1929, the only son of an uneasy marriage between a Welsh commercial artist and a champion barmaid. He was educated erratically at various suburban schools and at a very minor public school in Devon. After being expelled he became a reporter on *Gas World*, stumbled into the theatre as an Assistant Stage Manager with a touring production of *No Room at the Inn* and spent several years as an actor in various repertory companies until *Look Back in Anger* was presented at the Royal Court Theatre on 8 May 1956. Since then he has written over twenty-five plays for the theatre and for television and won an Oscar for his screenplay of *Tom Jones*. He now lives in Kent.

JOHN OSBORNE

A Better Class of Person

AN AUTOBIOGRAPHY
1929 - 1956

PENGUIN BOOKS

Penguin Books Ltd, Harmondsworth, Middlesex, England
Penguin Books, 625 Madison Avenue, New York, New York 10022, U.S.A.
Penguin Books Australia Ltd, Ringwood, Victoria, Australia
Penguin Books Canada Ltd, 2801 John Street, Markham, Ontario, Canada L3R 1B4
Penguin Books (N.Z.) Ltd, 182–190 Wairau Road, Auckland 10, New Zealand

First published by Faber and Faber 1981
Published in Penguin Books 1982

Made and printed in Great Britain by
Richard Clay (The Chaucer Press) Ltd, Bungay, Suffolk
Set in Monophoto Ehrhardt

To Helen

Contents

Illustrations

A Better Class of Person

1. *No Pride in Real Gentry*

May 8th is the one unforgettable feast in my calendar. My father, Thomas Godfrey Osborne, was born in Newport, Monmouthshire, on May 8th. Had he lived he would now be the age of the century. The Second World War ended on 8 May 1945, a date which now passes as unremembered as 4 August 1914. On 8 May 1956, my first play to be produced in London, *Look Back in Anger*, had its opening at the Royal Court Theatre. This last particular date seems to have become fixed in the memories of theatrical historians.

In the summer of 1938 my father was compelled to give up his job through ill-health. He was a copywriter in an advertising agency in Shoe Lane, right beside the *Daily Express*. I was not sure what a copywriter was as my mother always insisted that he was an 'artist'. He had been given an imitation-oak clock and twenty pounds, which he spent taking us to his favourite seaside resort, Margate. A few weeks later the three of us stood on the Continental platform at Victoria Station waiting for the train to leave to take him on his way to a sanatorium in Menton. We stood there, in the way of these lifetime farewells, each impatient to see it over quickly. My mother was biting her long-gone finger nails, dressed in one of her all-one-colour 'rig-outs'. He leant out of the railway carriage, gave me a ten-shilling note and said, 'Take your mother to the pictures, son, and then go to Lyons Corner House.' The train drew out, and his head soon vanished into the carriage. Even I knew that the trappings of glamorous departure were taking him to an exile of pain of some sort and little hope or comfort whatsoever. My mother and I went to Lyons Corner House and then to a West End cinema for the first time, the newly opened Warner in Leicester Square. The film was *The Adventures of Robin Hood* with Errol Flynn. It banished the sight of my father's disappearing head for the rest of the day and some of the next.

I forget faces quickly, often alarmingly so. The images of people with whom I have spent long, intimate months, years even, become easily blurred, almost as if a deliberate act of censoring evasion takes place either through me or by some strange agency. But my father's appearance, even at this remove of forty years, is as clear as if I had seen him only a week ago.

His hair was almost completely white (at this time he would have been thirty-eight), but it had been that colour since he was in his early twenties. His skin was extremely pale, almost transparent. He had the whitest hands I think I have ever seen; Shalimar hands he called them. ('Pale hands I love beside the Lethe waters', of Shalimar. It was one of his favourite Sunday ballads.) The fingers were very long and, in contrast to the whiteness of the rest of the hand, the tips of every one were stained burnt ochre from years of Players Pleasing. His suit—as I remember he had only one, blue-striped suit—was usually unpressed but he was meticulous about the state of his cuffs and particularly his collars. The rest of his costume was unvariable: a rather greasy bowler hat and a mac which, on his insistence, was never sent to the cleaners although my mother once threw it, to his distress, into the dustbin. The edges of the collar and sleeves were an ingrained, shiny, mourning black, but his papery shoes were always brightly polished. In all, he must have seemed a little like a Welsh-sounding, prurient, reticent investigator of sorts from a small provincial town.

'As each of us looks back into his or her past, doors open upon darkness.'
E. M. Forster

In an essay on racial purity, Forster puts down this challenge:

Can you give the names of your eight great-grandparents?
The betting is at least eight to one against. The Royal Family could, some aristocrats could, and so could a few yeomen who have lived undisturbed in a quiet corner of England for a couple of hundred years. But most of the people I know (and probably most of the people who read these words) will fail.
... Two doors at first—the father and the mother—through each of these two more, then the eight great-grandparents, the sixteen great-greats, then thirty-two ancestors ... sixty-four ... one hundred and twenty-eight ... until the researcher reels.

'Racial Exercise', 1939

Most of the detail of my family background comes from hearsay. From dropped remarks, endlessly repeated anecdote, a roundabout of jokes, songs, moral stories, hints, gossip, conspiracies, implication, hymns. Just as children demand your instant familiarity with what is known only to them, you were expected at an early age to be able to identify members of the family—on both sides—even the dead. There were dark places in the filial landscape where figures would appear in a blazing memory of innuendo. This was especially so with my father's family, the Osbornes. There were

14

my grandfather's brothers, all thrashed regularly with a cane in their nightshirts by my great-grandmother. A widow, with four sons, she seemed to have come from what my mother called 'moneyed people'. 'There's no pride in real gentry,' she'd say. My great-grandmother was clearly proud, not Gentry but definitely Trade.

I spent years of unforced, curious listening in my boyhood, trying to establish hard details about what any of them actually *did* or were, but information was difficult to come by. It was rather like saying to a singer of ancient ballads, 'Yes, but what were the real *facts*?' Their memories were fixed in a chain of images, scraps of conversations, swift allusions to people or occasions which were dangled before you in the deft way of someone who has access to things you will never know nor understand. They were enjoined to their own past and a little with the present, in so far as it affected their comfort and prospect. Recall was minute, examination perfunctory. They were like actors in a long run. The past held little mystery, the present only passing interest. As for the future, it was something to be dismissed with some holy satisfaction. 'I shan't be here to see it.'

Throughout my childhood no adult ever addressed a question to me. When I was at boarding school, when I went out to work, until the day she died when I was thirty, my father's mother never once asked me anything about myself. I think she had a glancing fondness for me. If I volunteered information, she would smile a thin winter of contempt and say nothing. Or change the subject firmly. To how well my cousin Tony was doing at Sandhurst. How her niece Jill was engaged to such a nice young man. Who had been to Blundells School and had a very high position in Lloyds Bank in Lombard Street. I was convinced that her dismissive smile was aimed only to chill my father's coffin yet again.

2. Uncalled-for Remarks

PHOEBE: I remember once my Mum promised to take us kids to the pantomime, and then something happened, she couldn't take us. I don't know what it was, she didn't have the money I expect. You could sit up in the gallery then for sixpence. Poor old Mum—she took us later, but it didn't seem the same to me. I was too disappointed. I'd been thinking about that pantomime for weeks. You shouldn't build things up. You're always disappointed really. That's Archie's trouble. He always builds everything up. And it never turns out.

The Entertainer, 1957

Fulham Palace Road was the first identifiable landscape of my life. A lady to whom I was once married described me without humour or affection as a Welsh Fulham upstart. I must say that I didn't mind the description at all. For one thing, it seemed accurate enough even if meant unkindly.

Fulham in the 1930s was a dismal district. It sprawled roughly across an area, at least as far as my territory was concerned, from Hammersmith to Chelsea to Walham Green—as it was then called, it is now Fulham Broadway—to Putney Bridge at the other end. It was full of pubs, convents, second-hand clothes shops, bagwash laundries and pawnbrokers. Everything seemed very broken down.

I was born at Number 2 Crookham Road off the Dawes Road, which is between Lillie Road and Fulham Broadway. Even today, with the odd Italian restaurant and boutique, the area is gloomy and uninteresting. The boundaries of my earliest territory extended from Hammersmith Broadway with its clattering trams and drunken Irishmen to the Fulham Palace Road, a long road leading to Putney Bridge. On the left there is a huge cemetery (containing first my sister and then my father), a stonemason's scrapyard of broken tombstones and dead daffodils in milk bottles. It stretches as far as Fulham Broadway, where my mother would walk past my sister's grave on her way to pay the bill at the Gas, Light and Coke Company and my father took me to the old Granville Theatre or dropped in at Lyons for his favourite black coffee and brown bread and butter on the way to his regular visits to Brompton Hospital.

On the right of Fulham Palace Road is a succession of identical streets, Victorian terraced houses with strange little gnarled cigar stubs of trees lining the pavements. A most depressing red-brick church stands on the right and here, in Harbord Street, my mother's mother—Grandma Grove—lived for some forty years. When I last visited this street it was to go to a party given by a successful young actor. He had just moved into a house a few doors away from where my grandmother had lived for so many years. He is very like most of his neighbours who now live in that resolutely unprepossessing area, backing as it does on to the Fulham Football Ground and Bishop's Park, which still has a little green Victorian bandstand. My mother, living apart from my father, and I lodged in a succession of digs in some seven or eight streets by the Fulham bank of the Thames: Harbord Street, Finlay Street, Ellerby Street, Donerail Street. She was always moving because the house was 'a dead-and-alive hole', and she would inevitably have had a row with the landlady.

The actor's house was just round the corner from my first school, Finlay Road Infants, where, as was my experience at every new school, I was casually beaten up in the playground on the first day. The actor had paid £15,000 for it. My grandmother paid eight shillings a week rent. She had no bathroom. The corridor from the front door into the kitchen was cold and gloomy and covered in a very metallic claret and gold linoleum. I could just make out the inscription on the wall of an illuminated address presented to my grandfather: 'To William Crawford Grove with All Best wishes and Gratitude from all His Customers at the Marquis of Granby, Peckham Rye.' The front parlour was even less inviting, looking on to Harbord Street with the blank walls of the Football Ground visible at the far end and tall cranes from the barges stooping over them like iron giraffes. Sometimes, when I was staying there, I would have to sleep in this alarming room with its musty smell of a disused sanctuary for small animals. On the wall above the mantelpiece was a picture of my grandfather's Uncle Arthur. It looked rather like a Gothic Spy cartoon. He was regarded with great respect by the family and was said to be a director of Abdulla cigarettes.

My grandfather's background was fairly misty, like the rest. He claimed that he and his brother had gone to Dulwich College. Whether it was true or not I don't know. My grandmother might or might not have told me. Below Uncle Arthur's picture was a gilt ornamental clock in a glass case and, beside this, photographs of soldiers with fierce moustaches, relatives too, possibly.

17

There were lace mats everywhere, an aspidistra in the window, which was shrouded with heavy lace curtains keeping out what little light ever filtered in from the cold length of Harbord Street. The dining-room was a different matter. Although it was shrouded in the same curtains, it hardly mattered as there was no light to come through from the view of the wall of the house next door and electricity burned all the winter and summer. The table in the centre was cheerfully lit with a low red-tasselled lamp, the chairs were old and comfortable, particularly my grandfather's which no one else ventured to sit in. The gas fire, with its saucer of water set before it, burned almost continuously, drinking innumerable shillings and coppers fed into it from a most imposing gas meter sited on the top of a cupboard. My grandmother, who was a tiny woman, fed this god by perching on a chair like a watchful acolyte. My grandfather would never have got up to do it, even if it went out when he was alone in the house. The scullery was a grey-green brown, the sort of thing one might associate with a Victorian mortuary. There was a bare table and, of course, a gas stove. The room was almost empty and scrubbed clean.

Grandma Grove's past was shadowy, too. Her maiden name was Ell. Her relatives were referred to somewhat contemptuously as the Tottenham Crowd. It was hinted—as everything was *hinted*—that old Mr Ell was a Wesleyan minister. But, in the face of such theological vagueness and innuendo, it was impossible to establish anything beyond approximate truth about these matters. The Tottenham Crowd, or some of them, lived beside the fire station in a row of villas long since demolished. They were dominated by my grandmother's eldest sister, Auntie Min. She was a very gloomy woman who appeared to spend much of her time collecting milk bottles, putting out milk bottles and complaining about the milkman. Her husband, Uncle Harry, was retired and had been a stoker in the Royal Navy. He said very little but was friendly enough, encouraging me to talk to his ferocious cockatoo. Then there was Grandma Ell, my great-grandmother, who was extremely old, something like a hundred. My mother's family seem to achieve great age. My grandmother lived to be 103 and my own mother seems appropriately hell bent on a similar score.

Before my great-grandmother's funeral, her coffin was placed in the middle of a table on trestles in the front parlour. On another table were the funeral baked meats of ham salad and sandwiches. One of her sons, Uncle Lod, was an undertaker. He was very tall, thin, taciturn and had a reputation for getting wildly drunk at the weekends and becoming involved in fights. It was he, I think, who lifted me up—I was four or five at the time—to look into the coffin where my great-grandmother lay in what seemed unthinkable luxury. Then there was Auntie Rose, who had the reputation of being some sort of ill-used beauty, but was very sullen and not very beautiful. She, too, had a husband who said very little, just like Uncle Harry. There was Uncle Henry, who, as far as I could make out, was Auntie Rose's father. The same story about him was repeated to me like all my family's anecdotes, and my mother's in particular, endlessly. It seemed that he was a well-known musician in Tottenham and played the piano with such loudly proclaimed feeling that crowds used to assemble outside his house to hear him. In the evenings, policemen had to be called to disperse them. He was said to have been one of the resident conductors at the Crystal Palace. His story, which made clear that he was a mysteriously unhappy man, was that one evening his wife asked him if he would deliver the children's shoes to be mended on his way to the Crystal Palace. He took them with him and they were later found on the line of the tube station. Uncle Henry had thrown himself in front of the train. No one ever questioned why he should have committed suicide in this way. The legend was enough.

Auntie Winnie, another of my grandmother's sisters, lived and worked all her life in a north London hospital. She was friendlier than any of them and I can remember her always sitting with a glass of stout or port. Most of them did. She called everyone 'mate', men and women. I don't know why it struck me as odd. She had very little hair and never married. Her affectionate nature didn't seem to be returned by her sisters who dismissed her with, 'Poor old Auntie Winn, she'll never leave that place.' No one made any effort to see that she might. They were all pushy in their way, tolerating one another peevishly rather than having any actual exchange of feelings. If one of them died, fell ill or short of money it was something to be talked about rather than experienced in common. It was as if they felt obliged to live within the literal confines of their emotional circumstances. The outlet for friendship or conviviality was narrow in spite of the drunken commiseration, endless ports and pints of beer and gin and Its. This may in part explain my mother's stillborn spontaneity and consistent calculation that affection had only to be bought or repaid in the commonest coinage. 'He doesn't owe you anything', or 'You don't owe him anything.' 'What's she ever done for you?' These were the entries that cooked the emotional and filial books. They were chill words, flaunting their loveless, inexorable impotence.

My grandfather would talk at great length and vehemently about Oscar Wilde and Lord Alfred Douglas without ever revealing to me what the whole affair was really about. For some reason, Lord Alfred Douglas seemed to escape censure. Possibly being a lord helped. In this obsession, my grandfather was of course a stock figure of the time. There was a similar scandal involving the Duke of Clarence and messenger boys which also intrigued him. In my father's family identical waxen figures were brought out and maintained unchallenged by mere curiosity, to be left intact in the common memory, sometimes not much more than names—like the Princes in the Tower, or Auntie Margery; like the Lady of Shalott, or Uncle Ted; like Horatio Bottomley, or Lord Alfred Douglas. They were all, public and private, creatures of personal legend.

In Harbord Street people were nailed to the edges of public events. For example, my grandmother had some knowing significance contained in the fact that she had been a waitress at the Franco-British Exhibition. It fixed her into a place in history rather as one marks out one's life in terms of Coronations or Royal Weddings or Churchill's Funeral or moments of national ritual. Perhaps most people check their private memories against such occasions just as I tally my daily life with the dates of plays I have had produced. I know, for example, a little of what I was doing in 1961 because *Luther* was produced in that year. Events match themselves.

> She is a tough, sly old Cockney, with a harsh, often cruel wit, who knows how to beat the bailiffs and the money-lenders which my grandfather managed to bring on to her. Almost every working day of her life, she has got up at five o'clock to go out to work, to walk down what has always seemed to me to be the most hideous and coldest street in London. Sometimes when I have walked with her, all young bones and shiver, she has grinned at me, her face blue with what I thought was cold. 'I never mind the cold—I like the wind in my face.' She'd put her head down, hold on to her hat and *push*.
>
> *They Call it Cricket* ('Declaration'), 1957

As a result of this, as I thought flattering description of Grandma Grove, some of her family threatened to sue me on the grounds of libel. An extract had been published in some Sunday newspaper like the *People* and did perhaps appear patronizing. In her early sixties she was very small and very round-shouldered, which made her little more than about five feet tall. Her movements were quick, unlike Grandma Osborne who was tall, straight-backed and moved slowly and with schoolmarm precision. Like both her sisters, and, indeed the rest of the Tottenham Crowd, she was dressed at that time during the thirties almost exactly as she must have been thirty years before: her straw hats, the flowers, her wispy hair long and resting up above her head, the very long skirts almost to the ankle, and the boots, the smell of lavender water and moth balls, a brooch at the high neck collar—all these were Edwardian, which I accepted as part of her character.

She was born Adelina Rowena Ell. At eighteen she married my grandfather who was nineteen, and they quickly had two children. The first, my aunt, Queenie Phoebe Adelina Rowena Grove. Then, eighteen months later, my mother Nellie Beatrice. There were hints of deaths in childbirth which I indeed believe were true and talk of puerperal fever, or 'prooperal', as they called it. Eight years later my Uncle Jack—John Henry—was born. My grandfather, as young William Crawford Grove, was said to be the Smartest Publican in London, becoming manager at an early age of a pub in Duncannon Street, alongside St Martin-in-the-Fields. The name of the pub was simply the Duncannon and it is still there, a rather anonymous fluorescent place clearly quite unlike the fashionable hostelry it had been during my grandparents' tenure. It was frequented by theatrical folk a good deal, including Marie Lloyd. A central part of the folklore of this period of their life was that my grandmother, pregnant with my mother, came down the stairs of the Duncannon one morning to find Miss Lloyd reeling around the sawdust-covered bar swearing and shouting. My grandmother drew herself up and ordered the doorman to escort Miss Lloyd out and hail her a hansom cab. Whereupon, the story continued, Miss Lloyd screamed up the stairs at the young mother-to-be, 'Don't you fucking well talk to me! I've just left your old man after a weekend in Brighton!' I don't know whether this part of the Ballad of Grandma is true, but it has an encouraging ring of tinsel fact about it. Anyway, it makes a nice family tableau, and is also the only recorded link I have with anything to do with the theatrical profession.

Profligacy seems to have been a strong characteristic with both my grandfathers, although Grandpa Grove was a far stronger, flamboyant personality than Grandpa Osborne, who lost the jeweller's shop entrusted to him by his mother because he 'Played cricket all day' when he 'Should have been in the shop'. When I knew him he had retreated into the role of unpaid family retainer, gardener and odd-job man, despised openly by his family for not getting work, and doing menial tasks about the house, like packing his daughter's trunks for her trips to Africa. He was goaded into perfunctory trips to the Labour Exchange but his heart was never in it. Hurt, I am sure he was. Grandpa Grove would never have been hurt. No one would have dared to jeer at him in the first place.

When I first knew her, Grandma Grove worked as an office cleaner in the main office of Woolworth's, which was then in Cork Street. She had become head cleaner after a few years and was in command of some thirty or forty women, her 'girls' as she called them. I don't think she did a great deal of actual cleaning herself, but acted as a sort of motherly sergeant major, reserving the top directors' offices with their flaming turkey carpets and heavy furniture for herself. She held this job until shortly after the war, often walking to work in the early hours of the morning when the Blitz had been particularly fierce, threading her way through rubble and glass, almost like a cartoonist's Cockney: 'We can take it!' Sometimes she took me up to Cork Street and I would sit in the staff room with its faded rattan chairs, surrounded by her admiring 'girls', who would feed me on all kinds of cakes, buns and sweets. They also gave me money, from pennies to threepenny bits and sixpences. By the end of the day my reward was considerable. Why they gave it to me was mysterious. They all had kids of their own. I must have been a mascot or something. Anyway, I was pleased if unsurprised.

This friendly, rather cloying treatment from young women as well as middle-aged ones, may have been partly due to the way that my mother insisted on dressing me for such public occasions. My uniform consisted of a suit, silk in summer or some kind of artificial silk which was extremely uncomfortable and seemed to be perpetually wet, and in a self-proclaiming bright colour like pink, yellow, or what my mother insisted on calling 'lemon'. All ensembles like this, including my own, she declared to be 'rig-outs'. She planned them down to the last detail, going through phases of passionate attachment to certain colours or materials. She would have, for example, a coral and nigger-brown period, or a blue and lemon period. Everything matched inexorably. There was one period of tan mania. The seven ages of tan. 'I'm going to get myself a tan hat, tan shoes, tan handbag'—tan *everything*.

The snooking badge of bohemianism in my own rig-out was the black beret that she insisted on my wearing. This had originally been a practical innovation when I had a mastoid operation and my head was almost entirely shaved. The beret did indeed cover up what she called 'my unslightly head'. She regarded almost everything about me as irredeemably unsightly, bald or not. However, the beret did attract attention, and it appealed slightly to my early rather coarse, dandyish instincts. I may have consciously cultivated what I thought of as a kind of quiet, serious-looking charm. A lot of people must have seen through it as a mere fawning wish to impress. I always wanted to get on with adults, to have access to the mysteries and excitements of their lives, which held out so much more promise than that of children of my own age. There was no cachet in youth at that time. One was merely a failed adult. I sought out the company of people like my grandparents and great-aunts and -uncles; they were infinitely more interesting. And I was an eager and attentive listener.

BILLY RICE is a spruce man in his seventies. He has great physical pride, the result of a life-time of being admired as a 'fine figure of a man'. He is slim, upright, athletic. He glows with scrubbed well-being. His hair is just grey, thick and silky from its vigorous daily brush. His clothes are probably twenty-five years old—including his pointed patent leather shoes—but well-pressed and smart. His watch chain gleams, his collar is fixed with a tie-pin beneath the tightly knotted black tie, his brown homburg is worn at a very slight angle. When he speaks it is with a dignified Edwardian diction—a kind of repudiation of both Oxford and Cockney that still rhymes 'cross' with 'force', and yet manages to avoid being exactly upper-class or effete. Indeed, it is not an accent of class but of period. One does not hear it often now.

The Entertainer, 1957

Indeed, one does not. This description (I used to shower my scripts with irrelevant stage directions; *Look Back in Anger* is full of them) is a part-portrait of my grandfather.

BILLY: We all had our own style, our own songs—and we were all English. What's more, we spoke English. It was different. We all knew what the rules were. We knew what the rules were, and even if we spent half our time making people laugh at 'em we never seriously suggested that anyone should break them. A real pro is a real man, all he needs is an old backcloth behind him and he can hold them on his own for half an hour. He's like the general run of people, only he's a lot more like them than they are themselves, if you understand me.

The Entertainer, 1957

Grandpa Grove certainly had his own style, but unlike Billy Rice he could not be regarded as having been a star, except in a very small way at the height of his career as a publican, when there were hansom cabs, cigars and his famous breakfast which was said to have consisted of half a bottle of 3-star brandy, a pound of porterhouse steak, oysters in season and a couple of chorus girls all year round.

Under the mantelshelf in Harbord Street there was one of those fringe-like curtain arrangements which failed to conceal his trusses, or 'trusts' as my mother called them, which I would gaze at while he talked about Henry Irving in *The Bells* and bawled various bits of the Old Testament at me. He was always dressed, apart from a well-worn cardigan, as if ready to go out at any moment. His patent shoes, cleaned by my grandmother, gleamed as did his hair and watch chain. He would sit toying with his sovereign case or buffing his carefully attended finger nails. He was the only man I met until I was in my late teens who habitually used a cigarette holder, usually containing Abdulla Egyptian cigarettes, doubtless cadged from Uncle Arthur.

He was most impressive, and convincing, in the way he would roll out names: names of stars as if they were either personal friends or members of his club—which he said was the National Sporting Club—Sir Edward Carson or Rufus Isaacs. Like so many people at that time he took as much interest in law-court proceedings as people do nowadays in football or pop singers and indeed the success charts of lawyers were followed in awe by the British public. It was not a matey, familiar business but a show laid on for the common people by their superiors and masters. His account of Carson's cross-examination of Oscar Wilde was one of his specialities. So it was, too, with King Edward, admired for his flash friends and racehorses and, later, the next Prince of Wales, once admired and then to be reviled after his disgrace with Mrs Simpson. There was constant invocation of the Lord Chief Justice, almost greater than God in his infinite wisdom and power; the Aga Khan ('Mum always likes me to put a shilling on the Black Man's horses'). Lord Beaverbrook was a particular favourite because Grandpa had seen him once emerging from his Rolls Royce: 'One of the finest men in England today.' He seemed to know everything about him. 'When I was with Beaverbrook during that time ...' he would say. He had worked as a canvasser in the north of England for the *Daily Express*, a miserable commission job which only the most desperate unemployed took on. Flushed with port and excitement, I would listen as he told me that he would live to see the day when one of two things would happen: one, I would be the Prime Minister of England; or, two, I would be the next George Bernard Shaw. His reverence for Shaw was almost as extreme as his hostility to Gandhi. As he disagreed grandiloquently with almost everything that Shaw ever uttered on any subject, except the benevolence of dictatorships, this was confusing.

When we visited the Groves, the rest of the family would be literally yelling news to each other. My grandmother would come in and out of the kitchen, picking exactly the wrong moment to interrupt my grandfather. I would be the only one listening to him, but then I was the only one who seemed to listen to anybody. They didn't talk to each other so much as barrack themselves. He would yell some humiliation or, if she were sitting near enough, kick her, imperceptibly but expertly, under the table. He was most adroit at this. Beside him on the dark red tablecloth would be the Bible, the *News of the World* and the *People*, the *Empire News* and, in later years, the *Watch Tower*. He would read from these aloud and everyone was

24

expected to listen. 'Now, hold your bloody noise while I'm talking and put the wood in th'ole.' He had an obsession with draughts and none of the windows was ever allowed to be opened. The gas fire was on summer and winter and often it was quite difficult to breathe through the haze of Abdulla, as he boomed his police-court rhetoric, invariably berating some Draconian judge for not giving a severe enough sentence, especially in cases concerned with sex. 'Bloody rogue, dirty bastard, rogue! Fourteen years! Men like that should be hanged. Worse!' Worse than hanging was God's word to Grandpa in such matters.

When I was dismissed from his presence or he was bored or tired, I would follow my grandmother into the tiny scullery and get a slice of 'dinner' (called 'chaw'; she was particularly good at dishes like braised heart, stewed eel and faggots). There would then be a lot of winking and whispering. 'Dirty old bugger,' she'd say. 'I don't like to think what *he'd* get. Do you know he has women in here every day when I'm at work? At *his* age.' He was then about seventy and was constantly seeking out and finding the rent money, insurance money or gas money that my grandmother had hidden away, to spend on taking one of his 'women' out for stout and oysters at the Clarendon in Hammersmith. Grandma Grove was ingenious in the way she discovered the addresses of these ladies and took a great deal of pleasure in hunting them down to their various houses. They all called themselves Mrs Grove when she confronted them at the door. I don't think any of them lasted for very long. She was understandably keen on recounting her triumph over Marie Lloyd and of casting her into the outer darkness of Duncannon Street. 'Of course, *he* doesn't know *we* know about it,' eased the pain in her shin bone. Happy recrimination and ill-feeling were never very far below the surface.

Religion was rather baffling. Auntie Queenie was very High Church, my father professed sickly atheism, and my mother never went to church at all. I was rather mystified by the meaning of all this, but it appeared to be something very exclusive and beyond the grasp of most. It was my mother who was the main antagonist in these matters, particularly during the brawls of Christmas, when she reacted fiercely to Auntie Queenie's over-heated and sentimental religiosity. Queenie assumed a royal, wounded aspect when these periodic fits came upon her. Even at that age I sensed that it was a very bogus performance indeed. In her most gushing periods of zealous charity she would use theatrical convent language, calling everyone, people like bus conductors and shop assistants, 'Dearest Heart', in the way that some priests matily invoke the Sacred Heart of Jesus.

Certainly, Auntie Queenie never felt any pernickity Anglican constraint.

Over her bed there hung not only a large cream-coloured crucifix but an even more prominent figure of the Virgin Mary. Also beside her bed was a white Common Prayer Book. Whether she used another one for her visits to church I don't know, but it was certainly new and unthumbed-looking. The basis of her belief seemed to consist of what she believed to be her capacity for more suffering than others and, in particular, the coarser members of her family. She had been brought up by a doting aunt and this apparently contributed to her feeling herself well above what should have been her natural station of Harbord Street. My mother was particularly resentful at this show of swank travail. The two of them would match suffering for suffering, pain for pain, blow for blow, strolling down separate memory lanes on to rival vales of tears. My mother pointed out that her sister's privations were nothing compared with her own. *She* had none of the advantages of being educated properly but of going out to work at the age of twelve to scrub a dining-room floor for six hundred orphans at the Foundling Hospital. This was no doubt true, and certainly no one ever contradicted her. She, my mother, had by her own efforts become head cashier at the age of sixteen of Lyons Corner House in the Strand. Queenie, on the other hand, had been levered by her pious, protective Auntie Phoebe, into an undemanding ladylike job, first in a milliner's then as a draper's assistant, becoming under-buyer and then head buyer at D. H. Evans. It was a common secret that she had been dismissed from this appointment when she was discovered taking home the firm's latest models and wearing them, not always temporarily it seemed. Later, at Peter Robinson's, she was similarly apprehended. She ended her career working in a small Jewish Madam shop in Richmond High Street. It was a cruel blow to her pride and most enjoyable for my mother to visit her there, taking hours to make up her mind what she might buy from her sister, now that she was no more than a small-time head assistant.

Comfort in the discomfort of others was an abiding family recreation and my grandmother shared her barmaid daughter's satisfaction. After all, she too had come down in the world, relegated to head cleaner of Woolworth's from being Mistress of the Duncannon and the Hammer of the Marie Lloyds of this world. Coming Down in the World was something the Groves had in common with the Osbornes, except that the Groves seemed to feel less sense of grievance, looking on it as the justified price of profligate living or getting above yourself, rather than as a cruel trick of destiny or a creeping army of upstarts Getting the Better of their Betters. Still, getting above yourself is a hazard open to many of us still and can be chastening. 'But there's no pride in Real Gentry—that's what I always say.' And they always did. They had a litany of elliptical sayings, almost biblical in their complexity, which, to the meanest mind or intelligence, combined accessibility and authority. Revealed family wisdom was expressed in sayings like, 'One door opens and another one always shuts' (the optimistic version—rare—was the same in reverse). 'I think I can say I've had my share of sorrows.' Like Jesus, they were all acquainted with grief. 'I can always read him like a book'; 'I've never owed anyone anything' (almost the Family Motto this); 'You can't get round him, he's like a Jew and his cash box'; 'Look at him, like Lockhart's elephant.' This meant someone was being inordinately clumsy, and apparently referred to a popular large bun that was sold in an establishment called Lockhart's in the Strand, long since disappeared and forgotten even then.

There were lots of references to Jews. One of my mother's favourites was, 'Listen to him, John Lawson's son. "Thank God, I'm only a Jew."' This was a reference to a very famous music-hall sketch called *Humanity*, performed by John Lawson at a time when, according to serious historians, music hall was well on the way down its pristine path to revue and 'variety'. My only link with this famous sketch was provided for me by my mother, whose memory was always definitively faulty. It was, according to her, about a highly reputable, rich and—it seemed—wholly virtuous Jew who struck up a full-hearted, passionate friendship with a Gentile who became his Best Friend. The wholesome Jew leaves home for some reason, the war perhaps, and his lovely wife in the care of Best Gentile Friend. Adultery, Close-Thing, but, most of all, Betrayal takes place before John Lawson reappears. My mother thought it good for a quick laugh to call me John Lawson's son—'Only a Jew!' As she was anti-Semitic in the sense that she thought all foreigners were Jews, it was meant unflatteringly. But she described in detail the roof-rending scene in which the Good Jew Thrashed his Best Friend. Quite apart from the horror of such untidy destruction, was the principal character—the Set. This, as she described it, consisted of a superb sitting-room, furnished in Taste-Beyond-Which. Which being mostly breakable—like ornate and irreplaceable chandeliers. Glass, blood, antiques, teeth, hair, tailoring all exploded everywhere. A ruined palace of a place, a disgraced wife, a treacherous friend, destroyed virtuous Jew. After the vicious fight between Gentile Snake and Jew, the virtuous one, bleeding in mouth, mud and spirit among all the despoil sang his song: 'Only a Jew'. Twenty years later it was this shaky fragment of theatrical memory that was to nudge me towards *The Entertainer*; not, as I was told authoritatively by others, the influence of Bertolt Brecht.

Sic: if one were looking for a word to describe the argot used generally by my mother's family and friends one might call it this; Sic—a self-conscious, disorderly babble, perhaps like Peter Brook's Orghast except that Sic is presumably more lucid and spontaneous. But only just. I grew up believing that there was a language one read in books and another one spoke, and that the divide between the two was impassable. I was in my early twenties before I realized that 'long' words could be inserted quite freely and naturally within ordinary conversation without remark or derisory comment. Talking expressively to strangers and more often intimates was perhaps the beginning of the long gritty road to addressing God Himself without hobbling embarrassment.

Queenie or, as she preferred to be called, Queen shared a flat with a friend known to me as Auntie Caddie, although her name was in fact May. Why she was called Caddie I have no idea. Perhaps it was something to do with golf as there seemed to be numerous snapshots of them together in what were then called sporting clothes. Auntie Caddie looked born to wear plus fours. She even referred to herself as a John Blunt woman ('person' hadn't occurred to her), and although most people poked fun at her, very few of them did so to her face. She always wore a tweedy suit or, rather, a 'costume', with a high collar and beefily knotted tie. She also wore Henry Heath hats which carried some authority in the name alone.

Anyway, Auntie Caddie would stand with her legs wide apart, her plump hands behind her back and boom questions at me, usually about why I wasn't at school. This was a hard one to answer and one repeatedly asked by probing adults. My mother for years kept me away from school as often as she dared on the pretext of my poor health; in reality, it was because she was bored with being on her own and needed even my childish company. Caddie and Queenie shared a Key Flat in Blythe Road, a plaster Virgin above their double bed, an Airedale and, of all unfamiliar things to come, a white telephone. There was also an intimidating porter. On the other side of Blythe Road was Cadby Hall, which was the headquarters of J. Lyons and Co., as well as being their biggest teashop. My mother and I used to have tea there before having to face the porter and Auntie Caddie. These visits were always uneasy and overpowered by the magnificence of Lyons Biggest Teashop, where I usually managed to faint, greatly to the annoyance of my mother.

These 'blooming fainting fits', as she called them, persisted for years. They nearly always seemed to happen in public places like cinemas or restaurants or where they would create the maximum of irritation and embarrassment for my mother. I was constantly taken into the offices of cinema managers after witnessing fairly innocent but distressful scenes on

28

the screen. One, I remember, was a childbirth sequence in a film called *The Citadel*, starring one of my father's favourite actors, Robert Donat. The climax involved the doctor holding up the newly-born child and slapping it into life. The spectacle was too much for me. Blood seemed to drain out of me and in no time my head would be between my knees and I would be sipping water from a kindly usherette or, in the case of Cadby Hall, waitress, who was certainly more sympathetic than my mother.

It was not until I was about sixteen that I was to have much contact with Uncle Sidney. During these Fulham days he was not much more than one of the Smaller Players of the Grove Repertory Company. As always, what little information I had was by implication and elaborately vague. Auntie Queenie, Caddie and Uncle Sidney took numerous holidays in Sidmouth together, where they all dressed in tennis clothes, consisting of white trousers, blazers and white pleated skirts. I think little tennis was played but there was a great deal of dressing up and snapping away with the Box Brownie. Even to me they presented a rather bizarre trio. Auntie Caddie with her dark flecked Eton crop, striped blazer and carefully starched collar and tie. Uncle Sidney with his Silverkrin crinkled hair, large flannel bags and very sheepish expression. And, finally, my Auntie Queenie who looked remarkably like the carefully posed theatrical photographs of Ivor Novello, with the same thin, rather accusing mouth. The first time I saw Ivor Novello in his Tyrolean *unterhosen* he immediately made me think of Auntie Queenie. She, not surprisingly, thought he too was wonderful.

The general verdict on Uncle Sidney seemed to be that he was a pretty decent sort but a bit of a cissy boy. He had his own flat, which he shared with his friend John and which was furnished almost entirely by coupons they both collected from Carreras cigarettes. After about seven years of courtship, Queenie and Uncle Sidney were married. I was later to grow quite fond of Uncle Sidney and his letters in particular.

'*Dear John*, Do so hope you have a very nice Christmas. Gosh how I wish I was with you all. I just hate the thought of it, all alone. Just had the Coalman deliver, another Bill £5. 6s. Ah well why worry. It's a rotten day here, very dull and raining. . . .

'*Dear John*, Queen seems about the same. Looks well in herself. They get her up for a while each day now, so that makes a break from Bed all the time. . . .

'*Dear John*, A few lines in haste. Don't get much time for letters these days. Was home on Spring Holiday last week, but busy with spring cleaning the home. Gave it all a good clean, Curtains down in all rooms, Windows clean, fresh Curtains put up, Ceilings, Walls cleaned, and Furniture polished, Pictures and Ornaments washed....

'*Dear John*, Queen keeps about the same, looks well in herself, but leg no better. Grandma Grove is supposed to come with Jack today to see Queen. Of course his Lordship would not write me to ask the best way. Queen has been in hospital now 6 months and he has never written me a line....

'*Dear John*, Just been doing some washing, so shall have to Iron when its all dry. Going out after that to have a little Drink, just feel I need it. Begin to get a bit fed up at home with no one to talk to, and all the work....

'*Dear John*, I used to think Mother a dear ole soul, but now realize she is as bad as the rest. Don't want to see any of them anymore. Queen goes on about the same, but tries to be the big I am, and the Sisters and Nurses have not much time for her. I've had a rotten cold in my head. Have to go to the Dr. tonight 6 pm, as my ear is bad with Wax. Hope he can get it out, and not have to go to Hospital the same as last time to see an Ear Specialist. Been busy since I've been home. My Lunch to get, then washing for Queen and myself. Just going to have a Cup of tea, then the Dr and Ironing when I get back. I feel so fed up today with it all. Do hope you are well....

'*Dear John*, Sorry I did not write you as usual on Sunday, but I felt so tired. Queen seems to be getting on quite well with the Walking Aid. She looks so well in herself, but I have to be so very careful what I say, otherwise she takes things in the wrong way. I've just been busy in the front garden, now broke off for a little rest. Have the Back to do later. Such a lot turns up to do in Gardens....

'*Dear John*, Have washing on the line, must be dry now, so have that to Iron. Nightdress, Knickers etc from the Hospital. Do hope you are keeping well. I'm alright—except for a little tired, but must get the Ironing done....

'*Dear John*, I can manage alright, just a little tired at times....

'*Dear John*, We shall be thinking of you at Christmas Day and no doubt have a little drink to your health from the Bottle of Gin we bought with your kind remittance, say 12 O/c.

All my love,
            Sidney   xxxxxxxx'

They were already self-parodies before they were popped in the box to me. I made a passable pastiche in *The Hotel in Amsterdam*, when they were singled out as being snobbish and anti-working class and apparently confirmed I did not know or understand my own background.

DAN: What are they?
LAURIE: Retired rotten, grafting publicans, shop assistants, ex-waitresses. They live on and on. Having hernias and arthritic hips and strokes. But they go on: writing poisonous letters to one another. Complaining and wheedling and paying off the same old scores with the same illiterate signs. 'Dear Laurie, thank you very kindly for the cheque. It was most welcome and I was able to get us one or two things we'd had to go without for quite some time, what with me having been off work all this time and the doctor sends me to the hospital twice a week. They tell me it's improving but I can't say I feel much improvement. How are you, old son? Old son? We saw your name in the paper about something you were doing the other day and the people next door said they thought you were on the telly one night but we didn't see it, and Rose won't buy the television papers so we always switch on to the same programme. Rose doesn't get any better, I'm afraid. I bought her a quarter bottle the other day with your kind remittance which served to buck her up a bit. Your Auntie Grace wrote and said she'd heard Margaret was having another baby. That must be very nice for you both. We send our best wishes to you both and the other little ones. Hope you're all well. Must close now as I have to take down the front room curtains and wash them as Rose can't do it any longer, but you know what she is. Bung ho and all the very best. Excuse writing but my hand is still bad. Ever. Your Uncle Ted. P.S. Rose says Auntie Grace said something about a letter from your mother which she sent on but I'm afraid she sent it back unopened. She just refuses to pass any comment. She told me not to say anything about it to you but I thought I'd just—*PASS IT ON TO YOU*!
    (*He gestures towards them.*)
    Pass that on!

The Hotel in Amsterdam, 1968

31

My Uncle Jack, eight years younger than my mother, might occasionally drop in at Harbord Street bringing with him an unusual feeling of dash and optimism. He appeared to take little part in the continuing story of Harbord Street, distributing generous presents and always leaving early with his son, Peter, a huge amiable boy who became a successful steward on the *Queen Elizabeth*. He rarely brought his first wife, Auntie Vi, known because of her swarthy appearance as the 'Gypsy Queen'. She made it quite clear that she didn't want to be mixed up in family 'squibbles'. Uncle Jack was what my mother called 'a bit woman mad'. He certainly seemed more cheerful and reassuring than either Auntie Queenie or Uncle Sidney, always bent on despondency and the theory that nothing good in this world, even if you should get it, ever lasted.

Nothing, indeed, is more revolting to English feelings, than the spectacle of a human being obtruding on our notice his moral ulcers or scars, and tearing away that 'decent drapery', which time, or indulgence to human frailty, may have drawn over them: accordingly, the greater part of *our* confessions (that is spontaneous and extra-judicial confessions) proceed from demireps, adventurers, or swindlers: and for any such acts of gratuitous self-humiliation from those who can be supposed in sympathy with the decent and self-respecting part of society, we must look to French literature, or to that part of the German, which is tainted with the spurious and defective sensibility of the French. And all this I feel so forcibly, and so nervously am I alive to reproach of this tendency, that I have for many months hesitated about the propriety of allowing this, or any part of my narrative, to come before the public eye, until after my death (when, for many reasons, the whole will be published): and it is not without an anxious review of the reasons for and against this step, that I have, at last, concluded on taking it.

Guilt and misery shrink, by a natural instinct, from public notice: they court privacy and solitude: and, even in their choice of a grave, will sometimes sequester themselves from the general population of the churchyard, as if declining to claim fellowship with the great family of man, and wishing (in the affecting language of Mr Wordsworth)

—humbly to express
A penitential loneliness.
Confessions of an English Opium Eater, Thomas de Quincey

According to my mother's shaky testimony she met my father when she was working as a barmaid in a pub called the Essex on the corner of Essex Street in the Strand: 'All the Press boys used to come in there.' Perhaps, to a young man recently up from South Wales, with no friends at work and only digs to go home to, the atmosphere of the Essex was comforting. Pubs are more than tolerable places in which to be lonely. My mother would throw bottles in the air, two bottles sometimes, catch them, throw up two more, catch them again, and pour off four bottles into four glasses at once with one hand. Soon he began talking to her about his work in the advertising agency, bringing in his drawings to show her, and they would go on to the all-night Lyons Corner House in the Strand, where she had worked as head cashier.

Living the first years of my life in Fulham meant mostly living with my mother. My parents saw little of each other. What had happened between them I have no way of knowing. My father, when he was not in Brompton Hospital or in Colindale Sanatorium, seemed to stay in digs a long way from us in Harrow or Hounslow on his own, and my mother would occasionally deliver a clean shirt and socks to his landlady. He would come over to see us when he was able and I have a vague remembrance of them hitting each other. They seldom took me out together. Apart from visits to the Shepherd's Bush Empire and walks in Bishop's Park and by the river, my father and I mostly visited pubs—the Spotted Horse in Putney High Street and the King's Head in Fulham Palace Road. Although he was frail (by this time he had only one lung), he enjoyed walking, saying very little. His own father was a great walker and taught him what was called the Countryman-Tramp's Walk, which consisted of putting all your weight on your forward foot, rather like wearing a surgical boot, and enabled you to walk for thirty miles a day, as he said he often did, without any discomfort. I practised this strange gait for years, much to the amusement of passers-by and sometimes catch myself experimenting with it now on long walks.

But most of the days in Fulham were spent with my mother, forced into bored idleness by having to look after me, and biting her finger nails to stumps. Heaven knows what she was living on. I was either too young or too sickly to go to school to give her some respite, not that she wanted to be on her own. I did spend a short time at Frimley Road Infants and was given the cut eye on enrolment. I still have the scar. My mother walked, too, not because she liked it but because she had no other alternative. Willis Road, King Street and Hammersmith Broadway are hardly tourist attractions even forty years on, and her walks were aimless expeditions to escape from digs with nothing to do in them and no one to talk to, pushing a small boy up to Fulham Road for his regular check-up at Brompton Hospital, or 'shopping' with no money in Kensington High Street.

The Brompton Hospital visits would take all day, from about nine o'clock in the morning to the end of the afternoon. For days before we set out my mother stoked my apprehension by telling me what they had done to my father, who had been shown off to the students like the prize pig at Skipton Fair. 'If only this man had come to us before,' said the house surgeon. I could imagine those eyes on my father's white, marble-veined body. 'Of course, they're very kind and *good* to you,' my mother would say. They didn't seem particularly kind or good to me, frightening certainly. This feeling established itself the moment we entered the door and passed the porter who acted like a policeman. I felt I had been arrested and was there because of some unknown transgression. The overpowering smell of the place reinforced the sense that it was like no other. We sat on long, dark, refectory-like benches and prepared to wait for the rest of the day in this dim, bustling crypt.

'They're all Scotch and Irish in here.' The Sister, who usually took charge of me, was indeed Scots. She wore a dark blue uniform with white dots on it and was about the only friendly face I could ever make out. But even she would make me take off my shirt almost immediately on arrival and I would be forced to walk without dawdling around the monastic corridors to my various X-rays and tests, and return to our bench wearing only my shorts with my braces chafing my salt-cellar shoulders. We had nothing to eat all day, as my mother obviously thought that to bring sandwiches or something of the sort would have been a little like munching away during Evensong. She had a reverential, almost mystical attitude towards medicine, an attitude very common at the time, and believed, for example, that doctors, exclusively, were the people who drove their own motor cars. If we saw one in the street, she'd say, 'Oh, look, there's a car outside. Must be the doctor.'

Shivering, hungry, largely ignored for hours, it was a little like waiting for the jury's verdict to come in, and the last visit of the afternoon was rather like being arraigned before the judge. In this case it was always Dr Henderson, another Scot. She thumped away at my tinny, inadequate body impatiently. Would I be reprieved? How squalid had I really been? Had it shown up on the X-ray screen? Eventually, throwing me a barley sugar, she would sit and write her report. The barley sugar seemed to indicate that I was on parole and soon would be let outside into the grey, free air of the Fulham Road. My mother, doubtful and bewildered, would lead me off to the dispensary to the next inevitable wait. At last, like the prisoner having his watch, keys and money returned, I was allowed to put on my clothes and cover myself up from any further fear of accusation. My release was not complete until the final interview with the Lady Almoner. I did not mind this so much because by this time I knew that I had got my ticket, at least for the next three months. My mother was having to go through it now, only she had it with smiles and nods of understanding and all from a very posh lady in overalls.

Kensington High Street was the Appian Way to the West End. The border ended at Barker's Store and we rarely ventured beyond it except for visits to Woolworth's in Cork Street, which was scarcely going Up West. Going Up West was something we didn't do until the later years of the war, when my mother was working full time and, with the aid of generous tips from GIs and Allied Servicemen, she was able to take me up with her on her days off. Up West in the 1940s was a very different affair from Kensington High Street in the thirties. For one thing, my mother seemed to have a great deal of money. The routine was almost always the same: lunch at the Trocadero, when she would complain about the menu being unintelligible and I struggled to explain with my inadequate French the concealed identity of the dishes. We invariably ended up having fish and chips. Her technique with waiters, as in life, was to either bully or fawn upon them. 'Oh, you really are very kind.' 'Oh yes, we *did* enjoy that very much. Very tasty. Really nutritious.' 'You *are* busy today, aren't you?' If this ladylike charm got no response from the waiter she would then resort to her usual domestic bad temper giving both the waiter and myself Black Looks. The waiter would be indifferent, or downright rude and unimpressed by my mother's current rig-out. If anything went wrong with the meal the blame was heaped upon me. The rest of her day off could be ruined almost at the outset in this way and if we could get through lunch without one of her Black Looks, when dark rivulets of rage and disappointment spread across her face, it was relief indeed. If I summoned up enough bravado I would sometimes—at the age of fifteen—order myself a cigar, choosing at random from the box ('That looks a nice one, dear'), looking around me as if my mother were not with me or even as if I were alone. Like Lyons Corner House, it seemed just the sort of place a gentleman would take a beautiful woman, but the Trocadero seemed unquestionably classier.

My mother's hair was very dark, occasionally hennaed. Her face was a floury dark mask, her eyes were an irritable brown, her ears small, so unlike her father's ('He's got Satan's ears, he has'), her nose surprisingly fine. Her remaining front teeth were large, yellow and strong. Her lips were a scarlet-black sliver covered in some sticky slime named Tahiti or Tattoo, which she bought with all her other make-up from Woolworth's. She wore it, or something like it, from the beginning of the First World War onwards. She had a cream base called Crème Simone, always covered up with a face powder called Tokalon, which she dabbed all over so that it almost showered off in little avalanches when she leant forward over her food. This was all topped off by a kind of knicker-bocker glory of rouge, which came in rather pretty little blue and white boxes—again from Woolworth's—and looked like a mixture of blackcurrant juice and brick dust. The final coup was an overgenerous dab of California Poppy, known to schoolboys as 'fleur des dustbins'.

Tea Up West would be cream cakes at the Regent Palace, gin and It for my mother, and then on to The Show! Ivor Novello, *Dancing Years*, *Perchance to Dream*, *Lisbon Story*, all of the George Black shows at the Hippodrome. Vic Oliver was my mother's favourite comedian. She thought he was marvellous. It was during these Black shows that huge chorus girls came down into the stalls and invited members of the audience to dance with them. My cream cakes almost churned as I thought one of them might approach me. I was about thirteen when I saw a revival of an old twenties' musical comedy, *The Lilac Domino*. I was overwhelmed by the beauty of the girls in it, longing to be on stage with them and take every one of them in turn to dinner at the Trocadero. It was the night before I went back to school and on my return I discovered that my headmaster had also been in the audience. I felt passionately that he had no business to be prying on such a world; one in which, unlike me, he could not possibly have any place.

But before these affluent, wartime days, we would come up the stairs from the District Line and walk straight into Ponting's, a superb store which preserved its *Kipps'*-like draper's atmosphere for many years. Going next door into Derry and Toms was like stepping from one century into another. Here there were blue carpets, everything looked very modern, rather like Auntie Queen's flat, white telephones and the girls behind the counter were not only as lofty as the Lady Almoner but all seemed to be casting smiling, seductive glances at me, just like the ravishing giants at the Hippodrome in later years. Any one of these creatures would surely be quietly flattered to sit beside me at a discreet table at the Trocadero.

Glorious Ponting's, Derry and Toms and Barker's. We would walk around these stores, hardly venturing anywhere else for almost the whole day. We went through miles of departments, floor by floor, my mother unable to buy anything, saying little except to complain about her feet aching. Often I felt that my own legs were going to drop off, something I dreaded in case I were to faint from fatigue, which occasionally I did. This meant coming round in a public place and looking up at a clouded, furious face and an aggrieved silence all the way back to the District Line, without even the consolation of baked beans for tea at Lyons at the end of it.

My sister, Fay, had died of TB and meningitis when I was two. She was reckoned to be a starry personality. 'Like a little fairy on top of the

Christmas Tree'. My father had managed to get her christened at St Martin-in-the-Fields by the Reverend Dick Sheppard, then a very popular star himself. She was spoken of as if she were some exquisite prodigy, but she exists to me only as a description of the last moments of her life, and my mother and father walking down the steps of Westminster Hospital afterwards with Big Ben chiming as they did so. This is really the only image I have of my sister at all. The remembrance was small, and later, as an adult, I often resented her wilful departure, leaving me alone to carry the burden of our mother. Perhaps she might have been some help and support, I thought. She was older, appeared to be beautiful and, from all unreliable accounts, affectionate. An ally, an affectionate one, and a woman, might have been helpful. Instead of making such a pious exit, so lovingly and medically described by Nellie Beatrice, so relished by Auntie Queenie, together we might have been an inseparable team on those aimless trips along the Appian Way to High Street, Kensington. There were no Black Looks in Heaven.

3. 'I Don't Want to End Up in a Dead-and-Alive Hole'

By 1936, my father's health had recovered enough for him to go back to his work as an advertising copywriter. Some kind of reconciliation must have been effected between my parents as they now set about living together under the same roof. We moved out of London, away from Fulham, the beginning of a change in things for all of us.

In the mid-1930s the Waterloo to Effingham Junction line fingered its way as so many others did into the Surrey countryside. Although it was still possible to keep sheep and cows in the East End during the Second World War it seemed to me that the railway led into an open, light and muted world without trams, with few buses—and those green instead of red. During the next ten years I grew to know almost every house and building and factory, the signs on them, the sheds in the back gardens, on the thirty-minute ride to our new house. Clapham Junction, home of Arding and Hobbs; Wimbledon with its stuffed St Bernard railway dog in his glass case on the platform (the grave gaze of this heroic animal made the change worthwhile); next, Raynes Park, with Carters Seed factory on the left, where my mother was later to work for a pittance during the early days of the war; Motspur Park, small factories and houses gathered round a pub, the Earl Beatty; then, Worcester Park, the village Neasden of its time. And Stoneleigh, where we came to live. The developers' fingers hesitated briefly before ploughing onwards, and paused to spread haphazard speculative tentacles. Beyond Stoneleigh were Ewell West and Epsom, a rather unappealing Victorian town being changed into a new, bright, brick-and-cement dormitory like others that became Reigate, Redhill, Leatherhead and Dorking. But beyond them lay the Downs; Effingham Junction nudged countryside which still had a few secrets left.

Stoneleigh itself was a station surrounded by groups of housing estates. Coming off the concrete railway bridge on either side were 'Shopping Parades'. In the middle was the Stoneleigh Hotel, which was not an hotel at

38

all but a by-pass Tudor pub where my mother was to work throughout the war and for several years after. The Parades consisted of a small Woolworth's, the dry cleaner's, newsagents and a twopenny library, butchers, florists and empty shops which had not yet been sold, gaps in the townscape, corners which had not yet been built on, patches of fields and stubble between houses and shops. It was not Stockbroker's Tudor but Bankclerk's Tudor. The ribbons of streets were empty most of the day except for occasional women on their way to the Parades, pushing prams along the clean pavements with their grass verges, fresh as last week's graves.

Grandma Osborne had been settled into this Byzantium of pre-war mediocrity by my father's sister Nancy. Aunt Nancy reminded me of Sister Ethel in the *William* books. She was flattered, fawned upon, almost beatified. To me she seemed affected, rude, snobbish and vain. She complained constantly that my cousin Tony might pick up my cockney accent. She had married Uncle Harry, who worked for the Unilever Company in Lagos, Nigeria. This meant that she spent a year at a time with him there, this being the span then allotted to wives in the White Man's Grave. Someone had to look after cousin Tony, and the obvious person was my grandmother.

Grandma Osborne's house was at the end of Clandon Close, a long cul-de-sac of pebble-dash counter clerk's Tudor with a back garden leading on to a large field encircled by exactly similar houses. At this time, houses in places like Stoneleigh cost something in the region of £300 to £600 to buy, but many were rented. My mother was insistent that we should not enter into buying because she didn't want to be 'tied down'. Thirty or forty times during the first seventeen years of my life we wrapped up dozens of china dogs and picture-hatted ladies with straining borzois—bought or won from fairgrounds like Dreamland in Margate—to move into another house or new digs until her snarling, raw-nailed boredom and dissatisfaction exploded again, driving her to make a dash for another lair. 'I'm fed up with this dead-and-alive hole.'

It was a just description of Stoneleigh and all other places like it. However, to a seven-year-old boy it could hold out promises of freedoms and discoveries that were not to be found in the streets of Fulham. Following the elder Osborne's exodus from South Wales, my parents moved into Number 68 Stoneleigh Park Road. What decided my father to forsake London, which he enjoyed as a true provincial, revelling in its variety and its mysteries and vastness, for the rolling acres of suburbia, upon which no countenance divine or otherwise would have shone, in ancient or any other time? His mother would certainly never have encouraged him to

39

feel his proximity would give her any pleasure. She was incapable of communicating such a thing and to her son above all. Filial guilt must have been uppermost, or perhaps the inner and physical fatigue that had led him to his healthless marriage.

Number 68 was half way down a very steep hill leading from the station. It must have been a patch of miniature downland before the concrete blotted it out a few years before. The descent on a bicycle from the top was thrilling. To hurtle down the switchback length of Stoneleigh Park Road without applying the brakes until it flattened out into the Ewell by-pass at the far end was heart-stopping. The chances of an accident were unlikely as cars were rare, vans few and the only regular traffic was the horse-drawn United Dairies cart or the Walls Ice Cream man on his bin bicycle. The house was similar to my grandparents' in Clandon Close but brighter and more airy, more toy box than Tudor. Instead of burnt oak there was an unlovely stab at modernity with black and cream for the almost uncarpentered woodwork and the staircase. Cream, not white, like Queen's crucifix. Cream was sophistication, like coloured telephones, telephones at all, as lemon to yellow. It had been, as my mother pointed out, a Show House, and some sales talk had been slapped on to the nasty edifice to make it look as though it had just been uprooted from the Ideal Home Exhibition. The estate agent had rubbed his hands and the dream descended. I liked the show house, and I hoped my mother's patience would hold out longer than usual this time. My father was now working regularly and seemed in better health and they appeared friendly to one another. Rows and silences were fewer.

Nellie Beatrice spent an inordinate time cleaning and polishing what was quite a small house for three people who didn't and were not allowed to create the merest untidiness. She had no reason to complain for my father was almost spinsterish in this respect, but every Friday was Black Friday for me, the day when we had what was called the Spring Clean. Sheets were draped over the furniture and chairs were piled on tables. Mattresses would be ripped from their beds, curtains taken down, washed and ironed. In the winter, when it was not possible to go outside, the Black Look clouding over the billowing dust bag of the Hoover was inescapable as it thrust its way into every corner, every bed or cupboard, bellowing and bullying a filthy uncomprehending world for hours. Handing over the Hoover to my mother was like distributing highly sophisticated nuclear weapons to an underdeveloped African nation. By the early evening she would be almost babbling with fatigue. A breathless interval at midday allowed us to bolt down an egg on mashed potatoes, frenziedly washed up so that she could 'get on' for the rest of the afternoon and a final burst to clear the field of this spotless battle and return everything to its gleaming, dustless place, raped by Mansion Polish and elbow grease, before my father returned home from work.

He soon came to prefer spending Friday evening in my grandmother's Fulham scullery rather than listen to my mother gibbering with irritability, as she shuddered with her life's bad back to prepare his evening meal. This fractious, jangling, indomitably Hoovered world was not a welcoming one. He always brought back a half-pound box of Terry's plain Brazil nut chocolates but it hardly placated her. No reward or show of gratitude would recognize her effort sufficiently. Besides, her attitude was that presents are given only either to buy affection or to make it clear that you are unbeholden. In this way you could alone face the world and say, 'I don't owe anyone anything.' So, if he hadn't decided to avoid coming home by drinking port with Grandma Grove at the Clarendon in Hammersmith, or with the 'Press boys' in Fleet Street, he would return back to all this with *Mickey Mouse*, *Rover*, *Hotspur*, the *Gem* for me and, after supper, and doubtless full of Waterloo buffet whisky, Guinness or Moussec, would sit down at the upright piano and sing. His piano playing was self-taught. He had a very pleasant light voice and would sing a few hymns, and songs like 'There's an Old-Fashioned House in an Old-Fashioned Street', 'It's My Mother's Birthday Today', 'Friend o'Mine', 'On the Road to Mandalay', 'On the Isle of Capri', 'Red Sails in the Sunset', Layton and Johnstone favourites, as well as a large repertory of music-hall songs: Harry Champion, George Robey, George Formby even, Paul Robeson, Peter Dawson, Melville Gideon, Jessie Matthews, Richard Tauber, Arthur Tracey—the Street Singer, who would have been smartly turned away from the forecourt of the Stoneleigh Hotel.

On Sunday mornings, braced by a visit to the Stoneleigh Hotel, he would take me around to Clandon Close. This weekly visit to his mother was something he dreaded and it was not difficult to see why. Her dismissive skill was subtle and brutal, sometimes no more than a thin smile, a watery upward look or an amused intake of breath, a scanning cauterizing instrument which rendered any endeavour puny or extravagantly indulgent. Her son was her prize victim.

There was one incident which she resurrected constantly with controlled, unabating bitterness. In the course of the Sunday lunchtime catechism of his present employment, preferably, or unemployment, his health and myself, she always struck back to her true course—Money. In particular, the money he, as a child, had cost his parents through wilful ill-health and some kind of applied original sin. The high point of this bitter retrospect was the South African Incident. She would take as her cue something like a glance at my new overcoat or pair of shoes, and say to him, 'Of course, when you had that trip to South Africa it cost your father and me a great deal of money . . . a great deal.' When he was about twelve my father had won the first prize in a drawing competition sponsored by the *Daily Mail*, a small sum of money and a round trip by boat to Cape Town. The prize was regarded as an outlandish and impractical one for him to accept because of his frailty and chronic asthma. Eventually and reluctantly he was allowed to board the steamer bound for Cape Town. A few days out in the Bay of Biscay he suffered a violent attack of asthma and was sent ashore to a hospital in Lisbon for some weeks before being shipped home with the bill of several hundred pounds. It was a mishap he was never allowed to forget. The account of the family borrowings and scrapings inflicted by his unhappy prize was repeated to him until he died and still recalled afterwards. Like a mark of inner folly the prize caught up with him in death, as she always knew it would. I never heard her say a kindly word to him or of him. When both her children died, both in their thirties, she spoke only of the bitter injustice of her daughter's early death.

If the pebble-dash house in Clandon Close was not exactly a dead-and-alive hole there was little activity inside or around it. It led nowhere, a terminus of semi-detached inertia. The houses in and around were a uniform standard, scattered in their ribbon millions all over England between the wars. There were occasional attempts at exotic variations such as extra bow windows in odd places or patio-type entrances which seemed to be useful for nothing but umbrellas. Bungalows, with concrete front gardens, had a sort of jaunty independence, inhabited by a somewhat younger set, often without children. My grandmother's house was not typical because it was the type itself. The hall was a small, unusable area flanked on one side by a tiny lavatory and bathroom and on the right side by a room which was usually called, for some reason, the Playroom. In most houses it was used as a cloakroom or for storing old toys and golf clubs. A few self-important husbands might even call it the Study or the Den, but there would be few books there, just *News Chronicle* give-away editions of Charles Dickens or the Waverley novels gathering dust behind the golf clubs.

Novels were read in other rooms, borrowed from the twopenny library in the Parade. Biographies of statesmen or soldiers came from the public library. Few letters were written except at Christmas and Easter, few dens contained a desk. Letter writing was a practice which was foreign to the people who lived here. They were immune or indifferent to contact, past or

42

present, as if they came from nowhere and wanted to keep it that way. Routine was Stoneleigh's altar, its liturgy Radio Normandy, its mother's milk a nice quiet hot drink as usual after yet another nice quiet evening. Casual entertaining or informal hospitality were like tolerating a smell on the landing or a blocked-up sink. Conviviality seldom went beyond planned visits from relatives. Whim or sudden impulse was unthinkable and blasphemed against the very idea of the God Routine. The litany read: 'I just have to have my routine. If I don't have my routine I don't know where I am,' or 'Well, before we start anything we've got to work out a routine.' I think Routine. Therefore I am Routine.

Spontaneity was bad breath to them. Certainly Grandma Osborne's conviction of her son's wanton instability would only have been confirmed if she had seen my maternal grandmother sitting long into the night with my father, my grandfather swearing over the *Watch Tower* and the *News of the World*, eating eel pie and faggots, drinking port and Guinness, disregarding time, health and tomorrow. What little social contact took place in Stoneleigh was mostly on the station platform and from the high-fenced back gardens on summer Sundays, when the air was broken in the early afternoon by repeated cries of 'Come on, it's getting cold; it's on the *table*', as if some sick or dying patient needed attention or the kiss of life. The few telephones, always beside the front door next to the coatstand in the hall, like an unwanted ornament or vacuum cleaner, can seldom have been used for idle conversation. Sited by the coldest draught with nowhere to sit, it was an instrument for discouraging communication, forbidding it in the interest of frugality of pocket and spirit, only to be used in the reporting of sickness, disaster or death.

Apart from the offensive notion of outside interferences like casual friendly visits, there was a similar attitude to religion which was looked upon largely as an intrusion from outside, better kept out of the house, like a muddy dog which would mark the furniture with its paws. The nearest church was up in the shopping parade by the railway station and the Stoneleigh Hotel. I can't remember what denomination it was but it looked like a steepled garage, less assured than the Great West Road factory Papist style, so it was probably Non-Conformist, a religion more suited to Stoneleigh, itself no place for Sunday drunkenness and large families. I had no contact with church at all until we went to live in Ewell Village, which had a reasonably ancient parish church where I became a choir member for a short time, purely for venal reasons. We were paid one and sixpence a week, plus funeral and wedding fees.

Although Grandma Grove had been brought up as a Wesleyan by her

43

minister father, she had given her daughter no religious instruction at all and never went near a church herself. 'We worked too hard to go to church.' As for the Christmas disputations between my mother and her sister, these were conducted on the Cavalier–Roundhead level of hypocrites versus the really good guys. My grandfather's religiosity was held to stem entirely from getting over the DTs and as a method of atoning for a lifetime's sexual voraciousness. It was accepted without question that Grandma Osborne, an ordinary Welsh Anglican, never went to church. God would not like her to risk her health by going out in the cold. Even in the height of summer her frailty demanded dispensation and was gladly given in His divine understanding of her. Instead, she would lie back in her chair, eyes closed, legs crossed and her high-heeled shoes tapping, as she listened to the Sunday evening hymns on the wireless. She seemed to know them all by heart. For all her show of austerity and undefined self-sacrifice, she was an incomparably lazy woman, as comfort-loving and selfish as a cat. Her husband did all her shopping for her and the wireless did her churchgoing.

My father was particularly contemptuous of clergymen, even more than civil servants. It must have had something to do with his experiences in hospital, when he never allowed them near him. His mother, too, had not bothered to give him any religious encouragement, possibly thinking he was unworthy of the effort. Grandma Grove didn't go to church because she worked too hard; Grandma Osborne didn't go because she hardly worked at all. Sponging off relatives was her God-given burden and her only daily toil.

The Bible was almost unknown to me until I later attended the Church of England school in Ewell. What distinguished this place was that more boys were caned more often during Scripture lessons than others. Sometimes it was for giggling at the salacious parts of the Old Testament, but often the result of divine, random whim of its instrument, the headmaster, Mr Jones, a fierce Welshman, whose lips would glisten with excitement as he swept around the classroom—all eyes lowered—looking for the next victim of unjust wrath. It was said that Mr Jones was very religious indeed because he was Welsh, and very Welsh at that. As the only other excessively Welsh person I knew was my grandmother with her feet-tapping and meticulous hymn singing, I assumed that being Welsh and believing in God were the darkest heart of religion. It was easy to imagine God with a firmament South Wales accent, whereas Jesus might easily come from Surrey; if not from Stoneleigh then from one of the larger houses in the better-still rural parts of Ewell, in the nice fresh air and certainly well away from any satanic mills.

There was something almost relaxing about the God Routine as practised with such ruthless self-containment by Grandma Osborne. It made a

44

comforting change from the chaos of my mother's irritability and snarling boredom. By comparison, she was kindly, blessedly consistent in her entrenched detachment, and unknown to lose her temper. A strange thing. To have lost her temper would have been a breach with routine and not to be countenanced. Through all the Family Rows I witnessed I never once heard her raise her voice. She withdrew like a Judo Black Belt, using the weight of her opponents' bluster and shouting to throw them over her shoulder with that watery smile.

Supported by her son-in-law for looking after his child, my grandmother ruled over their two up and two down as if it were a country house while my grandfather played the role of the docile retainer. I liked the old man very much, but he was a shambling, shy figure who said little. Throughout the day he made breathy whistling sounds as if he were talking to himself. The only thing I ever remember him saying to me was pointing out someone in the street. 'Do you know who that man is?' 'No,' I said. 'That man is a Socialist. Do you know what a Socialist is?' 'No.' 'Well, a Socialist is a man who never raises his cap to anyone.' It didn't occur to me then that no one in Clandon Close ever wore a cap except to play golf at weekends: caps worn in the pretence of golf playing. My grandfather wore the cloth sort, with a white muffler. His daughter, as if in conspiracy with her mother, gave him one for Christmas. He wore his badge gratefully. Perhaps it reminded him of the land of his mothers, where it would have gone unnoticed. Like my grandmother he was terminally lazy. He had not worked for many years and a fiction was kept up that he went to the Labour Exchange regularly to find odd jobs and gardening, which he may have done. No one took this very seriously, including my grandfather. He made occasional impassioned pleas that he was doing his best. He probably was; Stoneleigh, being little more than a settlement by the railway line, was not the kind of place where people employed jobbing gardeners or handymen. Self-containment was the rule. Self kept resolutely unto self. It was not merely a matter of income. Even a jobbing gardener in the shed or cleaning woman in the house would have threatened unwanted intimacy. His failure was doubtless genuine and his relief, too. He was allowed pocket money by my grandmother from Uncle Harry's allowance, which he was permitted to spend on an odd pint of beer and a packet of Woodbines.

Treated contemptuously as a servant, he managed to behave like a dignified one. Even my mother patronized him, something she could do to none of the other Osbornes, gleefully pressing the odd shilling into his hand. He was shown scant affection and I had the rarest pleasure of feeling sorry for an adult. The most responsible task he was given was packing his daughter's trunks when she was going back to Nigeria, and his skill in doing this was acknowledged even by my grandmother. Apart from his brief lessons in Socialism, a demonstration of the classical straight left in boxing, and of packing, the only other thing he tried to teach me was his Countryman-Tramp's Walk, the one my father had already inherited.

Disarmingly, in these four rooms his wife behaved like Mrs Danvers in *Rebecca*, keeping a firm eye on her tiny kitchen as if it were the butler's pantry. Although there was little to do apart from cleaning the fire grate, getting in wood and coal, Grandpa Osborne was not allowed to sit down or even light up a cigarette before lunch. He would often wait standing in the kitchen until he received his shopping instructions, which were small enough ('drop in at the Co-op . . . bakery up on the Parade') for three people, but were planned as if for a country-house weekend. Almost his most important errand was changing Grandma's library book at the twopenny library. She admitted that this was an extravagance but maintained that the public library didn't have the sort of books she liked, implying she had a special, refined taste. The truth was that she thought her husband incapable of even choosing a book for her whereas at the twopenny library they knew, of course: Ethel M. Dell, Netta Muskett and, that pre-war Dickens of them all, read and re-read again, Warwick Deeping. She didn't really want new books, rather the same books again. And, of course, she was also too lazy to either make the choice herself or walk a quarter of a mile to the Parade. Books had to be offered to her like an afternoon sweetie.

When the old man was finally given his instructions he would stay out for the rest of the morning. The shops were only ten minutes away and his list filled a small piece of paper. He was never asked what took him so long. He was out from under her feet. The Stoneleigh Hotel was not a place where unemployed old men are offered drinks, however long they sit in corners with near-empty glasses. Apart from going to the public library a mile or so away, he would sometimes mumble that he had been up to the Labour Exchange, knowing he was disbelieved. I think he just went for walks in Nonsuch Park on his own.

They never got up later than seven o'clock, breakfast was eaten and washed up by eight-thirty. The only reason it was necessary to keep to these spartan hours in such an otherwise indolent household was in order to have an Early Dinner, which was essential to the living of a Proper Normal Life, supposedly in the interests of my cousin Tony. The God Routine had to be obeyed even if, as in their case, it was to countenance sloth rather than endeavour. Its Prime Hours were as fixed as Sext, Nones and Compline, being Early Breakfast, Early Dinner, Early Tea, Early Supper and Early

Bed. To have even considered Late Breakfast or Late Supper would have broken the rule of Grandma's enclosed order. I'm sure she never had either in her life. Had she been there she would certainly have made sure that the Last Supper was an Early one. Whatever the old man pretended to be doing he was back in time for dinner. By saying Dinner rather than Lunch, she did not, like my mother, categorize the rich and privileged as people who had Dinner at Night. She regarded them as Late instead of Early, staying up Too Late and eating Too Much. Their own Early Dinner would be ready at half-past twelve or a quarter to one at the latest and would be washed up by one-thirty.

It was then time for grandfather to go upstairs to bed for his afternoon sleep, where he would lie down on his own in his long underwear until it was time for him to come down and make the tea. Meanwhile, she would have her Rest. One was supposed to make as little noise as possible during this, although she affected to be indulgent about it. She would read out from the *South Wales and Newport Argus*, the only paper she ever read at length, mostly the names of those in the Births, Marriages and Deaths columns.

Death received first attention. Birth announcements were a matter of counting months on fingers. A few marriages produced a sniff of respectful approval but most a sceptical intake of breath. It was as if almost everyone at home had committed some predictable foolishness, like the girlish mistake of her own marriage. My mother in one of her occasional prurient confidences told me that Auntie Annie, as Grandma Osborne was known, had only allowed Grandpa to touch her twice during their marriage. This was when they were both managing the King's Arms in Newport at the turn of the century, and she submitted herself to this unroutinelike ordeal solely after secret tippling while working behind the bar, a job she despised and held to be far beneath her. It rang true. Nancy was born in 1903. Grandpa Osborne, poor neutered old dog, was to die in 1941, going without his oats for thirty-eight years. I thought of them in their feather bed, of the old man lying upstairs alone every afternoon, Annie downstairs reading the *South Wales Argus*. What were his thoughts? Denied affection, sex, respect, even the work he shunned. Years later, George Devine told me a story about his own father. George's uncle was dying when he confided to him that George's mother had only allowed his father to approach her once. 'Only the once, George.' The result was George. Innocent of calculation, his father would sometimes give her presents of flowers or chocolates. Her response was always the same: 'Oh, I see. I know what you want. Well, you're *not* going to get it.' I always used to call him 'One shot George.'

After the *South Wales Argus* my grandmother would flip through the

47

Daily Mail which she thought a Good Sensible Paper and which contained her favourite journalist, Collie Knox, and her daughter's intellectual choice, Beverley Baxter, who she thought wrote wonderfully on the theatre. She said it as if it were self-evident, in spite of the fact that, apart from the pantomine, she had never been to a London theatre in her life. Beverley Nichols was another great favourite with both of them. Then, sinking her court shoes into the leathery squash of the pouffe, she would settle into her latest Warwick Deeping. Every afternoon for forty years the rigour of her daily regime was proclaimed by her uplifted court shoes. No one dared point out to her that she spent more than half the day sitting or snoozing in them.

The sitting-room itself (unlike my mother she knew better than to say Lounge) was shabby and dark, with a mixture of old sub-standard Harrods furniture and threadbare Victorian relics of middling monstrosity. The floor was covered with ancient Indian carpets, drained by time of any of their original colours. On the walls were aged Pre-Raphaelite prints, and the mantelshelf was littered with a selection of trophies from Nigeria—brass boxes in the shape of iguanas and monkeys, the sort of thing you see nowadays at African airports. The only thing of any possible value was a handsome carriage clock. A large turtle shell stood in the fireplace, a shield against anyone who might ever think of lighting the fire before the statutory seven o'clock. A huge walnut sideboard dominated the whole of one wall from floor to ceiling. It was the altarpiece, always covered with offerings contained in silver bowls, filled with a selection of nuts, fruit, tangerines, and her own home-made treacle toffee, which had its own silver salver and a silver toffee hammer. Quite delicious it was too. These luxuries, never available to me at home, were always to be had however hard the times were said to be. She had that masterly talent of the middle classes for complaining bitterly about her financial condition with no palpable change in her way of life. She must have achieved almost exactly what she wanted: a nice Early Night, a nice Early Life. It was certainly easy, easy and empty of spirit. She personified the terrible sin of sloth at its most paltry. Not the sloth of despair in the face of God. Despair would be like staying up spiritually too late. Every afternoon of this replete lifetime of self-conceit and cosseting, a bit of toffee or butterscotch went down a treat with Warwick Deeping.

After twenty minutes or so her head would fall back rather as if she was going to break into hymn singing. Her mouth would open, her teeth start sucking in the air and she would begin snoring lightly. I often sat with her during these afternoons, watching this unfailing event. Not daring to move, I would turn over the pages of my book or comic as carefully as possible. It was accepted without question that Grandma did not go to sleep in the afternoon. To have woken her would have broken the spell for me as well as for her, like rousing some mythic animal in a dark cave, and she would have had to go through the irritable charade of pretending she was still reading old Warwick and miss the rest of her frozen snooze. She thought that she could melt unobserved into something resembling a stone abbess prone upon her tomb.

The only person who ever had malice or nerve enough to challenge this delusion was my mother. She would watch in sneering anticipation waiting for her to wake up. When my grandmother did so, slowly rising like a lounge Lazarus, she would get her punch in before the old lady had time to come up from the count. 'Well, Mother, did you have a nice sleep? Nice sleep?' 'Sleep? I've not been asleep!' 'Oh, come off it, Mother, of course you've been asleep. Don't be silly, we could all *see* you. You had your mouth wide open and you were snoring.' 'I was not snoring.' 'Everybody heard you.' My mother would look at me appealingly, but she got no help from my corner. 'I *never* go to sleep in the afternoons.' 'But you *do*, mother. Everybody knows that.' 'I was *not* asleep.' 'Then what were you doing?' Contemptuous pause. 'I was just closing my eyes.' They were the few occasions my mother ever managed to score, almost her only satisfaction until her triumphant coup the day, years later, when she pitched the old lady from her pouffe into a local authority home.

Cousin Tony was also supposed to have his afternoon rest. Being a year older and the baser part of her son, I was allowed to sit and read. I had no wish to join him as I detested him. He was one of the few children in Clandon Close who used the Playroom as a playroom, but the only game I remember playing with him was that of King George's Funeral. This was done by arranging his vast army of toy soldiers on the floor of his room and into a procession leading to his toy fort which served as Westminster Abbey. He even had a magnificent gun-carriage. Behind it he placed the king's horse, with boots reversed and his little dog behind him. We were, at the ages of five and six, both well instructed in the minute details of that occasion. But when I say 'play', Tony ran a commentary and he moved the pieces about. I was a patronized spectator.

Tony was an ingenious and malevolent schemer, proudly encouraged by his grandmother, to whom he was undoubted heir apparent. No one, child or adult, was allowed to challenge his domain or his tantrums, flagrant lying and dwarfish bullying. Nurturing him, imposing him on any company, Grandma Osborne alone seemed to be aroused to excitement by him. I was repeatedly instructed by my mother never to retaliate whenever he surprised me with his armoury of kicks, finger twistings or rabbit punching. Having disabled me with one of these, he would howl off to Grandma, accusing me of his own offence. He was always believed. Later, of course, I found it to be a common technique among adults, particularly in marriage. After his father finally took him away from Clandon Close he went to a Welsh public school—Christ's College, Brecon—then to Sandhurst, where he contracted TB and was invalided out. As a schoolboy, he became very solemn and priggish. I had an argument with him one day about the advisability of free love. He looked at me sternly and said in a comic, Clive Jenkins-type Welsh accent, 'If God had intended men and women to have sexual intercourse together without marriage he would never have invented venereal disease.' When I met him years later, he had become a probation officer in Macclesfield, rather mild and thoughtful. It was hard to think of him as the odious child who had plotted to get me into trouble at all times. His name, incidentally, was Tony Porter. Perhaps it was a wry remembrance of his persecution to borrow his surname for a character in a play.

At almost exactly four o'clock my grandfather would come down the stairs, making his soundless whistle like a despairing kettle and go to the kitchen. Hearing him, my grandmother would slowly arouse herself like an alerted cat to resume her upright Deeping position, pushing her spectacles up on her nose and sucking the plate of her false teeth back into place. She would take the cup of tea proffered to her without thanks and without looking at him, avoiding the sight of the bare feet underneath his combinations. She would then go into the bathroom to rearrange her hair, which was a strange substance when dressed, like a saucepan scourer made of white spider's web. She belonged to the generation that boasted of sitting on its own hair, and indeed she could as I saw—rarely—in her bedroom. How she managed to gather up this strange filmy mass into what looked like a bearskin hair-net was most baffling. I was convinced that in the mildest breeze it must surely blow off and reveal a bald skull. As she hardly ventured out, even into the garden, I was never to know.

An elaborate tea followed, however delayed or inadequate Uncle Harry's monthly cheque might be. There were nearly always two kinds of bread and butter, two kinds of home-made jam, possibly a sponge cake, Dundee cake, rock cakes, eggs perhaps; soused mackerel was one of her specialities, as were her pickled onions, mussels and cabbage. *Children's Hour* was put on *exactly* at five o'clock—she wasn't going to waste electricity—and, while Grandpa puffed his first evening Woodbine in the kitchen, the three of us would sit down and listen to it until it was time for Tony to go to bed and for my grandfather to take me home, leaving Grandma to a nice play on the wireless or *Monday Night at Seven* before Early Supper—Marmite sandwiches or biscuits and cheese—then bed, Warwick Deeping and an Early Night.

When we grow too old to dream . . .

Jim and Annie Osborne were what my mother would call the 'wash outs' of the family. The old man's profligate days of playing cricket and rugby instead of looking after the jeweller's shop in Newport had come to a dead end in a pointless green circle of suburban grass. The Countryman-Tramp's walk had led to the cul-de-sac of family handyman, with little family and little to hand. His brother Harry, once the mayor of Newport and chairman of the Conservative Association, was long since dead. His older brother Tom had prospered moderately in the small ironworks that their mother had left him and was now retired to an hotel in Bournemouth with his wife, Lottie. They paid very occasional visits to Clandon Close, rather as if they were visiting an ailing relative in the workhouse. Grandma became skittishly attentive on these occasions and intent on pleasing Auntie Lottie, a huge woman like a balloon of flowered wallpaper in an enormous hat, who talked about her own money and her own bridge game. Trying to remember it, I feel that Auntie Lottie's heavily veiled message to the assembled company was that if there was ever anything to come, Jim and Annie must learn to live with little expectations. Jim said little, staying in the kitchen, preparing the tea and serving it while Annie admired Auntie Lottie's immense jewellery and the huge car outside. The two brothers said little to each other, possibly because Uncle Tom was almost stone deaf, although my mother, in one of her rare perceptive moments, told me that he exaggerated his deafness in order to avoid talking to Auntie Lottie.

Large, pink-faced, white-haired, Tom could have been a General's orderly. Lottie's common, boastful silliness was apparent even to me and enhanced her husband's dignity, if that's what it was and not deafness or stupidity. His deafness may have been a shield but it was worn with authority. His eyes seemed to be on me throughout the visit. I was unused to scrutiny from adults even in reproof. Grown-up boredom was most embarrassing when adults invariably feigned interest: 'And how are you getting on at school? . . . What subjects do you like best? . . . Want to be when you grow up?' Mercifully, Auntie Lottie was as uninterested in children as other grown-ups and ignored me, though she might acknowledge my cousin. But the old man's eyes stayed with me, disregarding Tony who whined, screamed and demanded, unchecked by his grandmother. It was

51

hard to look away, so I looked down. If he had some message for me he would give it to me in a secret manner. When they got up to leave, he would hang back at the sitting-room door, nudging his brother ahead of him and turn round to me. Staring down at me he would press a half-crown in to my palm, close it hard and say, 'Not a word to anyone', and go quickly. Tony Porter never got so much as a good-bye. It was a sweet conspiracy between the deaf and the silent.

Apart from Grandma's sisters from Newport there were other occasional visitors. There was Auntie Lulu, my father's cousin, who lived in, of all places, East Cheam, some four or five miles away. Stoneleigh was a world away from East Cheam's leafy roads, detached houses and surrounding gentle pastures. Lulu's husband, Uncle John, was an accountant, a pale weedy figure who looked obscenely exposed without his bowler hat, like a turtle without its shell. Somehow, my father made his own bowler seem degenerate, defiant and bohemian. I don't know how he managed it. Perhaps because his own hat had seen many a lovely Late Night. Uncle John's bowler was extra work, hung on the hook of Early Night forever. My father despised him: 'whey-faced, wormy little bank teller'. He usually concealed his rages with unconvincing politeness to contain his sparse energy, an instinct I may have inherited. He was a reluctant and poor dissembler, but his contempt for Uncle John was fearsome, even to an eight-year-old. John had a black saloon car, a telephone and 'such a pretty daughter', Jill, who was the first vaguely middle-class little girl I ever met. Twice I was asked to her East Cheam birthday parties. I had known nothing like it and had no idea of how to behave. Few little boys were invited and those that were ignored me. The little girls seemed quite vicious, their favourite word being 'spiteful', as they inflicted some physical or verbal nastiness on one another. I was prepared to be impressed by pretty cousin Jill in the same craven way as my grandmother with Auntie Lulu. When I arrived at the front door she was receiving her guests in a dress which was a cross between a velvet nappy and a tutu. My grandmother would obviously have thought it perfect for such a pretty little girl. She had an enormous velvet bow in her hair and looked like a slightly indecent ice-cream salesgirl at the Odeon. She stared at me so coldly I wondered if I had been invited.

I was never to go to any other of these children's parties, which were and are apparently such an unenviable feature of English middle-class life. Like most grown-up parties they seemed competitive gatherings planned to promote as much noise and ill-will as possible. I had never seen so much food, though I ate little, feeling that there must be some unwritten rules to break. The one rule I did absorb was that you must eat lots of bread and butter before your jelly or anything really delicious, so I obediently ate my bread and butter while the good things disappeared. Then came humiliating Pig in the Middle, the Farmer's Wife, Ring-a-Ring o' Roses, Musical Chairs, none of which I had heard of, let alone played. When the overseeing mothers decided these revels were becoming more like a frilly tribal riot we were ushered into a room to watch *Felix the Cat* and *Bonzo the Dog*. The projector stammered and the little girls screamed and punched and kicked the boys. In the future, only the school air-raid shelters were nearer to mayhem. I didn't like Felix or Bonzo anyway. Most comedy films that delighted other children disturbed and distressed me. Laurel and Hardy, Chaplin and later Abbott and Costello and the Three Stooges; circus clowns, Punch and Judy shows, all filled me with sick premonitions. I even sat gloomily through Cowboy films, before they were elevated into Westerns, while all around were cheering and stoking my dislike for them and what I was watching.

At Jill's party there was worse to come, that Strolling Player of the Nursery, the Party Uncle. His assumption that all children at heart are retarded four-year-olds was correct, for that was how he made his howling audience behave with scarcely any effort. His absurd tricks and, 'Come along, children' seemed like an invitation to Hell on Earth. I had scarcely ever felt such panic and loathing. I longed to get to the door, say good-bye to cousin Jill if she would speak to me, collect my bag with its orange and banana and remember to say thank you very much to Auntie Lulu and wormy Uncle John. For some reason, my mother forced me to go again, implying I was a lucky boy to be asked. The third year I refused. This time my mother didn't bother to argue.

Passing looks at Christmas

I remember some Christmases very vividly and some not at all. My early Christmases were spent between Harbord Street and Clandon Close. Christmas Day in one and Boxing Day in the other. When I was twelve I was in a nursing home for sick boys. When I was twenty-one I was drinking evaporated milk and eating brown bread and peanut butter on a camp bed in a theatre on Hayling Island.

The highlight of Christmas at both houses was the Family Row. The common acrimony and bitterness of generations would claim its victims long before the Christmas wrappings had been thrown away. It was impossible not to be caught in some cross-fire or stray flack at some points during these festive manoeuvres. I would be attacked through my mother for her profligate spending on the new clothes I might be wearing. You could be made to feel very foolish indeed standing in your new jacket or trousers which suddenly seemed to sprout pound-note signs all over them.

The Osborne Row differed from the Grove Row but they had their similarities. With the Groves at Tottenham or Harbord Street the atmosphere would be violent, even physically, and thick with accumulated melodrama. Religion was a favourite launching pad, even though only Grandpa Grove and Auntie Queenie seemed to have any religious beliefs at all. The Osborne Family Rows, in spite of the fact that they were unheedingly Christian, were centred on the related subject of money. Their disputations were on wills, testaments, entails; who had been left out, what some loved one's real intentions had been and how subsequently thwarted after death.

The Osborne Family Row was more reticent, subtle, bitter and less likely forgotten. It was stage-managed by my grandmother, like a child who alone knows the rules of a new game so that it is assured of winning. About four o'clock on Boxing Day, the appetite for muscatels and almonds and Chinese figs would begin to pall. A dawdling disappointment hung in the air. Into this let-down lull, Grandma would make the first throw. The game was hers and the name of the game was money and property. The property was mostly of a very small kind: a reference to some diamond engagement rings foolishly pawned at the wrong time; pawn tickets lost or unredeemed; fur coats handed on to the wrong recipient; wills misinterpreted; wills wrongful; unintended; insurance policies not taken out or allowed to lapse; stocks withheld; shares pledged. Nothing was beyond recall or valuation. Even my father's notorious Lisbon hospital bills were itemized yet again.

Having started the game rolling, the old woman would sit back in her hymnal posture, the corners of her mouth tucked into a smile and wait for all the other players to make wrong moves. My mother said little and when she did was ruled out of order and, by implication, stupid. My father seemed to become whiter and thinner than ever, watching his mother as she sat back, her eyes half-closed like a smug fakir. I could swear she was singing in her head contentedly, 'Say not the struggle naught availeth', or one of her favourite self-loving songs, which sucked up to the innocence of brave old age, like 'When We Grow Too Old to Dream' or 'Little Old Lady Passing By'. She regarded these songs as some kind of personal tribute to her own geriatric divinity. They were only two of the many Battle Hymns praising a world made in the image of Grandma.

The Grove Family Rows were not masterminded but emerged from a

54

port-wine haze of unsated disappointment. Grandma Grove was a stoic rather than an optimist. What the two families shared was the heart pumped from birth by misgiving. Not a proud misgiving of the spirit but a timid melancholy or dislike of joy, effort or courage: 'I don't suppose it'll last.' . . . 'I knew it wouldn't last.' . . . 'How do you know it'll work?' . . . 'But aren't you worried?' . . . 'Well, there's nothing we can do about it.' . . . 'No use crying over it.' . . . 'Can't expect too much, go too far, only get disappointed. . . .'

Disappointment was oxygen to them. Their motto might have been *ante coitum triste est*. The Grove despond was all chaos, shouting and tearful rebukes. Their battle cries were: 'You've always had it easy.' . . . 'You didn't have to go out to work like I did when I was twelve.' . . . 'You were always Dad's favourite.' . . . 'What about you and Mum then?' . . . 'I've worked hard for everything I've ever had.' The Osborne slough was full of sly casual strokes, all the more wounding to my mother because no one said openly what they meant, not about money and certainly not about property, but about emotional privilege, social advantage, hypocrisy and religiosity against ordinary plain dealing. The Osbornes appeared to preserve calm while being more succinct and specific. Their bitterness and sense of having been cheated from birth were certainly deeper. If my mother tried to wade in to an Osborne Row she was soon made speechless by the cold stare of Grandma and the passing looks of amusement between her and Nancy as my mother mangled the language and mispronounced words and became confused at their silences. 'Did you see that?' she'd say afterwards. 'They were *passing looks*.' She would flush through her flaking Tokalon powder, bite her nails and turn to my father for support, which seldom came.

For Boxing Day, Grandma Osborne had perfected a pumpkin trick which turned all the cold Christmas pudding and mince pies suddenly into funeral baked meats. She did it almost on the stroke of five and in one wand-like incantation. Lying back in the Hymnal position, she would close her eyes, smile her thin gruel of a smile and say, 'Ah, well, there's *another* Christmas over.' I dreaded the supreme satisfaction with which she laid the body of Christmas spirit to rest. In this one phrase she crushed the festive flower and the jubilant heart. On New Year's Eve she used less relish in confirming that there was little reason to feel good about the year passing and certainly less about the coming one.

Two days of bewilderment, betrayal, triumph and, above all, irredeemable and incurable disappointment ended. My parents gathered up our presents. A redemptive after-battle calm settled over the sitting-room strewn with wrapping paper and ribbon. We shuffled out in near silence back to Stoneleigh Park Road and my father's whisky bottle. Another Christmas Over. And in the beginning God created Grandma. To her the Inferno was as unthinkable as Paradise.

4. 'A Better Class of Person'

Early in 1938 we moved from Stoneleigh Park Road to a flat right beside Ewell by-pass, almost in Ewell itself, Number 8 Homedale. My mother was delighted. She liked the drudgery of moving for its own sake anyway, but she soon became bored when the move had been made and as soon as the new place was 'straight and nice' she wanted to push on. However, Homedale was a flat, which she regarded as being 'more modern' and less stuffy than a house. Not yet as chic as a bungalow but a step up from the dead-and-alive cul-de-sac.

My father was spending more and more time at home in the new flat. His employers at the advertising agency must have been patient, especially for the time, but after six months of almost constant absence he was sent the cheap High Street clock and a month's salary. He seemed relieved and grateful. 'We'll have a week at Margate,' he said. 'But don't tell your Grandma. She wouldn't understand.' We stayed in digs by the station. Morning breakfast was huge and delicious, the landlady as friendly as the best of barmaids, the weather was warm, even the sea. We spent half the day in Dreamland or on the beach, waded under the pier and went to nightclub-like entertainments in the evening, sitting at tables which seemed very grand and grown-up. When I first went to Las Vegas I immediately thought of those evenings in Margate and my parents, of fish and chips and Guinness. And the streams of girls. I had never seen a chorus line before. As they tap-danced and swung their legs they would sing 'Lullaby of Broadway' and 'Shuffle off to Buffalo', which seemed to be that year's most popular show numbers. I never tired of hearing them. They stayed in my head daily for months. It was the happiest week I can remember with my parents. They were friendly to one another. There were no moods and few black looks. I was unused to adult adventurousness, and it was exciting. Walking along the promenade towards Cliftonville under the coloured lights it felt as if all the songs belonged to Margate rather than Broadway or Buffalo, wherever or whatever they were. We would look up at the large hotels of Cliftonville. My father might suggest going in for a drink. But my mother would hurry on

57

ahead. 'This is where all the posh people stay,' she would say. 'You can't go in there.' 'Rich Jews,' my father added, following on behind with me. For a week, it was indeed Dreamland. For me, at least.

Homedale was a row of detached houses, each divided into two flats, set below an embankment beside Ewell by-pass. Ewell Castle School was beside it and opposite was the boundary of Nonsuch Park. The school was a Victorian-Tudor building and looked as if it had been built as a set for the film about Greyfriar's. It didn't seem to figure very largely in the life of Ewell Village. Whether it was a prep school or a private school masquerading as a public school I don't know. Homedale was flanked on its other side by yet another shopping parade which linked the surrounding suburbia like forts in a Roman wall. This particular Parade was just a curved corner consisting of a dozen small shops overlooking the busy roundabout at the junction of the roads to Kingston, Ewell Village, Epsom, North Cheam and London. On the other side of the roundabout was a pub similar to but even nastier than the Stoneleigh Hotel, oddly named the Organ Inn. Was it some Borough Architect's joke to call these shop-blocks Parades? Or did some Councillor think that the word itself would invest their dismal rows of newsagents and hairdressers with gaudy pomp, flaunting display and 'fond ostentation of riches', promenaded by prosperous Rotarians and Freemasons?

Some time ago I watched Michael Frayn on television describe his childhood in Ewell at what must have been roughly the same time. Although I recognized much of what he said, his experience of it seemed rather different from mine. He described it accurately and eloquently as the typical suburban outpost. However, to me, coming from Fulham and then Stoneleigh Park Road, it was a small rural island. On my way home from Heathrow Airport to Kent I have peered down at Homedale and wondered what it is like now. In 1938 it had a few remnants of charm, but the 406 bus to Kingston every twenty minutes and the frequent Green Line to Morden had ended its life as a village. It had become a timetable on a bus shelter, not lived in so much as passed through. Such places, however remote once, seem reluctantly on the move themselves. Stillness never returns to them. They are reduced to being thoroughfares, platforms for getting on and off. By the main bus stop there were a spring well and pond, backed by a large girls' school, Bourne Hall, which was surrounded by parkland. Its pupils, pouring out of the gates in boaters and swirling purple gym slips on summer afternoons, made the wait for a 406 an adventure. There was always the possibility of following one or two of them upstairs on the bus.

Opposite there was a church and in the churchyard a tomb

commemorating the man who invented the aeroplane propellor. Facing this was a blazer-and-tweed pub, the Spring Hotel, where my mother was to work after the war, although its unfamiliar gentility subdued her and she didn't stay long. 'Nice class of customer and the guvnor's a real gentleman. But a bit morbid—well, *quiet*.' In a narrow lane, rather like prints I had seen of nineteenth-century Eton, was Glyn House. I imagine it was eighteenth-century and it was occupied by a Sir Arthur Glyn who everyone spoke about as if he were the squire. Whoever he was or had been, he was pointed out as if he were a retired Prime Minister. Whether he was Ewell's last link with politics, empire or commerce, he was its last surviving Grand Old Man. The High Street was full of small grocers, the Gas, Light and Coke Company, a corn chandlers, the Olde Oake Chest Tea Shoppe and another 1930s pub. My school, Ewell Boys, lay back in Church Street in what seemed to be perpetual shade. Next to it was a sweet shop which sold liquorice sherbet and aniseed balls at a farthing for twenty, the best buy for an afternoon's reading aloud from *Pilgrim's Progress* or *Nicholas Nickleby*. Farther up was the recreation ground, the Rec., not to be entered alone and best avoided.

We left Homedale, either for financial reasons or because of my mother's restlessness and moved into Ewell Parade, another promontory of small shops with flats above, green iron railings at the back and tiny yards below. The 406 stopped outside on its way to the by-pass and to Epsom. Epsom had only recently been widened, scythed through and turned from a pokey country town into a municipal concourse able to accommodate traffic, with a new Woolworth's, pubs, and a brand new Odeon. I went there the week it opened with *A Star is Born*. Janet Gaynor, of course. I remember the title outside though, for some reason, not the film. Opposite the Odeon was the market place. Later I used to go every Saturday to buy books, old records and very early copies of the *Magnet* and *Gem*, which were links to my father. Number 2 Ewell Parade was above the twopenny library which was in the charge of two spinsters. Ewell was scattered with little shops run by single ladies or widows, often in pairs, selling confectionery, toys, tea and cakes, woollen goods, a milliner's with two hats and a handbag in its undressed windows. As a display of commerce it fitted the meagre imagination of a Parade perfectly.

Quiet tributaries led from what remained of the village, Drives, Ways, Avenues—Laurel Drive, Firtree Way, Linden Close—where you might stumble on a tiny footpath or green gap revealing a patch of the Old Ewell overlooked for a short while in the developers' haste. In between the new houses and beyond there were still steamy woods, thick with nesting birds, and ponds full of frogs. Only ten yards or so from Conway Drive or Edith Way I might pass in a few steps from suburbia into thick, silent copses, from civilization into the jungle, like passing from the palms and greenery of a florist's shop into a backroom of great primeval forests. The glimpse and plunge from the trim pavement to untrodden undergrowth was startling. For me, at least, Ewell had its scattered White Rabbit holes for the imagination, popping up all over the place, to follow obediently and headlong behind the stockade of fences and garden sheds. I suppose secrecy is childhood's great eroticism. These woods invited you to give yourself up to unimaginable private excesses. The depravity lay not in what you were doing—watching a toad or coupling rabbits—but the orgy of concealment itself. 'They can't find me. However hard they try.' Lying beneath a sea of fern the tumescence of brute secrecy triumphed and subsided only on the return home down Conway Drive and Edith Way.

It was a handy mixture of sport and perversion to be unseen, flat in the grass, and observe a group of tadpoling boys as if they were a hostile tribe. Or to track some unsuspecting District Commissioner of a grown-up who was walking his dog and unaware of your contemptuous scrutiny. Close by was Nonsuch Park, Henry VIII's hunting lodge, with huge oaks and elms strung across its parkland, empty most of the week except for elderly dog walkers. In the middle of it stood a Victorian-Tudor house where council employees served tea from urns on trestle tables, and buns and sweets from its empty rooms. Nowadays the whole place would probably be policed as a Leisure Area with play parks, sports and picnic facilities, information booths and every kind of organized amenity dear to the municipal imagination. No doubt it is. The glory of Nonsuch Park then was that there were no amenities at all, apart from one lavatory which was concealed behind the house. There were a few park-keepers, presumably there to see that small boys didn't chop down the oaks. I don't know how large it was, but to an eight-year-old boy it seemed the size of a county. In the dull flower gardens by the house women sat on benches with prams and in the parkland there were children but, astonishingly, never more than a few dozen. Surrounding it was a fortress of trees where I could actually get lost, and did occasionally. Not so many yards away the 93 bus passed on its way to Putney and Fulham. To see or hear it meant penetrating right up to the edge of the Park and peering through to the road beyond.

My father's parting gift at Victoria Station—sending me off to *The Adventures of Robin Hood*—paid off in months, years of excitement improvising the film which I knew almost frame by frame after two visits. Nonsuch Park and its turreted house were Sherwood Forest and

Nottingham Castle and the park-keepers unmistakably the Sheriff's Men. Armed with a bow and arrow made from garden cane and string, I crouched on thick branches ready to drop on any arrogant Guy de Gisbourne who would pass below. What I lacked was a Band of Merry Men. There were advantages to this. First, there were no arguments about casting. My role as Robin was as unchallenged as the scenario. I had bought a Victorian edition of the legends with Doré-like coloured illustrations which I knew almost by heart. There was a particularly poignant one of Robin, Christ-like, supported by Little John, aiming his final arrow into the air, from where it fell to mark his final resting place. It must have been familiar to almost every schoolboy although I thought it only revealed to me. Occasionally I did come upon groups of boys, Cubs or would-be Scouts who were curious rather than hostile. My costume consisted of little more than a dagger and belt at the waist, my bow and arrow, and cycling gauntlets, which made accurate aiming difficult but established the character. After a little explanation of character and plot, I could sometimes assemble my Merry Men for a day's outlawry. I tried to select younger boys who would not dispute my authority as casting director. Will Scarlett and Mick the Miller were pretty nondescript roles and could be distributed at random. There was usually someone taller than the rest who would be glad to revel in his superior height as Little John and a fat boy who could hardly turn down Friar Tuck.

Older boys often contested the leading role and disputed that it was My Game. If they were aggressive enough and clearly more powerful physically than myself, I would concede my rights as producer and consent to playing Sir Guy. It was a cowardly compromise but I decided that as Robin's adversary I was on an almost equal footing. Villainy had a sense of wicked superiority about it and I had a sneaking feeling that sometimes old Robin was a bit too good to be true. Perhaps I already had a vague sense that courting and, what's more, achieving popularity was not a gift I possessed. Sir Guy was contemptuous, feared and solitary. It was a close-run thing between him and Robin and he died bravely. Furthermore, Basil Rathbone, lean and lofty, spoke inevitably in a posh voice that was a good cut above Errol Flynn. It was pleasing to know that I must be the only acceptable aristocrat. Even if I were to be defeated by some bully from North Cheam or Ewell Village, I could despise Robin and his Band of Merry Louts, I could look down on them openly without challenge.

Maid Marion was the problem. What girl would let herself become lone hostage to a gang of rough little boys charging all day through inaccessible undergrowth in the Park? To almost every mother, Robin's exploits would have seemed like an adventure that must end in medical evidence about her daughter being read out in the Police Court. 'And where have you been all day, Gloria? I've been worried stiff. Where have you been?' 'Oh, to the Park.' 'On your own? Who with?' 'Oh, some boys.' Few girls could afford to be so daring, even if they had the inclination. Tomboys of independent mind were hard to come by. When I did discover my Maid Marion, she soon asserted her superiority by natural right. She also insisted that she should be Robin.

I don't know whether it is possible to identify early sexual quickening at particular moments. I dare say not. But the image of a young woman bending over a cot and taking out a baby lingered with me like the detail of a dream. I don't know who she was, only that the child was called Malcolm. Her skirt was black, her bare legs white, and it was exciting. I was about five. Then, the blur of twin girls called Daphne and Gloria and their plump younger sister, all four of us, smacking and touching on a cold leather sofa which stuck to our bare limbs, somehow stayed in my head and became vivid when I met my rebellious Maid Marion. She was no infantile mirage. She was present and became increasingly pressing. I was nine.

Joan Buffen lived at the far end of Ewell Parade. Mrs Buffen, a widow, ran the wool shop below the flat with her sister. Joan was an only child. The flat was small and cramped like all the others but its interior was very different. It was chintzy, comfortable and similar to the parlour room at the Olde Oake Chest Tea Shoppe. My mother thought Mrs Buffen was a bit stand-offish, but could never find anything specific to complain about. She was polite, rather abstracted and not one to stop and chat or borrow a cup of sugar. Running a wool shop implied that she had come down a few rungs, if only a few. But her puzzling other occupation lifted her above her admittedly genteel trade. She bred Staffordshire bull terriers, which even my mother realized was the kind of occupation pursued by people who most probably had dinner at night. She kept these unlovely, dangerous creatures in a yard behind the shop. Her daughter acted as full-time kennel maid when she was not at school.

Joan was three years older than myself, taller too, and dark. She usually wore a tweed divided skirt, a mean fashion which swathed her effectively from curiosity. When she climbed trees, which she did often, there were no fleeting rewards, only a coarse protective crotch. Joan and her mother were unmistakably different from the other residents of Ewell Parade. When I compared them with Auntie Lulu and my cousin Jill I began to see East Cheam differently. My mother had conceded that there was 'not much swank about her'. She dressed in old tweeds and heavy brogues or gumboots, striding in and out of the wool shop as if she had come in from the cow shed. They had no car like Uncle John. If they needed one to go to a dog show, they borrowed it from a relative. But I saw that compared to Mrs Buffen and Joan, Auntie Lulu and Jill were perceptibly Common. My grandmother would have been horrified at the suggestion. Mrs Buffen worked and was still undeniably a lady. Auntie Lulu was certainly full of swank. The frivolity of Jill contrasted with Joan's practical skills, grooming her charmless Bulls, cleaning them out, walking and training them.

It was weeks before I approached her about Maid Marion. I watched her every day from the end of the iron gallery, returning from school, walking her clutch of dogs like a circus performer. I ventured up to her flat. Being at the end, Mrs Buffen had been able to construct a wire fence to prevent her one domesticated dog, an old but still savage brindle, from mutilating the postman or other residents. Peering over the railings, I watched Joan carrying large buckets of food and sawdust, hosing out the kennels. They were big enough for me to stand up in. It occurred to me then that Joan and I could have lived in one together. If only she would look up at me, but she didn't. She must have seen me. But her attention never turned from the dogs. My mother soon noticed my absorption impatiently: 'I shouldn't bother trying to make friends with her—stuck-up little thing.' Besides, she thought that I had no business wanting to play with a girl, and an older one at that. Also, although she thought Joan was stuck-up, she might surely have reason to be. My mother always made it clear to me that my place in the world was unlikely to differ ever from her own. There was no reason why Mrs Buffen or her daughter should care to speak to me. I had nothing to offer people like the Buffens, therefore why should they bother to acknowledge my existence? It was consistent with her view of affection or friendship as a system of rewards, blackmail, calculation and aggrandizement in which people would only come off best or worst. Nothing ever strikes me with such despair and disbelief as the truly cold heart. It disarms utterly and never ceases to do so. I wish it were otherwise. Grandma Osborne's barrenness had some unyielding dignity. At least she didn't poison it with the unction of sentimentality.

But I was spared making the first move. One day, for the first time, she looked at me across the wire gate. 'Hello, do you want to come in?' She hardly looked at me. It was as casual as a stranger offering to light a cigarette. I was aware of a slightly impatient air—'Oh, well, he's been hanging about looking so stupid. I suppose I'd better ask him in.' When I hesitated, she unbolted the gate and held back the brindle beast beside her. Compared to the young dogs in the yard, he was almost benign. 'Don't let them see you're frightened.' I entered Buffendom prepared for anything. But at least I was inside. I had been noticed if not welcomed.

From then on, and for the next year, I spent hours sitting with Joan. We cooked meals of boiled sweets, fried with bananas, molasses and dog biscuits over a small fire, burning a hole in Mrs Buffen's saucepan. She accepted this with a calm that set her apart for me. At home, Nellie Beatrice would have sported a Black Look for a week. The dogs were constantly fighting, particularly the piggy-eyed White Staffordshires. They seemed to spend half the day, when they were not being fed, tearing each other to pieces. I have rarely encountered anything more terrifying but I determined not to show my fear in the face of their keeper's coolness. Mother and daughter shared this easy practicality in everything. Their assurance was enviable. I was bitten, sometimes quite badly, and began to take it as a matter of course and the Price of Love. Mrs Buffen would bandage my bites with such calm and lack of fuss that when she escorted me the few yards home my mother's ready hysteria was immediately deflated. It was like being given safe conduct by the Lady Almoner. I was saved the days of abuse and recrimination I ordinarily suffered if I returned bruised or bleeding from some encounter with boy or nature in Nonsuch Park. I relied on the uncomplaining aid of strange mothers or sisters. It softened the resentful onslaught when I got home, but none had Mrs Buffen's authority. She made no excuses for me like the others, 'It wasn't his fault. It was only an accident. Don't be *cross* with him.' And when we were left alone together my mother wasn't cross, she just hoped I was grateful to Mrs Buffen. I was, though not for being savaged by her dogs; but at least their bite was no worse than Nellie Beatrice's bark.

Joan went out of her way to draw my attention to sex. She was tantalizingly mysterious, refusing to be explicit and inflaming my bafflement. She had a narrow repertory of infantile jokes, mostly variations on the theme of a small boy and his sister being bathed by their mother, and the boy asking if he might put his train into the girl's tunnel. My father had once attempted to give me a very straightforward account of the whole reproductive process. He drew two detailed male and female figures and began explaining the functions of both at length but simply. The diagrams and the unlikely enormity of it all were too much for me. To his amusement, I rushed out of the room to be sick before he was half-finished. 'What did you want to go and start telling him all that for?' said my mother. 'You know what he's like.' He never brought the subject up again. One day, waist-deep in bull terriers, Joan made me look up the staircase at the enormous figure of Mrs Norman, the butcher's wife, who must have weighed about seventeen stone. Mr Norman, although not a particularly small man, was certainly half his wife's size. Joan's eyes watched me, smirking as she sometimes did when she gave me an unexpected punch in the back. 'What do you think of that?' 'What?' I said. 'What about Mr Norman getting on top of Mrs Norman?' she demanded. I had never thought of it. It was still difficult to imagine when it was put to me. I had only ever seen Mr Norman in his bloody apron and hard as it was to see him on top of Mrs Norman it was unthinkable without his apron. It took some time for me to make sense of the connection between the train and the tunnel.

On rare occasions, she would ask me up to her small, comfortable bedroom. It was more of a sitting-room, a place to talk and read. The lounge in our flat was like a doctor's waiting room without the magazines. Even the wireless was usually in the kitchen. Joan's room had hockey sticks, a well-used armchair, her toy animals, mementoes of holidays, school, jodhpur boots, pictures of flowers, animals and, of course, horses. All our walls at home were bare. There was hardly any evidence of a life already lived or being lived, a solitary enlarged snapshot of my sister hung on the walls of the lounge with a few china heads and flowers. A scattering of glass animals and swans from the Dinky Shop littered the mantelpiece. Magazines and books were cleared away as soon as read. The only permanent books in the house were *The Doctor's Book*, a popular encyclopaedic guide to all sorts of arcane and alarming ailments which could befall the average family, my father's copies of the *Boys' Own Annual* from 1908 to 1915 and Priestley's *Angel Pavement*. A large green volume was kept on the top shelf of the airing cupboard where I was unable to reach it. Years later I came upon it hidden beneath some blankets. It turned out to be *Contraception* by Marie Stopes. I spent days reading it, staring at the photographs, until my mother missed it. 'You haven't seen a big book around, have you? It's a *medical book*. One of the girls lent it to me.'

Joan had her own bookcase, and a full one. Anyone going into my bedroom would have had to guess who its occupant might be. Apart from the teddy bear allowed on my pillow it could have been a room reserved for the odd lodger rather than a child. My few books and comics were 'put away' in a cupboard along with toys. Meals were things prepared with the principal aim of being 'cleared away', washed up; beds, rooms, cushions existed for the sake of being 'tidied up', 'put straight'. The whole process reached its state of pristine perfection if we went on holiday and all hint of life or comfort was covered in immaculate sheets and clean newspapers. Joan's bookshelves contained the kind of things which, unknown to me, were cherished by most little girls of her class. There were girls' annuals, fairy tales, some poetry (Walter de la Mare I think), a few classics, Dickens, Stevenson, Lewis Carroll, Kipling, the *Jungle Books*, *Swallows and Amazons*, *Winnie the Pooh*. I had heard of few of them and read less. There were rows of books with titles like *Smokey—the story of an Exmoor Pony*.

In the holidays she was allowed to come with me to the pictures at the newly built Odeon in Epsom. Her family used the astonishing French pronunciation *O-Day-On*. It did seem a bit affected. Together we saw *Robin Hood* (yet again for me), *Sabu the Elephant Boy* (a particular favourite, this one), and *The Four Feathers*. As with *Robin Hood*, these were all re-enacted by us whenever we could find a willing cast. This was difficult because the nearest kids were a rough, uncooperative lot, but Joan could manage to intimidate a small group of usually younger children into taking part. I was allowed to be Sabu, a prince but a coloured one and therefore Other Ranks.

Before long, during our wanderings in Nonsuch Park alone together, she came to insist that I undo my fly buttons in front of her and achieve as big a trajectory stream over a bank of stinging nettles as I possibly could. I made feeble protests at first but she was able to blackmail me by threatening to refuse to let me come up to her bedroom ever again and read her books or even put my life at risk beside her in the kennels. Besides, I was flattered by her uncharacteristic curiosity. I tried to extract a promise from her that if I followed her command she would perform a similar service for me. Eventually, she agreed, but invariably went back on her word after having watched me with a kind of mocking encouragement. When she did at last relent and take her knickers down and crouch impatiently, I felt none of her exultation. It was a disappointing spectacle. Her demand had been triumphant, a sort of victory. Mine seemed childish and dirty. She allowed me into her room and to expose myself to her only when the caprice took her. Sometimes she would simply refuse without giving any reason. She could be spitefully snobbish, correcting my pronunciation of words. I was unhappy for days when this happened.

Joan was a girl, and I had accepted the role of her NCO, therefore I had to accept her whims. But dismay began to grow into resentment. When her cousin, who went to Epsom College, visited her in his grey shorts, school tie and striped cap, she would usually refuse to let me go out with them on the dogs' twice-daily walks. When I gave up pleading and probably looked abject enough, I would be allowed to accompany them, while they ignored every attempt I made to gain their attention. Such glee in the discomfort of others is one of the many contemptible aspects of childhood. I have encountered it in some adults and once, most overbearingly, in marriage. To look for generosity in a child is like expecting gratitude from a cat. Happily,

66

this predatory gloating usually passes from us as our own frailty becomes more evident than that of others. But the sight of Joan in jodhpurs, her boots gleaming as she strode around the kennel yard like an eleven-year-old Hunter Dunn was inflaming and unbearable. The gulf between us became only too clear and complete. Whenever she swung up on to her piebald pony she was lost to me. It was hard to know which was more hateful, the piebald pony or her cousin. The pony had Joan's thighs around his back. Her cousin was too wholesome and scrubbed to think or have any physical connection with Joan. *He* would never allow himself to be bullied by a girl into exposing himself in front of her. Nor would she have asked him.

I began to see that my longing for any scrap of affection, friendliness or even tolerance would come to nothing. The crumbs would diminish and be given with less and less grace until they were withdrawn altogether. I was a makeshift, and a poor and fleeting one at that. When her cousin left, I would be reprieved. For a day or two she would smile on my enthusiasm until her patience broke again. Seeing my misery only urged her on to throw me back to whence I came, like an amusing mongrel who quickly proves his dull breeding, untrained, untrainable and ultimately unrewarding.

My mother, her indifference melted by unkind curiosity, got the picture with unusual—if blind—accuracy. 'What do you want to go on moping about after Joan for? You just make yourself look silly. She's only laughing at you the whole time. They all are. What do you think a girl like that could see in you? Even if she were the same age, she's not ever going to be interested in someone like you. She'll get fed up with you in five minutes. You'll see. They're all the same. Time you learnt it now. Before you get *really* unhappy.' The prospect cheered her up for a little. The Black Look flaked its powdery surface and broke into a yellow grin.

Before the year was out, Joan told me that she was going away to Boarding School in September. It was 1939. She tried not to sound excited and I tried not to sound impressed. I had learned to protect myself a little. Later, I watched her pack. She showed me her new uniform, books, lacrosse stick. I had nothing to say, but it was unnecessary anyway. What existence I had been allowed was already discarded. When the day came for her to leave I went out of the flat before breakfast and went for a walk in Nonsuch Park. When I came back she was gone. My mother caught my red eyes at once. 'Joan came to say good-bye. I said I didn't know where you'd gone. She looked ever so nice in her posh uniform.'

In time I grew to convince myself that I could become ill with grief. Stricken with Sickness unto Death, I only waited for it to pass. It was vain to resist the excess of a faulty nature. It had to be endured along with the inheritance of a weak body, a blemished skin, ugly limbs, teeth and dandruff. Leaning against Robin's favourite tree in Sherwood that day, the tears falling into my mouth tasted as bitter and surprising as those that were to come. As I spluttered against a tree in a suburban park, an ordinary middle-class English girl in a gym-slip was happily making her way most willingly to school. A girl very like my own daughter now.

If Joan was my first girlfriend she was also for some time my only friend. The boys in the village were a hostile bunch, probably the remainder of what was once Ewell. Their encampment was bounded by the new by-pass on the one side and the growing collection of council houses in West Ewell on the other. The Rec. was their reservation. I dare say their tiny tribe was soon to be defeated by the London homesteaders. Ewell Boys' School, tucked away in its dark lane, was very much as I had dreaded. Like Brompton Hospital, the faded brick and tall windows held out nothing but the promise of harshness and pain. It was damp, dark and cold, even in the summer. The School Inspector—a figure in my life rather like the Income Tax Man in Archie Rice's—who was to follow me around for years to come, finally caught up with me. I don't know why my mother connived in absenting me from school. She was not protective when she protested that I was 'over-sensitive' or 'delicate'. It was as if I were a rather prestigious cripple. There was no question of tangling with authority on my account. Having drawn attention to herself she would have despatched me anywhere. My first day at Ewell Boys' School was much as I expected. Like hospitals, I knew that they were places where pain and humiliation were the rule. Every school and hospital I went to proved me right. With my packet of sandwiches deep in the pocket of the too-new raincoat which my mother insisted on my wearing, I attached myself to a file of boys who looked like prisoners but acted like eager recruits. A huge-chested man in a polo-necked pullover, running on the spot, blasting the whistle between his teeth, shrieked and chased us into the morning assembly. Mr Jones, the Welsh terror himself, already wet-lipped, cane dangling beside his hymnal, herded us through a couple of Ancient and Moderns. There was whipped-up retribution in the air, baiting everyone into a kind of happy expectant impotence.

Almost all the lessons in the class I'd been assigned to seemed to be taken by Mr Blundell, the polo-necked drill sergeant. He told us that he was a superb footballer and that he weighed thirteen stone. He had the instinct of the nerveless for putting his bullying finger on the quaking nerve. He constantly barked out my name, as if it were itself some damn silly bugger's attempt at deceit. The dread time for me at all these council schools was

Playtime. What I remember above all is the constant clash of boots on gravel. Most boys wore huge boots, gaping above the ankle, passed on from their brothers or even their fathers. Some wore no socks. Only a few of us wore shoes. I asked my mother if I might have a pair of these boots, second-hand preferably. They were the accoutrements of war, without them you were unarmed, unprotected. They had a war-like sound and a powerful look. The wearer of such boots had a clear advantage over an adversary wearing a light Freeman Hardy and Willis shoe. Walking the Barratt way was not for these warriors.

The classrooms may have been purgatory but the playtimes were undoubted hell. I always spent the whole twenty minutes longing for the bell which would rescue me back to the comparative safety of the classroom. Apart from physical timidity I was also rather girlishly fastidious. I was, and am still, almost spinsterish in my distaste for noise and personal disorder, although I am capable of initiating both. Because of my mother's instruction not to disturb my father and because of her 'nerves', I was always constrained to close doors with a surgical accuracy so that the lock went into its place without making a sound, or of taking my shoes off in the house and padding about in slippers or even stockinged feet. Creaking stairs had to be negotiated like minefields. These restrictions did not apply to my mother who could make the kitchen reverberate like a firing range. However, I did know that my father, trapped and sore in bed, could be reduced to fulminating pain by a carelessly slammed door or some beefy doctor slumping his carcass on his bed, even by a noisily folded newspaper.

Milk bottles in particular were anathema to my mother; the sight of one half empty on a table would bruise her face into the blackest of her looks, and she would sweep it away out of sight if she didn't actually pour the seamy liquid down the sink. This had a lasting effect on me. Playtime was the festival of the Milk Bottle and I thought it squalid. The smell of milk and the sight of small boys straining at their bottles with or without straws made me feel very queasy indeed. Most of the boys had free milk. I dare say I might have been entitled to it, but my mother gave me the few pence it cost to buy my own, which I pocketed. Apart from my absurd primness, I didn't like milk and loathed taking part in this headlong scramble.

She talked about germs always as if they were like ants that could be made to writhe in a miserable death, gasping on their backs, in the cauldrons of her fortress home. Whenever I emptied my money box she would insist on putting all the pennies, halfpennies, sixpences and threepenny bits into a large bowl, pouring boiling hot water and Dettol over them. They were, she said, full of 'germs' from other people. She was the same about my father's germs. He had 'dry TB' and not 'wet TB', she explained, so Dad's germs did not buzz around in the air like filthy moths. They stayed, presumably snugly, inside him in little sachets like dried cigarette tobacco, almost hygienic germs. Using anyone else's cup was as deadly as handling coins. She hurled pints of scalding water over any cups, plates or forks left behind by the rare visitor. Even the doctor's tea cup was sterilized. His patients' germs must have been jumping like fleas from it. The sight of children sharing the same bottle of Tizer or, worse, milk, made her almost delirious. If ever, afflicted by raging thirst, I was driven to share a bottle, I was to wipe the top of it as vigorously as possible, but only if boiling water were unobtainable.

From this induced aversion to the milk bottle, germ-ridden lucre and the healthy animal noise of everyday life, I developed an overwrought distaste for anything which might become a group or a crowd or threatened confusion. As for orderly groups, like queues, whether outside cinemas and bus stops or martialled, eager lines in the playground, they aroused me to a frenzy of helpless and bigoted malevolence. Later, I always refused, on principle, to buy duty-free goods on aeroplanes or at airports. It must seem a mincing kind of snobbery to those others set on an easy bargain. In any scramble for the best seats, rate of exchange or even for survival itself my prig's foot would be the first to step back. I would insist on the feeble dignity of being at the tail end of the bus queue, and be the first to fall back on the right to watch others pile into the lifeboat. It is neither courage nor politeness. Perhaps it is what is meant by *hubris*. If so, I am afraid it has displayed itself in more petty than heroic gestures. *Hubris* or morose misanthropy, it has been constantly and indeed continues to be tested, just as it was on that first day in the playground.

For a short while I was able to conceal myself behind the wash-house but I knew there was no escape, at least not from the ritual interrogations and trick questions like, 'Does your mother keep dripping?' Smart replies to this kind of cross-examination were more dangerous than silence or stupidity. In my new raincoat with its bourgeois room-for-growth, I was a conspicuous target in that pit of milling boys. The sound of boots on gravel, pitching limbs and shrieks was like nothing I had ever known. Suddenly I found myself watching an earnest, determined-looking boy about my own age who could almost have been cast as William in one of Richmal Crompton's books. He was at the head of a long line of careering boys. Behind him, a chain of them hanging on to coats and jerseys followed on an unsteady rampage all over the playground. Yelling with triumphant ferocity, they hurtled and snaked round, a little like the huge electric Caterpillar Ride in

Dreamland. The point of it was to hang on to the boy in front and not get thrown off the chain. The game was called, simply, Trains, and its inventor turned out later to be the boy at the front. He looked too solemn to lead, let alone enjoy, this kind of demented power. Later I came to realize that by diverting others into excitement, he could escape being manipulated, coerced or bullied himself. He could baffle a brutish little world with clowning, grapeshot energy. It was my first glimpse of Mickey Wall. I came to admire and envy his difference, his wholesome eccentricity which he managed to make acceptable even to the stampeding, booted herd of Ewell Boys' School.

Mickey Wall or, as he preferred, M. Geoffrey Wall was certainly odd if not, as it turned out perhaps, remarkable. For a boy of nine, he had an icy brain, quick and disarming. Such youthful shrewdness often betrays a calculating heart. There was little affection in him but it was to take years for my importunate spirit to realize this. As I watched him, I had no idea of the light-hearted contempt he felt for his companions. When he was about fourteen, a pedantic socialist and professed democrat, he enjoyed quoting Horace about the common herd of men and holding them at bay. *Odi Profanum Vulgus*. 'I loathe the uncouth, vulgar throng', he translated for me. Unlike me, with my patrician pretensions and genuine loathing, he was merely dismissive of meagre intelligence. Hatred would never rush that cool head. For the next five years he was to be my only friend and nobody's fool. Nobody's fool was what I aspired to be, though with little confidence. It was difficult enough to avoid becoming anybody's victim. The herd was about to strike.

Absorbed in watching Mickey Wall's progress across the playground, I was suddenly aware that I was surrounded by three boys. They were dirty, ragged and huge-booted. Their eyes were narrowed with curious hostility. This fixed look scarcely moved when they spoke, their lips and face muscles wired up into a mask of threat. Foolishly, I was slightly reassured by their height. I towered over them. They looked unhealthy, either hard but underfed or flabby and germ-ridden. My spirit stiffened very slightly; a little gasp of home-made *hubris*. One of the boys spoke. 'D'you want a fight?' I knew that there was only one answer to this question. Refusal was impossible and would lead to unending torment instead of isolated bouts of pain. 'All right then.' 'All right then. Take your pick.' I looked at the three of them and immediately chose the smallest. He was a good head shorter than myself, rather plump and unhealthy-looking with a closely shaved head (later I was told he had been a bad lice case). Nowadays he would be identified as a lesser punk. He was slug-like. A swift tap and he might spill

71

slime. Certainly a wet-germ carrier. My mistake was apparent within seconds.

Looking down at the suddenly contemptible slug, I stabbed at him with the classical straight left taught to me by Grandpa Osborne, who had sworn it was the ultimate defence and, with a long reach like mine, a safe, effective attack. Immediately, his fist, which seemed almost as large as his head, hammered into my stomach and ribs. I could see my own blood through the corners of my eyes, tear-like streams pouring down into my mouth, tasting thick and warm. I had no idea of what I was doing but mechanically went on jabbing my ponderously executed straight left well past his right ear. Perhaps twice I contacted his head, hurting my knuckles. The speed and power of his short fat body and bobbing asphalt head were astonishing. I had no idea that such physical strength might exist. It was an astounding experience.

Within seconds he had given out more energy than had escaped from Grandma Osborne for probably a whole half-century. I had lived for eight years without knowing that such animal power roamed the earth around me. Here was Robin Hood all right, cruel and pitiless. In a black and red swirl of faces, boots and asphalt, I looked down at the weaving scrub of the slug-head as I went on blindly miming Grandpa's South Wales amateur middleweight instructions. His fists, like tight pebble bats, pounded into me from forehead to groin. I don't know how long this went on, but presently I heard a voice saying, 'Had enough?' In the blood and darkness I managed to shake my head. He relaxed his speed and began to punch me casually, like a painter adding touches to a canvas. He fell back, just filling in the empty spaces in a diagram of pain. Then, like some cheeky circus dwarf, he butted me in the stomach, not so much with his head as with his whole body.

Suddenly it stopped. I could just make him out. He looked puzzled but not triumphant, then turned away with his two lieutenants to the sound of muted cheers. Such an abject match must have been disappointing, even to those who found the sight of blood its own reward. As a contest it was comparable to a blind-worm faced by a terrier. An older boy led me to the lavatory basins and washed my face clean with water from one of the dreaded milk bottles. My whole body seemed raw and inflamed, within and without. Indeed, all those furious blows seemed buried in my body, unseen. The pain was eased slightly by a glance at my face, which felt as if it had been scrubbed with a pumice-stone but which was not badly marked. I looked at myself, almost grateful for the slug's skill at inflicting inner damage. I needn't expect much more than a medium Black Look and suppertime sulk of sighs and reproach before I escaped early to bed.

The following morning I woke up wondering whether to feign one of my fainting fits or nervous attacks. I decided reluctantly that this would be a strategic mistake. I was right. The iron-headed slug never approached me or even glanced in my direction again. His lieutenants occasionally smirked and bumped into me deliberately in the corridors, but for the rest of the time I was at Ewell Boys' School I was never challenged again. My humiliation had been so complete it was a guarantee of safe conduct. What the slug had done with such ease needed no repetition, even if anyone cared to bother. I made neither friends nor enemies after that first day. Other playgrounds later were to be more dangerous, when my status was not so immediately fixed. I had been tested, found totally wanting and unfit even for occasional persecution. Perhaps the paralysis of shock and pain that had immobilized me had disguised my fear and even been interpreted as dumb courage. Everyone, including the staff (who never interfered in fights until the participants had all but killed each other), had watched the incident and no one ever referred to it. I was surprised and relieved. The slug had established my lowly place in the herd without fuss or feeling. There was a civilized constraint implicit in leaving the humilated or vanquished alone which I found wanting in later adversaries, both men and women. It was a closed incident and natural to the primitive, tribal mind. To the cultivated mind, the closed incident is often too sophisticated and unacceptable to accept graciously, particularly in the face of love or ambition.

For the next year or so my life at Ewell Boys was glum, anonymous and uneventful. Scarcely anyone spoke to me directly, staff or boys, for which I was grateful. Boredom and ratty apathy prevailed from nine till four. Enduring Mr Blundell's jokes and jingles ('When we all go to Chelsea, we shall all see what we shall see, shan't we?'), the present passed, hour by long hour. The extent of pleasure seemed a boiled sweet, excitement was the four o'clock sprint past the church to tea with my father if he were home in bed. Mr Jones continued to rumble during Assembly and Scripture classes, looking like Elijah and sounding like Clive Jenkins having a mild fit. I learnt nothing. We recited the twelve-times table endlessly and memorized Imperial measures, rods, poles and perches. Mr Blundell found I had not been taught either multiplication or short division so he mercifully ignored me. I think we must also have been taught Sellar and Yeatman history, King Alfred and the Cakes and King Canute, and we read Bunyan, Dickens and, of course, the Bible. Those who could read at all did so aloud. The majority, those who couldn't or barely, were left to stare at the pages unaided and in silence. I longed for Nonsuch Park, where Robin Hood was still a kindly soul, and the tales of Joan's Exmoor ponies. Even the treacherous bull terriers were preferable to the inferno of two Playtimes a day. It seemed madness to be doing literally nothing nearly all week when I could have been reading, listening to the wireless, even walking in the empty park or, best of all, talking to my father, Black Looks permitting.

Mickey Wall, the dashing driver of the Train Game, had not yet spoken to me. I would certainly not have approached him. He seemed very cheerful and friendly to everyone in an abstracted way. He had no particular comrades and usually read or carried a book at Playtime. No one bothered him so he had obviously secured his position in the school as surely as I had mine. One morning, going back up the stone stairs to the classroom, I looked behind and saw Mickey Wall making his way alone across the playground. It was a strange sight. He waddled forward, flapping his arms vigorously up and down against his sides like a penguin about to take impossible flight. His concentration was fierce and exhilarated. His palms pumped against his shorts in a deliberate, slow-motion rhythm. 'Wall, what do you think you're doing, for God's sake?' Mr Blundell's parade-ground bellow was startled. Mickey Wall's r.p.m. increased as he swooped downwards. 'I'm just flapping, sir.' 'What d'you mean, you're flapping?' 'I'm *flapping*, sir. I do it all the time.' Mr Blundell's sneer turned to distaste and then discomfort as if he had seen something very nasty indeed. 'Well, whatever it is, stop doing it. You're just looking bloody silly.' 'Yes, sir,' came the cheerful reply. If Mr Blundell hoped for a note of insolence there was none to detect. I had never witnessed such spontaneous and self-assured behaviour. Seemingly unaware of anything but his own joyful release, he did look as if he was having a thoroughly enjoyable time all to himself. Others might have suggested that he was merely acting daft but he seemed to wander the school and even the streets determinedly flapping, happy and unmoved. Here there must be an unusual spirit. He was certainly unique in Ewell Boys' School in 1938. The sound of one hand flapping.

It was forbidden to talk in the school corridors, but one day I found myself beside him as he was singing 'Some of These Days', and quite loudly at that. He gave a passable imitation of what was to me then an unknown Sophie Tucker. Turning, he said, 'D'you know I think that's my favourite song?' 'What is it?' I asked. (Listening to the smart, rented shilling-a-week Ekco wireless was only possible when my mother was out. Music, even turned down to the lowest volume, was too much for her nerves.) His gaiety was startling. '"*Some of These Days*". *Sophie Tucker*,' he said and whooped away into another verse. That afternoon we arranged to have a long talk during Playtime the next day. I wasn't sure I was yet ready to walk beside him in the street; besides, he lived in the opposite direction,

74

off the Kingston Road near the Rembrandt Cinema. Talking was hard to sustain during those dreadful twenty minutes. Shouting, yes, kicking, milk-gurgling, pinching, hurtling and lurching. Conversation was inconceivable. In the event, we were ignored. I might have thought that his petty eccentricity was a splint to support someone hobbled with shyness like myself. I was quite wrong. His extrovert oddity was simply the happy expression of an oddly uncomplicated spirit. He used it to his advantage as a tactical device against parents, relatives, teachers and other boys. For a nine-year-old to invent an enjoyable and acceptable persona cannot be a common achievement. For an Oxford graduate it is a commonplace path, but in a sprouting suburb of South London, eccentricity, like irony, is ineffective or resented. However, he was harmless and cheerful, neither rebellious nor conformist, nothing disconcerted or alarmed him. Polite, almost courtly, he seemed as modest as he was opinionated. Practical, full of cheeky mockery, he might have been dull, but he never seemed so to me. What he lacked in imagination he compensated with the bubbling enthusiasm of his confidence.

Most of the characteristics were ones that I came to suspect or despise in others. It was impossible to think of him brought down by doubt or regret. Doubt could be ignored as a technicality, and regret unlikely to a life conducted without risk. Experience was a series of fairly proscribed certainties and all the more enjoyable for that. He was blessed with the gift of painless accommodation. He would never be happy. It set him apart, and it did seem a rare gift for a boy rather than a common adult flaw. I knew none of these things then about M. Geoffrey Wall. I knew only one thing. I had found a friend. Mrs Buffen could feed the bull terriers herself.

5. O Wall!

Mickey Wall's flapping must have made a strong impression on me. Some thirty years later I found myself struggling to stand on a chair in a rather staid restaurant, the Hotel Metropole in Beaulieu. I then, I am told, for I remember very little of it, gave the assembled diners, English and French, a detailed lecture on how to take physical flight unaided except for a Nietzschean Concentration of the Will. I demonstrated the exact curve, the amount of pressure required, aided by the correct arm movements and supreme resolution needed to inch your feet from the ground, flapping ever more powerfully until you were triumphant astride the air, like a seagull resting on the wind. The next day the waiters were all smiles, and the English visitors cool. I had done it often enough in dreams.

Mickey Wall's technique of containing adults was the pre-emptive strike which left his victims instantly trivialized. With the patience of a sniper, he would pick off an unheeding grown-up with some tangled *non sequitur* or inscrutable nonsense that defused retaliation. Even when he gave voice to what seemed to me the unsayable, his gravity ensured that his reward was never more than a half-hearted cuff or brief banishment from the meal table. It is hard to convey the impact of these sallies, which certainly did not rely on wit but on transported cheekiness. Rude, naughty or invented words exploded with inevitable shock but his blandness belied mischief, let alone wickedness. Propriety and dignity had a whiff of shot and shock, as if innocence, in the form of Mickey, was keeping them on their toes. For those with sufficient style, he had compiled a nine-year-old's manual *pour épater le bourgeois*.

For example, he was ever ready to coin a meaningless phrase or invent a word by the mere addition of a letter. During a long fiery afternoon in Mr Jones's pit of Scripture and whacking, he was challenged about the contents of a toffee tin under his desk. 'What is that you are playing with, Wall?' 'It's my gzoo.' 'What's in that tin?' 'My gzoo, sir.' 'And what's that?' Mickey, looking eagerly helpful, held up the tin and took out the various toy animals, elephants, giraffes, lions, antelopes. 'These, sir. This is my gzoo.' Mr Jones looked upon Mickey's Ark as if it were of the Covenant rather than Noah. The creatures of the pit waited for the fork of Welsh flame to strike and consume the blasphemer. Mr Jones stared, nostrils flared for the whiff of evil. Instead of dragging Mickey to damnation by the ear he flung down his palsied cane and mumbled, 'Well, put it away again. We don't want to see it.' Elijah's chariot wheel had lost a small spoke.

His little guerrilla sorties weren't to be beaten off with retorts like, 'Can't you stop being so *childish*?' 'Why don't you grow up?' When he introduced me to his sister, Edna, a nice but slightly irritable nineteen-year-old, she was bending over the fire grate. 'This is my sister, Edna,' he said. She turned round politely and acknowledged me, all of ten years between us. I was prepared to be impressed both by her seniority and attractive appearance, but not for his comment. 'Hasn't she got a big arse?' he said thoughtfully. Edna aimed a token blow at him. She was used to his solemn insults but they still disconcerted her. Once, returning in his parents' car from a day trip to Eastbourne, he winked at me, as he usually did before he was about to take aim and, leaning forward to his mother's ear, yelled, 'Ma!' 'Yes.' Pause. 'You've blown off.' The consternation that resulted from this grenade slung into the front of the car was furious. Mr Wall almost stopped the motor as if some damage needed inspection. We all rode back in silence, Mr and Mrs Wall like the victims of a bomb attack and Mickey and I exploding with our easy rout. On our return he was packed off to bed without supper and I was reproachfully sent home.

On another occasion during a visit to his aunt's in Saffron Waldon, we had been particularly instructed to be quiet and well mannered, as Auntie was going through a difficult time. 'Don't play her up, lads,' said Mr Wall confidentially. 'She's a bit on the sensitive side. Anything'll bring on the old waterworks.' Then, man to man, he added, 'You know—woman's troubles.' We didn't know. I doubt if it would have stopped Mickey, winking at me over the tea table as she moved into his sights. She was a kindly woman, taking great pains to give us a huge, country tea with hams and unfamiliar delicacies. 'You're quiet, Mickey. What are you thinking?' There was the usual pause as he despatched yet another piece of cake or trifle before he lobbed over his reply. 'I was thinking ...' he turned to her husband. '... I was thinking she's an old cow.' I sat appalled at this gratuitous assault. Perhaps he'd expected the waterworks to explode but his aunt took it calmly. He must have realized his mistake as he almost immediately sent himself to bed. He was not so much willing to wound as unafraid to strike. No reference was made to it during the rest of our stay and if Auntie had been hurt she concealed it, pushing on to us all the good things we could carry when we left. Our fears that she would report the incident to Mr Wall were dispelled.

Mickey's father was a genial man, a minor clerk in some government department in Whitehall. He had a dry line in humour. When I proudly showed myself in my first pair of long trousers he said, 'Nice fit under the armpits.' Grandma Osborne and others had been insultingly scornful: I was too young for them. It was a relief to have them regarded so lightly and not as a social blunder. He was also about the only person I knew who drove a car, a 1938 Ford. My mother's insistence that cars were driven almost exclusively by doctors led me to believe that he must be well-off, although his appearance and way of living seemed unremarkable. He walked to the station and the car was mostly used for Bank and summer holidays. There was a telephone in its proper place behind the front door but, like those belonging to carless residents, its use was monitored and not encouraged. Mickey said his father earned eight pounds a week, which was the same as my father. However, as my mother pointed out bitterly, *they* hadn't got doctor's bills to pay. Added to this, Mickey's mother worked as a secretary in a newsagents and stationers in Epsom.

She seemed immeasurably older than her husband and Mickey was pleased to embarrass her by telling any company assembled that he was 'a change of life baby'. He surely must have been because she had been Lord Robert's secretary during the First World War, and her life must have changed especially late for she looked as if she were his grandmother. She was a busy, impatient woman, constantly typing in the otherwise unused front parlour, but she was always absent-mindedly welcoming. It was a relief to be accepted unthinkingly as just an extra place setting, without the resentful preparation of 'dainty' sandwiches, expensive shop cakes, and with no recriminations afterwards about the bother of it all. If Mickey or Joan came to tea they were fawned upon and then reviled after their departure. Hospitality was as unknown to Nellie Beatrice's nature as friendship. Her attempts at it were simply more excuses to put someone in her debt so that her social rent book was paid up and in credit. But then if you've never felt welcome in your heart for anyone, sharing a meal is no more than taking in Extra Catering. If my mother asked you to break bread with her she was only thinking of how long it would be before she could start clearing up crumbs after you.

I was soon spending almost every evening at the Walls' home at 39 Bradford Drive. There were no invitations at teatime. It was assumed I was staying. Even during the war, with rationing pinching hard, such a hungry family (unlike my mother, they would never have resorted to the Black

78

Market or the favours of spivs and GIs even if they might have had the opportunity) fed me as lavishly as they could. Nellie Beatrice could neither understand nor admire this behaviour. It was baffling, unmotivated and suspect. Like their house, which was untidy, shabby and none too clean, it paid no heed to her rent-book accounting. The kitchen at Ewell Parade was as bare as an empty operating theatre. The dishcloths were as sparkling as clean sheets and the scrubbing brushes looked scrubbed themselves. It would have taken a strange strain of germ to have entered there. The Walls' kitchen smelt of fat and burnt greens eroding the walls and woodwork, the saucepan enseamed and blackened like an industrial antique. What the bottom of the sink was like I never knew, as it was buried at all times beneath a cold greasy sea of floating china. If Ewell Parade was Auschwitz to germs, 39 Bradford Drive must have been Butlins with special terms for cockroaches.

Big-arsed Edna was a good-natured girl, rather plain and anxious. Saturday was the big night of the week at the Walls', though little happened except for a long and lavish tea when Edna's anxiety about the coming evening sometimes became oppressive. She and her friend would have a bath after tea and then rush up and down the stairs in curlers, half dressed for hours, in preparation for a dance at the Stoneleigh Hotel or the Toby Jug at Tolworth. It was a frantic, enjoyable event to watch. Few people I knew had a bath more than once a week. It was a fixed feast in the calendar, usually Friday or Saturday, and everyone took their turn. During the war it was unpatriotic and impractical to soak in more than the prescribed four inches, which barely covered the nether parts. It was a hardship easily borne. Most people shared Grandma Osborne's belief that immoderate bathing was 'weakening'. But before the demands of the war effort there were the claims of economy, health and even, in the Walls' case, a hint of morality—Mrs Wall insisted that Mickey bathed in a pair of bathing trunks to cover up what was known in that family as your 'tickle pot'. I was never sure whether this was one of his flights of flapping fancy. However we were not allowed to play cards on Sunday so it might have been a dark aspect of his mother's otherwise free and easy bearing. Similar Saturday-night fever must have been disrupting tea in lower middle-class households all over Britain, but at the Walls' it was simply rowdy and good tempered and Edna was a forgiving butt. After several hundred tantalized Saturdays Edna got married in the early part of the war to a French-speaking aircraftman from Guernsey. He left her after six months and nothing was said about the circumstances. I don't know whether or not she remarried. I hope so.

Mickey's brother, Alan, was a pupil at Tiffins School in Kingston. He was studious, amiable and looked uncritically upon his younger brother and even myself as temporary lunatics. The Walls were not, as my mother described them with sham admiration, a close-knit family. They were quite loosely knit, with dropped stitches all over the place, but as comfortable as an old pullover. To me, their trust seemed almost like indifference. The Osbornes and the Groves, with their common mistrust and carping, suspicious spirits, were neither close-knitted nor comfortable. The grudge that was their birthright they pursued with passionate despondency to the grave.

I had Saturday tea at the Walls', on and off, until I was nearly eighteen and went off to the provinces. Even at that age, even then, possibly from habit, Mickey and I behaved like a variety act, like giggling schoolgirls rather than teenagers who were curious about books and politics for no identifiable reasons. 'Come on, old man, out with it. If the joke's that good why don't you share it with everyone? Either that or get down from the table.' We would invariably have to 'get down', when we retreated to an emergency meeting of the Viper Gang in Mickey's room. The occasional cloud of disapproval or, even rarer, disgrace, was always preferable to hushed evenings at Clandon Close or the Old Black Look of Home.

M. Geoffrey Wall was president of the Viper Gang Club, membership two, myself being the secretary. The objects of the club were implicit in its name. It was formed to strike. Its targets needed no specification. It created a deterrent, although, as its existence was unknown except to us, its value in this respect was limited. We tried to remedy this by posting cards bearing an ill-drawn viper about to pounce above the words 'The Viper Gang is Watching You'. The teachers, schoolchildren and parents who received them can hardly have been alarmed. It was also frustrating, since no one could respond to the anonymous challenge, so postage was pointless as well as wasteful. However, the existence of a secret society can be sustained by the pursuit of pure secrecy itself like some abstract discipline. It was enough to be secret about being secret. The newsagent who refused to sell you five Woodies, even though you swore they were for your Dad, would have no idea that henceforth he was under permanent and clandestine malign scrutiny. Actual consumption of tuppeny ha'penny packets of Woodies, Weights or De Rezkes was indeed not only secret but subversive, risking deprivation of supper, privileges, pocket money, a possible thumping for Mickey or the Black Look of the Month Choice from my mother.

Soon I, too, became J. James Osborne, and survived for a while as the signature on the fly leaf of my school books. Later, when I began writing poetry and short stories I omitted the initial J. It sounded too American.

John was a boring, commonplace name. James was forthright and adult-sounding. We both came from homes where books and music were almost completely disregarded. Although no one said as much, people who went out to work every day had no time for such luxuries. Even in the Walls' house there was little to read apart from the dusty Waverley novels, a complete Dickens and an incomplete encyclopaedia. When I see the junk books on my sixteen-year-old daughter's shelves and hear the exclusively pop music she plays, I wonder at the catholicity of the Viper Gang's taste in music and literature. I find it hard to understand what influences made us cast out cultural nets so haphazardly. Our earliest reading, with grown-up encouragement for once, was the *Magnet* and the *Gem*. We became early archivists in this later rich field, acquiring the first issue of the *Magnet*, 1908, and of the *Gem*, 1912, for a few pence in Epsom and Kingston markets. Later, when I was out of work, I sold the whole collection, with its Nelson Lees, Sexton Blakes and Schoolboy's Own Libraries, for £8. It would be worth many hundreds more than that now. We read comics: the *Dandy*, *Hotspur*, the *Wizard*, clung still to Mickey Mouse and had a fondness for *Chips*, a pink comic beloved of my father. This featured two especially likeable characters in Weary Willy and Tired Tim, who glorified good-hearted laziness and friendship, unharassed by teachers threatening not only work but extra work, and adults demanding stints of weeding or burdensome shopping, and were the very ideal of friends. The *Dandy*, with Keyhole Kate, Desperate Dan, Homeless Hector and Ivor Clue, was popular with everyone. Possibly, for this reason, I decided it was rather coarse. Popularity didn't affect my taste for *Film Fun*, I had spent too many hours in the cinema to resist its spell, its cramped little drawings with its regular final tableau of two comedy heroes—Laurel and Hardy or Arthur Askey and Stinker—sitting down in triumph to a blow-out in a posh restaurant surrounded by attentive waiters. Diamond tie-pins as big as pebbles sparkled above napkins tucked into their collars, as they brandished knives and forks in front of a gorgeous mountain of mashed potatoes studded with sizzling sausages pointing outwards, like batteries of guns on a battle cruiser.

This dish, which no one ever seems to have seen in life on a real plate, was the ultimate metaphor of wealth and success. It was the still-life subject of ultimate poshness. I once tried to persuade my mother to create it for me but she refused. I tried it myself, but the potatoes were neither mountainous nor gorgeous and the sausages, limp and bready, sagged pathetically. The tie-pins and the waiters were missing. Lacking, too, was the essential ingredient of this fantasy dish—success. Secret celebration is all very well, but when the reason for it is inaccessible, even to its participants, it must taste unsatisfying.

Beside Mr Wall's unread Waverley novels, there were a few books that must have been bought by someone in the family in the last century. Together with these, we read or skipped and delved into the books Mickey was later introduced to at Tiffins. We puzzled over and sometimes enjoyed Harrison Ainsworth (*The Tower of London*, particularly) and Bulwer Lytton, both dusty Victorian historical novelists, *Gulliver's Travels, Tale of a Tub, Rape of the Lock*, Everyman editions of Tacitus and Suetonius (odd chapters), and *The Faerie Queen* (his set books). I still have a lot of the books we read then. Apart from politics, histories of the world by Wells (*Crux Ansata* was a favourite) and Winwood Read were popular. I suppose they were the common popular self-educational coinage of the time. Wells seemed a bit too much like a scrimping schoolteacher for me. I goaded myself through Shaw's dull novels once, when I was convalescing in Penzance, but we enjoyed the Prefaces to the plays almost more than the plays themselves. They were both frowned upon, unread, by most adults which made them essential to the Viper Gang. Also on our shelves were *The Scarlet Letter, Alice in Wonderland*—read many times—Edgar Allen Poe, Dumas, Hugo, Stevenson, Kipling, Belloc for some reason, but not Chesterton. We had a sneaking regard for Grandma Osborne's Warwick Deeping and despised what were probably the most popular of boys' stories at the time, the Biggles books.

A device common to many of us, even in later life, is that of appraising the character of others by their tastes in literature, films or art by marking them against your own. It is a superficial guide to personality but can be surprisingly accurate in the case of early allegiances. Or so it seemed to me. Biggles readers were unspeakable, as were admirers of the Three Stooges, a film comedy trio universally popular with schoolchildren at the time. But partisanship about comedians seems to lose little of its intensity with the advance in time. The schism between Chaplin men and Keaton men remains abiding. Most of us revere our comic angels and denounce the devils of others. It is possibly as well that we each take our stand on laughter, which is founded on our confusion. We only compound the chaos it expresses for us by dissembling, because we fear to confess that we may sit unhappy and baffled, unable to be coerced by the laughter of others.

I don't know why we were both intrigued by books as musty objects as much as ciphers to something that was being concealed from us. Mickey certainly had a complacent, academic nature, an immunity to imagination (in spite of his near-Surrealist, almost Lewis Carroll swoops) that pointed unmistakably to his ending up a polytechnic pundit or at least a school-teacher of sorts. As it turned out, he became a clerk in the Transport Department at County Hall. He probably did the crossword in four minutes on the 8.17 to Waterloo, but the *Telegraph* not *The Times*. At the age of nine he had all the blandness and inability to be aroused of the fully paid-up London Library card-carrying pedant, all characteristics locked into life-long combat with my own ungovernable choler. Our temperaments could hardly have been more dissimilar.

In spite of my admiration for Mickey's awesome curiosity, I developed a distaste for crossword wizards. Apart from envy of such indisputable cleverness, I also felt perhaps unwisely that intellectual facility of this order must be the mark of an impassive, untroubled spirit—a justification for my own inadequacy which persisted. A few years ago in the south of France, I was joined by a group of young, rich, successful men and their wives and girlfriends. Their bronzed bodies glimmered with health, wealth and a muscley, animal yet urban confidence. The men were the kind of lawyers, accountants, brokers or property dealers who were being tipped to become millionaires before they were twenty-eight. One of the girls noticing me, asked me with over-polite indifference, 'What did you do for 17 Down?' My brain, dimmed more than usual by several morning Ricards and sunshine, slowly concluded that she was referring to that day's *Times* crossword. 'I don't do the *Times* crossword.' 'You don't!' Her surprise, if that is what it was, seemed more hostile than curious. 'But how do you exercise your mind?' Discarding the coarse reply that sprung to mind—'I fuck intellectual girls'—possibly thinking it was too subtle for her and her companions, I mumbled something about letting my mind out for a swift turn round the block only when absolutely necessary.

When he was barely thirteen, Mickey declared he might become a philologist and walked about with two heavy works under his arm or in his satchel. One was Hogben's *Loom of Language* and another was by a Dane called Jespersen about the science of languages, and from these he would quote passages about the roots of Finnish or Icelandic verbs. Early on I had a rather morose taste for Grimms' tales and Oscar Wilde's fairy stories. Perhaps because of Grandpa Grove's prurient obsession with Wilde, I read all I could find about him, as well as the plays, *The Ballad of Reading Gaol*, *De Profundis* and *Soul of Man under Socialism*. Even then this last was surprising and intriguing and seemed to contradict the flabby voluptuous-ness of the fairy tales or my grandfather's judgement of his life. Later, before 1945, we both became intrigued with Socialism and the Labour Movement, reading indelibly dull books about people like George Lansbury and J. B.

Thomas, books about the General Strike, the Jarrow March and, of course, every available word of Orwell. We bought Strachey's *The Theory and Practice of Socialism*, *The Road to Wigan Pier*, *Guilty Men* and many another Gollancz orange-covered edition.

Somehow the excitement of the 1945 General Election filtered down to two schoolboys, possibly because it was the first Election we had experienced. The end of the buoyant days of the war was in sight and we must have looked for something to replace it. A new eager divisiveness was snatching in the air, increasingly evident in the *Mirror* and the *Daily Worker* which began to throw startling light for us on the attitudes of the *Mail* and *Telegraph*, and all the adults we knew read nothing else. We chortled over Quintin Hogg's book *The Case for Conservatism*. The case for Socialism appealed less to idealism than to the crude subversiveness of the early Viper Gang. We could acquire a populist chic with little more than slogans about the means of production, statistical runes about 1 per cent of the nation owning 90 per cent of the nation's wealth, and mere graffiti like 'Joe for King'. The practical mood of the country, sensed so accurately and crusaded by the *Mirror* with its Servicemen's readership, must have attracted an army of similar cheeky boys, to whom 'Jane' was not only a handmaiden to randiness but an Angel-General leading us out of the land of adolescent bondage.

Among such boys was Hugh, who later became a lecturer in politics at Keele. His was more of a Damascus awakening than our anarchic dissidence. At the age of thirteen or fourteen he was a passionate Christian Socialist and devotee of the works of Conrad Noel, whom he would quote almost word for word at great length, interspersed with long passages from Isaiah and *Prometheus Unbound*. Shelley and Isaiah were his twin Messiahs. Although we might have regarded ourselves as the Apostles of Ewell, there was little affinity otherwise between us and Hugh. His cleverness and the devoutness of his conversion were impressive but his solemnity clashed with our taste for cheap ridicule rather than systematic argument. There was a whiff of nocturnal emissionary zeal about the chap. We had the instincts of pillaging soldiery rather than missionaries.

Hugh's memory was prodigious, even by Mickey's standards. To me, having no gift of memory, it was miraculous. Our giggling Godlessness, bent on petty vexation rather than fierce vision, seemed and was shabby in the face of his Christian Socialism. Baring-Gould was another of his heroes. I got a little pleasure reading a passage from *Point Counter Point* in which the character based upon D. H. Lawrence suddenly reviles Shelley for canoodling with nauseating love-sick angels, ending up, 'I wish to God the bird [the skylark] had had as much sense as those sparrows in the book of Tobit and dropped a good large mess in his eye.' Hugh winced at my delight in Huxley's coarseness. 'You're so superficial,' he'd say. 'You sound just like Noel Coward.' I wasn't quite sure how to react to this. All I knew about Noel Coward was that he wore dressing gowns all day, played the Captain in the film *In Which We Serve*, which Mickey and I had enjoyed immensely, and had written the awful 'I'll See You Again', beloved of my mother. We made it clear that Baring-Gould gave us the pip and that Shelley was the victim of wanker's doom, without a decent limerick in him. Our ribaldry was doubtless the unthinking exuberance of commonplace minds. Whatever the truth of this might have been—and it could be justified—Old Hugh was mightily lacking in the salt of human scepticism. We all attended the local Labour Party meetings and Hugh was shocked at our mocking of the chairman who kept saying that the People had been Misled, a word that he pronounced as 'mizzled'. It was another example of our purblind failure to confine ourselves to what no doubt, in later years, Hugh would have called the Broader Issues.

Mickey and I were always joining, usually for a very short time, various societies or organizations. He persuaded me to join the Epsom Choral Society, which was affiliated to the Goldsmiths' Union. We both went for an audition. He read hardly any music and I none at all. Somehow we duped Mrs Ralph Vaughan Williams, who was in charge of the choir. We even took part in a concert in the Albert Hall and I found myself among a regiment of huge baritones struggling to make sure that I turned the pages over in the right place during the *Messiah* and the *St Matthew Passion*. Mickey joined something called the Linguists' Club for which I at least couldn't bluff my credentials. He discovered Bradlaugh, the Victorian atheist militant, and I subscribed to the Rationalist Press Association which published a monthly magazine, the *Freethinker*, which we read aloud eagerly, selecting the most offensive passages, to Hugh. Later, the office in which I worked in Fleet Street overlooked their headquarters in Johnson's Court and I could gaze down at the very temple of my unbelief. Another publication, *The Thinker's Library*, featured contributions by a renegade Catholic priest calling himself Father McCabe. As I remember, his tales were almost exclusively concerned with the lewd activities apparently raging in monasteries, and the depravities of nuns.

The BBC was our sole music mentor, or mine certainly. For almost a year when I was in bed with rheumatic fever, I listened all day to both Forces and Home programmes, discovering how to pronounce Dvořák and Dohnányi and what the mysterious 'Köchel' might be. During the war, gramophone records had a punitive Purchase Tax imposed on them, being classed as luxuries, along with furs and jewellery. Perhaps it was some gaggle of sour egalitarians protecting the people from elitists who clamped a higher tax on Mozart than Glenn Miller. Anyway, one twelve-inch scarlet-label record of a symphony (usually six to eight sides) cost nine and elevenpence three farthings, $33\frac{1}{3}$ per cent of which was tax. Collecting under these proscriptions was difficult so we pooled our money and saved for months to buy a symphony or concerto. We vowed to have a complete set of Beethoven and Vaughan Williams, all seventeen symphonies. We never achieved it partly because it was too tempting to buy single records rather than wait for weeks. The first one I ever bought was a Beecham recording of the 'Entry of the Queen of Sheba' and then Prokofiev's Classical Symphony.

The cinema was my church and academy. From about the age of four I went at least twice a week. In those days of double features I must have seen over two hundred films a year. It was the kind of thriftlessness that made Grandma Osborne and her tribe swear as indignantly as she did about the Welsh miners at home throwing legs of mutton to their whippets. When the insurance man, the clothing-club man or the milkman called and my mother was hiding in the bedroom, I would as often as not be sent to the front door to mumble, 'Mum's out'; but she could always lay hands on Money for the Pictures—the mainstay cultural benefit of a generation of children from similar backgrounds to my own. Picture Palaces, as Grandma Grove still called them, were aptly named. The warm luxury of Eastern or Egyptian Art Deco, the ascension of the cinema's organist like a matey angel, were preferable to a cold room with a mantelshelf lined with unpaid bills from doctors, coalmen and the Gas Light and Coke Company. To the profligate poor or near-poor, the priority of the Picture Palace was an unanswerable case.

Hollywood bit-players, now known by name only to cineastes, the elevator boys, gangsters, cab-drivers, bar-tenders, cops, butlers, Italian chefs and foreign counts were, I suppose, as real to us then as the characters of *Coronation Street* today. The difference lay in the kind of familiarity. For one thing, it was unmistakably foreign and beyond our reach. We had to learn to translate intuitively what Confederate money was, a sawbuck or even a hundred bucks, convert a dime or a nickel into something comparable, or the meaning of being behind the eight-ball, taking a raincheck or over and easy. These were elementary steps but they had to be mastered at an age when the grasp on your own language and birthplace was meagre enough.

But foreign, and specifically American, their very strangeness made the dreams of Hollywood accessible and open to identification and fantasy in a way that home-grown films were not. Surely few *Coronation Street* diehards could want to live there. The luxury and privilege of, say, living in Manhattan held more promise of imaginative fulfilment than the more familiar but remote English equivalents. The American model was unreal but attainable, the English model slightly more real but ultimately unattainable. A world of large gardens, tennis parties, housemaids, college scouts and Inns of Court might seem pleasant and comfortable enough but there was little impulse or point of dreaming yourself into it. You would watch it from without but never enter it even if you were inclined. What was not unimaginable or close to you was Eric Blore opening the door to your apartment, having William Powell recover your wife's jewellery for you, being made vice-president of a corporation by your father-in-law, Edward Arnold or Eugene Palette, handing your topper to the hat-check girl at the Stork Club as you escorted Carole Lombard or even, at a pinch, Gail Patrick into dinner, wearing a black shirt and white tie and black pin-stripe with a white carnation like Dan Duryea, or maybe taking a cab driven by Frank Jenkins to Penn Station. There was no need to have passed your Common Entrance, let alone have been to Eton or Oxford. It was available, to be admired, envied and even coveted, and most of all to those of us in the front seats who had sneaked in through a carelessly unbarred exit door.

Madeleine Carroll was my earliest favourite star, but then there were scores, year after year, never replacing, only enriching each other. Robert Donat reminded me of my father, although they were unalike. I saw *Thirty-Nine Steps* whenever I could and there was a time when I knew the dialogue of *The Four Feathers* and *The Prisoner of Zenda* by heart. The Rembrandt Cinema in Ewell was almost always full every evening during the war. On Fridays and Saturdays there was certain to be a queue. A Bette Davis film was almost impossible to get into all the week. Even Grandma Osborne was known to leave her Warwick Deeping for the afternoon and walk a hundred unaided yards to the Rembrandt to see *Now Voyager* or *Mr Skeffington*.

I can only remember one occasion when the Rembrandt was almost empty the whole week—apart from Mondays, which were unpopular. The word of mouth about the film showing around Ewell and Stoneleigh was resentful and indignant. In the Parades and saloon bars, there was talk of Speaking to the Manager, even of Writing to the Film People themselves. Later in the week, undeterred by those who said we were wasting our pocket money, Mickey and I went to see *Citizen Kane*. We came out afterwards from looming Gothic darkness into the bright Kingston Road, silent,

87

uncomprehending and deeply depressed. At tea the Walls asked if we had tummy ache. It had been nothing, even for two such eleven-year-olds as we were, to giggle about.

6. Bugger Bognor

My father was away in the sanatorium in Menton for a few months, leaving me without even a silent ally. I went home as little as I could, spending days or the short evenings first with Joan Buffen and later with the Walls. I avoided going back to the certainty of the Black Look, the reproach for being late when I had scrupulously made sure I was on time, the whine of complaints about selfishness, what was so special about the Walls? They were nobody; he was only a government clerk; worse than a guvnor's man; only with a pension. That stuck-up kid in her riding breeches, who did they think they were? Anyone could run a wool shop if you'd got the money; morbid job; no life; so bloody quiet; no one to talk to; dead and alive; nowhere to go; seen all the pictures on; walked to Epsom; just enough for a cup of tea and a bun; can't remember when I last had a drink.

Ewell, 1964

Dear John,

   They say if one can live here one can live anywhere, as one might express it: the English weather is always pulling down the blind on beauty. I would like to have a small cottage near the sea: and shops—*not* too remote as I have been so used to noise and lots of cars and people, when one is old and lives alone one does not want to be shut up at least, I don't; after all you're a long time dead. I like life and people and I think a change from this place and Stoneleigh would be rather nice. Please *don't* think I am discontented: *far from it.* Treated myself to a pair of curtains: cost nearly £2 gosh everything is a price: you could get the same ones for 10/- a few years back: but it will brighten it up a bit. Had a dam depressing letter from Queenie: so sent her £1 to cheer her up. What an unhappy woman she is.

Always in my thoughts,
Mother

p.s. Sorry ree the mistakes and writing—must get some more glasses my sight is not too good.

Fortunately, she let my room to a commercial traveller and spent hours preparing huge meals for him in the evenings with the result that she had a lodger *and* was well out of pocket at the week's end. When he offered to pay more she refused, saying to me, 'I can't help it. I'm just good hearted that's all. There it is—that's the way I am. Always have been.' This preposterous conviction was reward enough for her and she smiled at me knowingly when she gave Mr Evans his dinner, telling him what a quiet, good boy I was. However, it was more than worth my sleeping on the sofa and I hoped he would stay until my father returned.

I got regular postcards from the south of France with his drawings on one side of them, very detailed and spidery. They were mostly jokes constructed around current catch-phrases, using me as the principal character. He sent one of a 'skipper', which was his name for me, in a sou'wester and vast oilskins, staring up at an enormous giraffe, quoting Mae West, 'Come up and see me sometime.' 'Can't. I'm no angel,' replied Skipper. I had dozens of these with laconic messages in his tiny but legible handwriting, always in green ink and with a postscript for my mother. 'Dad's had his bum shot full of gold today so he's never been more valuable. The nurse is German and a proper Hun she is. Must be Mrs Hitler.' I kept them for twenty years until they were stolen from me by a vengeful lady of too intimate acquaintance who refused to return them.

Early in 1939 he returned, relieved to be free of the Hun's tortures. Sitting around the flat, fully dressed but always wearing his Sherlock Holmes-style check piped dressing gown and large carpet slippers, stroking the cat and reading, he said little but his presence silenced my mother somewhat and the atmosphere and tension calmed considerably. Occasionally he would venture out to a nearby pub and go for a short walk, but by the spring he was again spending most of the day in bed.

During that summer the Walls took me in their dinky claret and black Ford to Felpham near Bognor. It was their custom to rent a little semi-detached house in this seaside suburb which has now become an exclusively geriatric watering place. It was pleasant enough, a little like the leafier environs of Clandon Close with identical shopping parades catering for its mostly regular annual visitors. Nellie Beatrice reluctantly agreed to let me go after tactful pressure from my father. He was not yet so ill that she dared to ignore his fleeting will. As ever she was determined not to be beholden to anyone or tricked into making preparations for suspect favours. Naturally, the Walls thought nothing of it. The only money I needed was the price of a cheap bathing costume—one and sixpence—which I bought at the H. G. Wells draper's in Epsom with its smell of calico and overhead cash trolleys.

When I showed it to her, she said, 'Well, there goes my Sunday Guinness.' I decided the best course was to disbelieve her. She was to remind me of this sacrifice from time to time, probably in imitation of Grandma Osborne and the Lisbon Hospital bills. Immediately I returned she waited sullenly for me to finish my blurting account of Royal Bognor before she attacked me for not having brought back a present for her or my father. My father told me not to think about it, which is exactly what I had done. Eight days of Black Looks could not blow away the sunny freedom of those two weeks.

I had been to Bognor before in the winter of 1934. Bognor, made legend by the last words of the recently dead king. Three years ago I returned with my daughter. It seemed very much the same—pleasingly small, shabby and unassuming—with the same arcade of shops and stalls, the pier (now irreparably storm-damaged), a first-rate bookshop, Queen Victoria's comfortable old hotel. Apart from a huge Colditz Butlin's complex on the eastern shore, some concession to fashion and dress, a collection of foreign students hanging around the Victorian station and more traffic, it could almost have been 1939 again.

On my first visit I had been sent to recuperate from a mastoid operation, subsidized entirely by my father's charitable association, the National Advertising Benevolent Society, which was to steer both of us through the fiscal waters of repeated illnesses. Then, with my right ear smothered in one of my mother's absurd black berets, specially sent from Paris she boasted, we stayed in a very cheap boarding house where welcome was unknown, particularly during the day. Forbidden to return to our cold bedroom till high tea, we trailed around the town, a small enough place, in the March wind and rain waiting in cafés and promenade shelters for the cinemas to open. Munching ham rolls from Woolworth's, we would shiver until it was time for us to be allowed back for our soup, pink salmon and salad. I came out in a series of large ugly blisters which burst like watery boils and were extremely painful. The local doctor insisted that the only cure for them was to stand in the icy sea up to my knees. I was also to conceal them from the landlady in case she turned us out. Neither of us wanted to stay but my mother was afraid that we might be reported to Mrs Ure, the kindly secretary of the benevolent society, who had made our holiday arrangements for us.

My visit with the Walls was very different. We went for long drives in the black and claret Ford into the countryside for picnics, to Chichester to look over the Cathedral, empty and uncluttered by German tourists, unlike when I visited it some forty years later. We spent the long sunny days on the beach tucking into piles of tinned salmon, sardine and ham sandwiches, shivering in the cold sea, sustained by Tizer, blessed Tizer, the orange champagne bubbly of thirties' children, and the cooler mornings in amusement arcades, with fish and chips for tea, the end-of-the-pier show and then back to Felpham, as friendly and familiar as Bradford Drive. We could go back when we liked and stay up as long as our happy, tired bodies would allow us.

Only one incident marred my second visit to Bognor. For years I suffered the humiliation of being a fairly regular bed-wetter. I had not yet discovered that this was a common affliction and that the lone unfortunate bed-wetters themselves conspired unknowingly in their own isolation, each one intimidated into believing that he or she was a toad-like creature who made a swamp of beds in defiance of all that was decent. If it was hinted that a child had 'filthy habits' everyone knew at once what it meant—and it wasn't picking one's nose. To be exposed as one of these was hideous degradation, and left you permanently under threat of blackmail, revenge or gratuitous cruelty from any child or parent who might be privy to the sinful stream that insistently gushed forth from your possessed body. Certainly a majority of children at the schools I attended were such sinners, but working-class clothes smelt anyway and stale urine was little more than an ammonial additive. Parents and children from Bradford Drive and Clandon Close, with at least one ritual bath a week and neat washing lines, were more fastidious. Occasionally, some especially nasty boy—a customs officer, Inland Revenue Inspector or letter-writer to the *Daily Telegraph* in the making—would yell, 'Pooh! Blimey! Don't go near him, he's wet his bed!' And a few more inspectors, town hall toadies and form-serving bullies-to-be of post-war Britain would hold their noses and perhaps dance around the flushed-out victim. But some of the tormentors would be aware of the shame beneath their own noses.

Naturally, my mother was hot on to this gaping weakness, and it stoked her ingenuity to theatrical excess. She would settle for nothing less than an auditorium for my arraignment. She would expose me before the assembled school, the Headmaster, the lady teachers, the girls, indeed the entire world. Grim tales abounded about children forced to stand with their shameful sopping shrouds covering their bowed heads. It must have been a fairly common ritual, especially in institutions, but observed in lower middle-class homes as well. As usual, my father, when he was at home, came to my rescue. When he discovered this reign of blackmail he immediately and angrily put a stop to it. Brushing aside my mother's aggrieved self-righteousness, he took me to a doctor, who discussed the problem, all smiles, and diagnosed a general state of anxiety, which sounded more encouraging than wilful sloth. The doctor gave me a monthly diary in which I was to mark the dry days with a red pencil, rather like a church calendar. My father checked it with me regularly, but for months there were no red-letter days, High or Holy, and we quietly gave up the experiment. Nothing was said. Nellie Beatrice was not yet secure enough in my father's frailty to challenge him but she gave the clear impression of having been vindicated of cruelty.

So, I was unsurprised after a night's blissfully fatigued sleep in Felpham to wake early and find myself wet, cold and immediately awake and trembling. I was sharing a bed with Mickey but his place was empty. I lay wondering whether I had overflowed on to his side. Hoping it might dry up under the heat of my own body I got up and found that the guilty overflow seemed to have stayed in my own territory. I took off my wet pyjama trousers and looked up to find Mickey and his brother Alan staring at me and at the bed. Almost immediately, I ejected another pounding flood on to the bare floorboards. The sound of it seemed to splutter all over the small house and go on endlessly. Finally Alan said, rather calmly, 'You seem to have a weak bladder, old man.' I stared at the ragged grey stain, defeated. When they had gone to breakfast, I managed to approach Mrs Wall alone in the kitchen and began to explain the terrible event. She interrupted me almost at once, telling me to have my breakfast and not let it spoil my holiday. I knew the boys wouldn't have told her. They seemed no more than mildly curious about my bladder. It must have been Big Edna. To my unbelieving gratitude it was never referred to by anyone. I was especially appalled at the idea of Edna knowing about it and I was excessively polite to her, not only for the rest of the holiday but from then on.

On our last day Mickey and I became very gloomy at the prospect of returning to Ewell. Our lugubrious depression must have been comic for it amused everyone else. We packed up our buckets, spades and the toys bought for the beach and I put my collection of tiny crabs into a bucketful of stinking sandy water. I later emptied them into my frog Horace's tin bath. Whether it was the foul water that killed him or the crabs I don't know, but he only survived the creatures of the sea for a few hours, which added tragedy to the sorrow of my return home. We went down in the early September sunshine and looked out at the sea, hurling pebbles skilfully across the tops of the waves, bouncing out to the darkening, golden sea. 'Good-bye Bognor. See you next year.'

'No such undertaking has been received . . .'

I know the place to within a foot where I was standing when the material for countless comedians' later scripts incorporating Chamberlain's words came from out of my mother's kitchen into the air at eleven o'clock on that still Sunday morning. She was having her Sunday Guinness and I was standing on the green-iron landing waiting for Joan to come back from church. My father was in bed reading the *Sunday Express*. As the words came out from the window: 'No such undertaking has been received and we are now at a state of war with Germany', I had no idea that I would come to know them as well as the Lord's Prayer. I rather liked Mr Chamberlain, especially his butterfly collar and umbrella. He looked like the sympathetic headmaster of a posh school.

Almost immediately after Chamberlain's thin voice faded away and before the BBC launched into one of its fits of national solemnity with an orgy of Elgar and elegy, the air-raid siren sounded. It had begun. Herr Hitler hadn't wasted any time. This was the week when my father had read out the *Daily Express* banner headline: 'THERE WILL BE NO WAR'. My mother was saying something about it not being like the last time and thanked God Dad was too ill to be called up and I was too young. If I were to be left later on my own with my mother the prospect of going into the Army or, preferably, the Navy offered escape but not for almost nine years—my age over again. I think my father said the words which we were all to hear so often in the next few months that it would All Be Over By Christmas, but I was determined to be unconvinced. I looked out the pamphlets about what to do in the event of an air-raid and took my Identity Card from its drawer. I would doubtless need it when stopped in the street by suspicious policemen. I had already memorized its number—EPHA/64/3. Like so many official things at the time it was blessedly more simple than such a document would be today. An Identity Card number now would have at least forty digits instead of the mere seven. Some lunatics have recently advocated the reintroduction of these Identity Cards. It is certain they would be impossible to remember.

A whistle sounded from the road and I rushed to the window to see what was happening. It was like the beginning of an early Ealing Comedy. An elderly, blue tin-hatted policeman was labouring up the hill from the village on a bicycle, occasionally pausing to blow his whistle. His progress was extremely slow and breathless. Hanging around his neck was a placard with the message: 'TAKE COVER'. Take cover? Where? Stay indoors, I supposed he meant. Presently, he disappeared over the hill and the All Clear went. A false alarm or a trick of the enemy? Or Whitehall, whatever it was. Mickey's father, Mr Wall, worked for Whitehall. Perhaps he might know.

I resisted all this adult talk about it being all over by Christmas. It was rather the same attitude, I felt, as my grandmother's Boxing Day spoil-sporting. I don't know whether my father believed it. In the circumstances he can't have cared very much. Anyway, I was determined not to believe it. I didn't want to believe it. The war was like an extended Christmas, a festival of carolling warriors, or it might be with any luck. Invasion seemed like the idea of Christmas to me, better than the brawling, carping Christmases in Clandon Close or Harbord Street. My father seemed to know a great deal about the Great War. After all, it had only been over for twenty years. Of course, he had been like myself, too young to fight. He was fourteen years old when *the* great war was declared. I besieged him with questions about anything he might remember.

Mrs Ure wrote to my father saying that the Benevolent Society would make arrangements for us all to move to Ventnor in the Isle of Wight where we would be safer and the climate would be more suitable for his health. There was a famous sanatorium in the area where he could be looked after if and when it became necessary. On a bright September day, the 28th, a huge Daimler ambulance drew up at the back yard behind the shops and my father was lifted on a stretcher down the steep iron steps into it. It was enormous inside with great windows, and looked like a very comfortable upholstered hearse. My mother and I went in afterwards and sat down. It was thrilling. I would miss Mickey, but he was buoyant to flapping point at the new drama of our various lives. Everyone said I would make New Friends, but I didn't set much store either by their judgement or by the likelihood of meeting anyone as stimulating or amusing as M. Geoffrey Wall.

I had only been in Mr Wall's car before and the majestic trip across Surrey, over the Devil's Dyke, Hampshire and the New Forest was luxurious. It was enjoyable being stared at by people as we drove through towns and were observed like the Royal Family going up The Mall. We made Royal Progress to the ferry at Southampton. The sea looked dark and dangerous and we were surrounded in the harbour by grey, whooping destroyers. Would we be torpedoed? We arrived at Ventnor in the late sunny afternoon, going on a mile or two to a place called St Lawrence Halt where there was a tiny railway station and a gloomy, grey Victorian hotel called the Carfax, which I was to get to know well. Below the country road leading on to Black Gang Chine and Niton, a small village, was a little 1930-ish house with a large derelict garden and orchard that went down almost to the sea itself. From my bedroom I could see out into the Atlantic for miles. I went for a walk almost immediately in the fading autumn sunlight. The downland on the upper cliff was full of places to explore and trees to climb. There were a great many cattle and hardly a sign of anyone except the occasional dog walker on the beach far below the chalk cliffs. I hurried back into my father's bedroom to tell him what I had seen.

Soon there was very little to be seen as a few days later a black mist and enveloping fog settled over the whole island, only to be pierced by the flash of gunfire from the convoy attacks in the Channel, which took place frequently during the next few months. That unyielding icy mist must have bitten into my father's remaining lung immediately. No cars, let alone trams. I spent days wandering along the cliffs between Ventnor and Black Gang Chine, ancient shrine of smugglers, where I was soon to play constant truant from school. My introduction to the school was much the same in every detail as my initiation at Ewell Boys, only it seemed colder and more alien. Again, little work was done and we seemed to spend most of the time practising gas-mask drill and preparing for an air-raid. Air-Raid Drill in any school I ever went to was conducted with the same grim bullying tactics, although most children found it difficult to take seriously. The most popular use of the gas masks themselves was as megaphones for farting sounds made from within. They steamed up immediately when donned and it was almost impossible to see, let alone breathe. The possibility of surviving long inside one of these smelly, steamy rubber things, with or without a gas attack, seemed unlikely. Apart from this, the straps hurt your head.

My mother managed to get a few medical certificates from my father's sympathetic doctor, saying that I was too delicate to attend school during the island winter and the four-mile walk every day was too harsh for my health. This was untrue, but the walk itself was indeed long and bitterly cold and, in the almost black wintry evenings under arches of overhanging trees, rather frightening. I settled down to following the course of the conflict in the newspapers and on my own cheap portable wireless. My bedroom began to resemble a briefing room with photographs and drawings from the newspapers of anything to do with the war. On one wall was a map of Europe and the Western Front, with the Maginot Line and the Siegfried Line clearly marked, and Swastikas, French flags and Union Jacks dotted all over such places as Latvia, Lithuania, Estonia, Czechoslovakia. One of my particular favourite photographs was of Finnish soldiers looking like white-hooded monks on skis poised to fight off Russian troops. It was about this time that the P&O liner, *Rawalpindi*, sank. My father seemed affected by it. 'Look,' he said, 'the old '*Pindi*'s gone down.' There was a wonderfully dramatic drawing of it sinking, guns blasting the sky in the *Daily Mail*. 'Gone,' said my father, 'the old '*Pindi*.' It seemed to upset him.

A new schools' attendance officer, more zealous than the previous one,

discounted my mother's certificates and insisted that I go to St Boniface's
School in Ventnor. Again, it was very like the one before. Coming home
after the first day with blood on my collar there was a Black Look intensified
by the island's chill to greet me. I managed to keep away as much as possible
from the small enshadowed house and explored the beach which stretched
for miles, and hardly anyone in sight. It was in this way that I met Isabel
Sells, and fell in love for the second time. She was a tall, pretty girl, much
taller than I, and had just had her twenty-first birthday. I met her as she was
walking her dog along the beach and she was so immediately friendly and
easy that a wave of happiness overwhelmed me, as I had not felt since first
crouched on the kennel floor with Joan. Here, I was sure, I had found a true
friend and one who would allow me to love her. She told me that her mother
ran the Carfax Hotel, but because of the war there were hardly any visitors.
They lived there alone with her grandmother. The bad news was that she
had just become engaged to a young man called Raymond. He was twenty-
eight and wasn't in the Army because he was in a Reserved Occupation. In
the event, he turned out to be a very jolly, companionable young man who
always seemed astonishingly pleased for me to join them. At weekends the
three of us would set out enthusiastically along the beach and over the cliffs
together. For some reason I insisted on calling him Professor Huggem.
Perhaps it was because a lot of kissing and cuddling went on between the two
of them, which caused me to feel much more than envy. Still, my distress
was worth witnessing such trusting pleasure so easily passing from one to
another. I had the occasional consolation of holding Isabel's willing hand
when they finished.

She invited me to tea every Sunday and it became a regular occasion.
Sometimes I even went during the week when Raymond was claimed by his
Reserved Occupation, which was even more enjoyable. Her mother was a
warm woman—motherly, I would have called her, if the word did not have a
specific meaning for me. The third member of the Sells' family was the
grandmother who always dressed in black bombazine with a toque and a
huge black overcoat. She also had a black cane and a smelly black dog. She
was like a mixture between Queen Mary and Giles's cartoon Grandma. She
sat beside the fire in a vast, Spanish ebony armchair, never moving except to
say something disapproving, principally of Isabel but also of her daughter.
They took no notice of her and Isabel laughed openly, if kindly, at her. She
whispered in my ear, 'She hasn't had a bath for months. I don't think she's
taken her clothes off for *years*.' Certainly the old lady was more polite to me
than she was to her own relatives. In fact, she seemed to almost look forward
to my visits, as she always asked me lots of probing questions about myself

and what I was doing. This adult curiosity was most unusual, so I felt she couldn't be all that bad.

The Carfax was not as boisterous a retreat as 39 Bradford Drive, but it was a happy escape from the tiny kitchen down the road at our house, inappropriately called *Mon Abri*, My Refuge. The whole family seemed interested in me and treated me as if I were an equal, even the formidable old Giles woman seeking out my boyish opinions about anything. For example, when discussing the progress of the war or the state of the nation, I was able to find my voice and use it to some length, as I read the newspapers from cover to cover and, of course, there were the exhibits in my briefing room. I must have seemed oddly well informed on developments in every theatre of war and thoughout the Empire. During a discussion about when it would all end, the Sells and their friends had all agreed with my father about it being 'All Over By Christmas'. I confounded them with my firm opinion that it would last at least five years. Unknown to me at the time, it seems that Lloyds were offering odds in late October that the war would be over by Christmas. The national obsession with Christmas seemed to be very like my own.

The island was shrouded in silence apart from the whooping destroyers passing the island in convoy, out of sight in the thick mist. Something was going on out there and, whatever it was, I was missing it. Whenever their guns roared, the whole island seemed to shake as if it might disappear into the sea. I think my mother would have wished exactly that. She complained even more bitterly about her loneliness and this deadest of dead-and-alive holes. As far as I remember, the nearest cinema was a considerable bus-ride away in Shanklin. Ventnor seemed hardly as lively as Ewell Village, especially out of season as it was now. No doubt in the summer it was very different, but I was not to find out.

As my mother bit her nails to purplish stumps, my father grew weaker, and I was able to spend more time with him in his bedroom as she huddled over the kitchen grate. We read aloud from the papers to each other and, while his strength lasted, long adventure yarns from his old copies of *Boys' Own Paper*, 1908–12. When he grew tired I would read to him. November came and I began to become excited at the prospect of Christmas. I don't know why, because there seemed little to become exercised about, just the three of us together. However I was sure that lovely Isabel would ask me over, possibly on Boxing Day as I knew my mother wouldn't allow me out of the house on Christmas Day. She would say that I was leaving my father and her all on their own. It was, of course, only half a mile down the road. I think she also suspected that my feelings for Isabel were not just those of childish friendship. Anyway, she was disapproving of the Sells family, thinking that if they ran an hotel they must be rich and privileged, which they clearly were not. She soon developed an overweening jealousy of the family, Isabel in particular, and was always discouraging my visits. 'You're not to go down there and worry Mrs Sells. She's got quite enough to do looking after that hotel. I'm sure that they don't want you round the place—kid like you.' As much as I protested that they *liked* me being there, she wouldn't believe it. Well, Boxing Day would at least be free of Grandma Osborne's annual Christmas message.

Round about the end of November, an ambulance, an ordinary white one this time, took my father on a stretcher to the sanatorium between Ventnor and Shanklin. My mother and I accompanied him, helping him out into his wheelchair when we arrived there. It was a huge Edwardian affair, like a Continental hotel, with grand verandahs facing out to the sea, where patients coughed in their beds overlooking the black mist. I waited in a corridor while my mother and father went up to see a doctor. They were not away very long and we returned home in silence. While the ambulance men carried him back up the stairs, my mother said, 'Well, your father's only got six weeks. Six weeks to *live*, do you understand?' Would he be alive at Christmas? '*I* don't know, do I? Don't ask bloody silly questions.'

I didn't quite believe my mother. She was not to be trusted. I was determined to give him a nice present, something to keep him going, even alive. I scarcely bothered to think of what I might get for her. One evening I asked him what he would like for Christmas. He told me that there was a new series of books called Penguin Books that could be bought at W. H. Smith's and he said, 'I'll give you a list. They're only sixpence.' He gave me a selection, which included *Ariel* by André Maurois, a Pelican book in fact, and I think the first. The other two were *Death of a Hero* by Richard Aldington and *A Safety Match* by Ian Hay. I had saved some money from Ewell days, there being little to spend it on anyway on the island and went out and bought the three of them immediately.

Mon Abri, it turned out, was to be a very poor refuge from death and Christmas Day, when it arrived, was a morose affair. Money seemed to be shorter here than it had been in the suburbs and my pillowcase was limp, barely a quarter full. I never had the customary stocking. My mother did not have the thrifty middle-class imagination to attempt filling an inexpensive stocking with makeshift surprise delights. But there was a splendid model yacht, which I stupidly tried to convert into a three-master schooner, making it top-heavy and impossible to sail, a few odds and ends, comics and, best of all, *Boys' Own Annual* and the *Greyfriars Annual*. I gave my father the three books from his list. 'But I didn't mean you to get all three of them, Skipper. I only meant you to get me one.' But he seemed pleased with them.

Christmas dinner was fretful. My father put his dressing gown on and came down the few stairs into the sitting-room, where he hardly ate anything at all except his favourite bread sauce, saying that he would prefer to have the bird cold. He left nearly all of it while my mother scowled with heavy-breathing and pique. We listened to the King's Speech and toasted him sitting down. My father said this was a traditional custom in the Navy. The King himself was obliged to give up the Christmas 1939 forecast and said: 'We cannot tell what it [the New Year] will be. If it brings peace how happy we shall be.' Eating my own dinner eagerly, I was suddenly overcome with a panic sense of loneliness that I felt had descended on me for good. Sitting between my father and mother I burst into tears as he struggled to fan the tiny blue flame on Grandma Osborne's Christmas pudding. 'What's he grizzling on about?' said my mother. 'Leave him alone,' my father replied. 'The boy's upset. It's not surprising is it?' Or something like it. I left the remains of my dinner while my mother cluttered our plates noisily back into the kitchen. As I went up the stairs to my room I could hear her muttering about all the trouble she had gone to and nobody bothering, not so much as a bloody thank-you, at least she wouldn't have to spend another dead and alive Christmas in *Mon* bloody *Abri*. The following day she allowed me to go down to the Carfax and I almost forgot the sense of inescapable desertion I'd felt the previous day, consoling myself with kissing Isabel underneath the mistletoe, albeit egged on by laughing Raymond. I longed to enfold her passionately.

January 1940 came and I managed to keep away from school more than ever, although the attendance officer was a constant visitor. He was surprisingly friendly but kept pointing out with uncommon offical tact that school could not be put off for ever. It was at least a temporary reprieve. However, I was legitimately unwell for a while with a bad cough and often feverish, which prompted my mother to tell the attendance officer convincingly that I was going to be just like my father.

I was sitting in the kitchen reading about two weeks after Christmas, when I heard my mother scream from the foot of the uncarpeted staircase. I ran to see what was happening and stared up to the landing where my father was standing. He was completely naked with his silver hair and grey, black and red beard. He looked like a naked Christ. 'Look at him!' she screamed. 'Oh, my God, he's gone blind.' He stood quite still for a moment and then fell headlong down the stairs on top of us. Between us we carried him upstairs. She was right. He had gone blind.

A day or two later my grandfather arrived. The old man's presence seemed to restrain even my mother, although she still contrived to treat him as a begging tramp at the door, overfeeding him as if he were some wandering supplicant. My father seemed to recover and brighten up in his own father's presence and they spent some time talking to each other. I was curious to know what it was about but never ventured in when they were alone together. Grandfather was rather shyly apologetic about Grandma Osborne's absence, saying that she was, *of course*, not strong enough to make the journey. Besides, it was far too cold for her. Together we went for a few long walks up on the cliff. He said very little to me except to murmur about how I should have to Manage On My Own in future, putting ponderous emphasis on this fact. He was obviously thinking of my mother, who was already making no secret of her relief that it would all be over soon, when she could get out of this dead-and-alive hole and back to London or, at least, to the blacked-out lights of Ewell.

My father's condition soon deteriorated. When I saw him he croaked incoherently and the doctor suggested that it would be a good idea if I were to spend the next few days down at the Carfax with Mrs Sells and pay a short daily visit to my father. I found myself occupying a bedroom next to Isabel, full of dread for the time when I should soon have to leave it. The day my father died my mother came down to the Carfax and told Mrs Sells. She tried to insist on my immediate return but she was gently coaxed back. I threw myself into the arms of Isabel for the comfort I felt I would never receive again. The following day I was reluctantly sent back up to *Mon Abri*. My mother would need looking after. She was waiting excitedly for me and at once insisted that I go into my father's bedroom to look at him in his coffin. The smell in the room was strong and strange and, in his shroud, he was unrecognizable. As I looked down at him, she said, 'Of course, this room's got to be fumigated, you know that, don't you? Fumigated.' Frumigated was how she pronounced it. With my father's body lying in the bedroom across the landing, I had been obliged to share my briefing room with my mother, who spent hour upon hour reading last Sunday's *News of the World*, the bright light overhead, rustling the pages in my ear and sighing heavily. For the first time I felt the fatality of hatred.

A few days later, after hysterical hours of packing up and my grandfather being abused for his meticulous slowness, we left the house taking my father in yet another Daimler ambulance. The journey back to Southampton was unlike the journey out. I was going back to Ewell but nothing could be the same. Mickey Wall had won a scholarship to Tiffins Boys' Grammar School. Joan Buffen was lost for ever. The funeral in the crematorium in

Southampton was unremarkably eerie. From the faded pages of a pencilled diary I can read: 'January 31st. Father's funeral today.' And then a description of the coffin rattling on its rails, disappearing behind the purple curtains. 'I met the clergyman who is one of the nicest individuals I have ever met.' Who could I have been addressing so self-consciously?

We returned by train to Clandon Close where Grandma Osborne received us rather as if we had been obliged to cut short an unwise holiday. When her daughter Nancy had died two years before, she had worn a black armband in the house for twelve months. She wore no mourning sign now, even in her face, which looked as if the wafery skin had tightened with a repressed vindication. Her eyes seemed brightened and not by grief. My mother and I shared the second bedroom at the top of the stairs. During the next few months we paid constant visits to the headquarters of 'Dad's Society' in St Paul's Churchyard to discuss our future with Mrs Ure, what work my mother could do, and my schooling, followed by incessant talk of wills and insurance on the train home and in the bedroom. My father had taken out a life insurance policy with the Sun Alliance and Insurance Company of Canada for £400. It emerged that he signed a letter, under clear duress from his mother on one of his Sunday morning visits, stating that his entire estate, such as it was, was to go to her in repayment for the Bay of Biscay incident some thirty years before. He was finally to settle his debt.

My mother made as much show of resistance to this as she could. Letters to and from the Osborne family solicitors, Monson and Petty of Newport, Mon., dropped through the shared letter-box. After weeks of morning races to catch the postman first, my mother gave up and the old lady pocketed the money without a word said. Routed and intimidated, Nellie Beatrice smarted silently while Grandma's bearing quickened more brightly than ever. It was clear that we should have to find digs. The Grove pride, incapable of accepting kindness let alone charity and in spite of protests that it 'was unnecessary and a waste of money' to leave our room in Clandon Close, made a hasty, defiant move inevitable. I would have preferred to stay. Although I was in an exposed, neutralized position, my grandmother offered me some protection that would vanish as soon as I left the seething calm of the cul-de-sac.

Finding digs was disappointingly easy. The newsagents' boards in Stoneleigh Parade were full of cards offering accommodation and the ambiguous 'use of kitchen'. There were fewer bowler hats and more battledresses on the station platform in the early mornings. The 'business' trains became crowded with ex-filing clerks, shop assistants and senior storemen in khaki, often standing where they had once sat unchallenged.

Army boots scraped the polish from City shoes and crisp *Telegraphs* and *Daily Mails* were ruffled by hoisted kit bags. Street after street of two-ups, normally in siege against friends, let alone strangers, suddenly sought out occupants for their spare rooms. Confronted by paybooks and uncertainty, housewives who had scarcely ever nodded at next-door-but-one from the fastness of their latticed stockades openly touted for well-behaved hostages. Rarely, the motive was a desire for discreet 'company' and fear of being alone in the house surrounded by blacked-out deserted streets. Usually it was a reluctant concession enforced by the meagreness of Privates' pay. Like all amateur landladies, and many professionals, they sought the Invisible Lodger with visible rent books filled in unfailingly every Friday.

In her fury to 'get away from the Osbornes' my mother was in no mood to be discriminating. Taking with us little more than a suitcase of clothes, we were soon settled in with a Mrs Williams, at 120 Worcester Park Road. This was on the north side of Stoneleigh Station where the ribbon development at its highest looked back out upon the metropolis. On a clear day you could see the gasholders of south-west London. We had a double room and share of the kitchen. The sitting-room was theoretically at our disposal, but although Mrs Williams was quite a genial woman, it seemed implicit that we were not expected to ever take advantage of this amenity. Besides, my mother pointed out that we liked to keep ourselves to ourselves and John was a very quiet boy.

At this new address, I had no choice but to go to Elmsleigh Road School, which was some five minutes' walk away and near the north side of Sherwood Forest. My mother soon got a job working at Carters Seed Factory at Raynes Park, two stations away. This was piece-work, picking seeds, demanding a mechanical dexterity to achieve even a starvation wage. She would often come back with only twenty-two and sixpence a week. As our rent was something like twelve and sixpence excluding a shilling a week for the bath plus her fares, it was not adequate. After she had left, at about six o'clock, I would get up, listening to Billy Ternant on the radio and Freddy Grisewood *On the Kitchen Front*, before setting out with my sandwiches and gas mask for Elmsleigh Road. The school, which was mixed, was only different from the others in its modern buildings. The effective *Gauleiter* was a girl called Daphne, who held the balance of power between timid pupils and indifferent teachers. Tall and muscular, she wore a heavy stained gymslip and a great sash, which came in useful for bondage. She was always surrounded by her cohorts, usually all girls, who would select random victims for her, sometimes at mob whim, sometimes at her own unpredictable caprice. The victim, almost always a boy, was dragged to a suitably public place like the middle of the playground or playing field and, spread-eagled, he would have to endure the humiliation of Daphne lifting up her skirt and placing her navy blue gusset firmly on his head. She would sit like a conquering hunter for as long as it suited her, with the cold frenzy of a goddess on heat for sacrifice, while her prey gave up the struggle against asphyxiation. She might even urge her slaves to remove the victim's shorts. It came close to more than ritual castration, averted only by the bell for class. I witnessed these mass tribal seizures from the safest of distances. It was an all-girl exercise and even the toughest boys kept well away from the scene whenever it unexpectedly erupted, but there seemed no avoidance of the degradation once it had been decreed by Daphne. By some fluke, I was successful although I knew I was certainly on the goddess's list. The eyes of her warriors missed no one, particularly lone new boys. I fled their hounding scrutiny term after term, sniffing the air for some cunning ambush until the day I left the school two years later.

There was no black mist here to escape into or downland to wander over. The open roads back to Worcester Park Road offered no protection. The system of education differed little from what I had experienced before. The only thing I can remember learning at this school was a rude version of Thomas Moore's ballad 'The Harp that Once through Tara's Halls'. Again, lessons seemed drowsy interludes between the real business of Playtime, an underworld made more satanic by Daphne, its princess of Darkness. The blasting of whistles was louder and the gas-mask practice and air-raid and shelter drill consumed the day increasingly.

Sometimes I slept through *On the Kitchen Front* and was late. The punishment for this was a statutory caning of six strokes upon the hand, boy or girl, although the girls were sometimes overlooked. This took place almost daily, sometimes in front of the assembled school, sometimes in the headmaster's room. Mr Cotter looked, in retrospect, rather like a King Street Communist with a beret and pebble spectacles, and spent all his time doing woodwork and caning small boys. On being sent to him he asked your name, then enquired, 'Late?', or whatever the offence might be, and administered three strokes of the cane on each hand. They were delivered with abstracted intensity as if he were driving a rivet. It was particularly painful in the winter and some boys were foolish enough to yell—to the delight of the assembled girls. It was also regarded as an invitation for more. The slash of bamboo aimed at the tips of cold, mitten-clad fingers in the early morning was like the shock of an electric current, so much more telling than the palm, where presumably it was meant to be directed. If he was disturbed at his woodwork, the punishment was summary and quick, without need to play to the gallery of Assembly. He would relight his pipe afterwards and go back to the carpenter's bench without a word. Sometimes he sent you out to the corner shop to get him a fresh supply of his favourite tobacco. This seemed to be regarded as a favour. 'Say it's for me,' he would say, putting down his cane. 'They know what I smoke.'

Playtime was unavoidable; but I usually managed to escape the midday meal by running home, eating my sandwiches by the wireless and rushing back in time for lessons. A torment even worse than Playtime was the Shelter Drill which began to take up more time than anything else. More than the dead stretches in the classroom, I remember the shouting, whistling columns of children in corridors steaming with cold air, bobbing balaclava and woollen helmets, being swept into the black hole of the dripping shelter. It was a pit of unwashed, stinking boys and girls, fists, bones on shins, their inescapable flailing in crazed screaming darkness as you crouched for the All Clear that might never come. When the air-raids did in fact come with daily regularity, the penalities for running away from the shelter and going home as I did so often were made to sound unspeakable. Even this seldom prevented me from taking the risk. Mock or real raid, the terror was palpable. I spent hours running between home and school, once almost being machine-gunned by a low-flying German aeroplane; better to be mown down with some lone dignity out there in the open ribbon development than buried alive along with that mass of struggling young bodies, shrieking 'In the Stores' and 'Roll out the Barrel' till the kingdom might not come. 'In the stores, in the stores, in the sergeant major's stores/My eyes are dim I cannot see/I wish I'd brought my specs with me.' The school shelter was my only brush with fear in the war. My battle shock was puny enough but staged by Bosch and abetted by Daphne, its effect lingers enough after forty years to make me shun discos or nightclubs or football stadiums.

It was in the summer of 1940 that Mickey and I visited his aunt ('you're an old cow') at her small farm near Saffron Walden. Watching our balsa Hurricane gliders hovering above the open, flat fields, looking at sides of ham and eating more eggs, cream and butter than I had ever seen, even in the Home and Colonial window, it was like nothing I had known. We went on to a transformed, fortified Bognor, where it was impossible to go anywhere near the beach. It was sprayed with barbed wire and signs saying: 'KEEP OUT—MINEFIELDS'. Even the road from Felpham into Bognor was pitted with concrete tank traps and all approaches to the beach had sprouted pill boxes, already sandy and grassy. The town was almost empty, cafés closed, whelk stalls and gift shops shuttered, the few remaining dodgems attended by glum youths hanging around waiting to stack them away before season's end.

Wartime and weather drove us into the cinema in Chichester to see *Pinocchio*, which featured a character, a very raffish fox, who was an actor and sang a song called 'Hey-diddle-de-dee, an Actor's Life for Me'. I took to him at once and when we came out into the High Street looking vainly for egg and chips somewhere, I felt elated by the spry fox and his song. We must be two of a special kind. Later, they were called spivs. Suddenly we heard the air-raid siren, still an unfamiliar sound, and we ran aimlessly down the street. There were few people around and Mickey and I gave up running and stood to gawp hopefully up at the sky. Some cellar doors opened in the pavement outside a pub like a pantomine trap and we followed a small crowd lowering themselves unhurriedly into the vaults. The doors overhead thudded behind us and we sat among the barrels of sweet-smelling beer, waiting. Everyone looked up straining their ears but nothing happened. After about twenty minutes the All Clear went and we climbed back disappointedly into the street. When my daughter and I walked up this same street in the evening it was as quiet as it had been thirty-seven years before. There were one or two people going home from work and some foreign tourists trailing up to the Cathedral. Standing on the same cellar doors Mickey and I had crouched beneath, I thought of Bognor in 1940 and Elmsleigh Road. The trite tune of 'Hey-diddle-de-dee' sounded in my head like a snatch of enduring joylessness. I needed an immediate drink.

On the last day in Bognor we said our muted farewell to the beach, unable this time to cast our pebbles into the sea although we repeated the incantation of the previous year, 'Good-bye Bognor. See you next year!' Neither of us voiced our unbelief. We returned home in silence. Even Mickey was unmoved to rudery. The future held nothing more than endless Playtimes, Sirens and Black Looks. There was no imaginable relief. It was hot, mid-August and after only a few days it came.

7. Too Young to Fight and Too Old to Forget

Mickey and I were eating Victoria plums in the Walls' tiny orchard when the aircraft appeared out of the opposite ends of the sky, streaking high above us towards each other. Theirs shimmering black, ours silver. Or so it must have been. The blinding blue silence. Then the hurtling formation and symmetry exploded.

Throughout that autumn of 1940 we were charmed, privileged spectators at the most thrilling spectacular we could ever have imagined. Day after sunny day, I ran over to Bradford Drive to take my front seat in the moist shade at the bottom of the garden. We had the house to ourselves so there were no teachers or policemen to force us below ground. The sky was all ours and we were enclosed by it. Edna would come in for her dinner and scream hysterically at us to take cover but we ignored her. There would probably never be anything better than this at any time, ever, and no one could take it from us. We lay on our backs, spinning in the world, chomping on pounds of Victorias, secure and happy in our grassy cockpit, suffering no more than sore lips, stained teeth and stomach pains. The Battle of Britain exhausted everything, especially our appetite for tea. We knew our Dorniers from our Heinkels, and in the evenings in Mickey's briefing room we listened to the day's tally and moved our pins on the map of southern England. It seemed that those long days of blasting sunshine must go on until we dropped into something indescribably different, obliterating inert Stoneleigh and Ewell, inglorious cities of England's Southern Plain.

It ended with the shock of its beginning. The rush of blood was staunched, we looked up into the sky and saw only the unwarlike flab of barrage balloons. Numbed, we strained at the silence and longed for the day before yesterday and every bright minute. The darkening evenings of September, then the weeks, drew in and closed over us like the cellar doors in Chichester. Very soon they dwindled away into the flight from the school shelter and nightly prostration in Mrs Williams's Anderson, imprisoning dark, searchlights, ARP torchlights flashing in windows and irritable cries of, 'Put that light out!'

Mrs Williams spent much of her time at her daughter-in-law's house and as my mother was at work behind the bar at the Stoneleigh Hotel I passed most of these nights, which began unremittingly almost on the dot of six o'clock, on my own in the Anderson, listening to the plodding hum of German bombers. They were confined, uninspiring hours, very different from the free-for-all of being part of visible earth and sky. At least I was alone. When a bomb did shiver the darkness, the heart only faltered. It didn't overflow. The last crouch was not suitable for sharing. A rat has no comfort. My mother had refused to go into the Anderson anyway. 'I'm not going in that thing. Catch your bloody death of cold, you will. Rather get bombed.' Every evening for the next few months I would get into my pyjamas and dressing gown and take myself down to the Anderson with my copies of the *Magnet* and the *Gem* or some book like Mickey's *The Black Out Book* or *101 Things To Do In The Black Out* and the portable wireless, to lie in my narrow bunk until seven or so the following morning. On my mother's evening off, she insisted that we lie in a tiny triangular cupboard under the stairs, where we would read by the light of a candle. The wireless was forbidden as she believed that it might attract the attention of the German bombers.

Late into night in the cupboard, my mother, in her curlers and dressing gown, would read the *Daily Mirror*, hunched upright in a thick swirl of cigarette smoke, while Black Looks pierced the haze of the four or five feet of space we shared, daring me to sleep and leave her to hear the unremitting hum of the Hun. She fidgeted and kicked me awake until morning. Many nights passed without a bomb dropping. When they did it was difficult to guess how near it was to Number 120 Worcester Park Road. Sometimes the little cupboard would blur and seem to stretch and float an inch or two. On one particular evening she had hardly been able to glance at the *Mirror* 'for want of a gin'. The candle flickered, she stared and fidgeted me back to wakefulness:

MOTHER: Listen! No, listen. There. It's gone all quiet. Get me a drop of that gin. No, I'd better get it. I want to go anyway. Listen. D'you think it's quiet for a bit?

ME: They'll be back soon.

MOTHER: Oh, bloody cheerful as usual!

ME: Well they always are.

MOTHER: Well, I'm going to risk it. Don't you want to go?
ME: No.

She hesitated, possibly wondering whether to shove me out instead, then dashed up the stairs. No sooner had she closed the lavatory door than there was a shattering whizz and the house trembled as a bomb began its fall. The candle went out at the impact, followed by a scream from my mother. Deafened and groping I emerged from the cupboard into the mist of dust and plaster, found the matches and relit the candle. All the doors and windows had been blown out and the ceilings had collapsed. My mother was just visible, frozen to the lavatory seat. She moved forward to the head of the stairs bent at the knees, like a crazed gymnast, arms outstretched. I thought of my father's apparition at the top of the stairs a few months earlier. Her face sagged, powdered and gaping black, her mottled sloped chest heaving with her moans. Her knickers were flounced below her knees in a collapsed silky bag. The lost days of summer were recompensed for a few joyous moments as I looked on at the funniest, most enjoyable sight I had ever seen. When she tottered down to the hall, I was still laughing. Nothing could have stemmed my exploding delight. The Black Look had been blasted into a blob of stupidity and fear. Too shaken to aim a clout at me, she crawled back into the cupboard, curled up into a heap and left me to sleep undisturbed until the cold air from the rising dust of the street woke me and a neighbour in an ARP helmet appeared at the jagged porch. Everyone had their Best-Night-of-the-Blitz stories. I couldn't wait to tell mine to Mickey.

We spent the Christmas at Harbord Street. Grandma Grove, like thousands of others, had spent weeks walking to work through devastated streets, picking her way among rubble and broken glass to make her way up to the head offices of Woolworth's in Cork Street. She always left about four o'clock, long before the All Clear sounded, dodging posses of wardens and policemen to be sure of arriving on time, at six o'clock. A landmine had destroyed the nearby convent in Hammersmith and there was no gas or electricity. The festive chicken took hours to cook in a bucket over a cluster of candles. It was smoky but delicious, like Joan's kennel cooking. Even Grandpa was uncomplaining. The Dardanelles were to blame.

In 1941 I sat my Common Entrance examination. I knew it was hopeless and was astonished to get through the preparatory paper. Perhaps it had passed unmarked. But there could be no doubt about Part Two. Another four years of Elmsleigh Road loomed ahead, dull, unrelenting and unprofitable. The long, snug warren nights of the Blitz subsided. I had made no friends, seeing Mickey only at the weekends, which were interrupted by his increasing homework at Tiffins. Joan Buffen was gone, although I sometimes hung around Ewell Parade, looking up for a glimpse of her. Once, Mrs Buffen spotted me, and waved but, as she started to beckon, I ran round the corner. Once I saw Joan going into a sweetshop with her cousin. Later, she came towards me in the Village High Street. There was nowhere to hide. She was riding her pretty piebald pony and was flushed with strength and energy. I thought she wouldn't see me in her glow of concentration but, as she came alongside, she looked down with a brief, unsurprised smile, raised her cane and trotted on. I avoided the Village. It had never seemed a friendly place.

I wrote regularly to Isabel. If I could only live with the Sells at the Carfax, I would have willingly gone back to St Boniface Secondary School in Ventnor. I had never seen those beaches in the summer. Isabel and I could walk for hours along the open sands. The Germans wouldn't want to invade Ventnor. It wasn't Bognor. She wrote an affectionate letter in reply, full of questions about myself. She had got married to Raymond. Grandma had died at last and they were going to live near Southampton. They all sent lots of love and were always thinking of me.

'Don't you know there's a war on?'

By 1942 the Osborne–Grove family had shrunk. Aunt Nancy had died in 1938, of peritonitis it was said, but, according to my mother, really of 'Dad's complaint'. Grandpa Osborne died in 1940 shortly after my father of cancer of the bowel and Grandpa Grove followed soon after, possibly brought down by his youthful breakfast regime of porterhouse steaks, half-bottles of 3-star brandy and chorus girls. Grandma Grove emerged exhilarated and bustling from her adventurous Blitz into widowhood and was shortly pensioned off by Woolworth's with the unlooked-for sum of eight pounds a week for the rest of her lifetime, which was to span nearly another forty years. She was to be seen photographed in the local newspapers on her hundredth birthday brandishing her telegram from the Queen.

When I was first aware of Grandma Osborne she can scarcely have been much older than I am now, but she had already settled determinedly into iron-clad, impassive old age. After her husband's death, she left Clandon Close for a small flat above Tesco's store (more like a cheap-rate village shop then) in yet another Parade, Ewell Court, only five minutes' walk from Bradford Drive. Cousin Tony had moved on to Christ's College, Brecon and then to Sandhurst, his father having decided that he should be a professional soldier, no doubt to have undone the damage to his manly fibre wrought by his grandmother. Boasting loneliness, she graciously offered room to her sisters. After all, they were two widows and a spinster with little more than their pooled pensions to support them. Besides, with Grandpa gone, she needed someone to do the shopping and heavier housework. All of which was, of course, quite beyond her.

Auntie Bessie was a round, cheerful woman. She had married Great Uncle Frank, who was some kind of Cad or Bounder, having been obliged for unspoken scandalous reasons to emigrate hurriedly to Canada, leaving his wife and four sons to follow him later. She was kindly in a twinkling sort of way with a streak of Welsh deceit and petty vindictiveness which were harmless enough. She shocked her sisters by indulging in flights of nostalgia for the way she and Uncle Frank had enjoyed their sexual life, not in detail but revering an experience once enjoyed wholeheartedly and still, incredibly to them, at the age of seventy-one, relished. She was a tiny woman, a little over five foot. Uncle Frank had been six foot four inches and weighed some sixteen or seventeen stone, which might have fired the sisters' puzzled imagination whenever they cast their eyes upon her tiny round form.

Auntie Daisy was like an emaciated dwarf, a quick-moving cripple with a hunched back. She was a spinster, having lost her fiancé during the First War, in the way of the fact and legend of the time. She soon became the only sister left to look after their mother, and thoughts of marriage, if they had ever been, quickly receded. For twenty years she attended the old woman, heaving her deadly weight out of bed and into chairs. This was said to be the reason for her present condition, but it seemed more probable that when she entered this world it was as the perfect crabbed creature she was now. There was no hint from her sisters that her sacrifice, if indeed it was one, might have been wasted on what sounded like a charmless, unrewarding old bully. On the contrary, her grim frailty and intransigent character were admired as the acceptable scar of a Godly life. Now, humped off by a stronger hand, the ancient matriarch was gone, leaving Auntie Daisy with nowhere to live in Newport. Auntie Bessie's four sons were unable or unwilling to take her in, so both sisters winged back to their last days with sister Annie over Tesco's stores.

There were only three small rooms in the flat, including the kitchen, and the two younger sisters, Annie and Daisy, were soon ganging up on the once-nubile Bessie. She confided to me that they made sure that she had less rations, mixing margarine into her butter and watering her milk. Such low practices, true or not, would cloud whole days for her, driving her out walking for hours on her own. She did all the shopping while crippled Daisy did the heavier work. Annie cooked one meal a day of the lighter kind. Surprisingly, Bessie died several years before her two apparently frailer sisters. Her four giant sons—Dallas, Percy, Cecil and Basil—were either abroad or living somewhere in the provinces. Uncle Dallas was still in Canada, Cecil and Percy in Sheffield and Belfast, and Uncle Basil, who Annie seemed to imply had inherited his father's caddish tricks, was now a flight lieutenant in the RAF which, oddly, didn't impress her. Basil's wife had had a baby somewhat less than nine months after their marriage. Annie, a dab at counting on her fingers, tried to shame her sister with this fact but it only puffed her up. Perhaps it confirmed the continuity of Uncle Frank's vast prowess, something that cold, haughty little Annie could never have matched.

Meanwhile, back at the Groves, my Uncle Jack had suffered a motoring accident while he was working as a salesman for an ice-cream firm in Southend and had lost his right arm. Awarded over three thousand pounds, which in 1939 seemed a vast sum of money, he adapted himself to one arm with great ingenuity and dabbled with some style in what were always called 'risky ventures' by his family, mostly in catering and with small success. However, he always had a cigar to press on you carelessly. I never heard him complain about any of his unsupportive wives and mistresses or his falling circumstances. Today he lives in a council house in Salisbury, over eighty and with a back like a board, he looks like a retired sea-captain, cheerfully waiting for his next command. Ignored by his sisters, he seemed sweetly free of their malice and envy.

Stoneleigh

'*Dear John*, What a nasty jealous undesirable brother he has turned out to be. Frankly Johnnie its Mothers own fault. She has always made too much of him. Oh no he could do no wrong. He has caused those upsets with Mum and Dad for years. Thank God he is miles away from me. I could not stand his nonsense now; and cannot stand upsets of any kind. . . .

'*Dear John*, Regarding Mother I have written and asked Jack's permission for me to go and see her and if I went there would he allow me to go upstairs to see her if only for an hour, its no use me taking a chance going there and he refuses to let me see her, don't you agree, am standing by for a reply—*if* I get one shall go right away—but the mood he is in—I have my doubts. . . .

'*Dear John*, I don't want to blame my poor Mum too much: but it looks as though his Lordship [Jack] *did not* let her have my letter saying I was

112

waiting for his Consent for me to come along and see her—or *maybe is* afraid to say anything frankly I can't make it all out, have registered a letter to her this morning—I wonder if she will have it. I explained the position of things. I just let things stay as they are. I thought I must tell you and let you know everything. Such things: there will never be a cure for bitterness.

Always in my thoughts,
Mother'

As for Auntie Queenie, 'gone down in the world' as my mother had it, in the Richmond Jewish madams' shop, she was living in her pristine flat in a new mansion block overlooking Turnham Green with poor Uncle Sid, a clerk in a City firm of ribbon-makers which he had first joined at the age of fourteen until he became Aircraftman Bates in 1942. It was then that he met again his pre-war flat-mate and love-of-his-life, another aircraftman, John. Sid and Queen were married during a weekend leave in Queenie's church in Turnham Green. He was forty-two and the bride was fifty, wearing a new blue costume and veiled hat, wholesale price, from Madame Leons of Richmond. John was the best man.

'I don't know what I was doing when I asked her,' Sidney said years later, in a snatched simpering confidence. 'I must have been ever so tiddly. She made me go out and get the ring the first thing next morning. Bit of a cheek, I thought.' Technical manuals on *Married Love* and *Sex within Marriage* by a Mrs Renee McAndrew were left by the side of their twin beds next to the white-leather prayer book. During my lightning peeks into these manuals I learnt, amongst other things, that it was possible to achieve enormous satisfaction by being on top of the eiderdown as well as underneath it. Knowing Auntie Queenie, who could not bear the sight of even a creased cushion, I found it very hard indeed to imagine her contemplating crispy stains on her expensively dry-cleaned eiderdowns. 'She left these soppy books out while she was off in the bathroom for bloody hours. Sid Muggins supposed to be reading them. Have you read them? Well, *I* wouldn't. Lot of piffle. I tell you, I had half a bottle of gin while she was in the bloody bathroom—pardon my French—silly cow!' He looked around the pristine lounge. 'John and me had such a lovely flat pre-war. You'd have liked *that*.' It was not a welcoming place. 'More like a showroom,' as my mother said enviously.

Once married, Auntie Queenie became less like an Ivor Novello cast-off than a relentless home store-detective, steaming open Sidney's letters and monitoring his telephone calls to his friend John. She wrote to his commanding officer about their friendship and even went to the lengths of consulting their family doctor about his inadequacies, unimproved by the counsel of Renee McAndrew. At Chiswick she presented a package of letters from LAC2 John to the desk sergeant at the police station. But, we all learnt in disbelief, 'There was nothing the Police could do about it. Nothing.'

Auntie Queenie put great onus on her rare guests, demanding incessantly what they wanted to *do*. Did one want to read a book or the paper or why did one look bored or why didn't one go out for a walk—anything to get them off the furniture. The Chiswick Empire on the other side of the Green was the only lure to visiting Sid and Queen. Sid sometimes timidly slipped me a shilling. I could get Black Looks at home.

After her disastrous weeks at Carters Seed factory my mother threw all her frayed energies into her job at the Stoneleigh Hotel, earning a basic four pounds a week plus a great deal of overtime for Masonic dinners and Ladies' Nights. I saw less and less of her, sometimes only while I was trying to listen to *On the Kitchen Front* before school. When I got back she gave me my tea, to be eaten and washed up before going back to the pub. While the Blitz continued she often spent the night under the saloon billiard table with the rest of the staff. When she did attempt to get home and burst in on my candle-lit solitude in the Anderson, she was often thwarted by the air-raid warden. 'But my little boy's on his own down the shelter.' 'I can't help that, madam, you should have made some arrangements.' Fortunately for me, she never did.

For many people like her, the war was a free-wheeling, careless time of opportunity and relatively easy money. Tips flew fast and foolishly across the bar from GIs impervious to English currency, and what she called her 'Dutch Boys', mostly sailors. At weekends she would come home with a purse gaping with half-crowns and ten-shilling notes. She had, after all, worked as a barmaid since the age of eighteen, when she left her cashier's job at Lyons Corner House and went to work, 'living in', in a pub in Eastbourne. The 'guvnor' there, Charlie Farrell, had attempted and perhaps, she hinted, succeeded in seducing her. Mrs Farrell, who had apparently treated her almost like a daughter, giving her her cast-off coats and hats, became hysterical and Grandpa Grove was sent down to Eastbourne with an army pistol from his Dardanelles days, threatening to shoot Mr Farrell. However, he was immediately recognized as the one-time smartest publican in London, all three of them got happily drunk together and my mother continued work there until Charlie died and she came back to Harbord Street.

With her long experience in the trade, including such lost arts as fining spirits, breaking down port with gold instruments (so she said) and other mysterious things that had to be done to barrels of beer in the cellar in those pre-keg days, she established herself as the Stoneleigh's star turn. Quick, anticipative with a lightning head for mental arithmetic, she was, as she put it, a very smart 'licensed victualler's assistant' indeed. '*I'm* not a barmaid I'm a victualler's assistant—*if* you please.' I have seen none better. No one could draw a pint with a more perfect head on it or pour out four glasses of beer at the same time, throwing bottles up in the air and catching them as she did so. New customers would watch her juggling skill with wonder and regulars with some pride. I always hoped she'd drop one. She never did. Tired and abstracted when I occasionally saw her for a few minutes, she seemed almost content, never enquiring after the course of my own day; her mounting self-absorption left me thankfully ignored and unobserved.

Five years of comparative plenty and activity opened up for her after the blundering misalliance with my father and the apathy and discontent of digs in Fulham and Ewell. No more dead-and-alive holes, lots of laughter, a great deal of noise, less time to squander on Black Looks. When she did turn her attention to me it was usually after she had a barney with Cheffie or one of the girls, never with the customers. Cheffie was always getting riled and took it out on my mother, niggling her for no reason. When I was still at school or, later, going out to work and leaving early in the morning, she would wake me up in the small hours to listen to her account of these endlessly sustained bouts of ill-feeling and resentment. When I yawned, usually unwittingly, at the third or fourth recount she would slam out of my room complaining that I didn't care what happened to her. The catering trade is largely given over to neurotic self-servers, as I was to discover during my brief experience of it later when I worked in hotel still-rooms and kitchens in Brighton. Arnold Wesker's metaphor of *The Kitchen* is an uncanny realization of that hopeless, unhappy world.

So, Nellie Beatrice, or 'Bobby' as she was known to her admiring customers, spent the next twenty years, lunchtime and evening, behind a succession of bars, shrieking at half-grasped jokes, bawling out her unvarying catch phrases: 'Get up them stairs' (the battlecry of the barmaid and indeed of the whole war it seemed); 'The second thing he did when he come home was to take his pack off'; 'One Yank and they're off'; and, when she could single me out as a target, 'He's like John Lawson's son. Only a Jew.' 'There's no separating a Jew from his cash box.' 'I couldn't laugh if I was crafty.' And so on. Uncurious though she was about me, my disclaiming attitude in front of others was irksome and she repaid it with mockery. After my father died, I addressed her obliquely, and never as 'Mum'. 'It's funny, you never call me "Mum" or "Mummy". People have remarked on it. Just "she" or "you". I'm not the cat's mother, you know.' Mickey Wall grinned, 'Perhaps you're what the Yanks mean by Sonofabitch.'

We had never eaten so well. Unlike the Walls and Grandma Osborne, my mother had no scruples at all about dealing openly in the Black Market for coupons, points for sweets and ration books. Throughout the war we always had more than enough butter, sugar, bacon and clothing coupons which cost, as I remember, three and sixpence each. These were peddled in the bar by Eric, who must have been one of the earliest spivs, for he began his operations at the beginning of the war, running a fruit stall in Berwick Market. I had all the oranges and bananas I could eat. Grandma O, who would not turn on the wireless if the licence was a day out of date, was appalled and refused to accept them even for frail Daisy or hungry Bessie. For once, I wholeheartedly approved mother's blinkered morality. It seemed stupid and goody-goody to go without for fear of reprisal from above. It was the attitude I later took in school towards the code of owning-up, telling the truth or being put on one's honour. The adult world was already over-endowed with prying privilege and all the aids to blackmail. If it was expedient and a reasonable gamble, I chose to lie in my teeth rather than be honest in the gutter.

Christmas 1941 came and went much as usual. Grandma Osborne's Boxing Day message was addressed to a depleted audience. The religious and moral debate raged more tepidly at Harbord Street, though Auntie Queen turned on me during a doctrinal thump-up when she discovered that I had finished reading the book she had given me for Christmas, while she was still in the middle of a mournful outburst against her sister. It was all about dogs—my passion at that time. Partly from my lingering love and loyalty to Joan, I had spoken of becoming a veterinary surgeon, at best, or a dog breeder at worst, a suggestion which was ridiculed by all as silly, and worse, presumptuous. 'Don't tell me you've read that book already. Not right the way through. That book cost seven and sixpence.' She snatched it away from me. I was a selfish, greedy little ingrate, who gobbled up expensive presents. 'Seven and sixpence,' she screamed and stuffed it into her shopping bag. The crumbs of *The World of Dogs* spattered all over me.

Early in 1942 we shunted from Worcester Park Road to Stangrove Road. The ceaseless discord about bath times, charges, petty nuisances like the late whisper of my wireless or the stairs creaking after midnight had come to a head, and we moved into the upper half of yet another semi-detached on the other side of the railway line. The landlady's name was Mrs Dawson, a woman in her early thirties, whose readiness to take offence matched that of Nellie Beatrice. Her husband was in the Western Desert with the 8th Army, and she made it clear that she abhorred company. With the true suburban charity of the wartime landlady, her rooms were urgently for rent and unwelcome to lodgers. Mrs Dawson seemed altogether sharper and tougher than Mrs Williams and I had little hope of us staying as long as we in fact did. She acknowledged our existence on rent days and contrived to be close behind her own door whenever we came in or out. The house was silent except for the howls coming from her naked three-year-old son as he received his daily caning. Apart from knitting, it seemed her solitary relaxation. Whenever Corporal Dawson returned on leave she would invite him to join in with her. Upstairs, I turned up the wireless volume to drown the frightening cries. But not for long. She would somehow hear it above her own uproar and scream up the stairs at me, cane in hand.

Some of the houses in the street had been bombed and had grown over to become miniature recreation patches for the less restricted children and, in particular, those of the Woman Opposite. She had seven children, which caused the neighbours to avoid her. Men had been observed coming and going by the whole street, and it was certain none of them was her husband. Apart from descriptions of the condition of her son's bottom, the Woman Opposite was the only subject which tempted Mrs Dawson into conversation. 'Someone should Write to the Council about her, get on to the school inspector, the police.' If her Les wasn't out in the Desert, he'd do it. That bombed bit should have barbed wire round it. In full view, some said, and without hindrance of police or barbed wire, the eldest daughter, a scornfully pretty girl, became pregnant. Pushing their cartload of shopping, the family seemed unaware of mounting scrutiny as the girl's shameless girth increased. My mother muttered blackly about what my father would have thought of any boy who did anything like that with a girl. I viewed the Woman Opposite with fresh respect. She had a cheerful look on her face, and her seven children, beaten or unbeaten, as far as one could see were ragged, dirty and happy.

8. Deathaboys

One evening I was kneeling on the floor of the sitting-room, listening to *Hi Gang* or *ITMA*, my ear pressed to the wireless so as not to disturb Mrs Dawson's evening relaxation. Thinking I heard her stirring downstairs, I tried to get up from the floor to listen at the door. I couldn't move. My legs seemed paralysed and I was just able to lever myself up on to the uncut moquette of the three-piece suite. I couldn't ask Mrs Dawson for assistance, so I turned the wireless up and waited for my mother to come back from the Stoneleigh. When she returned after midnight I told her what had happened. She was seething with Cheffie's latest infamies. I'd got cramp and it wasn't surprising, sitting in a draught all evening with that damn wireless. The next morning I was unable to get out of bed and she called the doctor. By this time I was running a very high temperature, which was to continue for months to come. I had rheumatic fever.

We had a 'lady' doctor who was kindly and overworked. I settled down with some curiosity to lying in bed twenty-four hours a day, my legs swathed in thick rolls of cotton wool throughout a very hot summer. I followed the course of the newly opened Russian Front, recording the difference in my temperature between morning and evening and accustoming myself to the exhausting sound of my heart, which hammered every time I moved my position, however gently. It was uncomfortable but had advantages over the pounding of Elmsleigh Road School. For ten months, I read all day and listened to the wireless. The lady from next door lent me the entire set of a 1919 edition of a children's encyclopaedia. She brought them in one at a time every week, so that I didn't skip through the lot at once. In the evenings I used to hear her throwing plates at her husband.

Apart from her and Mickey I saw no one, except for my mother after work. For a short while she insisted on giving up her job to 'look after me' during the day. Making and remaking the bed she thumped around the room, telling me that I was too much to look after and should rightly be in hospital. The idea appalled me, but I agreed. Anything would be preferable to her presence. Presently, she decided to go back to work and left me to myself. I became absorbed in the observable processes of my body. The texture of my hair began to change from being smooth, silky and very slightly wavy to becoming harsh and brittle and unpleasantly coarse and, in some places, falling out; I began to notice an unpleasant odour from my finger nails and toe nails which stayed with me for years. Later came boils, and dandruff cascading from my head, powdering my neck endlessly. It was as well that neither Joan nor Isabel could see me.

After some nine months, a wheelchair was obtained so that my mother could take me out. It was a cold November, the chair was flimsy and even painful to a body sore and bony from lying. I tried to discourage these outings but she persisted on showing me to the world, pushing, or rather, aiming me reproachfully at the shopping parades. She had the consolation of having the sympathy and admiration of her customers. I felt like a discarded litter basket or an old pramful of coal, waiting for her to stop chattering in the warmth inside the shops. People asked after her health rather than mine, which was a relief. There seemed to be an implicit feeling among her saloon-bar confidantes that a twelve-year-old boy bundled in a wheelchair must be either a malingerer taking advantage of his hard-working, indulgent mother or some sort of shameless cissy. Fortunately, her appetitie for the pity of the Parade was soon overcome by the pointlessness of jolting me past streets of identical houses. There was Nonsuch Park, but I thought better of it.

She did agree to take me to see *Gone with the Wind* at the Rembrandt. This was a big event. For one thing, the fame of the film was such that it was hard to believe it would be shown in Ewell. However, here it was at last, with increased prices and bookable-only seats. Apart from sitting outside Tesco's in the perennial wind of the Parade window-blind, it was my first outing for almost a year. I was assigned a place at the end of an aisle in my chair. There were a few old people similarly positioned in the packed cinema so I didn't feel as conspicuous as I had anticipated. Once the auditorium darkened, I gave myself up to the film. The excitement became so intense that I felt myself sweating and cold tremors rushing to my head. I gripped the chair, knowing that I was going to faint, which I did, once during Olivia de Havilland's labour (before the hot water had boiled or the ritual sheets had even been torn up) and again when the young Confederate soldier had his leg amputated without anaesthetic. Each time I came round, my head dripping and fallen on to my knees, I looked up to see if my mother had noticed. Fortunately, her eyes were on the screen. She wasn't able to complain afterwards that I had spoilt one of her few precious pleasures once again.

After my visit to *Gone with the Wind* I recovered quickly, although I was only able to move slowly. I think it must have had a blood-letting effect in its excitement, after being so long in confinement. I longed to be in the world again. School must surely be out of the question. A letter from Mrs Ure told us that arrangements had been made for me to be sent to a convalescent home for boys in Dorset. Even Stangrove Road and Mrs Dawson were preferable. My father knew these places. They were all prisons, he had said. But my mother insisted that after all the Benevolent Society had done for my father it would be selfish and ungrateful to refuse to go. On 23 December 1942 I arrived with my mother at Shaftesbury and looked over the iron stairs across the deserted platform. In the empty station yard we were met by an unsmiling nurse wearing pebble glasses. 'Osborne?' she enquired impatiently. 'That's right,' said my mother, almost grovelling. 'This is him.' 'I see.' 'He'll be a good boy.' She stared down at me, her eyes embedded pebble, and grabbed my hand. 'He'd better be,' she said, as if I'd been arrested already for trying to escape. 'Well, you'd better say good-bye.' My mother hugged me, in her usual ear, nose and throat crunch hold. Unsure whether I was more glad to leave her loveless clinch or loath to let myself be dragged off by Nurse Pebble Head, I found my suitcase dragged from my grasp as I was pushed into a tiny car.

My father had been right, as I knew he would. The convalescent home was more like a Borstal for sick or dying boys. As she drove to the house itself, Nurse Pebble Head grew less fearsome but made it only too clear that she regarded the boys in her care as little less than criminals who had fallen sick. There were about seventy of them, ranging from six to sixteen years old, all from the East End or the poorer parts of London, though not from Fulham. The home itself was a large mid-Victorian house off an almost traffic-free Dorsetshire road. The atmosphere within might not have resembled Borstal but it was cold, institutionally quiet and watchful as if one were taking part in a silent and endless Morning Assembly. If I had heard of such places then, Elmsleigh Road would have seemed like a holiday camp in comparison. A sparse tea was served from trestle tables by very slow moving, clearly local-yokel nurses. The bigger boys took almost all of the little jam on the tables to go with their bread and marge, unchallenged by staff or inmates. It was quickly despatched in silence. The new matron announced her arrival, striding into the middle of the room, her red and blue cloak swishing behind her. She had a distinctly martial, or rather nautical, manner, having just left several years' parade-ground experience behind her at the Royal Naval College in Dartmouth. There, she pointed out, the sons of gentlemen and officers were beaten regularly for the merest misdemeanours. Surveying her new rabble of skinny, unhealthy, underfed urchins with distaste for the contrast they must have made to the future officers of the Royal Navy, she made it clear that we were all to expect similar if not the same treatment. If healthy, decently brought-up boys could take this discipline why shouldn't we sickly, weedy mob of little street Arabs be treated with equal severity? We had lapsed into illness only through lack of discipline and could all regard ourselves as under close arrest. A good hiding was as likely to make an unhealthy boy healthy as not. She would surely spot me as a lifelong malingerer.

Pebble Head bustled with respect at this address from the bridge and took me tightly and unnecessarily by the arm up to my dormitory which I was to share with another thirty or so boys. One of the local-yokels shouted at us to hurry up cleaning our teeth and then put out the light without warning. I waited for something to happen, possibly unpleasant. After a while one or two of the younger children called out for their Mums and were told to shut up. One boy could be heard weeping. It soon became quiet. Like the others, overcome by cold and tiredness, I fell asleep before I could puzzle more over the word 'convalescent'.

I was wakened the following day very early. The small boy opposite me aged about eight, suffering from malnutrition, and looking like a wizened old man, had, as was apparently his habit, wet the bed and was ordered by the matron to stand with his wet sheets over his head until breakfast. He shivered like this on the bare linoleum, but after ten minutes Miss Pebble Head relented and took the sheet away from him allowing him to dress, forgoing a bath before breakfast. Matron didn't seem to notice. It was hard to believe she would have thought it better to smell than to starve.

It was Christmas Eve 1942, the first time I had ever been away from home apart from Bognor. In the evening some children from the local church came to sing carols and the following day I was presented with a small pencil box by the vicar. He and Matron had taken an immediate evangelical shine to each other. They reminded me of Mr and Mrs Squeers as they herded us from food and presents to carols. The strains of one of my least favourite, 'Star of Wonder, Star of Night', seemed to fill the gloomy house most of the evening. A few desultory games were attempted by the fitter children but were soon abandoned as too rowdy and physically taxing for convalescent boys or their bored overseers. Cousin Jill might have got a few old favourites together. Come to think of it, middle-class party games had not been much nicer or quieter than the shove-and-kick encounters of these sickly street Arabs.

The daily routine was unchanging. I was, according to my mother, 'a finicky eater', but I soon found myself thinking of little else but Eric's Black

Market goodies and the Walls' lengthy, easeful fry-ups. Food was sparse, ill-cooked, cold and for the most part commandeered by the bigger boys who were unchallenged by the young, frail and feeble. During the morning there was PT for those capable of taking part, which seemed to include the sick, crippled and near unto death. Matron would probably have considered physiotherapy a pretty cissy option for anyone. Mornings were supposed to be given over to lessons. We sat at desks while a young woman we called 'Miss' or 'Teacher' encouraged us to use the few writing or drawing materials. Most were unable or unwilling to do either and she read aloud to us—few of the boys could read themselves (I pretended to be unable to for fear of being penalized for suspect superiority, a deceit she kindly accepted)—or simply encouraged us to talk about our homes. This was unpromising as the common experience had few accounts to tell beyond Dad blacking Mum's eyes, getting bloody good hidings from Dad's belt, visiting him Inside, the Probation Officer, Cops and how the other kids at home thought *we* were lucky to be where we were. Everyone, including the teacher, thought this was funny. Even to me, the germ-ridden streets of Stepney sounded like teeming alleys of joy compared to Matron's antiseptic ship-shape brig. An early, quickly consumed lunch was followed by a compulsory rest period of a couple of hours, lying down on the school-room floor covered by a blanket, while a girl nurse tried with difficulty to read from Kipling's *Jungle Books*.

A Family Row would have been welcome that Christmas and I even missed the Boxing Day valediction from Clandon Close. On Christmas Day I was sent up to the dormitory to lie down properly on my own bed with a blanket. Pebble Head told me this was necessary because of the condition of the valves of my damaged heart. My stay was to be for at least six weeks, she warned. There were no short cuts, which meant being *good*. The only other occupant of the dormitory during my afternoon rests was a boy called Fiske. He was in a bed at the far end. We never spoke. I used to watch him shamble to and from his bed like an old man negotiating a park bench. Soon he took to walking with a stick. I asked Pebble Head what was the matter with him. 'Oh,' she said, 'he's got heart disease. He won't last another six weeks.' Sure enough, shortly afterwards, he was confined to his bed and then disappeared during the night. I didn't like to ask what had happened.

We went for long walks along the deserted Dorset roads. After weeks of this, I still found myself struggling up hills with some difficulty, my heart pounding in the rear of the bored, unruly crocodile of young recidivists. Soon, however, I was reluctantly playing football. Feeling stronger, I began to count the days to my release. This prospect was delayed by a boy picking a fight with me in the usual, familiar playground manner. As before, his appearance was misleading. Three or four years older and more powerful than myself, he looked as if he were dressed head to foot in his father's oldest clothes, and he may have taken a dislike to what Eric's clothing coupons had contributed to my own appearance. Anyway, he decided to call me a twat in front of my fellow convalescents. I wasn't sure what a twat was but I knew it must be perjorative. His casual aggression was a relief after weeks of lethargy and I found myself pitching into him with some sense of relief. He seemed to be on the verge of giving in and I was feeling a literally pulsing sense of triumph when Pebble Head came between, holding us apart like a couple of Mrs Buffen's dazed Staffordshires. Waiting outside Matron's office, I heard her talking to the other boy and then shouting at him. I wondered if we would both be flogged. Perhaps we were well enough for the yard-arm by now. However, when my turn came to see her, her manner was milder but unmistakably gloating and cryptic. I would have to see the doctor the following day and the consequences would certainly be unpleasant.

She was perfectly right. The penalty for my scuffling little victory was to have my stay lengthened by another month. I was like a prisoner losing remission. Pebble Head explained that it was not a punishment but treatment I had brought on myself by undoing the results of enforced rest, routine and good food in a foolish fight. On 27 January, the anniversary of my father's death, I felt very sorry for myself indeed. Pebble Head became quite chatty, confiding how bored she was and that she didn't approve Matron's unselective strictures. Still, unlike me, the other boys were all a right rough old lot. She said she had been down on me at first, thinking that I was 'a bit of a cissy', so she had secretly approved the violence of my unwise fight. My twathood and cissiness remained unproven.

This was not the first I had been accused of being a cissy—a heinous tag in those ungay days. I was accustomed to my grandmother saying to me that I looked like a street-corner nancy boy, but I took this to be part of her general puritanism and disapproval of my fugitive flamboyance. It was a time when drabness was synonymous with maleness. I was once jeered at for wearing a new yellow pullover given to me for my twelfth birthday. To the shouts of 'Tweet Tweet' and 'Blimey, there's a blooming canary', I hurried red-faced along the streets of Fulham and even sophisticated Ewell.

Shortly before I was to be released, a plot was laid in my dormitory by half a dozen boys bent on getting away from this hated place at any cost to health or comfort. It was entered into in no spirit of fun or adventure but despair. They asked me to join them but it was too late. Six weeks earlier I would have accepted immediately. The day of the great escape arrived and I helped them with knotted sheets and climbed out of the window on to a roof, taking the sheet back and lumping up the pillows in their beds to make them look occupied when Pebble Head came round to make her midnight inspection, or in case Matron made one of her unscheduled checks. This she did later, snapping her torch on each side of the empty beds while I pretended to be asleep. When she questioned me about the boys' absence I enjoyed lying to her. She deserved it. Perhaps *she* would get into trouble. Besides, even she couldn't keep me for ever. The following afternoon, six exhausted, ill-looking boys were brought back by the police. It seemed impossible that I could have thought they might succeed. Still, by some remarkable chance, hitch-hiking on those ever empty wartime roads they had managed to get as far as Hemel Hempstead, a distance of at least two hundred miles. Perhaps the sick urchins' determination to escape from her care reminded her a little of the Dartmouth Spirit. They were in Matron's office for hours and the air was thick with speculation about them being sent to the Real Borstal or even prison. Whatever did happen was concealed from us, even Pebble Head refusing to discuss their eventual fate. Anyway, *my* convalescence was over. For the next few days of my stay the atmosphere relaxed. Even Matron called out 'Good-night Boys' as she turned the lights out. Instead of, 'If I have to come in here again tonight, you won't be very happy to see me.' To her, the war on malnutrition was not to be conducted against the disease but its victims.

Don't fence me in

After my convalescence I returned home uncertain whether or not I would be going back to Elmsleigh Road. I had known that any chance of passing the Common Entrance examination was impossible, but the thought of another two years of running errands for Mr Cotter and dodging Daphne's gusset was dispiriting. My mother was absorbed in Cheffie, Eric and the Guvnor. She gave me a sick note when she wanted me for company on her day off. If I mentioned school, she responded as she had done about the daughter of the Woman Opposite, muttering at me not to do anything that would have upset my father. When I did go back to Elmsleigh Road I found that Daphne had left and was working in Woolworth's. Even that luring excitement had gone.

Some weeks later we were summoned by Mrs Ure to 'Dad's society' in St Paul's Churchyard. She explained, like a Scots magistrate delivering balanced judgement, that it had been decided that I should go to a boarding school where I would be able to work hard and try to make up for my non-existent education. In view of my poor health they had decided to send me somewhere with only moderate academic prestige but which put special emphasis on clean country air, wholesome food and a healthy, specifically Christian life. The St Michael's brochure showed pictures of rows of boys happily hoeing in the huge kitchen garden. I loathed gardening instinctively. I looked on amateur gardeners and, later, golfers, as people impossible for me to love.

I felt divided and uneasy about St Michael's. It was undoubtedly many steps up from any school I had known. It might even be grander than Tiffins, Mickey's school, like Greyfriars even, but it was clear that I was not being presented with a choice. The decision from above ('Dad would be ever so pleased. It's what he'd have liked for himself. But he was always so poorly') had been made. My mother was delighted and expected me to look abjectly grateful. Joan was gone, Isabel married, Mickey taken up with Tiffins and his arcane studies. I had made no friends. Perhaps St Michael's might not be such a bad place, more comfortable than the Convalescent Home and happier than nights with Mrs Dawson and the black days off with Nellie Beatrice. I did my best to smile gratefully at Mrs Ure. It was a perfunctory performance and my mother punched me in the back on the way out. We then went to celebrate with tea at the Regent Palace and on to the first house of a George Black show at the London Hippodrome, and there again were the ranks of huge chorus girls swarming into the auditorium to scoop up male members of the audience and dance with them in the aisles. Would one of these gorgeous plumed creatures swoop down on me? The merest brush from their long gowns promised some animal scented power from beyond. Far, far beyond Stangrove Road, and Daphne, a pasty lump of a schoolgirl in a Woolworth's overall.

I went to St Michael's for the summer term in 1943. My mother saw me off at Waterloo on the reserved coach with its bold St Michael's reservations on the window. The platform was filled with figures in black and yellow piped blazers with black and yellow caps, some wearing short trousers, some long. I had not thought to put on my own new uniform and I looked with some envy at those who had clearly ancient blazers, grubby, stained and unclean, feeling conspicuous in my mufti: a red, black and grey checked suit which aroused instant scorn, it being regarded as the sort of suit only a bookmaker would wear. The suit was a clear tactical blunder. Their handy snobbery had made me blush already but I tried comforting myself with the thought of their slavishness. Eric would have approved of my suit, so of course, and above all, would Max Miller. If only I could have a suit like one of his. I had seen a ukelele on display in W. H. Smith's on the platform and I decided on the spot to buy it for seven and sixpence. Armed with the sheet music of 'Don't Fence Me In' I determined to set about learning it when I got to St Michael's. This was another error. The uke was dismissed as a joke and I never got further than learning the fingering for 'Deep in the Heart of Texas'. I was reminded of it later, reading the account of Kipps being politely asked at tea by his demure hostess if he was interested in music and his reply, 'Well, I *am* learning to play the banjo.'

The headmaster, Mr Eric Pepper, was shepherding his boys on to the train. He looked like a solicitor's clerk, or something similar, with slightly stained striped trousers, black jacket and waistcoat, and an Anthony Eden homburg dented and most unrakishly worn, which made him resemble the popular figure of the time, Billy Brown of London Town or Mr Strube. Together with a yellow toothy smile, topped by a dense moustache my mother would have suspected of culturing germs, he could have been a bystander in a George Formby film. Unlike Mr Cotter, who seemed more like a grim shop-steward than a teacher, Eric Pepper's braying, pedantic vowels and dowdy, prissy appearance sniggered rather than proclaimed his calling. With more individual style, he might have made an unsavoury, unloveable Will Hay. Even then I had the notion that I could unerringly smoke out the prigs, hedgers and dissemblers. Eric Pepper looked at a glance to be all of these, a guvnor's man who happened to be also the guvnor. It was, of course, a glib judgement but schoolboys, especially new ones, need to invent fools gladly for their own protection. I may have felt already that if I had talent it was to vex rather than to entertain. Unlike Noel Coward's, it was not to amuse but to dissent, although I possibly thought I could do both.

Eric (or Little by Little as he was shortly to be christened by me), like so many teachers, understandably sought at all times the Easy Way Out. The technique was the simple one of appealing to the craven instincts, apparent in most boys and girls, of overweening, paltry ambition and desire to please. If I shared these instincts, as I undoubtedly did to some extent, they were thwarted by some sort of cynical defeatism that spared me the effort of competing. In the most wayward child there is often a snivelling conformist struggling to get out. Eric had a nose for this worm of cupidity within and thinking himself a Fisher of Boys he had become an efficient and respected Prig Farmer.

St Michael's had been evacuated from north London, with a skeleton staff and a depleted number of pupils to its present primitive village. From the top of the playing fields one could see a great stretch of the Taw and

Torridge estuary. The school itself was a pleasant early nineteenth-century, long, low house, approached by a drive and surrounded by parkland which served as playing fields. There were large vegetable gardens, a piggery, and outbuildings later to be converted into Eric's most cherished dream, the School Chapel. In appearance, comfort and amenities, it was certainly an advance on anything I had experienced before, possibly superior to the Gothic pretensions of Ewell Castle School. To my relief, none of the boys seemed to come from what might be called a posh background, although most of their fathers owned cars and telephones.

I soon became very friendly with a boy slightly older than myself, Greville Pelham Monserrat Watson. In spite of his Lord Snootyish name, his father was a civil engineer from Belfast. I told everyone that my father had been an artist, that is to say a painter, which seemed less dull than civil engineers, dentists or bank managers. The father of one of the prefects was a police inspector, which would have been impressive in Elmsleigh Road but not, I decided, at a school with its own colours. Perhaps Dad's Society had been duped by the school prospectus. Or, more probably, they had carefully chosen what was most suitable for me, like the Convalescent Home. I had been accurately placed for the cut-rate. St Michael's, I decided, must be well among the lower depths of boarding schools. Anyway, I certainly felt more comfortable with these boys than Daphne's bandits and the carpentering shop-steward. They were also less brutal. The ages ranged from about eight to seventeen and, once again to my surprise and relief, there seemed to be scarcely any bullying. For my own protection from various assaults I relied on my Viper Gang tongue, modelled somewhat from my father's but mostly from my grandmother's, more than willing to wound and rarely afraid to strike. A negligible athlete, I showed a certain muscle with my mouth which could disarm most lustreless spirits and even appear to belittle certain of the guvnors and their men. To those who might have bothered to subject me to any scrutiny, I was affected, self-regarding and striving after eluding style.

BILL: No, but I never seriously thought of myself being brilliant enough to sit in that company, with those men, among any of them with their fresh complexions from their playing fields and all that, with their ringing, effortless voice production and their quiet chambers, and tailors and mess bills and Oxford Colleges and going to the opera God knows where and the 400, whatever I used to think that was. I can't remember at the time. I have always been tolerably bright.

JUDGE: Always been?

BILL: Bright. *Only* tolerably bright, my lord. But, to start with, and potentially and finally, that is to say, irredeemably mediocre. Even at fifteen, when I started out in my profession. Oh no, before that. Before that. Mark. I have never had any but fugitive reasons—recurrent for all that—that this simple, uncomplicated, well, simple, assumption was correct.

Inadmissible Evidence, 1964

If vanity led me into actorish posturings, I was not helped by my physical appearance. After almost a year in bed, I felt myself to be what my mother called 'a bit unwholesome' within and without. My hair had become crinkly and wiry, almost Negroid. I tried to straighten it with careful applications of Vaseline and water and, when I could afford it, Brylcreem. I developed a hideous acne not only over my face but on my back, which persisted well into middle age. Any dandyish pretence was spoiled by these glowering pustules which later made shaving such a painful, bloody, morning exercise. Apart from the dandruff which fell in itchy scabs on my close-shaven neck, I cannot have been an engaging sight, with salt-cellar chest, elongated face, too long upper lip—I had what my mother termed a 'gummy smile'—eyes set deep but, as pointed out to me by a kindly young scholar, possibly too close together. And squinny-eyed, like Henry VIII. My only asset was fairly long legs. I longed for a barrel chest and a big head like the police inspector's son. I was a poor sort of whippet among bulls. Thinness was not then admired, but largeness, in men particularly, was regarded as the mark of health, manliness and affluence. Men who would nowadays be dismissed as overweight and misshapen were respected as 'a fine figure of a man'. Compared favourably to Edward VII, the caddish, embezzling Uncle Frank, had been grudgingly acknowledged in my grandfather's eyes as, 'a fine figure of a man'. At least my father had had a power of silky straight hair, unlike my new kinky stubble, and a superb flawless pale complexion. No one suggested any remedy for my scrofulous appearance and I could find none.

St Michael's was probably not much seedier or inefficient than many other schools of its kind, offering the merest, timid trappings of a fake public school for the minimum expense. No one from Dad's Society ever visited the school to see what a poor investment they had made in their choice of a bargain-basement education for me. The emphasis was not, as the prospectus claimed, upon lots of good food and healthy living but upon the vague but rigorous code of the time—Patriotism, Religion and Athleticism. Only in patriotism did it prosper. As for its academic standards, they were surely makeshift and erratic even by the standards of cheap boarding schools in wartime, rural England.

In spite of this, a small proportion of boys took the General School Certificate, as I did myself in six subjects after less than two years at the school. In recollection, it was a bloody-minded achievement on my part, pursued to show that I could prosper unaided and without the indignity of appearing to try, which was the very reverse of the truth. Boys could go on to Higher School Certificate and even, rarely, to the Redbrick or White Tile universities and colleges. Except those on the run from the police or recruiting officer, few teachers could have been so reduced as to accept Eric's pittance and posting to this remote corner of North Devon. Only the quiet desperation of both teachers and pupils can have sustained the day-to-day existence of the place at all. In sport there was barely enough aptitude among the whole school to raise teams in any game, even to play each other. Whenever we ventured out to play local boys' clubs the results were so humiliating that Eric was often moved more to pity than reproach. We were surrounded by schools, even humble preparatory schools, which were uniformly more excellent.

It was an isolated place which gave us little hope for the future and no possibility of pride. In spite of Eric's efforts, torpor took hold of the building like dry rot. As a school we were a collection of wash-outs, staff and pupils alike, which may have given us some uneasy sense of community. It was unpopular to point out, as I sometimes did, our patently wretched estate, but I doubt if many boys ever boasted of their St Michael's days in the years to come.

Eric was the only abiding vitality of a genteel sort amid this sea of inertia and indifference. It was hard not to award him nine out of ten for Effort, except for those hard-minded spirits like myself who were too ungenerous in our youthful cynicism to grant him even that. The effort showed increasingly in his shop-soiled appearance, his frayed shirts, the paper cuffs he wore until they were almost black with grime and ink. His accent was widely imitated, especially by me when I discovered I had a pretty good ear for such things. It was strangled and over-deliberate, pronouncing words like 'Boogie-Woogie' as 'Bogey Wogey', 'chance' as 'charnce', and a school was always a skol, a little like the lager of the same name. He came from Bungay in Suffolk which, for some reason in our determination to find him even more ridiculous than he was, we found funny. If he was aware of this concerted flimsy derision, thinly disguised in my case, he wisely ignored it, relying on some outlying remnants of loyalty. After all, we were all adrift in the St Michael's boat. Parents were unlikely to thow us any lifelines whether their money was profitably spent or not. They were those kind of parents, careless more than uncaring. Still, I was keenly disappointed at having been sent to such a third-rate establishment and not to a decent school like Mickey's. I knew I had been fobbed off with a specious and pathetic imitation.

9. Tomorrow, the Empire

THE

MICHAELIAN

Being the Official Organ of St. Michael's College

Vol. 1. No. 1.   APRIL, 1944.   Postage Inland 1½d.   Price 1/-

Donna è mobile

Arse holes are cheap today
Cheaper than yesterday
Little boys are half a crown
Standing up or lying down.

There were two 'Houses', but these had no separate physical existence. Boys were selected by what appeared to be Eric's whim to be in either School House or Gray's. He was the head of School House which had the implications of his authority over it and reflected his own taste and moral attitude in the selection of boys who were without exception, in my opinion, the most conscientious collection of future customs officers, civil servants or teachers. Gray House, on the other hand, to which I was assigned, was raffish and anarchic in comparison or, at least, so its members chose to believe.

For example, all the day boys—about a third of the school and despised heartily by the boarders—were allotted to School House. They were certainly a dull lot of dogs, suspicious North Devonians, an unforthcoming bunch, and two Jewish boys, the first I had ever met. One of them learnt Hebrew, which seemed a pretty exotic thing to be doing. Eric's attempts to establish separate identities and rivalries for the House were frustrated by a minority, including myself, which took pride in never making any competitive effort or caring about its results. Our motto might have been: 'Strive not for the laurels are not worth the blooming candles. Leave them to the Suckers.'

Gray House was in the charge of the senior maths master, a lanky Welshman who spoke with such lisping, donnish speed that he was almost impossible to understand. In the face of my near refusal to grasp mathematics, even simple arithmetic, he soon accepted the truth which was that I was by now unteachable. After a few dogged weeks, he graciously gave up and ignored me. St Michael's had its advantages, especially for the stubborn and indolent. Mr Ronald Furness-Bland, who had taught at a school in Bishop's Stortford and always walked around in a rather gamey blazer, took the lower-school boys for maths and sciences. However, the main burden of teaching fell upon Eric himself which, to be fair to him, he did amiably enough, taking us in French, English, modern English history, Geography and Latin. It was a full day for him.

The English literature was taught to us by an old toad-like man, Mr Prentiss, who called his lessons 'Literature and Living'. Most of the boys poked idle but open fun at him, paying little heed to his watery stare and encouraging his old dog to fart under the desk. He had been persuaded out of retirement to engage us in a course of moral improvement rather than literary appreciation. Eric heralded it unmistakably:

Character-Forming

The Headmaster of Ardingly, in a recent letter to 'The Times', writes: 'Public Schools regard the training of character as of more importance than the training of either mind or body.' In our course, 'Literature and Living', we follow the Public School tradition. Voltaire said: 'We shall leave the world as foolish and wicked as we found it.' But shall we? We believe that our L. and L. students will prove the great French cynic wrong. May we be right.

In spite of this Mr Prentiss made a strong impression on me and I looked forward to and enjoyed his growling passion for Dickens, Thackeray, Richardson, Fielding, Tennyson, Matthew Arnold. He read long poems, *In Memoriam*, *The Return of Eugene Aram*, doggerel poets like Barham, Thomas Hood and minor Victorians. He always carried the same two books in his pocket. One was the *Meditations of Marcus Aurelius* and the other Plato's *Republic*. He said that whenever he was out for a walk or on his own, he would have something to occupy him in the event of sudden injury or, I fancied, approaching death. He did little more than appearing to think aloud. If you wished, you were quite welcome to listen. His method was not as openly proselytizing as had been suggested by Eric. He hardly spoke to any of us directly, leaving us as abruptly as he arrived in class. In my first year he gave me a prize for my Literature and Living papers which I still have, a huge, dull book about the Austro-Hungarian Empire. I dipped into it later when I was writing *A Patriot for Me*. I wondered if Eric thought the course might yet be character-forming.

THE CHAPEL FUND CONCERT, MARCH 3rd.

We had a great treat on March 3rd when the Choir, assisted by a bevy of local talent, gave its very first concert, of sacred, classical, and traditional songs, in aid of the Chapel Fund, which has benefited in consequence to the extent of £22 16s.

Miss Edna Friend (soprano) delighted the audience with 'Love's a Merchant' (Molly Carew) and 'The Pipes of Pan' (from Lionel Moncton's 'Arcadians'); Miss Maria Beer (contralto) contributed 'Still as the Night' (Carl Bohm) and 'Spirit Song' (Haydn) in a voice of haunting richness; and Miss Dorothy Prideaux set everybody chuckling at her monologues, 'Speech Day' and 'The School Concert.'

Mr. Richard Russell, who so kindly organised the concert for us, was unfortunately indisposed, and Mr. Sydney Harper, M.B.E., efficiently deputised for him at the last moment, receiving a hearty ovation.

All these, and Miss Dorothy Shutler, L.R.A.M., who assisted Miss Tunks at the piano, contributed to a memorable evening's entertainment, and we are indeed grateful to them for so generously giving their services 'in the cause.'

The main part of the concert was, of course, undertaken by the Choir; who sang with a quality of tone, clarity, and power of contrast that were thrillingly beautiful. Their interpretation of 'The Border Ballad' and 'King Charles' was positively exciting, and that of the Bach Chorale, 'Jesu, Joy of Man's Desiring,' delightful in its soothing peacefulness. A two-part arrangement of 'On the Banks of Allan Water' was another gem, whilst a highly original arrangement of the hackneyed 'The Campbells are Coming' fairly brought the house down. 'Life's Short Tale' and 'The Lord High Executioner' (soloist, J. Osborne) were very well done, and D. Hammett sang 'God's Garden' and 'Swing Low, Sweet Chariot' with much feeling and command of tone and volume.

Music, an extra subject which I didn't take except for choral singing, was taught by a hunched, white-haired lady who reminded me of Auntie Daisy, and who looked as if she had incontinently wandered in from the Home for Distressed Gentlefolk. She had only a few piano pupils and would seek me out and encourage me to sing Peter Dawson-type ballads like 'Friend o'Mine' and 'The Story of Alkazaar' for our frequent patriotic concerts.

A group of songs entitled the 'River Scene' contained 'Swing Low Sweet Chariot' and 'Old Man River.' The solos here were taken by Miss Friend and Osborne. The finale was a tribute to the men and women of England who during these difficult years have kept alive the spark of liberty; the heritage for the coming generation. This tribute was borne out by pupils representing members of the Armed Forces, Civil Defence Units and Workers, and in a moving speech by Hornsby.

Ronald Furness-Bland would have made a passable Captain Grimes in *Vile Bodies*. It was obvious to us that he brought some unease to the staff room. He was a gin and tonic rather than a sherry man, someone Nellie Beatrice would have respectfully identified as a sporting type. Far from resembling this Edwardian paradigm he personified Metropolitan Man, awesomely to us unhappy, exiled boys and disconcertingly to his colleagues.

Some of them might have imagined him more at ease in a Frith Street drinking club than in the rustic bareness of the Bell in Market Street, or that he might have preferred the stand at Kempton Park to sipping tea in the School Pavilion wearing knife-edge flannels and pristine boots. Quickly aware of this attention, he assumed an air of swaggering reticence which led to constant speculation about his certain criminal past. Somehow, he also managed to communicate an aura of prodigious sexual power. This was soon confirmed when Eric employed a rather effeminate male secretary, Mr Wilson, and his wife who acted as matron. She was an attractive girl to me, like Madeleine Carroll of holiday memory. From the moment she arrived, almost the entire school was bent upon the wild but intent dream of having an affair with her or, at the very least, a fleeting stolen embrace. Fantasy tottered between chastest passion and mass rape. It was generally agreed that she was completely wasted on Mr Wilson, who was supposed to be a painter and looked far too much of a cissy to have such an attractive young wife. No one who seemed to be such a willy-wet-egg would possibly have served this lady as well as any one of the older and adventurous boys.

O Mores, O Directoires!

Sure enough, one day in one of the passages, I came upon Furness-Bland, his arms around Matron, crisp and crackling in her white overall. They glanced at me absently as if they were only intent on not becoming unstuck. My interruption may have amused rather than alarmed them for they both treated me with surprising un-staff-like friendliness. I felt like a privileged conspirator, the silent witness to full-throated adultery under Eric's own monkish roof. Sex filled our days if not our nights. Even the bovine Devon maids who waited on us in the dining-room were coveted itchily under the tablecloth as they bent over us, revealing the elastic Plimsoll line of desire. As far as I discovered there was no evidence of homosexuality. I may have been deceived as I thought little about it. Sex meant masturbation or girls, women, older women and, most coveted of all, married women like Mrs Wilson. This was the ultimate prize of the swashbuckling fornicator. There is an obvious piquancy in cuckolding seniority, power and privilege which recedes as one grows older. Grown-up cuckolds could excite little pity from deprived schoolboys. If Mr Wilson was aware of his wife's blatant infidelity, he must have recognized the contempt in a hundred young faces.

I did once witness a somewhat girlish boy being held down and summarily masturbated but it seemed more of a young animal lark than

Soloists:

D. Adams: **Keep on Hopin'.**

J. Osborne: **Cobbler's Song** (Chu Chin Chow).

N. King: Piano— **To a Wild Rose and Sur la Glace.**

Sketch, THE HARE'S SCUT (by permission of H. S. Joyce, Esq.):

The Husband: M. Gordon.

The Wife: J. Worthington.

The Gardener: J. Osborne.

The Maid: F. Glover.

Sketch, THE STOIC:

Lord Bunstead: J. Osborne.

Lady Bunstead: A. Burn.

Their Daughter: F. Glover.

The Butler: A. O'Dare.

bestial assault. One boy, inexplicably named Juicy Lemon, used to make regular evening visits to Ronald Furness-Bland's room for extra tuition. This was puzzling as he was one of Ronald's prize pupils and there was some doubt as to whether Mrs Wilson alone could satisfy the Furness-Bland brand of sexual versatility. However, no one put the question to Juicy himself who, if he was aware of our curiosity, was blithely unforthcoming about his mysterious cramming. I recognized him in an interval at the National Theatre thirty years later. He introduced me to his wife before I hurried to the bar. I wish I had asked him why we called him Juicy Lemon.

One or two local girls were said by some boys to be obliging. 'Give her a shilling and she'll be willing.' I fancy it was mere speculation. It's been my experience that only a minority of men, or boys for that matter, venture willingly beyond cautious innuendo into clinical sexual confidences. I have, however, been expected to listen with pleasure to tales of the calculated male conquest, inch by monstrous inch, of a multitude of last night's guardsmen or waiters. Garrulous or not, the cold, cruising stare of the marauding gay seeking to inflict or invite violation and defilement, often masquerading as love, is pretty unlike the wry gaze of the Male Quest for Crumpet. Homosexuals seldom acknowledge close seasons or protected species. Adultery, after all, is more often a matter of survival than sport.

Imprisoned in this dream of girls and married women, of looking up skirts on tennis courts and lying beneath hedges, each new term brought its challenge, recharged, more urgent and impatient. Its call came across the playing fields, a grassy sea of refuge for unhurried delights, longingly from across the Estuary and sea front at Ilfracombe, smothering the very air above the cricket pitch, mingling with the muddy pain of the scrum, its sinewy legs trampling blasphemously on the vision of the thousand plump thighs wrapping us around from the world only just outside.

The programme was interspersed with sketches entitled 'Nature Abhors a Vacuum.' 'The Way to Ware,' 'The Cure,' and 'Props.' The leads in these were taken by E. Platt, J. Worthington, J. Rose, S. Rose, Spittle, Hillman, Osborne, and G. Watson. Watson and Osborne deserve special mention for their playing in 'Props' and 'The Cure.'

Habitual possession of Durex was essential to sophistication and the rubber badge of courage. These could only be obtained from the barbers in the town and, for some strange reason, the corn chandler's. Sometimes a group of boys would approach a friendly looking GI or sailor in the street. There were thousands of them stationed in the district preparing for the Normandy Invasion. Hundreds of landing craft lay in the estuary and were visible for miles. We knew that the Yanks, pampered in all things, had their free issue of French Letters. These could be seen, stretched out on countless hedgerows like spidery cobwebs from a midsummer night's dream of permitted ravishment of the locals and of what were then called Officers' Groundsheets, in other words, any girl in the services. We had no uniforms, nylons or gins and orange, barely a shilling for even the most willing. We could usually run to a packet of heavenly delight between half a dozen of us—'like sucking a sweet with a wrapper on'—but incomparable to the guerrilla hand beneath the dormitory sheet. A few puritanical young warriors refused us, but we could occasionally persuade one to go into the barber's on our behalf and get three for two and sixpence. Failure meant a group of us drawing lots to go into the corn chandler's and risk being challenged in our school uniform and reported back to Eric, which would have been unthinkable and have led to almost instant expulsion—or at least so we believed.

It was Eric's custom after Evensong on Sunday to treat the school to one of his homilies about Christianity and how we should apply it to our everyday school life. Once, unaware of our coarse sophistication, he even treated us to the famous cautionary tale of the little Dutch boy who bravely kept his finger in the dyke. One dull Sunday, assuming our ignorance and innocence even more, in the course of familiar calls to uprightness and truthfulness, he made elliptical but identifiable reference to a scandal which had been reported in the local newspaper. All of us knew about it from kitchen and servants' gossip even if we had not read it. It was a stock *News of*

The Michaelian

MAY THE TWENTY-FOURTH.

As we write, the most ruthless enemy civilisation ever knew reels brokenly across the rocking landscape, thankfulness and hope fill the national heart.

Countless people, who include our own parents, have been called upon to face times of unprecedented trouble, and they have faced them. Some have endured privation and loss, some have exposed themselves to appalling peril, some have made the sublime sacrifice. These were the care-free, irresponsible youngsters of a handful of years ago, through whom our Empire has survived, and whose ardent hope is that the coming generation may never be called upon to face such trials as they have known.

Now, soon it will be our turn to take a hand in the destinies of Empire. To-day, scholars; to-morrow, the Empire. It is a solemn thought.

the World type story, dear to Grandpa Grove, involving a scoutmaster and several local boys in a rowing boat on the River Taw. The scoutmaster, known to us as a fairly wet but decent, friendly sort, had been sent to prison for sexual offences against them. It was the kind of thing we were all familiar with in the Sunday newspapers, and the general feeling was that the sentence was inordinately harsh. Why hadn't the silly little bastards whipped off his shorts and pushed him into the river?

Devon was not yet the hub of national sexual scandal that it was to become thirty-five years later and this particular case had caused frenzied reassessments in some genteel quarters, especially as the scoutmaster was an active churchman. Whether or not he was an active Liberal in that traditional stronghold I can't remember. Outside the grounds of St Michael's, the locals soon lost excitement and returned to their age-old peasant pursuit of amassing wealth beneath their goose-feather mattresses. Eric's references to the affair were so delicate as to be quite mystifying to the younger boys who had little idea of what he was talking about, except an uneasy feeling that it was unwise to go out on to the river at all and so get your name into the newspapers. Incantations to manliness, proudest and most watchful of virtues, rang out for weeks afterwards. During this solemn warning against sodomy stalking abroad, G. P. M. Watson whispered in my ear, 'What's he talking about? Some silly bastards being buggered is it?' 'Looks like it.' 'D'you think Eric's a bugger?' 'Don't know. He's not married.' 'No, but neither is Furness-Bland.' 'What about Juicy Lemon?' 'Well we don't know, do we? Not for certain.' In our beginning, manliness was the word and the word was manliness.

My first term at St Michael's was largely spent in the sanatorium, as after barely a week or so I was found to have measles and for the next six weeks was the sole patient. During the first few days I had been horrified by the high standard of the work in the third form where I had been assigned along with other boys three or four years younger than myself. They answered easily questions about English grammar and mysteries of parsing, Latin declensions and French verbs, things of which I had never even heard let alone understood. This public academic humiliation so casually administered on my first day by these little boys was incomparably more bitter and astonishing than any of my past playground initiations. Like the bullet-headed slug at Ewell Boys' School who had butted me contemptuously from below, my classmates barely reached my looming salt-cellared chest. Their fretless confidence, like his, was invincible. Unchallenging or gloating, they seemed merely apologetic or embarrassed on my account. Physically, each would appear to have been a match for Daphne. It was hard to imagine them cravenly avoiding her path.

Accordingly, confined to bed again, I set myself unhopefully to catching up. By the end of my confinement, I had managed to get myself up to a shaky Fourth Form standard in French and to have covered most of the period in history which was set from 1688–1815. The text books were surprisingly clear and I began to enjoy the unaccustomed daily rigour, forcibly feeding them into myself. It was the Latin and, in particular, the mathematics—algebra, geometry—which made the empty room almost spin with defeat. The geometry theorems, for example, I was obliged to learn parrot fashion without understanding them in any way. Algebra eluded me completely and I could never accept that two minuses might make a plus. Bellicose defeatism told me that it was all too much too late.

Eric did pay me occasional encouraging visits, talking to me rather warily but quite kindly. It did not change my first scratch assessment but relegated him to the natural role of adversary rather than tyrant. He lent me a copy of *The Good Companions*, and as Priestley was one of my father's heroes, *Angel Pavement* being one of his favourite books, I read it twice, casting myself as the young penniless graduate, Mr Jollifant. Tinkling the ivories in the carefree company of the Dinky Doos seemed to beckon paradise from Hall and Knight's tormenting incarceration by equations.

One of the earliest events of the term was a meeting of the St. Michaels Brains Trust. This consisted of Mr. Prentice, D. Roberts, K. Reynolds, J. Osborne, R. Spittle, and R. Mellor. The proceedings aroused the greatest interest, and it is regretted that lack of time prevented further meetings. We will just give one specimen question and answer as some illustration of the discussion:—

Q. What is the best way to convert the heathen to Christianity?

A. To live the true Christian life as General Gordon did. Nothing can be more convincing; that is the way to command others to be Christians. As Pliny said, 'We do not want precepts but patterns, for example is the gentlest and leat invidious way of commanding.'

It was a hot summer again and as I sat surrounded by books I could hear the friendly clack from the practice nets every evening. After weeks at St Michael's, I had not yet been able to establish my place, however distasteful it might turn out to be. Curiosity, even envy, slowly overcame my apprehension. I began to wonder whether my friend G. P. M. Watson had found another friend or had perhaps teamed up in some way with T. B. Williams, who seemed to have a stamp of tough-looking stardom about him. When I did return cautiously to my dormitory the term was almost over.

The fathers opened the batting, Mr Adams and Mr Friend staying in for three-quarters of an hour, and scoring a fine 45 between them. They both very sportingly retired. The rest of the team scored 10 between them, and with one wide and two byes, were all out for a total of 58.

The two opening St Michael's batsmen put up a good show, but when Gordon was dismissed for 11 things began to look black when Osborne went in at seventh wicket down. Together with M. Bird, Osborne put up a fine stand at the wicket, scoring 19, and enabling the school to draw with the fathers.

The fathers also gained a distinction, it being the first time they have not lost for many a long year.

The school doctor had told me that my heart had still not fully recovered from the strain imposed upon it and I would therefore have to be excused games for quite some time, certainly until the following term. This was some relief, although cricket attracted me slightly as being less given to physical risk than other games, and for its grace and style which I unaccountably believed I possessed in greater quantity than most others. I still found my heart pounding unexpectedly, immediately summoning up the image of purple curtain swallowing up a rattling coffin. Only swimming seemed to be untaxing, but as this involved a compulsory early-morning dip in the outside pool throughout the year it had its drawbacks. In winter it was often necessary to crack the ice before entering. Boys who were unable to swim were obliged to walk across the width, a sure-fire incentive to learn.

Perhaps because of my supposed sickliness, I seldom joined the band of malingerers and found myself among the hardy, foolish few who were eventually left still able to endure this first light shock in mid-January or February. I had no enthusiasm at all for football. The freezing mud and certain prospect of injury didn't suit my spinsterish instinct at all. My object was always discreet avoidance of both ball and the opponent whenever it could be done without detection or derision. Boxing, to my dismay, became compulsory. I found that my grandfather's tips were surprisingly successful in the more orthodox arena of St Michael's, where we were coached by the ex-amateur boxing champion of South Wales and the Royal Navy. He decided that I had the right sneaky speed, and my straight left, which had proved so inadequate in the playground, was now greatly admired for its classic accuracy and deadliness. What I feared was finding myself entered in tournaments and pitted against the certainly superior local boys of any half-decent school. There was no doubt in my mind that I would be ignominiously thrashed. So I again used my tactics of the football field, but with less success.

> M. Hill (Gray) boxed S. Mellor (School) in a most determined match, in which both received considerable punishment. Breakell (Gray) v. A. Davis (School) proved an evenly contested match. Breakell attacked hotly, but in the end Davis's steadiness won him the points. Osborne (Gray) then met K. Reynolds (School), delighting the spectators with a really good straight left and winning on a technical knock-out.

It became the only activity in which I was forced to take the offensive and denied retreat. It was a question of getting in there first and saying, 'All right, *do* it to me.' It was a rat-like narcotic strategy, dicing on the swift collapse of a more powerful, impressionable opponent. By a quixotic barrage of desperate contumely, over a short distance, it could often dupe superior weight and skill. It could later be applied over longer distances to hostile audiences in the theatre. It was a creative tactic I later employed consistently, to my own satisfaction at least, in a play, *A Sense of*

Detachment. Inviting punishment and fuelled by it, a bloody technical knock-out could result with negligible injury to oneself. 'You're really hating this, aren't you? Why don't you walk out?' Most of my work in the theatre has, at some time, lurched head on into the milling tattoo of clanging seats and often quite beefy booing. I must be one of the few playwrights to be barracked by an audience led into attack by a phalanx of standing theatrical knights bent on utter rout. I was also chased by a whooping mob down the length of Charing Cross Road. The sound of baying from dinner-jacketed patrons in the stalls used to be especially sweet. Nowadays one is merely attacked by a storm cloud of pot and B.O.

Whenever I went to the Theatre Royal, Brighton, the stage carpenter used to look at me in mock despair, 'Oh blimey, it's not you again!' One Thursday matinée I was booed by a few old ladies and what seemed to be a dog. Those were the *fin de siècle* funk days of Binkie Beaumont's lily empire with its praetorian guard of Godfreys, Terrys, scuttling agents, managers, poison bum-boys and their hacks. The lordlier ones, spinning down from town in their Rolls Royces for a ringside place at one of my preview exhibitions at the Theatre Royal, held out certain hope for them of retaining their divine title. One week, over at the Hippodrome, they were there in such number and so drilled that the manager was convinced that any bout in which I was billed was now the most popular royal bloodsport of following queens. It is one of the many reasons I hold Brighton in such affection. Once, during a performance of *A Sense of Detachment*, a lady got up and threw her boots on to the stage, triumphantly unaware that she had trodden accurately on one of the many devices sown in the minefield of the text. 'How can you do it, Lady Redgrave?' she bawled. Audiences were tricked astonishingly by a series of booby devices and would often blow them roof-high into explosions of, 'Rubbish. Take it off!', almost exactly where the script indicated it. Participants felt themselves blooded, regrouping joyfully against a flailing, weak enemy until the realization came to them that they had been sold a dummy. Their slow rage could be terrible. Not only ladies of Esher and Golders Green fought back, but their hairy *Time Out* sisters with their agit-prop weaponry of participation and improvisation joined battle in the common cause of democratic banality.

The pursuit of drink was more practical than that of sex, and this led us to the town's main station where a usually dim girl behind the bar would serve us unquestioningly all the strong cider we ordered. We made these trips fairly frequently, my friend GPMW being absorbed by British rolling stock, which he stared at rapturously from the empty platform. Still, it enlivened some blacker dog days of the term, especially when followed by egg and

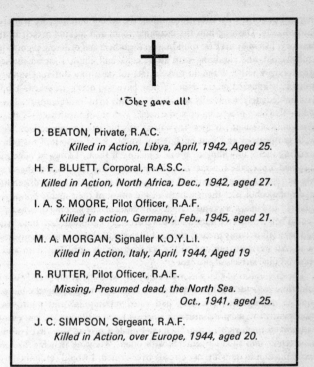

*'At the going down of the sun and in the mornings,
we will remember them.'*

chips at the Ice Cream Parlour, where a kindly GI might sometimes treat us to a second portion. It was essential to establish an alibi for these forays: practising at the nets or at some game or other, badminton, swimming. It was difficult for a complete check to be kept on every boy's whereabouts during an entire evening. The stakes were fairly well in our favour, but depended entirely upon everyone interrogated sticking to his story in the face of threat, bluff or blackmail, the stock arsenal of authority.

One evening several of us reeled back from the station through the school gates rather tipsily and unwisely singing. Suddenly confronted by Eric, who stepped out of the darkness surounding the school building, we scattered immediately. Dashing into the changing room and locking myself in the lavatory, I soon heard Eric rounding up the others and ordering them to his study. Cold, and rumbling with sweet cider and chips, I sat on the seat wondering whether I should make a tactical dash to a different vantage, when Eric knocked on the door. 'Where have you been?' he asked. 'Oh,' I said immediately, too loudly and clearly in reply to his quiet enquiry. 'Oh— well—I've been practising up at the nets.' 'Was anyone with you?' 'Yes, sir, Watson.' Or was it Mellor? Anyway, it was too late for correction. 'Very well. Go upstairs and wait outside my study.' I did so to find the others standing there, unwilling to speak. Looking at them, I knew at once that they had broken the contract to a man and that only I had kept to the story. My outrage and gaping betrayal were sponged up by the tiring, distending effect of alcohol. Let them wallow in the vomit of their manly honesty, a quality I had manifestly and dramatically disowned by keeping to our sacred pact. Their instinct for mitigation was correct, as I guessed. Last in to bat, I had been left not only to carry the can but to stumble into Eric with my head in it. We were all confined to the school grounds until half term and I received nine strokes of the cane.

The discomfort of this was muffled by my writhing at the perfidy of my sometime comrades. When I confronted them they were apologetic but not contrite, taking the view they had acted on impulse and improvised intelligently to a surprise situation whereas I had misjudged it, and events had proved them right. From then on I made a private vow that I would never enter into such agreements with others, knowing that few had my determination to outwit those already over-armed. I would certainly never own up like a man but practice every deceit which might reasonably result in outwitting any adversary. These guvnor's men might intimidate with their corrupt cant of manly honesty but not with my cowed connivance. Eric would occasionally drop little sneering parentheses into remarks during class. 'Well, of course, we all know Osborne's reputation for the truth. So perhaps we should take that observation with a pinch of salt.' And, sure enough, some arse-creeping little hack conformist would cackle back at him for reward.

Oh, Directoires of the world unite
In one great gusset of delight

The boys in the Upper School were allowed to go out in groups of not less

1
John Osborne,
aged three

2 Father – Thomas Godfrey   **3** Mother – Nellie Beatrice

4 Grandma Grove on her
hundredth birthday

5 Sister – Fay

6 Auntie Queenie,
aged twenty-four

7 Auntie Nancy and Uncle Harry in
'The White Man's Grave'

8 At Hampton Court, 1946
John Osborne with Grandma Grove,
Uncle Jack and Nellie Beatrice

Somers & Smith

9
Pamela Lane

10
John Osborne,
1950

Lisel Haas

11
In rep
(a) at Kidderminster

(b) at Derby with
Pamela Lane (*left*)

Raymonds News Agency

12 and 13
John Osborne,
playwright

14 At the Royal Court: Writers, actors and directors

1. Joan Plowright, 2. Anna Manahan,
3. Jacqueline Hussey, 4. Frances Cuka,
5. John Osborne, 6. Tony Richardson,
7. Wilfred Lawson, 8. John Dexter,
9. Margaretta D'Arcy, 10. John Arden,
11. Anthony Page, 12. Robert Shaw,
13. N. F. Simpson, 14. William Gaskill,
15. Miriam Brickman, 16. Michael Hastings,
17. Tom Maschler, 18. Alex Jacobs,
19. Alan Dobie, 20. George Devine,
21. A. L. Lloyd, 22. Mary Ure,
23. Alan Tagg

than two at a time. GPMW and I would take a train to Ilfracombe, eating in the equivalent of the Ice Cream Parlour, braving the breakers over the open beach with ever an eye out for likely girls who might spend an afternoon with a couple of impressive-looking boys from some unimpressive but unknown school. We always ended up at the pictures, with wet socks hung steaming on the radiators and a bag of buns and cakes. Deprived of the pictures after a boyhood of constant exposure, I had suffered severe withdrawal symptoms at St Michael's where we were only occasionally allowed to see propaganda films like *Western Approaches* or *One of Our Aircraft is Missing*. In the tiny cinema at Ilfracombe I was reunited with the best of the outside world with films like *Double Indemnity*. Deep in wartime Devon, Southern California with Barbara Stanwyck and Fred McMurray was like a sinister blow-out, a forbidden tuck-in. One couldn't imagine Eric cheating for monkey nuts let alone murdering for sex or money.

To our short-lived delight, a few day girls were allowed to attend the school as an apparent gesture to the exigencies of war, apart from those of Eric's pocket. I found myself sitting beside Jane Gregg, a rather vapid girl who lived with her sister Betty nearby, and who was said to have been screwed by T. B. Williams fairly regularly in the playing fields and even in her house before she transferred her attention to the GIs. The pleasures of inserting my hands deep up into the silky recesses beneath Jane's dress, and staring out at Eric while doing so and risking her denouncement, slowly palled in the face of her sulky refusal to acknowledge me.

However, Eric had also admitted several of his nieces, the most interesting of whom were two sisters, Jenny and Sheila. Jenny was a fine swimmer, stronger than many of the boys, and on the tennis court she blacked out my fading image of scrawny Joan Buffen. Jenny and her younger sister were no callow tomboys. We lay on the ground watching their defiant underwear flutter in the wind as they pulled down their skirts with useless modesty. Sheila, with her red hair and green knickers, was the more voluptuous and popular of the two, but Jenny who seemed more modest surely promised more. When I found myself playing one of the young lovers from *A Midsummer Night's Dream*, Demetrius, opposite her, only my irritation with the undimmed manliness of the character could conceal my confusion.

We exchanged a few implied intimacies and notes, but this was clearly something that would be conducted strictly according to the code I had adopted since the drinking betrayal incident had all but outlawed me. To my surprise, Jenny's mother made an application to Eric for permission for me to go to Sunday tea at their fisherman's cottage in Instow, where row

145

upon row of craft were lined up in preparation for the Normandy landings. Even more to my surprise, he readily agreed. It became a fairly regular idyll and I would walk over on Sundays meeting Jenny half way, walking across the fields and looking out at the estuary, holding hands and saying very little. I was certain that she was surely consumed with the same kind of feeling as myself. We both seemed to have the patience of prone certainty and it would soon express itself extraordinarily.

During the next holidays I wrote her long passionate letters, starting early on 'Dear Jenny' and ending later, finally, 'My dearest darling'. She was worryingly slow to respond to this show but when she did it seemed to tally unquestionably in identical passionate coinage. After the separated fervour of the holiday, the following term progressed confidently as far as I'd hoped, mostly in silent walks and punctuated with occasional ear-flushing kisses and probing embraces. For the present I was happy, almost palpitating, as I had as a convalescent prisoner, on the way to meet her on our regular Sunday walks and tea at the little cottage by the harbour. Weeks passed with little thought beyond the next Sabbath's clasp of palms. I had never felt such physical fever and I was certain it was flowing back to me with the same exhausting fire. Her silences couldn't conceal indifference let alone treachery.

Suddenly, our shared furnace silence blew up into wreckage her abrupt, complete absence. Without explanation she didn't appear. Was she ill? Should I write to her at home? I daren't ask but the explanation was soon coming. I had been sufficiently flushed into carelessness to drop a wallet full of Jenny's letters somewhere in the school. Eric presented these to me as damning evidence of my unspecified sin. The letters were absurdly innocent. My almost tearful request for their return was refused with what passed for relish in Eric. He had spoken to Jenny and her parents, he said. They all agreed with him that it was best that Jenny should leave the school at the end of the term and in the meantime she and I were not to communicate with each other in any form. I said, as bravely as I could, that I could not find it possible to agree with this. But that bit of unmanly bravado be as it might, Jenny had already agreed to the conditions without any pressure being put upon her. It was not to be believed, but Eric observed his own ludicrous code. He may have been a sworn dissembler but he was no liar. For the next few weeks until the term ended I stared at her miserably, willing even a whisper of regret or farewell from her. She never glanced at me. For the first time existence itself seemed deliberately pumped out from my being.

I heard little from Mickey. He was deep in exams, and while I was preparing for my General School Certificate, distracted by the bitter wreck of my love affair, he was preparing himself for the Higher School Certificate, something which seemed well beyond my reach. I was soon beginning to wonder where indeed the path from St Michael's was going to lead. One day I approached Eric, who seemed now to have banished the Jenny incident from his mind and was prepared to be polite to me, as to what he thought my possibilities were after I left school. What did I have in mind? I asked if he thought there was a remote possibility I might get a place at Oxford. Might I, for instance, perhaps become an historian? He smiled at me curiously and pointed out my virtual ineradicable academic inadequacies. Perhaps, with my enthusiasm for English and my father's background, a career in journalism was practical. However, it required a skill in shorthand and typing and, above all, the capacity for self-discipline without supervision. Did I have that? He implied that it had not yet shown itself.

Despising him as I did, I don't know why I was disappointed at his light-hearted lack of interest. One way and another, the approaching end of St Michael's for me was going to be, in Nellie Beatrice's words, A Proper Let Down.

After the School Certificate exams were held and over, we were three-quarters of the way through the summer term in 1945. In a way, it may have matched the weary, impatient mood of the country at the fading stage of the war. There was a general air of restlessness throughout the school and of longing to get back home and be free from the results of the exams and Eric's routine, which he however seemed determined to keep up until the last possible moment, overloading us with more and more provocative regulations. VE Day, 8 May, seemed frantic, disconcerting to me anyway, neither celebration nor sorrow. No more pins on wall maps. Victory in Europe: was it the glad end or a possibly bad beginning? I remember little of the events of the day, but they don't seem to match the hindsight description in the *Michaelian*. I do remember helping to drag a piano from the music room up to the playing fields and setting fire to it, the sight of its red-hot strings twanging and snapping back into the rising flames, a strange noise breaking over the shimmer of the summer air. There was a free holiday the following day which was slightly clouded by the piano incident, especially for those who had taken part in it. But Eric, in the wisdom of his patriotism, was lenient and decided magnanimously to let us off with a reprimand. However, he added that although the war in Europe had ended, the war itself had not yet come to its close and that anyway the school and its work must go on until its allotted span.

It was fair warning but I was in no mood to stay still. For once, my own

VE DAY AT ST MICHAEL'S

VE Day was celebrated fittingly at St Michael's, which had somehow become gaily beflagged with decorations from unexpected and mysterious sources.

After a preliminary speech, in which our Headmaster touched on the historic nature of the occasion, the boarders found their way to the gaily decorated streets of the town, where, we understand, a rousing trade was done at the Ice Cream Parlour!

Lunch was followed by a treasure hunt with plenty of prizes (and not a few surprises!), after which the school assembled to hear the Prime Minister's Declaration of Peace in Europe. During the day full advantage was taken of the glorious weather to make good use of the swimming pool.

The College attended the crowded and moving Service of Thanksgiving and of Dedication at the Parish Church, returning in time to hear His Majesty's speech, and then gave itself whole-heartedly to the construction of a bonfire, which should out-shine all the other beacons now twinkling merrily on surrounding hill-tops. And with the memory of that blaze in our minds we crept tired, but triumphant (for our bonfire **was** the biggest and best) to bed.

The second day—the first day of peace and the very first day of peace in the lives of our youngest—was a day of excursions, and many boarders attended The Gaumont Cinema as the guests of R. Perplow, Esq., whose generous treat was greatly appreciated.

Footnote.—A very small boy wanted to know if Monday's holiday was given for the end of the war of Europe, how many days would there be to celebrate the end of the whole war! A nice problem in proportion! Anyway, he should know now!

poised impatience was generally shared. About a week before the end of term tempers worsened throughout the school. Eric was evidently feeling the strain and I thought I could detect a rabbit-twitch of apprehension coming from him. As he became more bland and affected, I took to watching him for weakness. One night a large crowd was gathered round the radio listening to Frank Sinatra, then a baffling phenomenon with his armies of screaming girls and the uncertainty of whether or not he actually dropped his trousers to engineer this incredible hysteria. Evening cocoa was being handed out from huge chipped aluminium jugs, cold with skin on top. Eric suddenly entered and most voices lowered somewhat except for mine. He strode over to the wireless and turned it off, looking round, defying a response. Seeing my upturned, smirking scorn he lunged forward and slapped me very hard across the face. This shocked me, as I had never seen him do anything so unconsidered and spontaneous. My own reaction was equally spontaneous. I drew back my fist, not a straight gentlemanly left this time, and smashed my wild right into his moustache. He went flying over two trestle tables, which collapsed in a pile at the far end of the room, spilling the cloudless cocoa all over the place. Slowly, dripping blood and cocoa, he rose to his feet, to my infuriated dismay, helped by several boys. He swayed and quivered. 'Go to the sanatorium,' he said.

I was to stay in the sanatorium for the next day or so, visited only by the new matron. Eric telephoned my mother saying that it was essential that I should leave the school, as it was in a rebellious state after what had taken place. His implication, as she later reported it to me, was that the entire school was united in my support. True, a few braver spirits did manage to slip notes of encouragement and gratitude under my door. But the shifting St Michael's code would soon reassert its old shaky, despised self. My bag was packed, I was refused cider by an unfamiliar girl before getting on the train back to London. I stared out of the window at the huge placards by the track: 'You are Now Leaving the Strong Country'. I wasn't entering it for sure. All I could be sure of seeing was the Black Look of Waterloo. Behind me I had left nothing.

EXCELSIOR

And how time has marched on since our last issue. VE-Day, VJ-Day, a Socialist Parliament, the Atomic Bomb. What next? Has the world sufficient moral intelligence to withstand the temptation to unleash the forces of destruction it now commands? It seems incredible that it should not ... And in 1939 it was incredible that Germany would deliberately encompass the organised destruction of millions of innocents. It is doubtful if any of us realise the extent of the horror that has occurred. Perhaps it is a mercy we do not. But even the blindest of us must see the utter necessity of holding on to decent ideals and humane principles, each and every one of us, as never before. May we ourselves never fail in the humble part we play as units in this fantastic world-embracing scene.

10. 'Must Leave Now to Take Down the Front-room Curtains'

My mother was quite unprepared for my return, foresight being unknown to her kind. It was easy for us to avoid each other. When she was not at work, I could visit Mickey Wall or the Rembrandt Cinema or join Grandma Osborne listening to *Saturday Night Music Hall*. An advantage of her refusal to enquire about my life was that she ignored the bad as well as what might have been the good. The news came from Eric that I had passed my School Certificate—a passport to nowhere as it turned out. More important, the matter of Jenny came out. 'Oh my God,' said my mother, poring over the letter. 'There's a *girl* in it! He says something clan- . . . something was *going on*.' 'Clandestine,' I said. 'What's that mean?' 'It means he didn't know. Except that it's not true because he let me go to tea with her.' 'Oh dear,' she looked at me with some bitter satisfaction. 'How upset your father would be.' No, he wouldn't, I thought to myself, he might even have said Jolly Good Luck.

Mrs Ure also seemed uncertain as to what should be done with me. Prompted or not by Eric, it was decided that journalism was my only hope and I should be sent to Clark's College, where I would learn rudimentary shorthand and typing. It was made to seem both prosaic and unattainable. I cycled every day some five or six miles to the college, a large Victorian house in a leafy Surbiton street, where I was the only boy in the class of some thirty or forty girls. Day after day passed and no one, including the mild little teacher, addressed a word to me. After three months I had mastered enough shorthand to get me through an official 100 words a minute, which I was unable to read back, and an unverified typing speed. Mrs Ure provided me with introductions to local newspapers in Croydon, Sutton, Cheam and Barnes, but it was soon made clear to me that my chances of reporting a wedding in Norwood were as unlikely as phoning in an exclusive account of a military coup from some unheard of trouble-spot. 'He'll be a thousand-a-year man, he will. You'll see. He'll be a thousand-a-year man', even Cheffie put in a word for me. A thousand a year was more than twice the amount my father had ever earned.

During this period of charade interviews, I woke up one morning with violent pains in the stomach and complained to my mother, who gave me three brimming tablespoons of castor oil. When she came back from work in the afternoon, I lay sweating on the bed, doubled up and she sent for a doctor. He was encouraging but did nothing to ease my agony and insisted on 'A Second Opinion', which seemed to be something available, like the Second Coming, even to the humblest like myself. The Second Opinion confirmed that I had a twisted burst appendix and peritonitis, urged on by Nellie Beatrice's castor-oil chaser. A few weeks later I had an appendectomy at the Epsom Cottage Hospital, a cosy little place which nevertheless could do little to ease the ordinary unpleasantness of operations at that time, most of all the administration of the anaesthetic. This sensation, like being held down on a table and slowly stifled to death by numbers, was ineradicable. Even the painful abdominal after-effects were almost a reassurance of outraged life still within me. For once, my grandmother ventured out, as she had failed to do for my father's funeral, and came to see me.

Convalescence seemed inevitable but the NABS had either lost interest or felt, understandably, that they had done enough for my career. I embarked instead on a two-week trip to Penzance with Uncle Sid and Auntie Queen who had unaccountably visited me in the Cottage Hospital. They seemed to have decided to adopt me like bemused foster parents, taking me to the theatre, visiting third-rate opera companies and concerts at the Albert Hall. Queen's employer, Captain Leon, had a drawerful of free tickets amassed for charity by the theatre-loving customers of Richmond, enabling me to sit in ten-guinea seats and watch *Don Pasquale* or *Crime and Punishment* with John Gielgud. Queen and Sid found it all a bit too 'highbrow', until the time would arrive when he urged her to go on and be a sport, snap out of it and have another drink.

Sid and Queen booked rooms for their week's summer holiday in Penzance. Before the war they had always gone to Sidmouth with Auntie Caddie, in their tennis-playing days. Now, with Auntie Queenie, bride of a few years standing, in her early fifties and Sid in his mid-forties, they seemed frightened that Caddie might catch up with them. I enjoyed myself tremendously. Penzance was a cosy place, not boisterous like Margate or sleepy like Bognor, but what I imagined Ventnor to have been like in summer—hot, palmy and drowsy—like Isabel. Queen scrutinized every move Uncle Sid and I made together, although the three of us were almost always in company. Occasionally Sid would come into my room in the evening, sit on the bed and try to talk about what he called 'highbrow books and things'. Listening outside, her ear placed to the door as she had done on my mother's wedding night, Auntie Queen could have heard nothing compromising, only what she regarded as an excess of attention to a young boy.

At the end of the week they had decided to go home. It had been 'very nice' but they had had 'quite enough'. The high spot had been a visit to the film *The Bells of St Mary's*, with Bing Crosby and the adulterous Ingrid Bergman as a nun, which possibly appealed to Queen's nostalgia for Renee McAndrew. I said good-bye to them, excited at the prospect of a whole week without their bickering and hourly disappointment with Penzance, and a world loured over by Auntie Caddie. I longed for them to go, leaving me to explore the fishing villages and rocky beaches on my own. Sid dared not show his regret. Queen was impatient and their preparations to leave were like disassembling a siege. I had not had such a sense of freedom since walking on the beach in the Isle of Wight and there was no Black Look to return to at teatime.

I wandered among the rock pools, perhaps thinking of Isabel or Mickey and the undisclosed future, but only slightly missing a companion. At least the circumscribed tedium of St Michael's was over. Towards the end of the week, feeling stronger after long walks to Mousehole and Lamorna Cove, my acne dried up and improved under the burning sun. I found myself on what seemed to be a deserted beach, and in the shelter of a huge pile of rocks I took off my bathing suit and began to cauterize my appendicitis wound with a stick, rather like a crayon, which I had been given for this purpose. It was six months since my operation but my scar had refused to heal and was still partially open with patches of wormy flesh protruding from it. The cauterizing was not painful but the sight of my exposed abdomen was depressing.

Scraping away at a piece of hanging flesh, I noticed that I was being watched and quickly hoisted up my trunks. I went to make off in another direction where I could carry on undisturbed. I looked towards the figure on the beach, a handsome, grey-haired man, possibly in his late thirties, who was lying on the sand near the sea. He looked extremely relaxed, rather amused and very brown. Covering myself up, I tried to hurry past him, but he stopped me and spoke in a very confident, educated voice. He asked me about myself and what I was doing on my own. His name was J. Wood Palmer and he had just come out of the army, a major in the Army Educational Corps, 'trying to bash a little poetry into the heads of squaddies'. He asked me what was the book I was holding in my hand. It was Shaw's forgettable novel, *An Unsocial Socialist*. He too was a writer and had had several short stories published in international collections. He invited me to have tea at his cottage.

The cottage was small but very comfortable, lined with books and exactly what I imagined a writer's cottage to be, lacking only the spaniels and a wife. 'This village is called Sheffield,' he said. 'Rather piquant I think, don't you? There's only one small post office and a pub. You might think of it next time you buy something inscribed "Made in Sheffield".' I was puzzled that someone so worldly should find something barely remarkable so amusing. Unsure how to react, I studied the books on his shelves, while he made tea. He was indeed a famous writer; there were editions of proper books, no Penguins, inscribed *International Short Stories of the World*, a great many volumes on history, poetry, novels, first editions. There was more to read in his small sitting-room than I had seen outside my favourite bookshops in Bognor and Kingston, only here everything was covered in the scent of flowers from the open doorway.

As he made the tea, he sang pleasantly in a baritone voice from something I identified as being from Italian Opera though not precisely. He sounded happily occupied and the sounds of his preparations were very different from the noise of impatient, resentful drudgery I was used to hearing from kitchens. His kitchen was clearly a retreat, a place to put up your feet in, rather than a coven of grease, elbow grease and bad temper. Presently, he put on a record of *The Miracle in the Gorbals*. 'Listen to this,' he said. 'The first thing is the theme of the lovers which in the next scene is played as the theme but in a different key as that of the prostitute's. Rather interesting I think. Amusing. Don't you?' I wasn't sure what he meant, or, rather, just how really interesting it was. Perhaps there was more to it than an obvious musical trick. As it was I had actually heard of *Miracle in the Gorbals* and of Arthur Bliss. There had been a long article about him in *Picture Post*. After a week with Queen and Sid it seemed amazing that I should strike up an acquaintance with a cultured and apparently famous writer so easily.

During tea he talked a little about himself, about his own experiences teaching young soldiers about civics and politics. He asked me about my own politics and my friends. He was so courteous, casually encouraging me to tackle his effortlessly prepared tea (my mother would have taken heavy-breathing hours over it). The delicious scented tea, the pretty china cups and bowls, the silver trays and flowered knife-handles were friendly and obviously used every day and not mummified in serviettes among new-smelling drawers in the lounge sideboard. His ease and attentiveness, the absence of any sense of hurry, behind or to come, was heady. There was no washing-up to be got out of the way before you'd finished, no summoning bell or waiting landlady. I soon began to feel that if I did say anything foolish, he would generously find it 'interesting', like the lovers' theme. I told him about Mickey Wall, Eric, trying to be a journalist. 'Perhaps you're really a poet,' he said. Could he be serious? Yes, he was. I said little about Queen and Sid and nothing about my mother. I didn't want to be found *too* amusing.

The light was beginning to fade and, clearing the table, he suggested that I might like to stay the weekend here at the cottage. My heart stopped. I was quite unprepared for invitations so lightly offered. Such things were usually mulled over suspiciously like will-readings. I was due to go back the following day. What could I do? 'Why don't you ring up your mother?' To the famous writer it was quite clear, but I knew there was no point in doing that as she would only raise difficulties. A cloud of changed plans was unthinkable to her wellbeing and would be proof of my selfish caprice. I explained that we had no telephone. 'In that case, why don't you get me to send her a telegram from the Post Office? We can do it in the morning.' It seemed worth the certainty of a week's Black Looks for the chance of a few days in this civilized man's company. I agreed eagerly. 'Very well then,' he said. 'It's all fixed. I have a young friend coming at the weekend. I think you might find him quite amusing. He's a poet, too, but sometimes he gets very sulky and goes outside and sits by himself, so you and I can talk together if necessary.' It was all fixed. Short-stories and their writers seemed very important then. My father had written them sometimes and read them constantly.

Before it got quite dark, I was sitting comfortably, reading one of his contributions to *International Short Story*. 'Before I send a telegram tomorrow I do think that I must tell you that I shall almost certainly try to seduce you.' This time I could think of no reply at all. He was smiling but he was also serious. The back of my itchy neck and chin were wet and burning. I felt immediately transformed from a welcome visitor to an oafish shoplifter. Above all, I felt pitiful gratitude for his honesty and good manners. It was what I knew to be *Good Behaviour*, a rare sight in myself and others. I mumbled a few excuses about my mother after all really expecting me and that she would be cross. He took me across the fields and showed me the quickest way back to Penzance. 'If you ever change your mind—remember Wood's Ha'pence and Made in Sheffield.' Unable to express my mixed feelings of admiration and relief, I escaped back to High Tea and my cheerful, unlettered landlady.

I looked later for the works of J. Wood Palmer without success. He had told me that he was a descendant of the famous Wood in Ireland, he of Wood's Ha'pence, the subject of Swift's *Drapier's Letters*. It was the one reference he had made over tea which I had instantly recognized. Eric had taken me over it a few months earlier. That afternoon was the first time I had ever felt indebted to him.

11. Hold the Front Page

In January 1947, Dad's Society sent me to work for Benn Brothers, which was a glum building, grey outside and white tile within. However, the *Daily Telegraph* offices were only a few yards farther down so it was better than being sandwiched between Kennard's and Dorothy Perkins in Croydon High Street. Benn Brothers was a subsidiary of Sir Ernest Benn Ltd. Sir Ernest, it seemed, was a near Fascist Evangelist who principally published educational and religious works and, through his other companies, a host of technical journals like the *Electrician*, *Nursery World*, *Engineering World* and so on.

Benn Brothers was controlled by his sons, Mr Glanville and Mr John. Perhaps this identification by Christian name was to give it the feel of a family firm, implying a filial, cosy atmosphere which it certainly did not fulfil. Benn Brothers was an old-maidish, anonymous organization and its employees, doubtless most of them failures in the mainstream of journalism, were rather like the boys at St Michael's, aware of the drab hopelessness they had settled for so defeatedly. Defensive and prickly, they were scornful of the big stars on the Street, implying that they were casting-couch upstart scribblers and inferior to real 'working journalists'. I never understood this phrase but I took it to imply seriousness and permanence. The big by-liners, like myself, probably couldn't read back their own shorthand outlines and were unlikely to bother, as I saw it.

Mr Glanville, who seemed rather like a cleaner and more prosperous Eric, sent me to Mr Silcox, the Editor-in-Chief of the *Gas World*. Mr Silcox had a very high opinion of himself and immediately and eagerly gave me long lectures on the ethics and responsibilities of journalism. He would occasionally take me pottering around to conferences or to the offices of the British Gas Corporation in Hyde Park Corner in his rotund little Austin with a huge placard on the window proclaiming: PRESS. The Editorial staff numbered four, including myself. His daughter, Primrose, acted as his secretary, fawning on him with the admiration of an ambitious wife rather than a daughter and was seldom away from his side. I was soon given the impression that every lurking eye in the building was after Primrose's body. It was clear that I was not yet a serious candidate, but Mr Silcox was on the look-out for a suitably serious working journalist son-in-law who might one day step into the Editor-in-Chief's chair at the *Gas World* and display PRESS on the window of his baby Austin.

I was assigned to a tiny desk in the adjoining room, which was even smaller than the Editor-in-Chief's. This contained the Assistant Editor, a large gloomy man rather like Mr Prentiss, who said little but wheezed and grunted on a running sewer of a pipe all day. By the end of the day the little room was almost black, like a railway tunnel in mid-winter. Apart from myself the only other occupant was the Chief Reporter, a foxy-faced man who wandered in and out on various assignments which he increasingly handed over to me. These 'assignments' included summonses to press conferences at Ministries about anything that had to do with industry, engineering or the Gas Council. At first I enjoyed these expeditions, especially when I found myself sitting next to some scruffy authoritative expert, like the Industrial Correspondent of the *Daily Herald* or the *Daily Telegraph*, watching Sir Stafford Cripps or Emanuel Shinwell conferring with their Eric-like heads of departments, trying to answer cheeky questions from the back-of-the-class Press. They were hugely unlike smarmy Silcox with his hair parted in the middle and Primrose's hand on his working journalist's shoulder. The only man who later reminded me of him was Ernest Marples, a most famous Minister of Transport, which must be the Working Journalist's idea of a plum political appointment. I have no son and am unlikely to father one now but it is more than passing comfort not to have begotten a future Transport Minister, Golf Club Secretary or Royal Court actor.

Even Mr Silcox found it hard to conceal how little work there was for me to do. There was little enough for anyone except the Assistant Editor, preserved like a sweating kipper in his own pipe smoke, who hardly ever looked up from his proofreading all day long. The Editor-in-Chief spent most of the day out of the office. He would announce half way through the morning that he was going out on an assignment, confirmed by the commissionaire who checked all our movements, in his Press car. Primrose was kept busy typing letters which her father dictated to her first thing in the morning, and the Chief Reporter opposite me was also out most of the day. He would come in for about an hour, type up his little bits of copy and then disappear.

My first task of the day was to read a large selection of provincial newspapers, the *Glasgow Herald*, the *Scotsman*, the *Yorkshire Post*, the

Liverpool Post, the *Manchester Guardian* and one or two others to see if there was anything about the gas industry that might startle some of our readers. I could make this enjoyably last the morning with ease. There were never more than a few buried column inches about gas, and provincial life seemed vastly richer than Ewell's or, indeed, Fleet Street's. Mr Silcox had given me a book on how to proofread and I got through this without much difficulty, although I was never entrusted with any proofs to actually read. All the copy was of such a highly technical nature, mostly by experts in the world of gas that it would have been difficult enough to understand let alone correct. The only two contributions made by the staff were Mr Silcox's weekly leading article, almost always inveighing against the Labour Government, its nationalization of the gas industry and the coal mines, and the Chief Reporter's column called 'Round the Showrooms', which was supposed to be bright and snappy stuff giving information about how to evangelize the gas cause in showrooms, cinema foyers and restaurants. He fobbed this off on to me, with the Press Conferences, but it helped to release me from Primrose and her father. I became 'Round the Showrooms, by Onlooker', and it offered me new scope for going past the commissionaire without explanation. I spent almost a week wandering round the Ideal Home Exhibition, sampling healthful drinks, midday drinks, sleep-inducing drinks, fruit drinks, along with dozens of different breakfast cereals. Stuffed in the cheeks with honey, milk, malt and wheat I watched demonstrations of cleaning, sweeping, beating, stain removing and polishing available to the ingoing tenants of Attlee Buildings and Stafford Cripps Estate.

During my twelve months' spell in bed with rheumatic fever I had subscribed to a correspondence course conducted by the British Institute of Fiction Writing Science. I received weekly lessons on thick blue paper. The syllabus was mostly concerned with disciplines like How to Choose Your Market, the Correct Size of Your Margins, Spacing, Letters to Editors, Dealing with Rejection Slips, Essential Information, and so on. When it came to the art of fiction writing itself this turned out to be a simple matter of observing a narrative pattern which was something like 1a), 1b), 1c), 2a) and 2c). This iron formula was inviolable and simple, based on self-evident principles of exposition, conflict, exposition of second conflict, conflict and resolution of both conflicts, or variations on these. One's efforts were tolerated only by the most slavish adherence to these scientifically proven standards of fiction writing.

Not daring to send in anything of my own, I submitted two short stories written by my father. One was called 'Crawshay-Bailey Had an Engine', a story about a small boy's obsession with a Great Western steam engine, and another one called 'Mouse Pie', which I read after his death and was obviously about me and the problem of bed-wetting. Eating Mouse Pie was a traditional old Welsh cure for this habit. I submitted these under my own name and waited. The replies of the Fiction Editor were fulsome in their praise of my promise, but he made it plain that without the expert tuition of his Institute my chafing genius would never find an 'outlet', even in the 'class' market that I was aiming at, like *Argosy*. I was already aiming too high to affect a sale. When I started sending in my own efforts, the response from the Head Fiction Editor soon became reproachful, impatient and eventually ill-used and sorrowful. I was quickly disheartened, gave up sending my five-shilling subscription to the British Institute, grateful that no more was demanded of me than my original ten guineas deposit. Now, with an empty desk facing me all day, I decided to take up my writing again, wondering if I had retained any of the craft that could make a success out of fiction untutored by scientific method.

Silcox and Primrose kept a sharp eye on me and there was not much opportunity for me to persevere with my British Institute of Fiction Writing Science training at my exposed desk. However, the Editor was often away for days at a time to attend some conference vital to the future of the gas industry, and I could then invent some showroom exhibition far enough away to get a chit for my two-shilling bus fare and go off for the rest of the day, wandering about the City lanes looking at churches. I seemed to be installed in the St Michael's of Journalism and Mr Silcox was its Eric, the *Daily Telegraph* a closed fortress like an Oxford college or the Inns of Court. But already thoughts of a huge office rattling with telephones and delivering copy to order were unattractive. I didn't fancy being yelled at as a copy boy. My spirit was cheeky certainly, but my irreverence was not the pushy, imperturbable kind necessary to a young reporter. Even at the highest level, it seemed a striving, unrelenting pursuit, untroubled by inner life or dignity. It was a priggish response but accurate enough about my own deficiencies.

In spite of these gloomy conclusions during my afternoon walks in the City lanes, I was soon to become the Ace Reporter of the *Gas World*, following up a scoop which led to my almost immediate promotion. The winter of 1947 was an historically harsh one, ushering in the first post-war fuel crisis. Everyone, particularly at the *Gas World*, blamed every bleak succeeding day on the Labour Government, Mr Attlee, and our own office villain, Mr Shinwell. Mickey Wall took his *Daily Worker* without incident to Tiffins, but on the 8.17 up to Waterloo there was no avoiding unfriendly stares or the brusque reception when I arrived at the office, particularly from Primrose. Silcox would have me in his office on some pretext and give me more lectures about the ethics of journalism and what a fine profession it was, making it clear that the Royal Road to Working Journalism did not lie through the columns of the *Daily Worker*. He also made it blandly clear that if either Mr Glanville or Mr John were made aware of the existence of this publication in the building the culprit would probably be summarily dismissed. Sir Ernest would come down from Leatherhead or somewhere and strike fire into our little corner of the building.

In February there were heavy floods in the Home Counties and I was told to take a train to a hard-hit region and report on the situation as it affected the gas industry. I set out idly enough, regarding the 'assignment' as a day's paid holiday. However, I had not yet abandoned the ethics of Working Journalism and took a ticket to Windsor, where flooding had been reported to have been especially heavy. I got out with very little idea of what to do with the rest of the day. Being near the river, even I was easily able to acquire a boat and, astonished by my own enterprise, found myself rowing enjoyably down a main street in Windsor, asking people from upstairs windows where I might find the local gas works. I soon found it and made for what I took to be the coke ovens, where I was welcomed enthusiastically by Mr Shinwell's New Army. I took down a lot of technical details about what had happened to the ovens, knowing that it made no sort of sense but that when I tidied it all up it might become A Story. By this time I had so enjoyed my own undiscovered, untapped resourcefulness that the outcome was unimportant anyway. Benn Brothers seldom sacked anyone. They didn't employ sackable people. Rowing myself back to the station I telephoned the Assistant Editor, telling him what had happened, saying that I was more or less stranded and would have to go home. The next day I wrote up my story and gave it to Silcox, who was delighted at my enterprise and immediately gave me a special recommendation to Mr Glanville. I decided then and there that he must be a bigger prick even than Eric. I couldn't believe that even a reader of the *Gas World* could be interested in my rowing trip to the gas ovens of Windsor. Within a few days I was summoned by Mr Glanville and told that my weekly salary of forty-five shillings was going to be raised to four pounds. He asked me how I was getting on at the *Gas World* and I replied warily something to the effect that there was not enough writing to do. He said he would look into it.

Encouraged by my huge rise of almost 100 per cent I decided to buy myself a typewriter. These were not very much in supply just after the war and I could find only one within my price range at a second-hand shop in Fleet Street. It was a pre-1914 government model which had been rehabilitated. The keys clanked down in a sideways, lurching motion. It was

£14 and I borrowed the money from my mother, promising to repay her out of my new rise. It seemed to be built of iron for use in an Austro-Hungarian fortification, and I almost ruptured myself carrying it across Waterloo Bridge to the station. When I staggered into the house, my mother said, 'That's a funny-looking thing to spend all that money on'. Ace Reporter or not, I now had the basic equipment for a writer.

I seldom went into the staff canteen which was always full of typists and boys of about my own age, dull sub-Silcox men and women all incestuously working on the various journals. Often I ate sandwiches in one of the Inns of Court or the Temple. But one figure at Benns' struck me at once as being quite different from the rest. He would occasionally stride into the canteen. Tall, with a bushy moustache, reddish hair, very athletic looking, he was about thirty and was the only man in the building who wore what was then considered to be long hair—in other words, nearly down to his collar. He was extremely handsome, I thought, a little like an American-footballer version of my father. I was very curious about him, and asked the Assistant Editor who he was. He was the editor of a magazine called the *Miller*, he said, and volunteered no more.

After a short spell with the *Nursery World*, where I was treated very coldly by the female staff, I was summoned to Mr Glanville again who told me that Mr Silcox felt there was not enough work for me to do on the *Gas World*, especially as it was even more technical than most of the other journals published by Benn Brothers. He asked me if there was any other journal I would like to join. I couldn't think of one that held any remote interest to me. 'What about the *Miller*?' I suggested. He seemed puzzled. 'Well, I was brought up in the country, you see,' I explained. 'We'll see what we can do.' After a few days I was transferred with Mr Silcox's benign blessing and slight puzzlement to the *Miller*.

Arnold Running, the editor, more than lived up to my expectations. For one thing he was Canadian, racy and quick-witted. Apart from this he used the dirtiest language I had ever heard. At first he seemed slightly unfriendly, and suspicious. Later he explained that he was sure I was a bit of a 'panty-waist'. After the circumlocution of one of Silcox's Weybridge lectures, the delight of hearing, 'Jesus Christ, Osborne, more horse shit comes out of your mouth than out of a horse's ass' or 'You fucking stupid little ass-hole', all delivered with utmost, unfamiliar friendliness and a broad grin was more encouraging than anything I could remember. Arnold's candour was gruff, overwhelming and delightful. On my first Monday in his dark little office, which overlooked the white-tile well of the building and received little light, he looked at me appraisingly and said something like, 'Jesus Christ, this firm really makes my balls ache. There's sweet fuck-all for anyone to do here and I get paid forty quid a week for that and then they send me some shit-head ass-hole like you to help me do it.' Forty pounds a week! He was only twenty-nine it turned out, and already he was a thousand-a-year man. 'Well, as long as you don't get restless, give me any bullshit or generally get up my ass you can stay. But no bullshit. I can't stand bullshit. That's why I keep away from everyone here. Too many panty-waists and ass-holes. Just when anyone's around look as if you're doing something, for Christ's sake.' 'Yes, sir.' 'And for Christ's sake don't give me that Sir bullshit. My name's Arnold. Right?' It certainly was more than all right.

The contrast with Eric and Mr Silcox was total. There was probably even less work for me to do on the *Miller* than on the *Gas World*. Arnold's job as editor simply consisted of reading long articles on milling, correcting proofs and giving them to me to recorrect. He also typed a few letters to subscribers and contributors which were taken down by his secretary, Josie, a very plump, nubile and provocative girl quite unlike most of the silly gigglers up in the canteen. Arnold was open in his contempt for the *Miller* ('Just a load of horse shit'), and for Benn Brothers and everyone in it. Everyone there was just 'a horse's ass'. He was impressively educated, having a degree in English at the University of Saskatoon. The document testifying to this was framed on his sitting-room wall at home—'Universitatas Saskatooniensis'. ('Quit your laughing, you fucking little shit head.')

I had scarcely anything to do most of the week except assist him make up the pages and go down to the printer's in Liverpool Street and help him put the paper to bed on Thursdays, something I had never been allowed to participate in on the *Gas World*. The work of the *Miller* could have been done by one man in about two days, including the day spent at the printer's. It was a Time and Motion nightmare. The routine was simple. Josie came in to do Arnold's letters which should have taken about ten minutes but stretched into an hour-long exchange of sexual repartee. We talked of little else. Josie was as different from Primrose as Silcox from Arnold, who kept calling me a 'horny little bastard' in front of her which seemed to please everyone, including her. She dressed in very short skirts in defiance of the recently introduced New Look, slavishly worn by the girls in the canteen. Over-painted with vast eye make-up, deepest black red lipstick and lurid finger nails, she seemed the perfect, sophisticated, lecherous, sublimely common barmaid the heart could imagine. Her favourite colour was a particularly whorish dark green, which she wore with over-reckless insistence like Wilde's carnation. Some of the staff, particularly the older women and those on the *Nursing World*, had complained about her wanton appearance. How she ever got past the commissionaire let alone Mr Glanville or Mr John was inexplicable. But Arnold would listen to no one, including Mr Glanville. 'So what the hell! She just looks like she's a good fuck.'

Arnold's snorting, effervescent spirits, which sparked over the office all day, were soon dampened when he got home. Mrs Running even contrived to make his moustache, which seemed so sprightly in the white-tile corridors of Benn Bros, tame in her presence. They lived in a mansion block between Cheyne Walk and King's Road, which felt extremely smart to me, but she had no liking for it and wanted Arnold to go back to Canada where there was a better life, with lots of 'fancy gadgets', as he put it, and modern kitchens and Chevvys with automatic gear shifts. England had none of these desirable things then. Arnold was reluctant to go until he had written his novel, which he felt could only succeed if he stayed in London. There was a lot of open bickering between them about it and a few years later he gave in. He wrote to me from Toronto in 1957, where his wife had decided they should live: 'The ass-hole of Canada,' he said, adding, 'Come to that, it's the ass-hole of anywhere. Always knew you were a clever little prick, panty-waist or not.' He was working on some newspaper and now had a couple of novels published. He didn't sound very cheerful and kept referring to being middle-aged, missing London and no longer being able to 'horse around'.

I knew him for less than a year but I grew fond of him and dependent on his advice. No one had shown me such consistent, energetic kindness. His locker-room gaiety was melancholy, touching and encouraging to me and probably no one else. He was all for me going into the theatre and turning my back on Ace Reporting for Mr Glanville. 'Get the hell out of it while you can. I *have* to stay in it. I'm married. You're too full of highbrow horse shit for Fleet Street. You better get rid of it someplace else.' His soft, attractive Canadian accent was reassuring in itself and there was no doubt about its seriousness or considered concern. He was to be trusted. It became clear that there would be pricks like Eric and Silcox in the world, and men like Arnold. From then on it was a beholden duty at all times for me to kick against the pricks.

Slow quick quick slow

Arnold would work for a token hour or so during the day (he had a most puritan conscience), while I made a pretence of correcting proofs, which he would do himself later anyway. He gave me the less technical articles to go through which were mostly scientific arguments for and against certain ingredients used in the process of milling going on at that time, like the wheatgerm itself, riboflavin and Vitamin B. Then there was the weekly article on windmills, of which there still seemed to be hundreds in those days, particularly in East Anglia. These articles, too, were highly technical as well as historical. Unlike the *Gas World* no one ever seemed to come in snooping, except for the advertisement manager, who was no match for Arnold. There was no Mr Silcox or Eric to make us mime a day's work, so we spent most of our time talking about politics, sex and writing. I told him of my attempts at the short story and he seemed to think that I would have better luck trying, as he was, with a novel, which might easily become a best-seller. Short stories were mostly written by highbrow shit heads.

His taste in literature was almost exclusively American and he lent me his favourite books, including Melville, Hawthorne, Thomas Wolfe, Elmer Rice, Eugene O'Neill, John Dos Passos and Hemingway. I had read some of these already, but he also gave me books that had been on the American best-seller list, such as *Anthony Adverse, Gone with the Wind* and *King's Row*, all of which had made huge sums as successful novels, vastly enjoyed by Mickey Wall and myself. Arnold, too, had his idea of getting to know one's market and his choice seemed shrewd. He was also very interested in philosophy. I had been reading popularizers like C.E.M. Joad and knew the identities if not the doctrines of Locke, Berkeley and Hume. He was very keen on Schopenhauer and Nietzsche. I had just tried to read *Thus Spake Zarathustra*; Hugh had presented it as a challenge to my suspect intellect. *The Decline and Fall of the West* by Oswald Spengler was very popular at the time and Arnold lent me this too. In his view, Spengler was borne out by present events and I was prepared to take it on trust from him. It was impressive to me at the time.

National Service lurked beyond the *Miller*'s friendly den. Boys like Hugh, who certainly had none of Mickey's inventive resilience, told tales of lads driven to suicide. The spirit of Shelley and Baring-Gould had proved an ineffective protection against the corps of crop-headed NCOs who seemed to have been recruited from the Gestapo to administer a system of misery for National Servicemen. To make it worse, it was a system that was gleefully endorsed by secure middle-class adults, the kind who nowadays talk yearningly of short sharp shocks. Unfortunately, National Service seemed neither short nor sharp but two years of unremitting, abject misery. The prevailing sour climate of austerity encouraged these attitudes, and its shortages often seemed to extend to ordinary human patience, sometimes even kindness. Wartime dreams of being a Jolly Jack, obligingly serviced by a fleet of randy Wrens, being entertained by concert parties of Hollywood Stage Door stars and flattered and cosseted by a grateful nation, had died with the twang of burning piano strings on 8 May, gone with the matey Churchillian past. Mr Attlee's cowering recruits were the forgotten army of post-war adolescents, despised outsiders with no glorious recent past to distinguish them, a shamble of nuisances, irrelevant to the present and of no particular account to the uninspiring future.

They were not to know the privilege or status of Teenager, an American word and a foreign concept like 'Mother's Day'. They were certainly not a market for goods. There were no goods and they had no money. No one fawned upon them, feigned affection for them or, above all, feared them for their one irrefutable, unattainable gift—youth. Rarely did the nation's leaders ask, as they do now, with toadying anxiety, 'What about the *Young* People?' If they ever did, the hostile inflection would have read, 'What *about* the Young People?'

We had heard comforting but unlikely stories of lads successfully convincing blimpish psychiatrists that they were undesirable homosexuals, but I knew that this was a fantasy I had neither the talent or nerve to explore seriously. So, like thousands of other displaced, pimply youths, I waited, dimly hoping that a Labour Government, surely dedicated to libertarian compassion, would dramatically abolish conscription before my number came up, or even that a short, glorious war would turn us overnight from disregarded, snotty-nosed little erks into Our Gallant Boys in Uniform.

There was no doubt that I was indeed marking time, not only at Benn Brothers but waiting to undergo my Army medical and enter another period of undefined expectations. Mickey Wall had gone into the Army Educational Corps and seemed to be enjoying himself, but he, after all, had a cheerful, improvisational spirit. As I had often seen, his spontaneous eccentricity could disarm the most rigid imagination. His bland apparent conformism would protect him from the ugly harassment to which the National Service seemed dedicated. This was regularly confirmed to me by highly coloured, alarming accounts of basic training in places like RAF Padgate. In the meantime, life with Arnold was pleasant, a pocket of subversive idleness in the very crypt of Sir Ernest Benn's temple of industry, dedicated to the ethic of Hard Work is Good for all the Others. Often he would say, 'Fuck off, you little bastard,' in the middle of the still afternoon and I was able to wander around the City. I usually chose the City rather than go home early and disturb my mother's afternoon rest and hear about Cheffie's latest iniquity. I also had an arrangement with the commissionaire, whereby I and a few others were allowed to sign the book after the rest of the law-abiding staff and get in a half an hour or so later in the morning.

One lunchtime, having been told to fuck off early, I was walking down the Strand and passed the Vaudeville Theatre, where a play called *Now Barabbas* was being presented. It was by William Douglas-Home and I was aware that it had created something of a stir as being a very 'serious' play, a description which in those days would inflame the Gallery First Nighters and give a boost to those box offices where it was not playing. I can't remember the name of the leading actor, but outside was a photograph of the leading actress, Jill Bennett.

Walking further along, a girl emerged from the Halifax Building Society. She smiled shyly, waved and hurried down the Strand. All I knew about her was that her name was Renee, that I saw her on Tuesday and Friday evenings and that she lived somewhere in Elmsleigh Road, almost opposite the school. I had seen her regularly waiting for the 8.17 at Stoneleigh, when she would smile at me in the same shy way before she got into the same carriage every morning a few yards down the platform from my own.

One of the reasons for not returning home early was to avoid my mother's parting accusation when she left for work, 'Why don't you get out of the house of an evening instead of sitting around being a bloody misery just reading and listening to that bloody wireless and records. Bloody good thing when you do get in the Army if you ask me.' I was not bloody miserable doing these things but was eager indeed to get out. The thought of my having the room to myself, even without much likelihood of putting it to immoral purposes, irked her increasingly. Mickey was by this time promoted to sergeant, posted to Norwich and his leaves were infrequent. I went on my own to a few Saturday-night dances, but soon left early discouraged by the lines of sulky, scornful-looking girls, the usually empty floor separating them from gangs of strutting Brylcreemed boys. Also, I seemed to have unaccountably ignored one fact—I couldn't dance. I must have felt that you went to a dance and then, with luck, the social process took over technicalities like where to put your feet while you were thinking of what to say or of whether the bathroom mirror had let you down.

I left the dance hall of the Victoria Inn at North Cheam one evening, having danced with no one, spoken to no one and after hastily drinking one beer. Staring into a shop window framed with lace curtains and displaying photographs of young women, some dressed in ball gowns, some in *tutus*, and young men in dinner jackets or white tie and tails, the answer seemed clear. It was the premises of the Gaycroft School of Music, Dancing (Classical, Exhibition and Modern Ballroom), Speech, Elocution and

Drama, proprietor Mrs Elizabeth Garrett. The following week I enrolled in the beginners' course. Arnold allowed me to fiddle about ten shillings a week on bus fares and miscellaneous expenses. With my train fare costing fourteen shillings a week, twenty-five shillings a week handed over to my mother, I had a little over two pounds a week left to pay for dancing lessons at two and sixpence an evening, and the odd private one thrown in. My freezing sense of foolishness left me within minutes of my first lesson. I could see that I was quicker-witted and more adroit than most of the pupils, a pretty clumsy, dullard lot mostly in their late twenties, older and crippled by lack of rhythm, instinct and ineptitude of bearing and character. Week after week they struggled with their joyless, fumbled formations and I soon became snobbishly encouraged by the sight of proclaimed mediocrity concentrating such mountainous effort on so little. Among the few of my own age was Renee Shippard of the Halifax Building Society.

She seemed to be a quiet but open, affectionate girl without any of the whining inert suspicion that marked so many girls like the ones at Clark's College or in Benns' canteen, trusting yet responsive without being avid. However, the light-on-her-feet prurience of Mrs Shippard, the black suspicions of Nellie Beatrice, and the English winter hampering brief experiments in Nonsuch Park, reduced us to snatched pelvic felicities during the Quickstep, what I came later to know as a Dry Fuck on the Floor. Slow, slow, quick, quick, slow. But soon we were seeing each other almost every evening even if only for a few short minutes on her doorstep. (Mrs Shippard: 'Perhaps you should have a little rest from each other sometime, dear. You don't want to get tired of each other too soon, do you?') She didn't mean it. Her enthusiastic, prying coyness was too obvious. But what we so simply wanted was denied to us. Apart from Mr Attlee's weather or watchful park-keepers, more vigilant than the Sheriff of Nottingham in keeping Maid Marion off her back in the ferns and bushes, sex itself was the most unobtainable luxury in the winter of our post-war austerity. Even Eric the Spiv couldn't help me. As for 120 Elmsleigh Road, there was nowhere to go except the sitting-room, Renee's bedroom being open only to a glimpse on the way to the toilet. After a short evening listening to the wireless or my classical gramophone records, which the Shippards tolerated in polite boredom while Renee and I held hands, we were left a statutorily timed ten minutes as Mr Shippard 'turned the lights off', an exercise which in such a house could take not more than two minutes. What we both wanted was buried not in a waste of grinding shame but of perfervid fumbling.

Nellie Beatrice did not welcome the idea of a girl being alone with me in 'our' house. She said the word 'girl' as if it were synonymous with prostitute, although she was unable to fault Renee's respectability. Her father had a 'good position' in the Strand branch of the Chase Manhattan Bank, something Grandma Osborne could approve, if pressed. My father, I knew, would have despised Mr Shippard, a non-smoker and a Christmas-only tippler, and his wife for her importunate lower middle-class gentility. My own abiding snobbishness emerged: I wanted Renee's body, her friendliness and uncapricious affection, and I had begun to cherish the idea of her daily, fleshy, unfailing comfort. But what about the misty goal of a thousand words a day before lunch, home to the wife and children for lunch and walks with the spaniels before tea, revision of the novel, then maybe a few friends for dinner at *night*, perhaps even in dinner jackets? Renee didn't quite fit in with that picture, even if she were allowed to contemplate it. The dream was insubstantial and silly enough as it was but it would need her blind devotion if I was to set out somewhere in my undefined, uncharted future to achieve it. At present, the only certain prospect I could anticipate was that of National Service squalor, followed by almost certain unemployment.

Seeing Renee in the suburban, frantic neatness of Elmsleigh Road was one thing, but spending a darkened Sunday in a terraced house in Westcliff with her relatives was discouraging. The Shippards had unbelievably raised themselves upwards. But her Uncle Jack lived in Westcliff, the dispiriting 'over-spill' of Southend, a word not yet invented; the sort of place where incipient Thompson and Bywaters might have once been trapped by the gods who look down upon the godless, and drove them to front-parlour madness—all before the days of housing estates and wife swapping over Bacardi and Chinese Take Away. The front-parlour gloom was the same I had known at Tottenham and Fulham, with the odour of anaemic self-righteousness, the lifeless whine, the lack of rigour or gift of even petty decision. Union with Renee soon appeared a consummation more devoutly to be escaped than contemplated and the Royal Road to Mere Content between Renee's legs looked less inviting after a high tea in Westcliff with relatives even duller and more commonplace than my own. Even a dutiful escape to the Odeon in Southend to hear the *Messiah* and then a windy fruitless fumble on the beach back to Westcliff were not reassuring.

In spite of this December storm warning, clear even to my muddled, protective sense, I found myself being encouraged by Renee and her mother to willingly buy her an engagement ring, a solitaire diamond, if that it was, for £12 from Bravingtons, celebrated in every tube train like Tiffin chocolate. Bravingtons in the Strand, a few yards from the site of Miss Bennett's debut in the West End. My mother disobligingly lent me the money. However, it was mildly gratifying to feel that if I was pledging myself to the most untrue marriage of unlike minds I was at least being seen to give in my notice to Nellie Beatrice for good and all. Renee and her mother were kindly, good tempered and agreeable, virtues as remote from my mother's crabbed nature as dog shit and fag ends to the daily discontent of *Guardian*-reading women. Mr Shippard seemed prepared to go along with his wife's rather flighty fancies, even if they presented him with an eighteen-year-old prospective son-in-law earning four pounds a week in a job with no clear prospects. Mr Silcox, in a good mood, might have reassured him, but Arnold would have taken care of that: 'Jesus Christ, your daughter must be some kind of ass-hole to want to marry a fuckin' panty-waist like little Osborne.' Arnold's admiration for me was genuine but impossible to call upon in Station Road, Westcliff.

Somehow, the Shippards became protective of my alleged intentions towards Renee in the circumspect, cautious way of the Ratepayers' Association of Elmsleigh Road. I was at once titillated and alarmed by the pattern of events I had so blithely set in train. Mrs Shippard became more girlish and flirtatious, her Sunday teas more lovingly elaborate and her daughter's engagement ring was the table centrepiece. She emerged as a lifelong Bride, born a Bride, a practising Bride. Nuptials were a garment she drew on every day, like underwear, never the bridesmaid always the bride. Her attention was centred forever on the Central Act of the wedding feast as if it were regular Holy Communion. Impregnation, live issue and age were consumed in the transubstantiation of Holy Matrimony, endlessly administered until they spotlessly reached happiest descent in a girl's life into the grave, where Virgo was for ever Intacta.

As for Renee, her hesitant, rather maidenly affection looked already 'contented', precipitately sated into matronly tenderness. Instead of browsing round the stalls and bookshops of Kingston and Epsom, I was being led gently to gaze into High Street furniture shops. I had not dissembled my doggy, lecherous, sentimental feeling for Renee, but I knew also that it was fired by a wholly selfish desire for comfort and flattery. Perhaps RAF Padgate or Catterick would provide an escape route after all. My snobbery and embarrassment made certain that I confided in neither Arnold nor Mickey Wall. The Shippards were kindly, simple, attentive and I had no reason to despise or hurt them, but I knew that I would have to, and with the least cost to myself.

Two things changed this headlong turn of events for me. My engagement lasted three months into 1948. In October 1947 I had gone to Kingston upon Thames to undergo my Army medical, quite certain that in a few weeks I should be wearing a uniform malevolently designed by the authorities to proclaim to the world the patent inadequacies of mortals like myself or lesser breeds from nowhere. The only law we were to know was that imposed upon us by our betters. It was not to be. My mother's careless castor oil, the possible imprecision of the Epsom Cottage Hospital and my sustained jabbing with the purple cauterizing stick paid off. Pressed for details by the doctors about my medical history I found myself enjoyably reciting the list of ailments I had in all truth endured, if not suffered, from childish diseases, glandular fever to the dreaded TB, father and sister both having been struck down by the White Plague, and so on. After a couple of hours of standing—a naked postulant—peered at, mumbled about, pulled and poked painfully in what seemed like clinical rape, I began to be alarmed. It made me wonder if my refusal to keep up my regular visits to Brompton had not been a mistake. Was I a physical wreck? Did I have the Osborne Plague? That might be worse than RAF Padgate where, even if I were certain to suffer, I was unlikely to die.

Clutching panic about me I faced the medical officer for his verdict. I was Not Guilty. It was not merely a reprieve but an unconditional dismissal. Because of the abdominal damage I had sustained I would be unable to engage in any of the likely tasks that the Army might call upon me to do. In no circumstances of National Emergency would I ever at any time be called upon to serve in His Majesty's Armed Services in any capacity. With this terse pronouncement I was free not only to leave home but to choose my destination, to be neither a military nor a suburban hostage.

12. Kindly Leave the Stage

The three greatest lies in the world:
I hate money.
I'm glad I'm a Jew.
I'll only put it a little way in.

Preserve me from the carping spirit. I say it almost daily now when the captious refusal to be pleased or assured by ordinary modesty or reticence is general. Charity is hard to come by, certainly in youth and was missing in me then. I hope I extended little to myself. No doubt I did, but, in flight from what I feared as defective imagination, supine passion, I was at least aware that the snobbery of my feelings towards the Shippards was not only unworthy but a reflection of my own inadequacies.

Existentialism was the macro-biotic food of the day and Mickey Wall and I were 'into' the impenetrable brown rice of Heidegger, Kierkegaard, Jaspers and, of course, Sartre. Uncomprehended concepts of freedom, will and choice floundered to act in the face of concrete possibilities like two up and down in Stoneleigh with Renee and Mrs Shippard. My untutored understanding told me that I was standing at a crucially Existential crossroads. The problem was simple: how to get rid of Renee without causing her too much pain and me too much guilt, and how to leave home and my mother and manage to support myself. I suspected that any resistance Nellie Beatrice put up would be counter-weighed by her pleasure in my broken engagement. My calculations were vulgar but shrewd in knowing when to strike to the most disadvantage to others and the greatest benefit to myself.

One of the older, more serious pupils of the Gaycroft School of Dancing had encouraged me to join an amateur dramatic society in Leatherhead. It was directed by a young lady called Terry Tapper, which had a merry theatrical ring about it, like the Dinky Doos. She accepted me eagerly and we began rehearsals for one of J. B. Priestley's 'Time Plays', *I Have Been*

Here Before. The rest of the cast were not only maladroit and unenthusiastic, but bewildered by the play, a gloomy affair which no one could understand. I suggested that we do a production of *Blithe Spirit* instead. Everyone agreed thankfully as they had seen it as a film and enjoyed it. Seeing the film myself about half a dozen times, I gave what I thought was an astonishing reproduction of Rex Harrison's performance. However, after a few short weeks rehearsals were abandoned. I was the only one who seemed to have any instinct for walking round the furniture or learning any of the lines and the production was shelved to everyone's relief except mine.

But the fumbling of others had given me some confidence. I knew that my impersonation had been an accurate one which everyone agreed was professional. In fact my aptitude seemed to have confirmed them happily in the knowledge that they could never become even amateurs. Added to this, Mrs Shippard insisted that I looked and sounded exactly like Rex Harrison, her favourite actor, in spite of the fact that she had not even seen my performance. I had no respect for her taste but I felt she could represent a popular opinion which might help overlook my natural deficiencies. But real encouragement was to come from within the outlying fringes of the profession in North Cheam. My dancing teacher, Betty, took a very flattering fancy to me, especially in view of the fact that she was twenty-nine. While she put me through the parade-ground drill of the Quickstep, Foxtrot, Samba and Pasodoble, she would thrust her heavy erotic frame against me and talk of her husband's inordinate sexual demands. Her mother, Mrs Garrett, said I looked like Leslie Howard and should certainly go into films. She was certain that it could be done. Leslie Howard was indeed a little like my father but I suspected he had a certain wet-egg appeal to middle-aged ladies. My father was no Rhett Butler, but he was no Ashley either. With the right wardrobe, Rex Harrison was nearer my style. Better still than any, but for age and accent, would have been Conrad Veidt.

Renee and her mother were impressed by Mrs Garrett's ambitions for me but disconcerted. Reaching for the stars might mean lifting one's dedicated gaze from Renee's flowing bottom drawer. In the meantime, Mrs Garrett seemed benignly confident about my future. She made no attempt to thrust drama or elocution lessons on me. Her belief was astonishing. My star was to be ripped most timely from Gaycroft's by a few sittings with a reputable wedding photographer in Sutton High Street. My studio portraits were mounted and displayed in the Gaycroft window and sent off to whatever agent might be looking out for failed aircraftmen from the suburbs of South London. I was to be put up for the leading part in a film, *The Blue Lagoon*, starring a girl called Jean Simmons, a romantic story about two innocent teenagers alone on a desert island. It was patently unthinkable, but whatever grafting Mrs Garrett may have done on my behalf must undoubtedly have been undermined by my photograph. The part went to a hefty young man called Donald Houston.

An audition for pirates in *Peter Pan* followed and then I was sent for an interview with a Mr Michael Hamilton who was a producer for a management called Barry O'Brien. He was moving into a large Edwardian block of flats near Harrods and, with the aid of a young man, capriciously and irritably directing a cast of removal men to arrange an enormous selection of antique furniture. He was the first man I had ever met who was openly camp, and in the unblinking, self-travestying tradition of the time. The subtleties, degrees and form of camp had not yet been revealed to me. This was the everyday, cooking camp of actors and hairdressers which I soon found myself half-consciously imitating, leading to a lifetime of random misunderstandings. Mrs Garrett had told him all about me so he asked me no questions. She had only seen me perform a passable Quickstep and a flashy Pasodoble, but it was enough to get me the job of ASM, touring in Hamilton's production of *No Room at the Inn*.

Barry O'Brien Productions specialized in what were then called Number Two Tours of West End successes. *No Room at the Inn* was a melodrama about wartime evacuees being farmed out to unscrupulous foster-parents. The wartime memory was still vivid enough to make it seem topical, and there was a bravura part for a leading actress, of a tart in a provincial town, which had been played three years before with great success in the West End by Freda Jackson, then an unknown actress from Nottingham. (Its author was a woman called Joan Temple.)

The likeable villainess, Mrs Voray, was a readily identifiable archetype. A careless, rather than wicked foster-mother to a bunch of irrepressible East End evacuees, she was a figure of melodramatic tragedy rather than a calculating, depraved monster. Although she neglected and railed at the foul-mouthed urchins she had taken in for a few shillings a week, it was hard not to sympathize with her. Harassed by smug clergymen and social workers with posh voices, priggish school teachers and overworked billeting officers, she seemed more put upon than the repellent charges she was supposed to be exploiting. When she pulled on her old 'Sailor Beware' hat with its limp, bright feather, her slit black skirt and garters, jeered at by strident child actresses, her drunken ignoble death was more pitiable than morally justified, which the script seemed to imply.

Anyway, given a roistering performance by the doomed Mrs Voray, cheered on to her destruction by cute kids who said 'bleeding' every few minutes (led by fifteen-year-old Rita Garnsey, the dramatic star of Gaycroft) to the excitement of their elders, it struck the theatrical gong squarely between Moss Empires and Shaftesbury Avenue. With its short scenes of melodramatic information, sentiment and broad humour, it was a skilful example of music-hall drama. It is sometimes overlooked that the halls relied so much on undiluted drama, where laughter was interrupted perhaps for twenty minutes at a time by very simple appeals to emotions like jealousy, crude patriotism, lost love, poverty, death. John Lawson had done it, obviously, so did the embarrassing Wee Georgie Wood and Dolly Harmer, Elsie and Doris Waters, ventriloquists with their surreal dummies, Thora Hird in her second-act silent monologues and curtain calls, Hylda Baker in her working-man impersonations.

No Room at the Inn was a series of broad sketches mounted on a ninety minutes' narrative with time for two intervals. It let the orchestra go to the pub while getting the second house in and effecting the simple but necessary changes of scenery. I say necessary because they were, essential to the succession-of-sketches formula which distinguished its style from most three-act plays. Even a nude backcloth with new actors every ten minutes or so provided the driving rhythm of dramatic 'turns' and changes of mood and response. My mother, for instance, always asked in advance of seeing a play or show, 'How many scenes are there?' A play with one set offered no renewed hope every few minutes. As with Shakespeare, if one set of characters or action bored you, there was the certainty of something different forthcoming shortly while you ate an orange or studied the rest of the programme.

The tour was to last for six months going first to Cardiff, Southport, Cambridge, Lewisham and Wimbledon. If I proved satisfactory during that period I would stay on with the company until the tour ended the following Christmas. My duties were to be Assistant Stage Manager, understudying the five men and teaching the children. Mr Hamilton didn't make it very clear to me what this task required except to say that it was the company's responsibility to see that they were—unlike the children in the play—not morally deprived or improperly fed. The company chaperone was Mrs Garnsey, mother of the child star. I was to tutor them during the mornings, except Mondays when I would be doing the 'Get-In'. It sounded daunting but more exhilarating than being Ace Reporter for Benn Brothers. I was being offered the almost certain guarantee of a year's work with no qualifications or experience needed and seven pounds a week. It was explained to me that I would be able to live comfortably in digs for about three pounds a week. I was determined to believe him. I could and would.

The Shippards were not quite defeatist about my offer, as I knew my grandmother, Nellie Beatrice and even the Walls would be, but they were certainly dubious. Mr Shippard seemed even more shrewdly suspicious. His daughter was unmistakably cast down and looked for comfort to Mrs Shippard who fluttered and brought out the sherry decanter. I pointed out irrelevantly to my fiancée that if I had passed my Army medical, I would have had to leave her anyway, and told her of the dates when I would be in London and able to be with her.

The real problem would be my mother, so I decided to enlist Arnold's support in by-passing her objections. She insisted on believing that Arnold was an American, a gentleman, and one who possessed a quaint foreign wisdom about big decisions. Arnold artfully managed to strike the right note, pointing out that I would be able to send her home two pounds a week, which was what I had been giving her up till now, except that I would in future be self-supporting. He even tried a sly appeal to her vanity. 'Well, you see, Mrs Osborne, the little bastard's a kind of genius in my humble opinion.' This homely verdict may have been a reassuring explanation of why I was so unrewarding to have around except to accompany her ungratefully to the pictures on her days off. 'Oh, Daddy would have liked to have heard you say that, Mr Running,' she simpered. And it was fixed.

Stoneleigh

Dear John,

Mother is so disappointed in Queenie as she always thought she would be a great Some body: as she was clever as a child and so liked by everyone. I was not very pretty like her, and Mum said I was always crying and got hurt very quickly. Well, as my Dad always told me I turned out to be a real gem: although at times I had a bitter tongue which was not always my fault. So you see one must never have great expectations or demand so much from one's children.

Always in my thoughts,
Mother

I began rehearsals on 5 January (her birthday) for *No Room at the Inn* at the Winter Garden Theatre. 'Just my luck,' she said. 'On my birthday and my one day off.' In my diary for the month an entry reads: 'Monday 5th: Started rehearsals. Tuesday 6th: Gaycroft. Wednesday 7th: Write for an hour or so. Thursday 8th: Writing.' I don't remember what I can have been writing. Perhaps it was just a resolve not to break faith with the future novelist and his spaniels now that I had left Fleet Street behind. Two weeks later Renee and I spent a tearfully flailing evening on the floor in front of the fire in my mother's sitting-room. The following morning, Sunday 18 January 1948, I joined the midday company train call for the first date of the new tour, the Theatre Royal Cardiff. Instead of getting a train up to the Big Smoke, I was getting into one and Away From It.

> Brutus and Cato might discharge their souls,
> And give them furloughs for another world;
> But we, like sentries, are obliged to stand
> In starless nights, and wait the 'pointed hour.

Dryden

1948, January 20th: Cardiff. Not good digs. Getting good address.
    „   „   21st: Letter from Renee.
    „   „   22nd: Matinee.
    „   „   23rd: Letter from Renee.
    „   „   24th: Letter from Renee.
    „   „   25th: Cardiff depart 12.40. Crewe. Liverpool for Southport. Arrive 6.45.

Diary

Apart from the leading lady, Diana King, I was the only new member of the company. The young Irishman who played a sailor client joined us the following day. There were four second-class carriages reserved for the company. I was claimed on arrival by Bert, the stage carpenter, and his wife, the wardrobe mistress, and bustled into one of the two carriages that appeared to be reserved for the staff and stage management—wardrobe mistress; stage carpenter; two ASMs, including myself; stage director; Mrs Garnsey, mother of the leading child actress; the three older girls and a small boy. The actors had their own carriages and it was soon clear that there was an accepted system of Officers and Other Ranks in the operation of company train calls. Bert made it obvious that my place was among the Ranks, with the *News Of the World, Sunday Pictorial* and Mrs Garnsey's charges, who reminded me of the most deprived and appalling inmates of the convalescent home. Apart from the star, Rita, they too looked as if they were plagued with lice, bed-wetting and malnutrition, like the inmates at Deathaboys Hall.

The actors' carriages were littered with folded copies of the *Observer* and

Sunday Times. The young juvenile, Sheila, a twenty-two-year-old who played the leading evacuee with elfin Elstree winsomeness, swooped in during the journey. With her Joan Buffen accent, unteased schoolgirl's hair, above all her enthusiasm, goshing rather than gushing, she was almost a shock after the memory of Renee, hair carefully rolled, her corsage—for that is what it was—flattened on what was already a bosom. It was a shape I had found exciting as well as comforting, but it would soon burgeon into what was then known as a roll-top desk; not something to be despised, but Renee was still barely eighteen. Sheila was twenty-two and her own roll-top seemed some more careless years away. Childhood still beckoned to her from behind at a time when the word 'gamin' was popular with film publicists.

Bert was quite agreeable, although his wife, Lily, was a very bad-tempered crone. He was a dedicated Tory voter ('*You* put them in, *you* get them out,' he would intone every time he read something about the Labour Government in the papers). He sucked up to the actors shamelessly. The stage staff were itinerant forelock-pullers, and lucky to be so. Bert would rush out on to the platform on our frequent stops offering one of the more haughty actors a choice of sandwiches or tea. 'Can I get you something more, Miss Atkins?' he would wheedle. 'No thank you, Bert. That's very kind of you.' Miss Atkins turned out to be a particularly churlish actress given to waspish tea-shop outbursts, which she may have intended to be Mrs Patrick Campbell gestures to style.

One of my jobs as ASM was to act as call boy, not only calling the half-hour, quarter, five and Beginners, but giving individual calls throughout the play. It was undemanding enough, simply requiring the actor's acknowledgement. This established, he had no excuse for missing his cue. An ASM, I was told, should always wait for the acknowledging 'Thank You' or accept responsibility for a missed entrance. However, actors rarely blamed dozy lads for their own unpreparedness. Calling the artists seemed a gratuitously servile and unnecessary tradition to me but I soon found it was a friendly, bantering business. Not so with Miss Atkins. She had a trick of occasionally ignoring the most insistent knock, deliberately missing her cue, hurling insults like stale scones at the Prompt Corner and demanding abject apologies in her dressing-room, when her artistic sensibilities had recovered. She was extremely cunning about when and how often she chose not to answer the call. Someone should have warned me against her for I soon discovered that a couple of ill reports to the company manager could, in theory, cost me my job. The only remedy was to knock relentlessly until she was forced to snap back a reply. I won this war of attrition at the

Hippodrome Theatre, Bristol, by knocking on the door and entering immediately as she was inserting a Tampax. She never tried the trick again. I once found myself needing to provide an actor with a prop fountain pen. Asking him at the dress rehearsal if he could do this for me, he replied, 'I have eight fountain pens. But it is your job to provide me with one.' It was this sort of actor's kitchen *hubris* that nowadays would bring subsidized companies to a standstill.

The rest of the company were not so irksome, all secretly thankful to be working in a third-rate but long-running tour. The leading lady, Diana, was as friendly as her billing permitted. There was a rather vain and vague old queen who had worked for Martin Harvey and sounded like him; a neurotic, chain-smoking Christian Scientist, a Welshman called Davis; a gloomy hypochondriac Jewish character actress who carried a huge and heavy suitcase full of medicines and pills which I found myself obliged to carry for her; and an amusing, morose young Irishman who had me full of envy with his tales of very different travels with the famous Irish actor-manager, Anew McMaster, which made the *No Room at the Inn* company seem about as carefree and adventurous as Mr Shippard. It was difficult to understand how anyone could have thought me capable of understudying five actors aged between twenty-one and seventy. However, it was never questioned and, fortunately, only twice put to the test. Besides, the actors, selected on the principle of being the cheapest and most replaceable, were reliably immune to accident or caprice almost unto death.

Number 18 Tudor Street, Cardiff, was depressing. Thirty-five shillings a week, bed and breakfast. It consisted of a bed in the front parlour in a back-to-back street, with a white stuffed fox terrier staring down from a glass case on the sideboard. The landlady insisted on payment in advance. This, it turned out, was against all theatrical custom but she had a drunken merchant seaman in the kitchen to encourage her aggression and I paid up without hesitation. I was guided through my Actors' Church Union and Equity lists of theatrical lodgings and consequently did much better the following week in Southport. Bert was my most reliable authority in this essential knowledge, always aware of the cheapest and usually the best digs in all the forty-eight different towns we were to visit. It was hard to grasp that there would be so many places eager to watch Mrs Voray's downfall six or often twelve times a week.

Three pounds a week breakfast, tea and supper after the show was a fair average price. Fifteen shillings a week could get you bed and breakfast in places like Glasgow, but you might find yourself enacting the old gag of leaning against the wall in your overcoat to feel the warmth from the fire in the house next door. Three guineas a week usually guaranteed warmth in Victorian comfort, plenty of proudly prepared food, especially in Lancashire, Yorkshire and Scotland, and served with a gaiety to coax the most weary, beery stomach. The cook's confidence and concern made supper especially seem like a hungry hero's welcome home. They were very unlike Mrs Shippard's or Nellie Beatrice's formal meals, drudged over deliberately and eaten in polite anxiety. There were, of course, exceptions: the sullen amateur landladies unused to the ways of theatricals' late-night eating and midday rising were resentfully tolerated at such addresses and were struck off by those unworthy enough to spend an unwelcome week at them. A week in these circumstances would be ultimately expensive as well as dispiriting, so the matter of digs was crucial.

I found the best bargain of all was something called Room and Service. This meant paying thirty shillings a week for a bed sitting-room, providing your landlady with a list of your requirements for the week, which she would buy and cook for you provided it was 'nothing fancy'. If you chose wisely, it was easy to live very cheaply indeed. Grimsby was my first attempt at this experiment. Arriving, wet and tired, with aching arms from carrying my case down the dark streets from the station, I found my recommended address. The door was opened by a startled woman who looked as if she might burst into tears. Wondering if I had gone to the wrong house, I followed her into the front parlour where I was to eat my meals. Once again, a stuffed dog stared at me forsakenly from the sideboard while she silently made a list of my requirements for the week.

The following day I was too busy and lazy to look elsewhere. Throughout the week she served me sumptuous meals obviously beyond the budget of the list I had given her. Shy, watchful, she could hardly have been more attentive or different from what I had come to expect. Midnight bravura and eccentricity were customary in most digs but her silent stare, enjoined with that of her frozen fox terrier, sent me to bed promptly, wondering about my bill for the week. When I came back from Treasury Call at Friday lunchtime and asked to settle up, she refused to let me pay for my room but only for the food I had ordered. When I pressed her, she said she had been unable to speak to me all the week because I reminded her of her dead son. On the following Sunday she brought me a lavish breakfast. My train call was early, the parlour was damp and still and I was anxious to be away. The dog's stare from its landscaped glass booth and her silence discouraged lingering. I looked for her in the kitchen, but she must have gone back upstairs. I was about to call out when I realized I might wake her husband. I assumed she had one. There was a man's coat in the hall. Husbands in digs were often elusive creatures, carefully kept out of sight from embarrassment or diplomacy. Leaving a note, I let myself out as quietly as I could and walked quickly up the street, empty except for a couple of Salvation Army bandsmen assembling their instruments. I felt I had done right to leave without seeing her but it seemed unkind to have left most of the elaborate breakfast.

Every Sunday morning I hurried past houses, the moist curtains in their windows drawn behind limp grey lace, hearing only the sound of my dragging footsteps. My suitcase was always heavier than I had remembered. By the evening, in another town, I would have passed through an almost exactly similar darkened porch into what I came to feel was the domestic back parlour of Music Hall itself, full of laughter, coarse comfort and the defeat and melodrama of stuffed fox terriers. Some streets were given over almost entirely to the profession, like the dreaded Ackers Street in Manchester. Actors rarely wasted their salaries on hotels and the big stars especially had their favourite addresses where they stayed unfailingly. Every other place I stayed at had a signed photograph of G. H. Elliott or George Formby Senior on the piano. A line or two from them, hardly varying from year to year, in the Visitor's Book was the equivalent of five spoons in the Michelin Guide. 'Thanks again Rosie for a grand week. Usual lovely grub, lashings of it and plenty of good old giggles. Here's to the next time!'

Theatrical landladies were usually stage-struck, parlour performers, discriminating on the whole, and their opinion after the Monday performance carried some weight. The landladies' thumbs down could make itself felt at the box office the following day. Praise would be warm but cautious. 'Ooh, you were a bugger in that. I said to Albert, "He's a real *bugger* in that." ' This would be her husband or fancy man who lurked collarless in shirt sleeves reading the racing papers in the only armchair in the kitchen. A fiction was sometimes maintained that he was head of the house, particularly in matters of morality. If you contemplated nocturnal bedroom visits or discreetly sharing a room, it was rash not to consult or be advised by your landlady. Deprived of her conspiratorial rights, she might become very ugly indeed, not by turning you out of the house but by displaying her contempt in the contrasting treatment received by her undeceiving favoured guests. However, a circumspect approach made, married protocol was observed. 'Well, I'll have to ask Albert. *I* don't mind, you see. But Albert is a bit on the religious side.' Albert might spend Sunday and most of the week at the dog track or with the local tart. Out of the house during opening hours, his approval, if it was ever sought, was invariably confirmed. Rarely glimpsed or heard, he was given respectful precedence by everyone.

Once, in Kidderminster, a few of us wanted to watch a Sunday night play. The television set stood in the front parlour and, like the room itself, was seldom in use, kept silent for some unique occasion. Our request for permission to switch on was considered politely as if it were connivance at a night's adultery. 'Well, it's perfectly all right with me, but I'll have to ask Archie.' She went out into the kitchen where she could be heard shouting at Archie in a crisp Welsh voice. 'Archie, the boys want to stay and watch the television tonight, so you'll have to get out and bugger off to the pub.' We heard a grunt and Beattie returned. 'Yes,' she smiled, 'Archie says that'll be perfectly all right.'

Some were shy women wanting company, others high spirited ex-pros, frequently battened off by their men folk. Their gentlemen or 'boys'— preferred to girls, with their dripping 'smalls'—were lifelines to a world which, shared weekly, might seem less desperate and more companionable than that just beyond the terrace. Feelings were open, often raw, and most frailty smiled on or laughed away. The cast of *Soldiers in Skirts* were universally popular. ('Oh, they're such fun. They all call each other Elsie and Doris and Ada.') This show toured for seven years, subsidized by its exploitation of a company of hard-worked, underpaid queens. With their special but commonplace talents, they were hard put to refuse a guaranteed unrising pittance, less than my own. Cheap digs and loving landladies might have been their only comforts on those often cottageless provincial nights. After a fry-up supper and beer, the family might bring ukelele, violin, accordian, guitar into the parlour and another evening would begin for us, fired with the actor's late-night expectation of reprieve from dull sleep and the bonus of energy returned in full payment. The road into England might have been the noblest prospect that a Scotsman ever faced, but in my case it was the railway line that led out of Euston.

Nowhere in England seemed willing to feed a stranger on Sundays except the local Odeon in the late afternoon. On Monday morning at seven-thirty I went down to the railway yard to see the scenery and props unloaded, transported into the theatre and set up. In time, I managed to get some nightly changes down to twenty-one seconds from thirty-eight. Miss Atkins's behaviour was untypical. Rough democracy ruled, notably between sexes—equal pay, billing and no favours asked, shared expenses. Twice-nightly dates were tiring but the Variety Pit sparked the Prompt Corner into another life. Percy, the stage director, hardly ever bothered to have understudy calls. He locked up the prompt copy after each performance until the next. I had to rely on scripts then known as 'Sides' to learn my lines. These were the size of a pub menu and contained only the last few words of your cue followed by the speech. I was often given these later in weekly rep and they were nightmarish for someone with no special gift for memorization like myself. Admittedly, I heard the play word for word every night and knew the moves, but I had lighting, music cues and changes to distract me. I discovered *répétiteur's* skill with the prompt book, knowing the how and when of helping an actor deserted by memory or improvisation. I enjoyed presiding alone over the Prompt Corner, umpire and captain in one.

I was surprised, elated and eager about almost everything except going through the farce of giving lessons to Rita Garnsey and her pals each morning. No one seemed concerned except Mrs Garnsey, who, having bullied her sleepy, quarrelling charges into the dressing-room, settled down to knit, make tea and chat till lunchtime. I had bought several text books including some I had used at school, all equipped with answers at the back. Thinking that I might be asked at some stage to provide evidence that I was doing my job, I made perfunctory efforts to persuade them to at least copy out passages from books that were familiar. They were barely literate, but knew instinctively that I had no competence let alone real authority and I soon gave up. I was scarcely credible as an ASM. Besides, no one seemed to be concerned about even the pretence of observing the regulations, which varied bewilderingly from town to town. The children's education was a more onerous and pointless task than calling Miss Atkins. Proven inadequacy seemed the only way I could look forward to lying late in bed after the long, happy nights with the landladies. But if I were exposed by the authorities, would the company manager, Miss Dalton, be obliged to fire me?

However, apart from occasionally checking that we were all assembled with our books in the dressing-room at 10.00 a.m., she showed no interest in what we were doing. The problem was solved precipitately a few weeks later in Newcastle. Walking into the dressing-room on Tuesday morning, handing out my ancient text books, I was confronted by an official from the local educational authority who politely asked me to carry on with my tuition. If I had been asked to go on for one of the five actors without the book, I might have been forgiven for failure. I knew I could expect no indulgence from Newcastle. I made some sort of mime show of instruction for a miserable hour or so under the inspector's eye, while Mrs Garnsey's needles clacked in silence for the first time. The children were loyally attentive, sensing that my job might be at stake. Certain that my theatrical career was about to be destroyed by a council official, my gratitude to them made our charade possible only by its solemn absurdity. The Education Officer rang me the following day and asked me to go and see him. 'You see,' he explained, 'we don't teach children in that way any longer. Besides, you have no qualifications and no aptitude. I'm afraid your employers will have to make some fresh arrangements.' Astonishingly, arrangements were made immediately that Mrs Garnsey should take her children to the local school every week. More important, my job and salary were unthreatened, my amateur standing gone. By the end of the tour I would be a full member of Equity. I was free to explore unknown heartlands after all. The future was now open. There remained the matter of Renee.

I had made no arrangements the following week in Cambridge. University towns, Cathedral towns and seaside towns in season were traditionally ones where actors could expect small comfort or welcome. By about nine in the evening I was still stumbling around with my huge suitcase. It was the beginning of the Lent term and even Bert had been discouraging about finding a bed for the night. Almost in tears with the thought that Mrs Shippard might yet be serving me tea, hand held by Renee beneath the table, I was suddenly aware of a tall don in a dog collar striding towards me. Perhaps I was breaking some ancient statute with my vagabond presence. 'Are you a member of this university?' 'No, sir, I'm not,' I said, putting down my suitcase. If only I had been. 'Have you nowhere to go? That case must be very heavy for you.' 'It is. No, I can't find anywhere.' 'Well it is the beginning of term and it's sure to be difficult.' He introduced himself as Duckworth. He looked me up and down smilingly and said, 'Well look here, if you don't find anywhere by 11.30 you're welcome to come over and stay on my sofa if you care to.' He turned away quickly into the crowd without waiting for me to reply. 'You'll find me at St John's,' he said. 'I'm just off to speak to the heathen at Peterhouse.'

Two hours later I managed to find the police station, where I was given the address of a doss house in Portugal Street. I stood outside, contemplating the choice between St John's and Portugal Street. The college would certainly be warm, interesting and I could be sure of some sherry or, with any luck, whisky. I wondered what the Reverend Duckworth's opening preamble would be, possibly not *Miracle in the Gorbals* but something more recondite. My head throbbed and the thought of his tall, athletic, healthy frame and manner led me wearily to Portugal Street. I had a feeling that the Rev. Duckworth would be less frank that J. Wood Palmer. I paid one and sixpence for my bed and groped in the dark towards it, cursing my lack of foresight and undoubted timidity in shunning the comfort of St John's.

On Monday morning I left my suitcase at the stage door and went to the station to load the scenery for the Get-In. There was no sympathy for my digless condition except from Sheila. I was working all that day and evening and would have no chance of finding an alternative to Portugal Street. Her concern welled over as I told her and she promised that she would fix me up with her own landlady. That night I fell asleep exhaustedly in a room beside hers. The landlady was not the theatrical sort but almost as solicitous as Mrs Shippard. Sheila and I shared a late, delicious breakfast, while she chatted away with gamin laughter and welling eyes to match. Elmsleigh Road, a memory of refuge in the arm-aching hours outside St John's the night before, had to be exorcized after breakfast with Sheila, quilted and flowery from the nursery warmth of her landlady's bed. Something clearly had to be done and fairly soon. Even my sluggardly resolve had been fixed by Sheila and the remembrance and steamy promise of tales of Exmoor ponies.

Renee had written to me every day, sometimes twice. Even a few weeks before I would have been touched by her letters, no less simple or trusting than my own had been to Jenny. Now I thrust them quickly into my pocket at the stage door before Sheila could see them. The following week it was back to the Smoke, to Lewisham and Wimbledon. My job was apparently secure. I needed to dissemble for three weeks until it was back to the Heartland, to the Empire, Sunderland. I had no qualms about Mr Shippard's feelings. He was the kind of man I knew my father would have despised out of hand from his deathbed. My panicky determination to get the train from Euston and take myself off to the care of Mrs Ellis of 21 Turnstile Lane, Sunderland, was increased by the knowledge of my calculated treachery towards two people whose affection, however it might be dismissed, I had sought in my friendlessness and then abused. Guilt and some sense of my headlong absurdity warned me a little against Sheila's Elstree overflow. As with Renee, my eagerness and talent for unscrupulous compromise outfaced my own mean and common spirit, but I could not quite shake it from its course.

Renee and her parents came to see the play in Wimbledon. They could find little to say about it. I knew that the next week I would be safely in Sunderland.

GEORGE: Oh, don't be so innocent, Ruth. This house! This room! This hideous God-awful room!

RUTH: Aren't you being just a little insulting?

GEORGE: I'm simply telling you what you very well know. They may be your relations, but have you honestly got one tiny thing in common with any of them? These people—

RUTH: Oh, no! Not 'these people'! Please—not that! After all, they don't still keep coals in the bath.

GEORGE: I didn't notice. Have you looked at them? Have you listened to them? They don't merely act and talk like caricatures, they *are* caricatures! That's what's so terrifying. Put any one of them on a stage, and no one would take them seriously for one minute! They think in clichés, they talk in them, they even feel in them—and, brother, that's an achievement! Their existence is one great cliché that they carry about with them like a snail in his little house—and they live in it and die in it!

RUTH: Even if it's true—and I don't say it is—you still sound pretty cheap saying it.

GEORGE: Look at that wedding group. Look at it! It's like a million other grisly groups—all tinted in unbelievable pastels: round-shouldered girls with crinkled-up hair, open mouths, and bad teeth. The bridegroom looks as gormless as he's feeling lecherous, and the bride— the bride's looking as though she's just been thrown out of an orgy at a Druids' reunion! Mr and Mrs Elliot at their wedding. It stands there like a comic monument to the macabre farce that has gone on between them in this house ever since that greatest day in a girl's life thirty-five years ago.

Epitaph for George Dillon, 1958

In the dressing-room at the Empire, Sunderland, I began writing my first play, a melodrama about a poetic Welsh loon called *Resting Deep*. It had nothing to do with my own experience and certainly none of what might be occasionally found in the drab world of George Dillon. Thick envelopes came daily from Renee. There was no Gaycroft gossip, the Halifax and the 8.17 unmentioned, even her parents seemed unbelievably to have given place to me, *our* future, when I returned to London and got another different sort of job. Her speculation and plans put the Pasodoble back in its rightful place. The following week on Good Friday, in front of Mrs Coleman's gas fire in Number 70 Dudley Road, Wolverhampton, after an evening lying on the rug with Sheila's welling Anglo-Catholicism and our reading of Aldous Huxley, I began to compose the letter that must be sent off to Elmsleigh Road.

I had told no one of my dilemma. It was unthinkable to write to Arnold or Mickey Wall. I decided to confide in the young Irish actor, Sean. He was sympathetic but gloomy. The callous indecency of what I was proposing to do to a nice girl, who had acted towards me in good faith, was inexcusable. However, he made a characteristically morose suggestion. He had decided to go to Spain after the tour was over and enter a monastic order until such

185

time as he might return to Ireland and Anew McMaster's touring company. I could accompany him. I didn't take the suggestion about the Spanish monastery very seriously but the possibility of entry to McMaster was convincing. Religious conversion as a provision against marriage, like homosexuality against conscription, looked too difficult to sustain, but more worthy of a try. After all, Mr and Mrs Shippard were not Army psychiatrists who were authorized to poke me about in the nude and interrogate me about my failed attentions to Renee. Also, I had no intention of mentioning Sheila, who was already proving to be neurotically frigid—which possibly accounted for her constant Anglo-Catholic welling-up at the sight of my tumescent belief that being an actress she was likely to be even more responsive than my fiancée.

After a few days I received Mr Shippard's reply to my letter. He was not impressed, nor was he disappointed but quite unsurprised at my behaviour. He had always suspected something of the sort from the outset and regretted ever having agreed to his daughter becoming engaged to someone like myself. The tone became even clearer. 'The country's well rid of the likes of you and the sooner you get out of it the better and leave girls like Renee alone. Naturally, in the circumstances, we will not be returning your engagement ring. Never try to communicate with her again. Yours faithfully, D. Shippard. P.S. Renee has been crying her eyes out ever since she got your letter. It's a disgrace. Your mother must be ashamed of you.' Or something very like it.

My mother could only have been consoled by an incident that had ended in distress for everyone involved. After a few readings of the letter, I told myself I was puzzled by the rather vulgar reference to the returning of the ring. My letter, long-winded, dishonest and evasive, larded with banalities about Life, Art and God, had been lost on Mr Shippard. But lying to myself was no comfort. My reprieve left me in no need of it.

Wednesday, March 31st: Sheila's 22nd birthday.
Thursday, April 1st: Letter from Mr Shippard.
Saturday, April 3rd: Act II *Resting Deep* finished.

The following Saturday in Leeds, there is a note reading: 'The play should be finished by now. If not, why not?' And, underneath, a memo: 'Start on comedy.'

13. Dead-and-Alive Holes

CHAP: Then there was Rosemary.

GIRL: (*To the* INTERRUPTER] There's Rosemary for *you*.

INTERRUPTER: We don't know who any of these people *are*. What they're *doing*. Where it's taking *place*. Or anything!

OLDER LADY: Give the boy a chance.

CHAP: What? Oh, Rosemary.

GIRL: Yes, Rosemary.

CHAP: Ah yes, well, she had the rags up all the time.

GRANDFATHER: Well, they can't help it, you know.

CHAIRMAN: Well, he's got a point there.

CHAP: No, but she had it all the bloody time. I mean like all over the graveyard in Norwich Cathedral.

GIRL: Norwich—you mean like—

CHAIRMAN: Yes. (*Wearily*) Knickers off ready when I come home.

CHAP: I mean, Women's *Insides*. I've been walled up in them and their despairs and agony ever since I can remember.

GIRL: Perhaps you should try it yourself.

CHAP: I'm not strong enough.

GIRL: No, you're not.

INTERRUPTER: I think this sort of talk is highly embarrassing. My own wife is in the audience and I may say that she is undergoing what I can only call to someone like you, an extremely difficult—

GIRL: Period—

INTERRUPTER: No. I would say more than that. Expected but dramatic experience in her life.

GIRL: You mean she's got the Hot Flushes?

CHAP: Well, let me tell you mate, *I've* had them for forty years.

GIRL: And you look it . . . So we've got to Rosemary.

CHAIRMAN: Yes.

A Sense of Detachment, 1972

OLDER LADY: Thank you. May I say first that I have no particular personal complaint. In some ways, I was born into a good time. And because of my natural intelligence, have managed to cope with what to most *men* would be an intolerable situation. My young friend here has complained, if I heard him correctly, of one of his earlier girl friends being sick in the ground of Norwich Cathedral. However, I would just say to him and others like him that it is a mere fact of life that women at all times and at all ages have suffered from, and in many cases died from, not merely childbirth but from what you would no doubt call the inbuilt tedium of organs such as the cervix, the vulvae, the vagina and the womb.

BOX MAN: Disgusting.

OLDER LADY: If men had to undergo what they so cheerfully call 'the curse'—

BOX MAN: Period pains—

OLDER LADY: —They would have long ago invented some alleviation.

BOX MAN: Invent it yourself. Sing us a song.

OLDER LADY: I'm afraid our young friend here has let him delude himself into dreaming about something he thinks of as 'Eternal Woman'.

BOX MAN: Who doesn't?

OLDER LADY: That is because she is only valued by the excitement she may or may not arouse.

BOX MAN: Get off out of it, you old bag.

OLDER LADY: In short, she has to be desirable.

BOX MAN: Well, it does help, lady.

OLDER LADY: In the case of men, it appears not to be necessary. We women can be put down, if that is the expression, by the flimsiest physical or intellectual failing. We have been eternally abandoned from the Old Testament onwards. All I say to you now is that we may all probably totally abandon you. Men, I mean.

A Sense of Detachment, 1972

Nearly every town we visited until the middle of the summer had, if not a cathedral, a famous or commended church or churches. With Sheila, I explored the ecclesiastical wonders of Norwich, Peterborough, Liverpool, Leeds, Manchester, Newcastle, Aberdeen, Edinburgh, Plymouth, Coventry. Her mind stuffed with Pugin and Perpendicular, Sheila's spirit was made tranquil in transept and cloister in a dozen cities, as I thought of the coverlets in our digs crinkled and crying out for an afternoon turn down. When the rain washed us out of the deserted Close we would take our Equity cards to the nearest cinema for a free seat, where I could enjoy the warm darkness instead of the afternoon chill of nave and apse. Incense was to warm her spirit more than the steam of damp unfamiliar sheets. By the midsummer our score for the tour was: Burnes Oates: 9; Oats: Nil.

Apart from bouts of light, sparrow melancholy, Sheila seemed happy with our weekly progress through English cathedrals. I had no way of knowing whether her fluttery chill was merely wilful boredom, but I began to wonder whether her vague languor and spasms of terror might have once been dismissed in the novels she admired as 'the vapours'. She was not content and neither was I. My Welsh melodrama lay untouched since Wolverhampton. Once again, Mrs Garnsey's girls were helpful, mocking me ungently but playfully about Miss Tight-arsed Bossy-drawers having got me where she wanted. Their dirty-minded derision seemed kindly and sensible as I faced Sheila's outbursts in and out of the dressing-room and back into our digs. Her flaunted helplessness and demands fuelled from misty recollections of Exmoor, an ideal of Elstree, were becoming resistible. After nine cathedrals we were back on what now seemed home ground at the Empire, Kingston. We began rehearsals for replacements for the next stage of the tour. For no reason, I felt open to new confidence and any kind of possibility.

Barney and the yellow pyjamas

You should choose your theatre like you choose a religion. Make sure you don't get into the wrong temple. For me the theatre is really a religion or way of life. You must decide what you feel the world is about and what you want to say about it, so that everything in the theatre you work in is saying the same thing. For me the theatre is a temple of ideas and ideas so well expressed it may be called art. So always look for quality in the writing above what is being said.

George Devine

BARNEY: This the first play you've written?

GEORGE: My seventh—

BARNEY: Dialogue's not bad, but these great long speeches—that's a mistake. People want action, excitement. I know—*you* think you're Bernard Shaw. But where's he today? Eh? People won't listen to him. Anyway, politics are out—you ought to know that. Now, take *My Skin is my Enemy!* I've got that on the road at the moment. That and *Slasher Girl!*

GEORGE: *My Skin is my*—Oh yes, it's about the colour bar problem, isn't it?

BARNEY: Well, yes—but you see it's first-class entertainment! Played to £600 at Llandridnod Wells last week. Got the returns in my pocket now. It's controversial, I grant you, but it's the kind of thing people pay money to see. That's the kind of thing you want to write.

GEORGE: Still, I imagine you've got to be just a bit liberal-minded to back a thing like that.

BARNEY: Eh?

GEORGE: I mean—putting on a play about coloured people.

BARNEY: Coloured people? I hate the bastards!

.   .   .

BARNEY: You spend your time dabbling in politics and vote in some ragged-arsed bunch of nobodies, who can't hardly pronounce the Queen's English properly, and where are you? Where are you? Nowhere. Crushed down in the mob, indistinguishable from the masses. What's the good of that to a young man with talent?

.   .   .

BARNEY: To get back to this play of yours. I think it's got possibilities, but it needs rewriting. Act One and Two won't be so bad, provided you cut out all the highbrow stuff, give it pace—you know: dirty it up a bit, you see.

GEORGE: I see.

BARNEY: Third Act's construction is weak. I could help you there—and I'd do it for quite a small consideration because I think you've got something. You know that's a very good idea—getting the girl in the family way.

GEORGE: You think so?

BARNEY: Never fails. Get someone in the family way in the Third Act— you're half way there. I suppose you saw *I Was a Drug Fiend?*

GEORGE: No.

BARNEY: Didn't you really? No wonder you write like you do! I thought everyone had seen that! That was my show too. Why, we were playing to three and four thousand a week on the twice-nightly circuit with that. That's the sort of money you want to play to. Same thing in that: Third Act—girl's in the family way.

Epitaph for George Dillon, 1958

I wrote that scene with Barney Evans, the entrepreneur, one winter evening in a Hammersmith flat seven years later. As usual, with better things that I have done, it was written quickly almost without pause, my pen tripping clumsily behind swift memory. It was a scene which pleased me to write but left audiences slightly baffled. They were not familiar with the Barney Evans type, which is unsurprising. Self-caricature is so general that it makes the task of the writer very difficult, particularly in the theatre. Barney was probably unacceptable in a play, being so likely in life, embodying the cliché, 'If you put him on the stage, no one would believe it.' Improbability is writ large over half the nation, making restraint almost the first necessity of art, defending the truthfulness of drama against the distortions of documentary and social realism. In the face of life—notably English life with its cultivated eccentricity and anomaly—reticence is almost the first discipline a writer must assume. Theatricality is an elusive refinement which may be why Dickens adapted to the stage seems invariably gross, with character overwhelming landscape. Barney Evans was the hybrid of a type I was to meet constantly. The first of this species, ranging from Barney to Binkie, I was to meet through one of the new replacements. Her name was Stella Linden and her husband was indeed very like the whale of Barney, Patrick Desmond, sometime producer, actor, agent, theatrical entrepreneur and play doctor.

The next few weeks were all London-based, Moss Empire, music-hall dates, where my idols had trodden the boards, soon about to creak away for good. I contrived to stay in digs instead of going home to Stoneleigh where I felt the Shippards might be lying in wait for me. I was also able to see less of Sheila, saying that I was living with my mother. Stella was about thirty, very dark with a large, handsome head and a very fine striking nose. To me, she had the appearance and authority of what was thought to be a Leading Lady. Even in adolescence, she could never have strived as an eternal slip of a girl, which was Sheila's pride and forte. Stella was a woman, all right, with a pelvic arch like the skull of an ox, a slippery slope of hips and the shoulders of a Channel swimmer. It was a body which looked capable of snapping up an intruder in a jawbone of flesh. In the phrase of a friend, 'She could draw you in and blow you out in bubbles.'

During rehearsals I scarcely followed the prompt book. Fortunately, she knew her lines and moves from the first day. She was taking over the role of the earnest social worker. Like all the parts in the play, it was small but vital to the tale of Mrs Voray's downfall, with one showy scene where she pleaded the evacuees' case for them. Mr Hamilton came in once briefly and left bored but apparently satisfied. There was no attempt to redirect the scene or bother with interpretation. It was not required and would have irked the

191

other actors. Only the children had been called in to run in the replacements. I read in for the rest of the cast. By now I knew the entire play almost word for word but fumbled even as I carried the book. Stella's effortless, instant polish suggested that she was more familiar with the text and production than I should have been. Unsurprisingly, it must have been pretty cold and mechanical. The previous actress had been competent and seemed to have gushed unnecessarily for sympathy. This performance had, to my eager eyes, a firmness which must come from intelligence rather than a chill spirit.

I convinced myself that here was an almost masculine, stalking power. She was no walking wounded woman, pleading for love like Sheila or weaning tamely like poor Renee, but arrogantly lubricious. Already no slouch at whistling up enigma, I was impelled to pursue whatever it might be. A weakness for pursuing siren sphinxes without secrets was already in full flight. I had an unfortunate tendency to regard instinct as merely a trick of reversed hindsight revealed only to myself. It was to produce fewer particular insights than rollicking blunders.

This overvalued instinct may have led me to the ploy of the Yellow Pyjamas. Free from Sheila, Shippards and Black Looks for the five London weeks, I wandered into Simpson's in Piccadilly. The basics of my Rex Harrison wardrobe were there but the weekly deposits I had made in provincial post offices, confined me to one agonized choice only. It was a pair of silk poplin pyjamas. They were yellow, not Nellie Beatrice lemon but yellow, the colour of the pullover that had been mocked in the street. Thinking I might soon be charged with loitering with intent, I asked the price. They were a week's salary and more—eight pounds. Having asked the price, there was no hanging back. I paid for them and went out into the sunshine of Piccadilly, to get on the bus for the first house at the Hackney Empire, clutching my new investment. Unlike some of my pushy impulses it was to pay off.

Stella had said little during the rehearsals, refusing proffered cups of tea politely and unsmilingly. The first night of the new tour with the replacements was at the Kingston Empire and I could think of nothing but her looming presence at the theatre. Besides, by this time I was no longer intimidated by the simple technical requirements of the show and had more or less taken over from Percy, who spent the evening reading in the staff room. I had got the changes down to a fine turn and knew how to get the stage staff to perform with only token disinclination. Unlike the printers at Bishopsgate they were unable to foul me up by exploiting my ignorance even in fun. I 'knew' the show and they didn't.

I called Miss Linden in good time, went back to the Prompt Corner and waited for her to tiptoe her way past the gloom of counterweights and prop tables towards her entrance. I waved encouragingly but she was intent on edging her way over to the dim outline of the knob just visible from the cracks of light from either side of the door flats. She stood poised, minutes early and, instinct and commonsense both awry, I crept up to her. 'Good luck,' I said, 'you're going to be smashing. Much better than the other.' She seemed to nod. I went back to my corner and waited for the flat to rattle exactly on cue, as it did. I hardly glanced at the book, knowing anyway that she would never look to the corner for aid. If only she had it would have been our first shared secret.

During my flash scene change immediately after her exit she brushed me aside among the charge of stage hands. Throughout the rest of the play I thought of the hours in the coming months which I would spend isolated in my corner watching that jaw bone of desire sit and stride across the stage. The set had to be changed back to the first act and I was unable to approach her until I called her for her entrance in the second house. This time I put my head in eagerly. Her own dark powerful head turned and the lubricious jaw bone opened over me from six paces. 'Don't you ever dare to do that to an actor again and don't you dare do it to me.' What did she mean? Her contempt was terrible. 'Don't you ever dare do that in any theatre again. I *mean* going up to an actor and talking to him just before he is about to make his entrance. And I don't just mean on a First Night. I mean now, at any time. Here or anywhere you may ever happen to find yourself in the future. I should get back to your corner.' I was snapped in two. My crass blunder was ineradicable.

I watched the second house in misery, the prospect of the next six months in what should have been Pleasure Corner destroyed. I knew that flowers or a contrite letter would only stiffen that stern nature. Appeals to sentiment from such a quarter might be won by honest graft but not feeble obsequiousness. The instruction was fierce and unmistakable. I had broken a self-evident theatrical rule. It was like a soldier dropping his rifle. I had dreaded calling her for the line-up but she anticipated it. Ignoring Percy, she slipped behind me on my stool and whispered, 'Forget it. I don't think you'll ever do it again. If you do, you won't last for very long.' Gratitude cast out everything but the thrill of her chastening. Schooled as I had been within a lifetime ethic of reproach, her unaffected forgiveness was startling.

Instead of banishing me to certain nonentity, she then seemed to seek me out. She came into the theatre long before the rest of the cast and sat reading in her dressing-room while the stage management prepared for the performance. Getting in early, she explained, was one of the hallmarks of professionalism, and I was anxious to believe her, collecting and delivering props to her long before necessary but with time to be encouraged to linger. She became quickly confidential without the condescension I might have felt deserved but with a needling curiosity about myself. Her low opinion of the company, the management and, to some extent, the play itself was disarmingly casual (actually her husband would have been only too pleased to have had such a rattling money spinner on the road as *No Room at the Inn*). It was, she said, a tatty production but she had agreed to do a six months' tour because she and Pat needed the money either to start their own company or to put a similar show, of better quality, on the road. Neither their talents nor the prospect seemed in doubt.

She insisted proudly on her husband's prescient gift for the theatre. His flair was phenomenal. I was unclear what either of them had been doing in the three years since the war. He had been in the RAF until 1946 and she had been a teenage housewife in Coventry with a child before she had been divorced by her upper middle-class husband. Directness is more invigorating than the ambiguity of truthfulness, the jawbone of an asp more plausible than the jawbone of an honest ass. When you are eighteen, hedged in by evasion and timidity, it is exhilarating, at the least. Whether directness, or deception, combined with unassumed sexual pride, Stella's theatrical sales talk was irresistible. She catechized me about Sheila, my feelings for her, and inability to contain her elfin tantrums and self-absorption. Like a television interviewer, her opinions were masquerading as questions, although I was unaware of it. She seemed to know more about my predicament than I did myself. She turned my groping game with Sheila on to its beetle back of callow posturing, exposed and futile. It was fortunate that she had not witnessed me floundering with Renee on her back. As it was, I said nothing about my enforced trail around England's premier cathedrals with the walking-wounded juvenile, disabled for eternity by Anglican menstrual mysticism.

I did tell her about *Resting Deep* and she asked me for the script as if it were a menu. Like a waiter, I gave it to her. Her verdict was no sterner than I had expected. Directness prevailed. Speeches were too long; wordy scenes; slack; audiences left hanging in the air; ending unresolved. Then there was the matter of characters being discussed who never appeared, leaving the audience wondering, 'Who are they talking about?' This critical trip-wire was one I was to encounter many times. Could wondering ever lead to wonderment? I was too gratified to ask. She went on a great deal about construction. Had I read *The Second Mrs Tanqueray*? I had not. There was

194

the key. What I needed was a short sharp lesson in Pinero.

I had not been too cast down by Stella's verdict on my play. I knew there was little merit in it although I thought she had disregarded its flashes of poetry. As *The Times* was to say of *Look Back in Anger*, it did, I was sure, 'contain some good passages of violent writing'. 'Fine writing' is no doubt what they were. Besides, intimations of poetry in the theatre was pornography to her. If she were to nose it, she would eliminate it as gleefully as Mrs Whitehouse would crush a smutty innuendo. Quick to offend, she not only believed in Dr Johnson's ruling that the drama's laws the drama's patrons give, but that they were to be administered without mercy and favour to any. Like all agents and managers of the time, she had no doubts that her own perception of public taste was a working primer for any form of dramatic activity. If I had said 'art', she would have reached for her hatpin.

When such powerful people talked about immutable theatrical laws, they gave the impression that their divine conformity was about to be outlawed. Nothing is noisier than a philistine in pain. If they despised the original imagination, they worshipped nebulous rules. These were almost elevated to a metaphysic in Moss Hart's *Principia, Act One*. The Broadway system still thrives scarcely troubled by the schisms and heresies that have split the rock of established theatre in England. But in New York the articles of theatrical faith are rarely challenged. Dissident murmurs may be heard from aggrieved dramatists, but few, even of these, would court excommunication. They cannot plead creative conscience and disown the faith they were born into, which means adherence to what might be called the Hart of Mystery. To some it might seem to be the Hart of Commercial Darkness but it survives as the only true faith. Its doctrine is unmodified and is expressed in the litany that includes 'Being Bombed in New Haven' and 'Getting the Second Act Right'—night-long vigils in hotel rooms with coffee and typewriters. The frenzy of these ceremonies conducted in semi-secrecy; producers, directors, writers, actors are locked out from the gaze of the world (except New Haven or wherever has been chosen) like disputants in an electoral college. They cannot emerge until the puffs of smoke rise from the printed reviews rushed to the tables of the waiting faithful in Sardi's. Half an hour after midnight the celebrants in the theatre will know the public's edict, whether they have toiled and brought forth a palpable hit or a flop. Thumbs up light the Broadway sky while their downward thrust can make the sidewalks tremble. The world between is grey and lonely.

West End managers were and are charged by the same beliefs and motives but they have never been so systematic and efficient in putting them to work. Stella, with her regard for creaky, Edwardian melodrama, was more literate than most, her husband certainly, who regarded Frederick Lonsdale as a cerebral taste. Artifice concealing any art could be whipped out by what critics often called the 'director's judicious [that is to say, butchering] scissors'. Construction was the centre of all their faith and was invoked like the Resurrection or Redemption. To me it has always been far more elusive than either. In Pinero's case and possibly Rattigan's it appeared to mean the construction of an artefact like a carriage clock, which revealed its beautiful precision to all, particularly for the benefit of those who were obliged to write and explain its workings to their readers. This made an otherwise tiresome task easy and even enjoyable and didn't apply only to critics but to those who were unlikely enough to read the plays themselves in the first place. Agents and managers like their popular models to be annually unchanged. If the new Ayckbourn or Stoppard is too unlike the last one there will be complaints from those who had got such reliable mileage from previous makes.

I mucked about on the drawing board with Pinero and soon accepted— without saying so to Stella—that if I would never make it as a theatrical draughtsman, I could never be so dull either. I was not even dismayed by the thought that I might not have the right kind of mind for writing plays just as I lacked the right one for doing crossword puzzles. The spaniels would be as happy walking beside a novelist as a playwright. An irate agent once ordered me to get out and about and learn by heart the Newtonian principles of theatre embodied in *The Winslow Boy*. The most perfect play ever written, he roared. I was also, oddly, directed to the feet of the Master; but Coward on Construction seemed pretty wobbly. Yet playmaking, a home craft like fretwork or pottery, demanded kits and models. It was hard to understand why Stella was intent on encouraging me. She still assured me that I needed a crash course in Playmaking at Home as urgently as anaemic girls were said, on railway hoardings, to need Virol.

She went on to tell me what possibilities might become open to me. She and Pat were both determined to return to Actor–Management and were negotiating an almost certain takeover of a theatre called the Granville at Walham Green. This was a famous music-hall theatre which had been floundering for many years and a lot of people had tried without success to revive its fortunes. If anybody was capable of doing it, she assured me, it was Pat, and then went on to give me an explanation of how it could be done, with a breakdown about the rent, percentages, house charges, salaries and all kinds of unfamiliar things. If I was willing to sit down with Stella and start to rework the play from scratch they would be prepared to include it in a new season which they projected. Was I willing to agree? I most certainly was.

For the next few months I would not be merely peering at Stella from the Prompt Corner but Home Playmaking with her. The close confines of digs shared with her was certainly preferable to the gynaecological agonies of the cathedral close.

Stella was emphatic that we should spend all possible time together from now on. There was no telling when the Walham Green deal might come through but not before the tour's end at Christmas. Sheila's insides would certainly protest as violently against making plays as love. I knew I could look to my new mentor to sort out these troublesome trifles for me. As an ambitious actress, Sheila must be moved by the plea, 'My Career Must Come First.' I was to hear it often enough in future. As a career person I may have lacked all passionate intensity, but this time I would get it in first—albeit something different from the nature of my first intention. The next stage of the tour looked like being a considerable improvement on the first.

14. *I'm Forever Blowing Bubbles*

During the weeks in London I had wondered if I might one evening find Mr Shippard waiting for me at the stage door. Already I felt I could put Stella on to him too. I was able to visit my mother only once and was rewarded with a couple of pounds. She was surprised and relieved that I was still in work and, for some reason, she had decided that I was safely away from 'girls'. Actresses, even young ones, were not girls, but likely ladies at least. Also, there was no need to leave out the warmed-up leftovers from one of Cheffie's lunchtime ruckings.

I visited Grandma Osborne, who pretended she didn't know what I was doing and asked me no questions at all. She talked about the news from Newport, who had died, Auntie Daisy's back, her own aching eyes particularly and her inability to sleep; Mr Attlee, horrible Bevan (a disgrace to Tredegar), *The Archers* and Warwick Deeping. Cousin Tony was doing very well at Sandhurst and Cousin Jill had entered a very nice secretarial school in preparation for getting a good steady position with her father's firm until such time as she got married. The room over Tesco's contained the furniture from Clandon Close, the same huge walnut sideboard, the silver bowls still full of home-made toffee and nuts, the props of many a Sunday night. Visiting her now in the suburban afternoon it was hard to believe that I had ever found her company comforting. Still with no reference to how I was spending my life, we said good-bye on the iron staircase. She wiped her eyes, as she would put it, discreetly, and kissed me, barely brushing my acne. 'Oh dear,' she said. 'Life seems to be full of good-byes.' Which is what she always said when I visited her.

She watched me for several minutes before I disappeared behind the Rembrandt Cinema. I went inside to see if any of the girls were there. Only one was left. Lily in the box office with her dark ringlets and strawberry lips and green dresses, who had allowed me in for nothing and let me take her home, had left to get married. The girl who had replaced her looked at me coldly, barring me the privilege I had known before. There were no occasional free Cambridge steaks to be had in the restaurant upstairs and

198

only the one usherette left to sit beside you cosily among the old-age familiars before the ice-cream interval.

Grandma Grove, Auntie Queenie and Sid came to see the play at the Chiswick Empire. Grandma thoroughly enjoyed herself, especially the bits with the sailor ('Your grandfather would have liked that'); Queenie thought it was a bit suggestive and Uncle Sid said it went too far. I toyed with the idea of taking them round to see Stella, and immediately abandoned it. The beginning of the tour consisted mostly of seaside dates—Margate, Eastbourne, Bournemouth, Torquay. It was back to familiar territory but no less exciting than the first time around and offering new promises. There was still a gazetteer of Midland and Northern towns to follow. We seldom progressed logically from one southern seaside town to another, but would go from Torquay to Hanley to Eastbourne to Sheffield, making for long, wearisome Sunday train calls.

Stella proved to be serious about the playmaking which I soon found irksome and unrewarding. However, I was not prepared to oppose her at this stage. What did concern me was that she seemed unaware of me except as a likely journeyman in dramatic construction. Sympathy among the company for Sheila's abandoned plight was general and Stella was regarded as a cynical older woman, spoiling whatever they thought a young girl like Sheila possessed to be spoilt. Even Bert became more churlish than ever, forgetting to chide me with having Put Them In and Not Getting Them Out. In Sheffield, I was summoned after Treasury Call to the room of the company manager, Miss Dalton. She was a huge, taciturn Australian and like all that recidivist race not given to praise or the willing expression of pleasure. She had never spoken to me about my work except over the school inspector incident, which she had thought of no importance. I had assumed that everything was satisfactory. I knew that my playmaking had not interfered with my professional work. With Stella's eyes upon me in the Corner I made sure of that. I had become a passable stage manager, a lowly calling which I despised and longed to leave behind. It required a bland, conscientious temperament that expected abuse and never admiration. The best stage managers are usually women, who bear indignity for the historical necessity of continuity itself.

Miss Dalton handed me my wage packet, letting out a deep sigh as if from some lonely marsupial pocket, saying that certain things had been passed on to her about my conduct, from the company. She didn't have to tell me what they were, et cetera. But she would just like to point out, although she, of course, had no jurisdiction, as such, over my moral behaviour, she would like my attention drawn to the fact that it had been noted. Was she going to

199

write to Mr Hamilton? Or Barry O'Brien and Jack Hylton? From what I had heard of Jack's reputation it could scarcely have been of any interest to him. Or perhaps Barry O'Brien and Michael Hamilton had a policy of discouraging heterosexuality within their touring companies? Surely she wasn't threatening me with the sack? Miss Dalton looked at me wearily. I found myself blushing beneath my acne, thinking that she must be wondering how an attractive and mature actress like Stella could even consider dallying with an unprepossessing eighteen-year-old ASM. Perhaps she would think that the stories were possibly idle rumour after all, because she ended rather lamely, 'Well, I just suggest you might think about what your mother might feel if she knew that there was any kind of truth in this kind of goings-on. None of my business, but I felt I had to say something.'

There was as yet no truth in her suspicion, that most Australian of all traits, and anyway I felt unthreatened. Obviously my job was not at stake and it was flattering to have been the object of gossip, but exasperating that someone in the company could be so suburban as to draw her attention to what must surely be a way of theatrical life. Here was the manager of a touring theatrical company talking to me about moral lapses like Eric or Mr Silcox. I had two prime suspects. One was Beatrice, the character actress, who was Jewish and therefore might have prompted concern for my mother's feelings. The other was Davis, the Christian Scientist, whose Welshness and puritanism made him a likely double dealer. Had he been more shifty than usual, glancing anxiously at my acne, muttering that he was working on it and fumbling all the while with his cigarette packet? Mrs Baker Eddy might have attributed my worsening condition to the turpitude of mortal mind.

Whether or not it was Mary Baker Eddy's reproof to his own mortal mind, Davis was too ill to go on as the billeting officer a couple of days later. I wished fervently that I were making the calls instead of listening to them as I made up. Stella came in, gave me a small whisky, and didn't wish me luck. I went through the performance mechanically, following the moves to within an inch and shouting the lines to the back of the auditorium. I made a slavish imitation of Davis's boring Welsh trades union lilt. I had discarded any idea of trying on my Rex Harrison as risky and inappropriate, and the billeting officer was not Leslie Howard material. Little was said afterwards. Percy gave me an absent-minded pat. Sheila said I was wonderful and Stella said I hadn't done badly for an amateur. I played it twice more and began to enjoy it. Miss Dalton beamed her spade-like chin in my direction. Viewed upside down it might have been antipodean approval. My job must be safe, immorality or not.

The physical possibilities of mutual playmaking were still unexplored. In Llandudno, I had the chance to draw on my investment in Simpson's. Sean and I were asked to leave our digs on Saturday. The landlady had some holidaymakers arriving early, and her Welsh cupidity delighted in turning out a drunken Irishman and his friend without argument. We protested but she was adamant. Stella came to the rescue. She was staying in a vegetarian hotel at great and unthinkable expense, but she could get us both in for one night at ten shillings. After the performance I struck the set and got the show out on to the waiting lorries in particularly quick time. Miss Dalton could not have complained. Getting back to the vegetarian hotel I found Stella in her bedroom eating chips from a newspaper, with Sean. I was worn out as usual after a Saturday get-out and looked, I hoped, appealingly at Stella, too tired to pretend about my needs. Sean seemed bent on reminiscences of Anew McMaster for the rest of the night, but by this time I had heard most of them several times over. The three of us lay on the bed drinking Irish whiskey. As if she were challenging the billeting officer, Stella said very firmly, 'Sean, do you think you could go to bed?' Sean looked baffled and a little hurt. She went on patiently. 'Can't you see that John and I want to be alone together.' He flushed almost angrily, as if she were revealed to him like a flasher in the confessional. I could never have been so direct.

He stumbled out and Stella began making love to me at alarming speed, but I was still sober and self-conscious enough to insist on going to my own room to get my pyjamas. I went into the bathroom down the corridor and put on the yellow rig-out for the first time. When I came back I got into bed, Stella turned out the light and I burst into tears almost immediately, not stopping for what seemed to be hours. The pyjamas peeled away like clothing cut through before surgery. I had never known anything like it.

CHAP: Then there was Jean, I suppose.
GIRL: (*Dances and sings*) 'Jean, Jean . . .'
BOX MAN: You'll get no awards for *this* lot.
CHAP: She was really good and big and well-stacked and knew how to—
GIRL: Get you on the job.
CHAP: Christ, I was only nineteen! I could do it *nine times* in the morning.
CHAIRMAN: Nine times. Could you really?
GIRL: There's not much impressive in that.
CHAP: (*In bad Scots accent*) 'Oh, there's not much impressive in that.' We've all had *colds*.
GIRL: And then there are all those dreary wives of yours.

CHAP: That's right. Those dreary wives of mine ... They all think I'm a pouve.

GIRL: I'm not surprised.

A Sense of Detachment, 1972

After Llandudno Stella and I became more or less official company lovers. Even the burly Dalton seemed intimidated by her, everyone treated me respectfully and Sheila took on a paler shade of piety, treating me in the theatre more like a wayward younger brother than a would-be lover. Like so many awesome decisions, once taken, the subsequent mechanics were bewilderingly simple. Outside the theatre, Stella and I spent all our time together. For a long time to come lovemaking preceded and often took the place of playmaking. Banished one afternoon from our landlady's bedsprings, we broke our way into the dressing-room floor of the Theatre Royal, Hanley, which burned down the following week. Stella dealt with all the landladies and the scruples of their husbands with no trouble at all. We often spent whole days in bed with the connivance of some landladies who attended to us like trainers sustaining their athletes. 'You're only young once, love!' For three months my play was almost forgotten as we progressed to a different town each week, Treasury Call every Friday, cheap delicious food, northern beer, sleeping in till noon, feather beds, free films and fucks.

I dreaded the end of the tour in Wood Green in December. The Granville theatre project had come to nothing. However, Pat had acquired a basement flat in Brighton and he would promote his theatrical productions from there. It would not interfere with Stella and I living there together. The marriage, explained Stella, was a mutual benefit based on their professional compatibility and affectionate friendship. They did seem fond and tolerant of each other and with respect for the other's fragile qualities. Pat's personality was less like Barney Evans than Ronald Furness-Bland, but his aspirations and opinions were Barney's exactly.

Stella and I had finished work on *Resting Deep*, which had now been retitled *The Devil Inside*. Stella had give it a Pinero uplift and added a few coarse jokes, one of which I remember was someone coming on and singing a song called, 'I love to play with your snowballs. There are no balls like your snowballs'. How this got past the Lord Chamberlain at the time is a mystery. However, it did, as Pat was determined to get the play presented, putting it on at the Theatre Royal, Huddersfield, later the following year. I couldn't think why.

'He was a popular hero more than a comic. He was cheeky because he was a genius. All genius is cheek. You get away with your nodding little vision and the world holds its breath or applauds. Max took your breath away altogether and we applauded. When I was at school he was popular only with the more sophisticated boys, and girls seemed bored by him altogether although I suspected that the girls I longed to know—big, beautiful WAAFs or landgirls—would adore an evening with him. I loved him as fiercely as I detested the Three Stooges and Abbott and Costello. He was not a great clown like Sid Field nor did he make me laugh so much. The Cheeky Chappie was not theatrically inventive in any profound sense. His fantasy was bone simple, traditional, predictable and parochial.

'It is said that he hit his insolent peak during the early forties at the Holborn Empire. I saw him there only twice, but during the next twenty years his style slackened very little and he never looked less than what he was—the proper champion of his type.

'What type?

'He was the type of flashiness. He was flashiness perfected and present in all things visible and invisible. The common, cheap and mean parodied and seized on as a style of life in face of the world's dullards. Maxie would have been in his element in the Boar's Head. Just to begin: his suits were superb. My favourite was the blue silk one with enormous plus-fours and daisies spluttered all over them. With his white upturned hat on one side and co-respondent shoes he looked magnificent, perfectly dressed for bar parlour or Royal Enclosure. In those days of clothing coupons, I longed to wear such suits, although a weakness for clothes was likely to get you called nancy boy. Someone called out after me in the street once because I was wearing a dull but yellow pullover. No doubt he grew up to be a customs officer or on the staff of the *Daily Telegraph*. No one would have dared to jeer at anyone who could wear a suit like Maxie's. He was constantly being banned by the BBC, then the voice of High Court Judges, Ministries and schoolteachers. Sometimes he was fined £5 for a blue joke which became immediately immortal. I knew the truth was that Max was too good for the BBC, and all the people like it. But this was just.

'He went on telling them from the *Blue Book*, wearing his smashing clothes, looking better than anyone else, and smelling of sea air, the open doors of public houses and whelks. He talked endlessly and with a fluency that made me spin. He was Jewish, which made him racy and with blasphemy implicit in his blood. He sang his own compositions in an enviable voice and with a pride I thought both touching and justified. "This little song . . . this little song I wrote . . . you won't hear anyone else singin' it. No one else dare sing it!" Nor would they.

'He seemed to talk supercharged filth and no one could put him in prison or tell him to hold his tongue. He appeared to live in pubs, digs, race-courses and theatre bars. Naturally, he never worked. On top of all this, he had his own Rolls Royce and a yacht, and was rumoured to own most of Brighton. I discounted stories about his alleged meanness and never buying anyone a drink. He was simply holding on to what he'd got and he deserved it more than anyone else in the world.

'Above all, he talked about girls. Unwilling girls, give-her-a-shilling-and-she'll-be-willing girls, Annie and Fanny, girls who hadn't found out, girls on their honeymoon, fan dancers minus their fans, pregnant girls and barmaids the stork put the wind up every six weeks. You always felt with Maxie that he didn't go too much on birth control, but if anything went wrong the girls would be pretty good-tempered about it. As for their mothers, he could always give them a little welcome present, too. In the same way, the wife was complaisant, just another cheerful barmaid at home, reading the *News of the World* till Max felt like coming back for "coffee and games". Except that Max could always do without the coffee.

'One always acknowledged his copyright to a joke. You could do nothing else. Some of his jokes are still school folklore. There's the immortal story of the man on a narrow ledge and didn't know what to do about it. That one cost £5 and worth every penny of it. There are incomplete lines like:

> "When roses are red
>   They're ready for plucking.
> When a girl is sixteen,
>   She's ready for—'ere!"

'You could repeat the line but not the master's timing over his swivelling grin of outrage at the audience. "You can't help likin' him, can yer?" They couldn't. They daren't. He handled his rare shafts of silence like—a word he would have approved—a weapon. When he paused to sit down to play his guitar and watched the detumescent microphone disappear, he waited till the last bearable moment to thrust in his blade with "D'you see that, Ivor? D'you? Must be the cold weather!" He was a beautiful, cheeky god of flashiness who looked as if he'd just exposed himself on stage. "There'll never be another!" There wouldn't, and he knew it and we knew it.

'As soon as the orchestra played "Mary from the Dairy", I usually began to cry before he came on. And when he did appear, I went on doing so, crying and laughing till the end. Even his rather grotesque physical appearance couldn't belie his godliness. You could see his wig join from the back of the stalls and his toupée looked as if his wife had knitted it over a glass of stout before the Second House. His make-up was white and feminine, and his skin was soft like a dowager's. This steely suggestion of ambivalence was very powerful and certainly more seductive than the common run of manhood then. He even made his fleshy, round shoulders seem like the happy result of prodigious and sophisticated sexual athletics—the only form of exercise he acknowledged.

'Some people have suggested to me that I modelled Archie Rice on Max. This is not so. Archie was a man. Max was a god, a saloon-bar Priapus. Archie never got away with anything properly. Life cost him dearly always. When he came on, the audience was immediately suspicious or indifferent. Archie's cheek was less than ordinary. Max didn't have to be lovable like Chaplin or pathetic like a clown. His humanity was in his cheek. Max got fined £5 and the rest of the world laughed with him. Archie would have got six months and no option.

'I loved him because he embodied a kind of theatre I admire most. His method was danger. "Mary from the Dairy" was an overture to the danger that he might go too far.

'And occasionally he did, God bless him, and the devil with all nagging magistrates and censors and their wives-who-won't. Whenever anyone tells me that a scene or a line in a play of mine goes too far in some way then I know my instinct has been functioning as it should. When such people tell you a particular passage will make the audience "uneasy" or "restless" they seem as cautious and absurd as landladies and girls-who-won't. Maxie was right. And hardly a week passes when I don't miss his pointing star among us.'

Max Miller—The Cheeky Chappie, 1965

Brighton meant Max Miller to me as well as licence and liberty. Hardly a month goes by when I don't spend at least one whole day there, but 1949 is, to me, the year of Brighton. I was not looking forward to the prospect of Christmas with Grandma Osborne and Auntie Daisy or the Yuletide Dance at the Stoneleigh Hotel. Leaving Wood Green, I moved with Stella into Number 7a Arundel Terrace. It was at the far end of Brighton, opposite Black Rock swimming pool, then unblighted by the Marina. The flat was the basement of a huge Regency house the size of an embassy, clean, newly painted and the rent was £8 a week. In the flat above was a very successful actor, Robert Flemyng, and his South American wife. Now it's owned by a waiter from Wheeler's in Market Street.

We were living in Brighton, Terence Rattigan was around the corner, stars were above and around us. In Kemp Town there was a tiny theatre called the Playhouse. They were putting on *Treasure Island* for Christmas and urged on by Stella I reluctantly went to see the director who gave me a job as one of the pirates. At least I was not in stage management and I could truthfully tell my mother that I was working over the holiday. Apart from the sick boys' Borstal, it was my first Christmas away from home. After the tour, *Treasure Island* was dull and amateurish. It also took me away from Stella when I wanted to be with her. However, we were sharing a flat, we had a vegetarian Christmas dinner of nut cutlets and vegetables and I was happier than I had ever been before.

'*A memory of Mondays*'

In January, we were both out of work and content. Pat offered to subsidize our playmaking by letting us live rent-free. Food was our only requirement. We ignored heat and light. Stella, for some bureaucratic reason, was unable to collect her unemployment benefit, having an almost unheard-of record of non-contributions. However, with my dole money and an occasional ten shillings from my mother we improvised exultantly. I went to Stoneleigh every Friday, eating as much as I could while there and returning with a selection of mostly tinned foods which helped to keep us going for the rest of the following week.

'I think of those who worship the physical side of life, but whose bodies have betrayed them.

'Lawrence took the 1914–18 war personally. And if train travel in Mexico was made difficult because of bandits, he took it as a personal affront. So it is with the bus that does not arrive at precisely the moment she starts to wait at the stop, or, which should be so overbearingly thoughtless as to overrun her destination: and so it is with the sun that fails to appear on her day off, and the umbrella that has to be lost because it is hers. There is always a scene, shouting and bullying, the vicious sulking and gratuituous insults. And, above all, the terrible blackmail of her remorse. That is the worst of all. For she owes the world nothing, it is gasping with humiliation, self-convicted, grasping all it can from her. It owes everything to her.

'My grandmother's apothecary: Dutch drops, Beecham's pills and peroxide. With these, she too can reject any approach from a sympathetic world. "I owe nothing to anybody. I have always paid for everything I have ever done or received. I have accepted no gifts from anyone. And if I have, at any time (and I am quite sure I never did), picked up sixpence, I have never failed to lose half a crown shortly afterwards."'

'He has no curiosity, and is a terrible bore.'

Notebook, July 1953

I would return on Tuesday, having to spend Monday with my mother on her day off as the price for our stocked larder. My mother resolutely shunned friendship in spite of being the life and soul of the bar. She hinted to me about men who had asked her to go out with them and even some who had offered to marry her. No one, she said, would ever take the place of dear old Dad. I found these offers difficult to believe. Perhaps some lonely soul might have been deluded by her bar-room gaiety and mistaken her fulsomeness for generosity of spirit. These Monday excursions were held sacrosanct. She grumbled about my being out of work, but no one else was acceptable to accompany her. I suggested that one of the girls at work might like to share the day with her. The company of a stranger was like an indecent suggestion. God had indeed always paid debts without money, or whatever she meant by that. What it meant was never to be beholden to anyone for the smallest favour. 'You don't owe them anything.'

Stoneleigh

Dear John,

I live here on my own: think well of those I love so dearly and it helps to make my life worth while. I would rather live on an island all alone than have any more upsets, all my life I can remember nothing but trouble. Tottenham people, the Osbornes. There was always jealousy of some kind; none of it was nothing to do with me at the time: but there was always this dam family bickering about who said, who or who done what: if Mother wants to get away from Jack (which Queen says she does) she is welcome to come with me: but it must come from her. I have asked her and she doesn't even answer—so there is nothing I can do now. You bet your life if he goes too far Sid will let Jack have it: but he does not want to upset or hurt Mother as he said her life is hell as it is.

Always in my thoughts,
Mother

For the next six or seven years I gave myself up to these Black Mondays. It was a guarantee of two meals in Joe Lyons and the reprieve from having to speak to each other in the cinema or music hall. We got on the bus to Epsom, Kingston or on the train to Wimbledon, trailed a while through Bentall's or Kennard's, looking, as we had once done in Kensington High Street, like foot-sore eunuchs in a brothel. An early lunch was followed by the pictures. We would then come out, have tea and perhaps ice cream before going on to another film. Often she would stare into windows, planning her next rig-out. Sometimes she insisted on buying me a jacket or a pair of trousers, saying that I looked like a 'down and out'. 'What a pity you couldn't have been something like a barrister or a doctor,' she said in front of some smirking salesman, 'instead of an actor.' There was no doubt about who was paying. Even if the day had offered up a couple of enjoyable pictures and a meal, the journey home, the queue for the bus, the bad back or headache, would obliterate the memory until the following Monday.

As the word Brompton was to pain, Brighton was to pleasure. If I were to choose a way to die it would be after a drunken, fish-eating day ending up at the end of the Palace Pier. Brighton is like nowhere else. No other resort has its simple raffishness. At that time in Brighton and Hove there were nearly forty cinemas and eight theatres. Two unemployed actors with Equity cards could keep themselves entertained constantly at no cost. It was still the Mecca of the dirty weekend. Before the Arundel Terrace days, Stella and I had spent a whole week in a place called Moss Mansions, which was a temple reserved entirely for this purpose. The whole building smelt of salty sex and frying pans. The stamping ground of Binkie, Terry Rattigan, Cuthbert Worsley, an entrenched outpost of the theatrical homosexual prevailing cadre, Brighton had randiness hanging in the air throughout the year. There was no close season on sex; sex was all year round. There was no drowsiness in the air as in Bournemouth, only randiness. Ozone in Eastbourne was spermatozoa in Brighton, burning brightly like little tadpoles of evening light across the front. Whenever I have lunch in Brighton, I always want to take someone to bed in the afternoon. To shudder one's last, thrusting, replete gasp between the sheets at 4 and 6 o'clock in Brighton, would be the most perfect last earthly delight.

Stella and I were supposed to work on our next venture from Tuesday until Friday. She had decided that we should write a play which was to be called *Happy Birthday*. It was to take place in a middle-class house and concerned the events during the birthday celebrations of a middle-aged woman. Using a family celebration where people gather and are reunited was a favourite device in the playmaking manual. Weddings (not funerals), birthdays, weekends, Christmas, even honeymoons, had all been used successfully as a dramatic structure from Dodie Smith to Coward, Priestley, Ben Travers, N. C. Hunter. The form solved a lot of dramatic problems. For instance, characters could confide themselves, explain their pasts under the duress of a special occasion and react quickly and, with their bourgeois emotions usually well under control, it could all be expressed in short, 'effective' (instantly grasped) scenes. Strangers or families who had seen little of each other for years could bare their hearts at a rattling speed during the preparations for weddings, birthdays, Christmas, the New Year, which provided lots of useful stage business with packages or plates. These plays with their meals, drinks, parcels and decorations, were repertory stage managers' nightmares.

Stella had fixed the formula for us immediately in her choice of title, *Happy Birthday*. Now that sounded like a comfortable evening with a nice, instantly recognizable family, a long, busy part for a middle-aged star organizing everything and everyone all the evening, sweeping the stage with flower arrangements, giving instructions, reading lists to cook and housemaids. She could commiserate with adulterous daughters or love-lorn undergraduates, upbraid returned family cads, unearth unsuitable affairs, listen to confessions of wasted, wicked or empty lives, dispense smiles, forgiveness, understanding, innocence and bestow her ultimate great gifts of overbearing middle-class decency and tolerance all round.

The models for the play itself were numerous. Some playmakers had even used Stella's trick of embodying the formula concretely in the title: *Quiet Weekend*, *Quiet Wedding*, *Spring Meeting*, *The Fourth of June* or, implicitly, *Autumn Crocus* and *The Holly and the Ivy*—all identifiable class gatherings. *Dinner Dance*, for instance, would have been unsuitable. *Saturday Knees Up* or *Dinner at Night* would have been playmaking folly. T. S. Eliot got the idea perfectly, beckoning audiences to watch Greek Furies enter from French windows, in tweed skirts, gardening gloves and brandishing trugs and secateurs by shrewdly calling his play *Family Reunion*. That didn't sound like an evening of myth and theology at all—just a Nice Play.

The leading woman in *Happy Birthday* was to be based on Stella's mother, a vain, complaining woman with an older, sponging lover. She, too, was an evangelistic vegetarian as well as Christian Scientist, and examined my spots as badges of animal toxics and mortal mind. She could hardly criticize her daughter for living with me except for my youth and distasteful unhealthy appearance. She was puzzled by Stella's description of me as common-camp. So was I, and none too pleased, either. Pat was eccentric and a bugger, according to her lover, but he was middle class in a remittance man sort of way. Stella, however, refused to let her mother patronize or bully me. 'You'll be hearing a lot of him later on,' she said. 'For the moment he's my fledgeling.' I had never heard the word used before, certainly not about myself. She said it so carelessly that my heart almost stopped again.

Her mother's life was sustained by Mary Baker Eddy, Gaylord Hauser and a substantial private income. Fearing neither death nor illness, she lived in terror only of the Labour Government. For someone who dismissed mortal mind, she was most addicted to mortal money. She seemed packed and poised to fight her way on to the next boat to escape the Socialist holocaust. It was a state of deepest dread very common among people like herself at that time. Stella wouldn't permit any Viper Gang jeers at her mother, saying, correctly, that I was incapable of understanding her feelings. Besides, Stella herself had no time for youthful Socialism. Her vegetarianism was of the most self-interested kind. My own motives in this respect were similarly funk, dictated by a desire to fend off the White Plague and clear up my skin. Stella had pointed out that I should make myself attractive to other girls, something which was not then on my mind, being so preoccupied nine times a day. But I did become more dismayed by our playmaking. Collaboration was making us both impatient and tetchy. My disinclination and Stella's growing irritation at my wilfulness and sulky bouts of pride made it easy to find excuses not to work. In Brighton there seemed so much to do.

Sometimes Stella would spend the weekend at Pat's flat in London and we would catch the last bus from Victoria back to Arundel Terrace. This cost five shillings, a considerable saving on the train fare. Underneath the rugs provided, we also contrived yoga-like postures between Crawley and Brighton that could have earned us founder membership of the Southdown Mile High Club. From Tuesday to Friday we spent drowsy marathon mornings in bed before wandering through Kemp Town to Joe Lyons in Old Steine for coffee and a fruit bun. In the early afternoons we attempted work on *Happy Birthday*. I disliked everything about it including the meaty but inaccurate, sentimental portrait of Stella's mother. I favoured characterizing her as slothful, selfish, grasping, snobbish, true to her class; a shameful anachronism and traitor to her country. This was pitching it a bit strong for a play with such a homely title. It would be like going to a sale of work and being faced by abusive WI pickets. Besides, creating a middle-class monster defied every rule of playmaking. No audience would tolerate or believe in such a creature or accept its authenticity.

Above all, no character who was unsympathetic could ever dominate a play. It was a point to be made to me endlessly, even when, years later, I and others seemed to have long since disproved it. A captive minority audience was to emerge, which was induced to come in to the Playhouse so that they might enjoy walking out. The playmaker's manual had no entry for 'Walking out'. Leading ladies loved being lovable and their public insisted on it. There was nothing like a dame and an unlovable dame was nothing.

Stella accused me of amateurism and inexperience, of poeticizing instead of dramatizing. They were fair criticisms. Aggrieved, I hinted insolently that she was an untried commercial hack, tone-deaf to literary sensibility. These nagging discontentments were becoming patently plain to both of us. Every time we tried to carry on with the play, we began berating and patronizing each other. Accusation and disappointment sent us to bed for relief but even that unfailing well of comfort became poisoned by such bitterness. The harshness of her resentment alarmed and angered me. Everything I did or said seemed to provoke her to venomous impatience. If I had ever seemed to possess some tender promise, it was no longer youthful or touching but the trite posturings of a tetchy, spotty teenager. I was, she said, lazy, arrogant, dishonest and ungrateful, particularly to Pat. Again, she was right in everything. Even my gratitude was backsliding. Regular sex had not dimmed desire but had ceased to make me feel beholden. Nine times and nine times nine must earn its due. Furthermore, she was anxious about having nothing to show Pat in return for keeping us rent free, in some comfort and, in my case, in blissful sexual affluence for the first time.

By the middle of summer we had produced little more than one act which was unsatisfactory as both matter and output. I knew almost at the outset that collaboration was abhorrent to my nature. As she had said, I was too arrogant. Besides, I was over-absorbed and distracted by my feeling for her. I dreaded that having lost heart in our work, her interest in me would wane. If I were a fledgeling I had turned out to be a disappointing, wayward one, flying tiresomely in all the wrong directions. For my part, her playmaking was more onerous and absurd than the formulas of the British Institute of Fiction Writing Science, being neither science nor art. A little later, it bore into me that Pat and Stella were only, if kindly, interested in my contributing vehicles for their seedy ventures. If I were to issue a challenge of my own to Binkie it was evident that it would never come from the lower depths of Kemp Town.

The summer visitors intruded beyond Black Rock, and Brighton seemed less of a friendly fortress than it had been when we had felt protected by the empty front and the wind across the beach. Stella was restless, constantly reminding me that we couldn't go on exploiting Pat's good nature. They were both overdrawn at the bank. Mr Attlee had made a loan from her mother unthinkable. We would have to do something. She had no doubts about her own ability to get some sort of job, but was discouraging about my own chances. Pat had promised to see what he could do but it was clear, even to me, that he was in no position to help anyone, including his wife.

Pat had shown no enthusiasm for what he had seen of the play. There was little doubt that it was to be an abandoned enterprise. My relief was tempered by justified apprehension. Stella was brutally realistic. One day, watching the trippers alight from their tiny train on the beach, she said to me, 'You know, the day will certainly come when I have to get up and go. It will be painful, possibly more for me than for you because you will recover more quickly. But I can be ruthless in these things if it's necessary and I will do it without hesitation, like discarding a limb. I can always grow another one. I've proved it to myself.' Her words struck at me, baffling my reluctance to believe her.

After returning from one of my Black Mondays I was dismayed to find that Stella had taken a job in a Greek restaurant just beyond the Palace Pier. Her employers were vile, the hours long, but she seemed exhilarated. It would help to feed us, she said, and put something towards the rent. An unmistakable barrier of honest self-help had been put down between us. At her suggestion there was no escape from the course of enforced endeavour. I went around to the kitchen entrance of the Hotel Metropole and was immediately taken on as a temporary dishwasher. Thankfully this lasted barely a week, when I was dismissed by the restaurant manager who said curtly that they were overstaffed. There were vacancies for the unemployable elsewhere and goaded by Stella I got a job, again as a washer-up at an hotel in Rottingdean. It was called something like Fitzherbert Court, catering particularly for Pinewood-based adultery. Film stars like Margaret Lockwood or Pat Roc, however, spent chaste, pruriently observed weekends there. Cameramen, in blazers during the day, danced the night away with continuity girls, as I loped home wearily after midnight.

15. Holy Ghost for Four

DIMITRI: They all wanted to fight. Listen, you put a man in the plate
room all day, he's got dishes to make clean and stinking bins to
take away and floors to sweep, what else there is for him to do—he
wants to fight. He got to show he is a man someway. So—blame
him!

The Kitchen, Arnold Wesker, 1959

Arnold Wesker's metaphor was accurate, although Fitzherbert Court might
not have recognized itself. It was inadequate in every respect. The staff were
all seasonal or casual labour like myself. Hysteria, neurosis and bad temper
dominated, and guests were despised above all others. It was a hell's kitchen
of Black Looks, hypochondria, an eternity of whining self-aggrandizement.
My mother would have been the goddess of such a place and Cheffie could
have rucked the fires of hell cheerfully for ever. Human kindness or concern
must melt in a steam of heat and frenzy. I had no choice but to stick it out.
Stella received a telegram offering her a job as leading lady in Kendal. She
left suddenly with disconcerting enthusiasm. I was to keep the flat as clean
as possible and not incur bills of any kind. As I was now out all day and half
the night there was little time even to switch on the light or answer the
telephone. She would 'send for me' as soon as she could.

'They eat what they want, don't they? I don't know what more to give a
man. He works, he eats, I give him money. This is life, isn't it? I haven't
made a mistake, have I? I live in the right world, don't I?' Nearly twenty
years later I heard these words of Wesker's restaurant proprietor uttered in
the famous clipped vowels of Noel Coward when we were both playing in a
bizarre charity performance of *The Kitchen* at the Old Vic. One thing was
certain—I was not living in the right world.

I became staff waiter, laying out the meals in the staff room and waiting
on its members. A supposed soft option, it turned out to be as disagreeable
as sweating in the grease and steam of the kitchen sink. The staff, to a

person, were as bullying, churlish, capricious and impossible to please as Nellie Beatrice on her day off. When they were not complaining about my inadequacies or slowness ('You'll have to do better than that, my lad. Look sharpish'), they wailed about their ailments and spouses. Most of the waiters spent their afternoons at the races where they would lose several hundred pounds of their tips. They chafed peevishly about the rest of the staff, the management and, above all, about health. They all had bad backs or some faulty-functioning organ, were 'bags of nerves' and perpetually 'run down' and 'in need of a tonic'. The staff room was like a squalling warehouse stacked with bags of nerves, longing to be moved elsewhere.

I was soon found to be quite unsatisfactory and was demoted to the still room. This was lorded over by a proudly self-confessed psychopath—who had spent most of the war in the Glasshouse—and his chubby, benign wife. They only spoke to issue orders to me at first, having decided I was both their personal slave and too snooty for the job anyway. She spent most of the day doing undemanding tasks like cutting sandwiches by the hundred as she sang 'Ghost Riders in the Sky'. Her husband's attitude to me was hostile if not downright frightening. He muttered about Rampton, which I knew to be a famous bin for the very likes of him. On the rare occasions he spoke it was to tell me the number of military policemen he had despatched with his bare hands. 'Bare hands mind.' Between them they ensured that I had scarcely a free minute during the day, without even a flop on the beach for respite. I now had to be in at six in the morning in time to prepare the early breakfasts, and as there was no bus service between Kemp Town and Rottingdean at that hour I had to leave at four-thirty and walk the four miles. Breakfast was like the beginning of the day in *The Kitchen*. Life seemed in tatters and violence and despair hummed in the air as waiters began screaming, 'Holy Ghost for Two', 'Holy Ghost for Four' until it exploded and receded by about nine-thirty. The rising, frantic tempo was exactly the same as in Wesker's play. My simple task was to provide toast demanded from the bedrooms, where the famous occupants were hungry after the delights of the night and screamed for instant attention. As I lit my oven, using my new dexterity to extract hundreds of slices of Holy Ghost and thrust them at the shrieking line of waiters, my lie-abed mornings in Arundel Terrace seemed irrecoverable.

I felt ill-used by Stella, but too physically tired to think of much except sleep. With the flat to myself I had toyed with the idea of going into Edlin's or an equally inviting pub, getting drunk on five-penny cider and picking up someone. However, on my one day off a week, my willing flesh and spirit were both too tired and too downcast to leave Stella's bed. There was a most attractive redhead who had served me in the chemists' when I had gone in to buy Stella's spermicidal jelly, an errand which I loathed but which she sometimes insisted I do for her. My lower middle-class discomfiture seemed to give her some amusement as a required part of my training for life as well as the theatre. The redhead had always smiled at me with what I thought was intrigued sympathy whenever she handed over the tube. In Edlin's, when she was always accompanied by an older man, I had thought her eyes were picking me out. One evening I followed her when she was alone but I failed to approach her.

Before the end of the season everyone working at Fitzherbert Court seemed to collapse with inertia at the prospect of the winter and their departure to the lower depths of some other catering underworld. There was talk of bankruptcy and closure and I was dismissed without explanation and given my cards peremptorily. The Still Room Terror and his wife said good-bye to me, saying that I hadn't been such a bad lad or so toffee-nosed as they'd thought. They gave me their address in case I should ever want a job in another still room with them.

My cards were insufficiently stamped so I was ineligible for the dole. I had been earning about £14 a week and had saved enough to see me through the next month or so. But this depended on my being able to continue living rent-free at Arundel Terrace. After a few nights hungrily watching the redhead in Edlin's and going back to my empty bed, I received a telegram from Stella. It read: 'Pat closing up flat. Please turn off electricity, close all windows, lock all doors. Writing. Love Stella'. I decided to wait until Pat turned up and see if he had anything to suggest. When he did, he was characteristically vague about the future in general and mine in particular. He only seemed interested in talking about *The Devil Inside*, saying that he thought he had found a theatre in which to open it in the provinces and an exciting new actor to play the leading part. By this time, I realized that this would be someone inexperienced and cheap, like myself. But as usual he was engaging, and infected me with his ferrety, genteel enthusiasm.

He took me to a bar where he insisted on buying pints of draught Bass. It was, he explained, like Archie Rice, impossible to get in Canada, one of the reasons for getting himself discharged from the RAF by truthfully informing the Commanding Officer that he was a practising homosexual. He had, he confided over Bass, become a vegetarian and now a Vegan not because of any high falutin' moral or health reasons but because the irrefutable attraction and logic of vegetarianism was that it enabled you to get pissed quickly and cheaply. Your system, uncoked by toxins, thrust you into drunken over-drive miles ahead of any poisoned meat-eater. That evening he told me Archie Rice's story about being caught up with by the Inland Revenue after twenty years, when he had been ambushed in a hospital while being treated for a hernia, by two men in bowler hats who appeared uninvited from behind the screens.

He had a list of projects, including the tour of a play called *Because I Am Black*. He talked about the author enthusiastically and I felt that I had been superceded. *Because I Am Black* was a sure money-spinner according to Pat. It was about black people who had come to settle in England. He soon dispelled any idea that this might be a liberal treatment of a new social problem, but insisted it was sensational stuff and really good theatre. Perfect for the twice-nightly music-hall circuit. He showed me a grubby copy of the play and I could see that although the principal character was drawn more or less sympathetically, according to the playmaking precept, the appeal of the piece lay in rattling bones of hatred and envy all over the place. He had already tried it out at somewhere like the Q Theatre and the production was triggered for the rightly selected dates. The author had agreed that the uppity leading man should be replaced. Blacks in *Because I Am Black*, like the queens in *Soldiers in Skirts*, were poorly placed to negotiate with the likes of Pat Desmond.

After closing time, he piled a few things into some newspaper and a brown carrier bag and rushed off to catch the last train to Victoria, saying that I'd be hearing from him as soon as he'd got something fixed. I decided to hang on at Arundel Terrace and see if anything happened. *No Room at the Inn* had only just finished its last tour and I decided to write to Michael Hamilton. Apart from looking in the *Stage* there was little else I could do. Mrs Garrett belonged to my amateur past. Besides, Nellie Beatrice told me that she had died. The North Cheam School of Music, Dancing, Speech, Elocution and Drama had drawn its lace curtains finally and for ever.

A few days later a letter came from Stella. She reminded me of her words about being able to cut herself off from me like a wasted limb. She had, after all, decided to do this. She had also been unable to find me a job in Kendal. There was a little gossip about the work and a casual reference to the fact that she was sharing a caravan with a young man in the company. For the next few days I walked about Kemp Town and Brighton with her letter in my pocket reciting it to myself and trying to salvage comfort between the lines. I knew she was speaking the truth. Her warning to me had been made in good faith and possibly out of hurt regard, a reminder of my obvious lack of enterprise or conviction. I certainly felt neither, only that both Stella and the theatre itself had turned their backs on me, that the Shippards, Grandma Osborne and Nellie Beatrice had triumphed, and so soon.

There was no alternative but to go back to the Black Looks. I sent what was surely a self-righteous, reproachful letter to Stella. When I left Arundel Terrace I took great care to see that the electricity was still turned on and that the windows and door were not locked. It was the only sweetness I could find in my farewell to my Brighton year. Michael Hamilton had nothing for me and the *Stage* produced nothing either. With my lack of experience or contacts I had little to offer. Stella wrote back unsympathetically, scornful about my complaining letter, but most of all enraged by my failure to follow her instructions about leaving the flat. Rightly, she never forgave me for that spiteful, graceless little act, infecting some little pain with most puny revenge.

For adults only

My mother had had one of her 'flare ups' with the tenants where we had been living before. In other words, as usual, she nursed minuscule grudges against the people living there. She was now living in an almost exactly similar house with Yvette, an amiable, volatile Frenchwoman who worked in the kitchen of the Stoneleigh Hotel. She was friendly, with two attractive teenage children whom she used to threaten with the cat o'nine tails, and was certainly a relief from the dull bank clerk and his wife we had left around the corner. Furthermore, she turned out to be an amused ally in the face of Nellie Beatrice's darkening temperament.

If Arnold had been still working for Benn Brothers I would certainly have gone back, if only to escape for the present, but by this time he had returned to Canada. Apart from Stella, he was the only adult who had befriended me, and I missed them both. It was not until the New Year that anything turned up, when Pat, good as his non-toxic word, sent me a telegram saying that he had arranged a job as ASM at Leicester. The pay was only six pounds a week and I was to start at once. It didn't sound like an advancement, but I accepted immediately. Yvette thrust a few pounds on me, which she made clear were a non-returnable loan as long as I said nothing to Nellie Beatrice. Between them I collected enough for my fare and first week's rent.

Arriving in Leicester I went straight to the theatre management, Mr and Mrs McTaggart, a depressed couple who ran the Theatre Royal's weekly repertory company. They reluctantly gave me the address of the room that they had booked for me and asked me to come back as soon as possible and start work. I dragged my suitcase to a back street, fortunately not far from the railway station. The landlady pointed me to a bedroom and washbasin. Needless to say, Mr and Mrs McTaggart, with the stubborn defeatism of lives nurtured in the Midlands, had seen to it that meals were not available, nor was food to be brought in.

The theatre itself was pretty and the market lively, but the McTaggarts were palpably unattractive and bent on ill-feeling. I was to discover that there were three kinds of repertory companies to be avoided: those which were twice-nightly; those run by married couples; and the local amateur dramatic society. Both the last almost guaranteed an unappreciative parsimony and this also often went with the first. The company itself was as despondent as the management. As always, with theatre companies, the prevailing climate emanated from those above. The leading man was a bald, morose actor called Wilfred Brambell, who managed to acquire some kind of star status from having been the standing understudy to Robertson Hare. The rest of the company also seemed smugly drab and particularly the women, who would have looked familiar on the 8.17 to Waterloo every morning. They were *Daily Telegraph* readers to a person and easily impressed by the prevailing atmosphere of unease which came from the knowledge, consciously encouraged by the management, that they were at all times replaceable by any one of an army waiting in the wings.

The first production was a play called *The Wind and the Rain*. In addition to my duties as stage manager, I played the small part of a student who comes on at the end of the play, which is about the life and love of a medical student in Edinburgh. It was identical to another role I was to play later, more than once, in *White Cargo*. Such parts seemed to have been written with stage managers specifically in mind. In *The Wind and the Rain* the leading man, the young student, appears in the first minutes of the play, which is devoted entirely to him until the last five minutes, when another young medical student comes on uttering almost exactly the same stock lines the audience has heard two hours before. It was consummate playmaking but demanded an entire evening spent waiting to make a derisory appearance in the dying minutes. It seemed also to be a measure of lowly status, like being the hind legs of a pantomime horse. In *White Cargo* the exact formula is used again. In that play the character is a raw young chap sent out from the Old Country to the White Man's Grave. In this case there was one guaranteed laugh, which was, 'Gosh [mopping brow and taking off topee], damn hot, isn't it?' This had been repeated by some buffoon throughout the play and even the most hardened amateur could hardly fail to get his rewarding laugh.

The season's programme at Leicester consisted of the staple repertory diet of the time: Home Counties comedies and murder mysteries; plays with maids and middle-class girls compromised in their cami-knickers; and the occasional northern comedy. Many of these northern comedies were written in a northern house style which hardly ever penetrated below Nottingham. They had titles like *Jobs for the Boy* or *Jack's the Lad*. Whoever wrote them knew their audience. Lines which were uttered by RADA-trained actors at rehearsal in utter disbelief were greeted in performance with howls of happy recognition. One I remember particularly involved a character getting his hands stuck in a vase. After struggling with it for long minutes, his line expelled itself into the audience: 'Eeh, I've got me 'and stook in't jug. . . .' Wait thirty seconds for laughter to swell and subside. . . . 'Come 'ere lad, get t' Vaseline. . . .' Instructions: stare at scenery for at least one minute, while the audience recomposes itself.

The management soon decided that I was incompetent and unwilling. They were right. I had put most of the day-to-day burden of collecting props and furniture from unfriendly shopkeepers, sewing curtains and repairing scenery on to my girl ASM who was unaccountably grateful. Leaving Leicester I would have welcomed 'Ghost Riders in the Sky' at six o'clock in the morning and the cries for 'Holy Ghost!'

Pat Desmond had had predictable problems with his coloured actors. I guessed that his scruffy, patronizing air, which was tiresome enough to ordinary theatrical white trash like myself, would probably be inflaming to some ill-paid black actor. Consequently, *Because I Am Black* was postponed until a more slavish replacement was found. Until then, another money spinner was to be set on the road in its place. This was a stage version of the *Blue Angel*, which had been adapted by a florid old actor rather like Robert Atkins, called Edgar K. Bruce, as a vehicle for himself in the original Emile Jannings part. The Marlene Dietrich role was bravely played by an attractive young girl married to the actor Jack Watling. There was little scope for her apart from showing her legs, as the play was a *tour de force* for Mr Bruce, whose acting style was not so much Regent's Park as Hyde Park Corner. Pat offered me a part as a student and ASM which I gladly accepted. It was clear from the outset that Pat himself had very little faith in the show, and for all the right reasons. He had only become involved in the venture because Mr Bruce had supplied the investment in the hope of recapturing his supposedly popular loyal following between Carlisle and Huddersfield. After a few weeks it was clear that his following was no longer loyal or popular. Few people had heard of the film, there was no Marlene and very little sex at all. Mr Bruce spouted whole passages of Shakespeare *ex tempore* for no reason except to prove what a fine neglected actor the tiny

219

audience was privileged to see. Pat lost interest in trying to drum up support, and the end came like a damp dawn execution, swift and expected.

In the meantime, he had managed to mount a production for one week of *The Devil Inside* at the Theatre Royal, Huddersfield. There was to be one week's rehearsal which I was unable to attend, being still with the tour. However, I was to go there for the opening the following week in case of rewrites. I had played Huddersfield before, although I had yet to be bombed in New Haven. Stella was in the theatre when I arrived. She seemed enthusiastic and confident. Rehearsals had gone well. The young actor playing the lead, Reginald Barrett, was a real discovery. Bookings were thin, but we were assured of at least a couple of good nights, it being Easter week. I sat through the dress rehearsal in a confusion of feelings, trying to relate what I was watching not only to myself but to Stella and our months in Brighton together. It seemed to have only dismembered resemblance to what I dimly remembered having written in Sunderland or even after. I thought the 'real discovery' was disastrous, but was too timid to say so, thinking how much better I would have been in the part myself.

On Easter Monday 1950 I sat in the stalls of the Theatre Royal, Huddersfield, watching the world opening performance of my play, holding hands with my co-author. Surging gratitude, excitement returned, I relented with myself as well as with Stella. After less than eighteen months in the theatre, I was watching my own play—or a version of it—being performed in a professional theatre. I was getting paid and I had an ex-mistress saying affectionate encouraging things to me. Stella's coarse jokes worked, as she said they would, but my remaining wastegrounds of poetry palled even for me. However, the reception at the end was friendly and the character actor brought forward the young man playing my part and said something like, 'I think, ladies and gentlemen, you will agree with me that tonight we have discovered a new star.' This absurdity was applauded politely, which I knew must be a recognition of the power of the role and not its feeble interpretation.

Afterwards both Pat and Stella were optimistic and there was talk about who they would bring over to see it during the week. The business had been good, nearly £400, but then of course it was Easter Monday. As it turned out, it was a little more than we took the rest of the week, and my share of the royalty was just over nine pounds. Stella tried to persuade me to stay until the Saturday night performance but, protecting myself from further disappointment and demands for pointless rewriting, I returned to Stoneleigh. I was pleased that the play had been performed but some pain had been expended for small reward. I had had one minimally gratifying evening in Huddersfield as an author with an ex-mistress and collaborator. And there was nine pounds to show for it, a week's salary.

16. Fall of a Sparrow

Wanted: Scarborough twice nightly
one leading M one F two juv char M
one char. Own wardrobe evening
clothes. Start immediately. No
Fancy salaries and no queer folk

Discouraging advertisements of this kind appeared regularly in the *Stage*. Only desperate folk, queer or not, could have felt bold enough to answer such an intimidating invitation. Even as an escape from Nellie Beatrice it sounded like self-immolation. Shortly after the *Blue Angel* tour I saw another advertisement, cautiously worded but almost matey in comparison. It read something like, 'Saga Repertory Company, Ilfracombe. Wanted: enthusiastic young actor to muck in with co-operative company. No salary but expenses, accommodation and sharing.' Instead of threatening no fancy salaries, it disarmingly offered none at all. But it sounded as if any folk sufficiently cast down by penury and despondency to accept such terms might expect some sort of welcome. Enthusiasm could be dissembled if necessary, unless circumstances were truly intolerable. Also, the word 'Saga' had an optimistic sense of epic. I sent off a photograph with details of my experience, some discreetly invented. A telegram arrived the next day telling me to go to Ilfracombe immediately. It was signed 'St George'.

Unsure whether it might be some facetious code, I got on the train from Waterloo quite hopefully. The idea of an incompetent co-operative was preferable to some end-of-the-pier bully. The Saga Repertory Company might be a little like the Dinky Doos. I wanted to be back in the provinces. Ilfracombe hardly matched my idea of what they might be, but it was familiar from my half-terms with G.P.M. Watson and must be nicer than Leicester in any conditions. I found the company in the little theatre on the front, pounded by the sea from the promenade. They were dress rehearsing the week's play, Rattigan's *Flare Path*. It had to be abandoned during the second act as darkness descended on the box office and the remaining wintry light bulbs showed the way to a few dozen bent figures clutching blasted umbrellas. I sat among the sparse audience like a happy dog-owner watching its pet's ill-performed tricks. The piece was performed with such earnest sentimentality that its groggy honesty seemed to overcome its unpreparedness and deserve the respect and attention it undoubtedly received. The audience was unexcited but content.

The Saga Repertory Company was run by two young men, Anthony Creighton and the sender of the telegram, Clive St George. Clive was sandy-haired, balding, in his mid-thirties and the business manager and publicist. Anthony was the Artistic Director. The sentimental excess of *Flare Path* was clearly imposed by him. Short, stocky, he seemed a little like a gushy Battle of Britain pilot or a slightly spastic Auntie Queenie. He welcomed me as if I had bailed out only after dropping a couple of bandits in the drink first. He had, in fact, been a Bomber Navigator and won the DFC for gallantly saving some crew members in a Halifax over Hamburg. After the war he had gone to RADA but, apart from this, appeared to have no professional experience, unlike myself. The average age of the company turned out to be about twenty-one, all of them almost immediately out of RADA or the Young Vic. Stella would have dismissed them all as amateurs.

Anthony, unable to find work after leaving drama school, had borrowed money from his mother and started the Saga Repertory Company with the vaguest intentions. Clive, his partner, was openly intent on making money with minimum effort. A corpulent, uncanny waxwork Terry Thomas, proffering his flair like a temperamental cigarette lighter, he was already a failure as a kind of used-play salesman. My short experience told me that he was a dedicated bankrupt, long set on a drifting, good-humoured, absent-minded course to the Scrubs, if he had not already made the trip. Addressing himself to some tricky matter of transport or publicity he would mutter darkly, 'Don't worry, we'll fix it. Don't forget *I've* got Coptic blood.' I thought this was some vague claim to fortune's destiny until I accompanied him on a visit to borrow money from his father, who was indeed a dignified and polite rich Egyptian. Clive's theatrical experience was less evident than his Coptic blood. Anthony, however, had toured extensively in an RAF drag show directed by Terence Rattigan. It was called something like *Boys in Blue* or *Things in Wings*. Anyway, it must have been a precursor to *Soldiers in Skirts*, the wartime makeshift of the Kenneth Clarks of drag. He showed me a photograph of himself with Rattigan, dressed in a *tutu*, carrying a wand, accompanied by a line of aircraftmen, during which Terry had sung his own show-stopper, 'I'm just about the oldest fairy in the business. I'm quite the oldest fairy that you've ever seen.' He had told

Anthony to go and see him after the war when he said he would be able to do something about his future. I wondered why he hadn't. Or perhaps he had.

The company consisted of three men, including myself, and three girls. There was a plump girl called Veronica Wells, who seemed physically flushed, or rather, mottled by her devotion to Marcel Proust. She had been trained at the Young Vic, George Devine's school, and, like all its students I had encountered, seemed tutored in solemnity, making one relish coarse pedlars such as Pat and Stella. A sour, nubile girl called Liz played most of the leading parts, allotted to her by Anthony to distract her from her preoccupation of being publicly in love with him and rousing and caring for his resistant needs. She fawned on him unaccountably, frantic, voluptuous and disturbing—to me, at least. She seemed over-ripe for violation, even defilement, from Anthony, who curled his own voluptuous lips with the disdain of a pantomime dame playing her Apache partner. The third female member of the company was Lynne Reid Banks—later author of a book and film called *The L-Shaped Room*, and fearless campaigner against dog shit in public parks. I already had some nose for such women, and her own oil met the iced water certain women draw from me. Not to be mixed, I became a poisoned well; charity was mutually and immediately interred.

The size of the company meant presenting only plays with casts of six or less, but they seemed to have found enough of these to keep them going for weeks past. Liz painted the scenery and there was no distinction or privilege between the actors and stage management. Business was treacherous and the weekly shareout was never more than a few shillings each. Liz was absorbed in Anthony and the other two girls, particularly Lynne, were given to continual carping about what they considered to be artistic as well as moral improprieties. Fresh from the sixth forms of Kenneth Barnes and George Devine, unexposed to the streets of Hartlepool or Grimsby, fornication on dressing-room floors in Hanley, the abiding scrutiny of grief stuffed into fox terriers, they enabled me to feel patronizing of others in my profession for the first time.

We lived in a large Edwardian hotel flanked with palms called the Grove Park. I remembered it from my half-terms at St. Michael's. It never seemed to have recovered from the war and its occupation by the US army, and still appeared from the outside to be derelict and unoccupied. Clive had made a deal with the proprietor for which we all stayed at a cost of about four pounds a week each. Whether we got our negotiated breakfast and late supper depended on both the caprice of the proprietor and our box-office return. The men slept in a large dormitory room and the girls in a similar one. We had the run of the entire place to ourselves, including a dozen bathrooms. The only other occupants were Gerald, the proprietor, always clad in the same dressing gown with a cigarette hanging out of the side of his mouth, in a state of laconic catatonia. Contributing to his iron inertia was Eric, his boyfriend, who worked in the kitchen with Calpurnia, an elusive crone who might have been incarcerated by Mr Rochester but was allowed instead to run the hotel and ease Gerald's nervous exhaustion.

Eric, too, was a figure of speculation, made more mysterious by Gerald's urgent confidences. 'Ooh, I can't tell you the trouble I had with Eric last night.' He would blink stoically, as the smoke from his drooping fag end invaded his eyeballs. 'I thought he was going to go crazy, my dear. Had to tie him down with ropes. Ropes! Silken ropes, my dear. Wanted to throw himself out of the window. I don't know why. He's such a sensitive boy. He's too good to be a kitchen boy. I keep telling him. Come into my room. He's such an artistic boy, he shouldn't be in the kitchen. Come and look at his underwear. Look at that!' He would open a drawer of Eric's tallboy to reveal rows of underpants, all ironed and wrapped individually in blue and pink tissue paper. 'Look at that. He does all that himself in his spare time. You can see—he's definitely artistic. Like you, my dear. Just like you.'

He was indeed convinced that I, too, was definitely artistic and was quick to notice that I was weighing up my slim chances among the three girls. Liz had eyes for no one except Anthony; Lynne was unspeakable (she may have unconsciously prompted me years later when I wrote a line in *Watch it Come Down*, describing an indiscriminating lecher: 'Some people will put it in a brick wall'); and Veronica was plump and motherly. On her back she might well cast out the spirit of Proust with a mask of Young Vic sexuality.

Whether or not he had been tying up Eric with silken ropes, Gerald would sink unexpectedly on the edge of one's bed for a chat at any time of the night. Anthony would have often disappeared into the town, while Clive wandered around the hotel in his long underwear with a glass of whisky in his hand like a sleepwalker to no unclear purpose. One night he, too, sat on the bed, frowning as if startled by some unsought pleasure. 'D'you know, I went down to the kitchen just now for a sandwich and as I was eating it, d'you know what happened? That old cow, Calpurnia, that dirty old cow, she came into the kitchen, took out my cock just while I was eating and sucked me off. What about that? What about that? Right in the middle of my sandwich.' The girls, too, wandered a little, but I could see that Lynne had cast herself as chaperone to the others, and my designs on either of them would be hurled aside like dog shit in the park threatening the frail children of *Guardian* readers. Gerald eyed me from the end of the bed, 'You should watch yourself, my dear. I've been watching you. You've got your eye on those young girls, you mark my words. You be careful. You don't know *what* you want. I think you know what I mean. At *your* age you just don't know.'

The first play I was to appear in was a melodrama called *Duet for Two Hands* by Mary Hayley Bell, the wife of John Mills. The part was that of a young pianist whose hands are severed at the wrist, replaced by the brilliant skill of a malevolent surgeon who sews on a natty pair of murderer's mitts, which have a nasty uncontrollable twitch to place themselves around the neck of haphazard victims. Clive drawled his scoundrelly way through the part of the surgeon while I clawed my way through the part of the pianist, thankful that Stella was unable to watch my confusion. I knew that I couldn't blame my lamentable performance entirely on the absurdity of the play. Clive was getting away with his part without apparently trying or caring. The company seemed relieved that I had got through it at all, implying that most weeks were far worse. Unlike Pat with his, 'No, laddie, you don't stand like that on the fucking stage in the professional theatre,' Anthony was even fulsome. By Friday I had become almost confident and the company manager from Minehead, who was in the house, came round to see me, saying that if ever I wanted a job I was to write to him at any time. My first week's share of the takings was something like ten shillings. I reckoned that I had done rather well.

The nights became more black and the sea hurled itself across the street on to the front of the theatre itself. Neither Rattigan nor Mary Hayley Bell could continue to compete with the warmth of the bridge rooms tucked away from the ice and spray of the front. Clive wheedled and Anthony pleaded. If we could get through the winter there would be pickings for all the following Easter. I was sceptical but happy until something better turned up. There was no word from Pat, most likely in full flight from the Inland Revenue or Equity. However, the girls were becoming sullen, particularly Lynne Reid Banks who disapproved of this wayward life as she would later of dog faeces and fag ends. Veronica, less aggressively, was yearning for the emotions she had kindled in herself at the Young Vic with Obey and Chekhov instead of Mary Hayley Bell. Lynne disapproved of each one of the men. She could detect the smell of male squalor in either cock-happy Copt or free-crapping labrador. Some time later at an improbably posh party in London I offered her a sandwich. I had taken some trouble to insert among the smoked salmon and cream cheese, like a worm in the bud, a used French letter. The unbelieving repulsion on her face, the prig struck by lightning, was fixed for ever for me, like Kean's Macbeth. Liz remained

226

loyal to Anthony, and seemed to relish the idea of wintering through a rent-free nervous breakdown at the Grove Park Hotel. Finally, Lynne and Veronica made the decision. We must disband.

Disappointed, I went back to Stoneleigh, but before I had time to write to Minehead, Clive rang me to tell me that he had arranged a tour of one-night stands. 'All *fixed*, old boy.' We were to be based in London using his second-hand car, with a trailer to transport our twelve-foot flats. We would be the same company, minus Lynne, playing towns and villages near London, all unserved by professional theatre, like East Grinstead, Hartley Wintney, Saffron Walden and Epsom. He was to prepare for our coming with saturation publicity for two of our biggest Ilfracombe successes, *Night Must Fall* by Emlyn Williams and *Springtime for Henry* by Benn Levy. The first which was, and still is, a classic thriller of its kind was a shrewd choice. It was most certainly what Pat and Stella would have called cracking good theatre and was almost actor-proof. Not so shrewd was Clive's Coptic saturation. In Hartley Wintney eight people turned up and in East Grinstead none at all. However, there is still something mysteriously wrong with that town. Perhaps, like the Royal Court, it should now be sold off to Sir Freddie Laker. Clive was as baffled as he must have been when he looked over his sandwich at the top of Calpurnia's thrusting head. 'Can't understand it, old boy. *Saturated* the whole town.' The eight people of Hartley Wintney were subjected to a pitiable presentation. Anthony Creighton played Danny, the psychopathic killer, investing every unlearned speech with the remembered vigour of a Night over Hamburg and enlivened by too much whisky. I was little better as the Inspector. After my experiences with *Duet for Two Hands* I was determined to try to avoid juvenile parts. I, too, had not bothered to learn my lines very well and relied on the script concealed in a hefty notebook which I carried all over the stage.

We were disgraceful, inexcusable and boring, as well as pleased with ourselves like a trio of saloon-bar drunks. Veronica played Mrs Bransome competently and was at least chillingly DLP (Dead Letter Perfect) as the phrase was then. Liz was creditable as a jealous wife (possibly thinking of Anthony) in *Springtime for Henry*, a modest but enjoyable farce, and I gave a passable imitation of Sid Field for no valid reason. For weeks we travelled from town to village in Clive's rusting Hudson, playing to never more than a dozen or so people. Clive's advance strategy had been as ineffective as the saturation bombing of Hamburg by Flight Lieutenant Creighton. There was no panic shift from cocktails and evening bridge. Even Anthony conceded that the Saga Repertory Company must disband yet again. Clive was anxious to join his father in scrap metal or something similar. Veronica had got herself a job at the George in Hammersmith and Liz seemed to have retreated into a withdrawn stage of depressive nymphomania.

Anthony, with a deficient sense of enterprise, would not consider alternatives. He still had some scenery and equipment and all he needed was the money to continue the course of his muddled indolence. This soon came from a young man called David Payne, tall, sandy-haired with a fanatic Papist smile. He was evidently eccentric, if not dangerously downright dotty, and was a lunchtime regular at the Salisbury in St Martin's Lane, at that time the Rialto for loud-mouthed actors and lounging fairies. Anthony came back one afternoon from the Salisbury with a cheque for £1,000 illegibly inscribed by David Payne. We went to the bank first thing in the morning and it was honoured without question. We emerged with money in our hands and went straight to the Builder's Arms in Hammersmith, dropping in later to see Veronica at the George.

Looking down the columns of the *Stage* we had noticed that the lease of a theatre was available at a place called Hayling Island. It appeared that the Victoria Theatre could be acquired for a weekly rental of only twenty pounds. Like the cheque, it seemed too good to be true and we went down immediately to see it. It was hardly recognizable as a theatre, being, in fact, the rear end of a small hotel. However, it had a sizeable auditorium, enough room to seat about 300 people, a proscenium with a twenty-foot opening and a reasonably deep stage. There was no flying space, but with our equipment that was not necessary. There were three sizeable dressing-rooms, one lighting batten and a set of floats. A monthly contract was drawn up for the lease of the theatre and David Payne's money was handed over for the first month's rental. We lunched lavishly in Portsmouth, toasting Dotty David in champagne. We even offered Veronica a job, which she refused. She felt more secure dipping into Proust with her Irish customers behind the bar of the George.

Hayling Island is not an island but an isthmus, a leafy, tight suburb with a long, empty beach, obscured in a blur of cold wind and sand. Adjoining it was Hayling Island Holiday Camp, a few windswept, exposed chalets, hemmed in by kiddies' roundabouts and pedal-driven trolleys for the campers to trundle themselves a few hundred yards to the tiny dodgem rink and ice-cream and doughnut hut. This was our literally captive audience. The nearest cinema was at Havant and the nearest place of any entertainment, Portsmouth. Car-owning democracy had not yet liberated campers from the confines of their site, and the motorcycle and sidecar were still the dream only of backyard ingenuity. In London we reported back to Dotty David who was vague, unsurprised and pleased. We made a list of available small-cast plays and set about getting a company together.

Clive was no longer available, so I became company manager. We would start from scratch. I would be able to ensure the selection of agreeable, uncensorious girls and Anthony would handpick the actors. His pipe-smoking, Johnny-head-in-the-air self-caricature concealed from almost no one that he was one of those luckless homosexuals, like J. R. Ackerley, who only fall in love with heterosexuals. I was quite fond of him, but his frequent references to 'the rough kiss of male Hamlets', made me eager for him to find some young actor who would command his whole attention. I had no taste nor aptitude for jealous melodrama, especially one like this, based upon a sexual fiction. My role in Sheila's soap opera was clear enough. I wanted to sleep with her. She didn't want to sleep with me but demanded chastity from me and the fervid pleasure of jealousy for herself. I had made it repeatedly clear to Anthony that rough male blankets had nothing on white bodies, like Stella's, in black silk sheets. The coarse prospect of the stubble of female armpits around my own bed sickened him, but it was one which he had to be made to accept if we were to work together with any harmony.

We placed a friendly-sounding-out advertisement in the *Stage*, like the one I had responded to myself. I had suggested we might employ Patrick Desmond's virtual confidence trick, which was to advertise for what were called 'students'. This meant that you could get your stage management at least to work for nothing, and in some cases someone dumb enough might even pay a premium of £50 for the privilege of working for an unscrupulous management. It was a practice frowned on by all respectable branches of the theatre and by the drama schools in particular. However, we decided against it, thinking, correctly, that we hadn't the sort of bravura and experience to get away with it. In the circumstances, we decided to offer £4 a week within the profit-sharing democracy of the company. For this kind of money, it was certain to me that no experienced or intelligent actor would be tempted. Anthony's sentimental faith was rewarded like a smug, supplicant cripple. The response was astonishingly enthusiastic. There seemed to be dozens of young men and girls eager to work for these wages, an unknown company and an unspecified vision.

We hired a studio in West Kensington and enjoyed ourselves hiring actors, as if we were furnishing a new house or buying a string of race horses. We went through what we judged to be the pick of the left-over flowers of RADA, Central School, the Webber Douglas and, of course, the Young Vic. Each drama school proclaimed its tenets. The St Denis–Devine graduates were still the most earnest and tiresome, especially in their criticism of our choice of plays, which were commercial and provenly popular. We still had

229

some £900 to play with, enabling us to get Anthony's scenery out of store, buy ourselves a few clothes, which we thought was a legitimate company expense, including a £10 dinner jacket for myself, an essential for a weekly repertory actor, and a few other personal presents for each other. We were in business.

A nice drop of cider

CHAP: Woman is dead! Long live Woman! ...

I do not believe it. She has always triumphed in *my* small corner of spirit, just as I have failed *her* image—my broken, misty, self-deceiving image you may say—during most of my life. And, remembering it, what a long time it has been. I believe in Woman, whatever that may be, just as I believe in God, because they were both invented by man. If I am their inventor, they are my creators, and they will continue to exist. During most of my life. What made me think of it? Watching a couple in a street late at night in a provincial town. Being in love, how many times and over such a period. Being in Love! What anathema to the Sexual Militant, the wicked interest on free capital.

Anathema because it involves waste, exploitation of resources, sacrifice, unplanned expenditure, both sides sitting down together in unequal desolation. *This* is the market place I have known and wandered in almost as long as I indecently remember or came to forget. Being in love, quaint expense of spirit, long over-ripe for the bulldozer; of negotiating from the strength of unmanning women's liberation. Those long-shore bullies with bale hooks in bras and trousers seamed with slogans and demands ... Being in love. Desolation in the sea of hope itself. Sentimental? False? Infantile? Possibly. And infantile because my memories of the phenomenon, if there be such a one, is or ever will be, start so *young*. From three, yes. I know it was three, even till the only twenty-one, there were so many girls, girl-women, women of all ages, I loved. Very few of them were in love with me, alas. Being in love blunders all negotiations and certainly differentials. I have been sometimes indecently moved to tears and if there were a court of justice in these things, I would have been dealt with summarily as a persistent offender, asking for innumerable, nameless and unspeakable offences to be taken into account. However, if I have been such a villain in this manor of feelings, I have tried to be as clever as I know how. Knowing, as we all know, that there is no such thing. If I have used blunt instruments and sophisticated gear, I've tried to avoid soft risks and only go for the big stuff. Naturally, I've made mistakes. In fact, when you look at it, the successful jobs have been far fewer than the fair cops. But that is the nature of crime itself, of *being in love*; you are incapable of adding up the obvious odds against you, unlike the law abider with his common sense and ability to discriminate between his own needs and that of the rest of society ... *Girls past*. If I ever yearned for a figment of England, so I yearned for *them*; for girls' past, fewer in the present and sadly, probably in the future. Who *were* they? All I remember most is their names, what they wore, sometimes what they looked like. Not very much.

A Sense of Detachment, 1972

We opened in June with *Springtime for Henry* and *Night Must Fall*. They were sound choices and saved us both the labour of having to learn lines, although in Anthony's case they rarely ever returned. Dotty David noticed but didn't seem to mind. He admired us like the new MG he had also bought out of his recent inheritance. He never enquired about how the money was being spent or about the receipts, which at first I insisted on presenting to him and then gave up gladly. During the next three months business was good, especially on Fridays and Saturdays when we were usually packed out. We played from Wednesday to Wednesday, which theoretically enabled holidaymakers, who were only staying one week, to see two plays. I used Patrick Desmond's trick of marking the posters 'For Adults Only'. Even plays like *Rookery Nook* or *Candida* could be hawked abroad in Hampshire as salacious.

With a weekly rental of twenty pounds and a company of eight, our get-out net figure was low and we managed to lower it still more by performing plays without licence, thus paying no author's royalties. We also avoided the entertainments duty which should have been levied by affixing Customs and Excise stamps on the back of each ticket that we issued from the tin box on the card table in the foyer. As a result, we were operating on a small profit almost from the opening of the season. The company became suspicious. I kept the books and issued no returns for them to check but distributed small, equal bonuses on Fridays which seemed to satisfy all of them except for one militant, who had also declared himself elected Equity representative, something I had not anticipated. Like all Equity representatives he was assuredly the least talented and most voluble member of the company. It is a job for failed guvnor's men which all but the most mediocre shun. I was determined to get rid of this particular actor before he aroused too much support or demands for investigation of our finances. He suspected, accurately, that we had not deposited the statutory two weeks' salary with Equity on behalf of their members. Although I was a full member, I had no more regard for Equity than authors' agents and the Customs and Excise. Besides, none of them had worked the forty-eight weeks necessary to obtain full membership as I had done. Their drama school privilege was a badge of snooty amateurism to me. I had to teach them how to cleat up a flat and adjust a counterweight. So much for Michel St Denis.

The company safe was a large tin box which I kept beneath the camp bed on which I slept in my dressing-room. We had no bank account. I regarded cheque books with as much suspicion as my mother did garlic. Anthony and I decided to sleep in the dressing-rooms, saving us the expense of a room in the adjoining hotel with the other actors. For several weeks we had House Full notices up outside the theatre almost every night. One particularly surprising success was a play called *Love in Albania* by Eric Linklater, which we put on solely because I wanted to play the part of an amiable, dumb GI, played originally by Peter Ustinov. But by the first week in September the holiday campers had almost gone and business dropped alarmingly. It was certain that we had made no impact upon the local elderly and retired residents. I pleaded with the company to be patient but they were all overtired, disillusioned and understandably unconvinced of our good faith. They were in no mood to be persuaded by a twenty-year-old Pat Desmond. Feeling was not good. Anthony was discounted as amiable and quite inadequate. I was aware that they looked on me resentfully, in some cases with a kind of revealed dislike, as an unteachable theatrical barrow-boy, to whom mask, mime or Copeau were the drama's despised Dinner at Night. The girls had turned out to be dull and I was encouraged by the certainty that every one of them was a lifelong prig. Better a spiv than a prig.

In defiance of them and in a bout of self-indulgence, I decided that we should finish the season with *Hamlet*, playing the Prince myself. I cut the play down to a running time of a little over two hours and threw myself into the part in manic defiance of the other dismayed actors and their mincing theorizing. It was a superb opportunity to express my contempt for them through Shakespeare. The women I taunted with vindictive relish, attacking them in the play with my own mind's eye of them. Ophelia, a vapid virgin from Leicester, no less, who had won prizes at RADA, asked me to leave her bedroom. As for Gertrude, I had quite capriciously decided to my own satisfaction that she was a prying lesbian who had prevailed on Ophelia to reject my attempts on the body she coveted herself. In the closet scene, I mauled her as lewdly as her costume allowed, which still gave me some clinical opportunities. She had a residual taste of the rank sweat of Claudius's enseamed bed and of all the monstrous regiment of women. My kisses were reeking with whisky as I paddled in her neck, and other places, and pinched wantonly on her low-slung cheeks.

As a Hamlet, it was a passable impersonation of Claudius after a night's carousing. I looked forward to Gertrude slapping my face during the scene or at least walking out afterwards. She would have been eagerly supported by the other actors on artistic if not moral grounds but, like them, she seemed almost intimidated by the low, lunging coarseness of the Osborne Prince, a leering milk roundsman of Denmark Hill, full of black looks rather than nighted colour. Seldom can a Hamlet have exemplified so wholeheartedly the vices mocked in the speech to the Players.

Anthony managed to remember a smattering of the Claudius I had left to him. I was almost unaware of the others. They were interruptions of a huge euphoria I was certain never to be allowed again. I persuaded the local schoolteacher to send some children, and about a dozen bought half-price tickets. Some of the retired folk from the Victoria Hotel and their friends walked the few yards into the theatre. There could never have been more than thirty altogether. They were patient and possibly too infirm to hobble out. One old gentleman told me I reminded him of Frank Benson but that I was much noisier. Mrs Creighton came proudly to watch her son's valiant attempts to drop his lines on some random target. She had somehow persuaded my own mother to see the last performance. Understandably, she was bored. She had accidentally seen the Olivier film, not knowing in advance it was Shakespeare. 'I've seen it before,' she said to Mrs Creighton, meanly giving away the plot. 'He dies in the end.' She thought my peroxided hair made me look a bit of a nancy boy and too thin. Watching the home audience and the surly embarrassed actors at the one scrambled curtain call, she said loudly, 'Well, he certainly puts a lot into it.' And, with a sigh, 'Poor kid.' It was unusually prescient.

The company broke up, jeered at and unchallenged from the stage by a Hamlet in a brawling, alcoholic stupor. The girls were gratifyingly acrimonious and genteel. They might have even said something like, 'Men are all the same—only after one thing' if they had the memory or perception to know what that might be. Savouring my defeat as a rogue actor-manager, their contempt was sweet, heady and welcome. The vengeful commissar from Equity was less comic but could never distrain on my godlike moments. I had resolved early not to dissipate my frugally displaced energy kicking against small pricks.

233

We were left to find two more girls and a list of four-handed plays. The girl stage manager loyally decided to stay with us but she was unable to act at all. We continued until Christmas, never playing to more than a few dozen people every week. Our reserve profits were soon absorbed in paying the new girls their literal subsistence expenses. Anthony and I lived largely on evaporated milk and boiled nettles. We congratulated ourselves on discovering this reasonably agreeable diet. Our gypsy resourcefulness contrasted significantly with the bourgeois expectations of drama-school townies. The owners of the hotel seemed unaware of our presence in the building and had no interest in the matter of rent, even when I pointed it out to them. Anthony had rented his flat in Hammersmith, so apart from going back to Stoneleigh there was nowhere for me to go. Then the local Customs and Excise man caught up with us after months of profitable evasion. In the foyer, I handed him an unstamped ticket, along with maybe ten others. When he asked to see me privately, I knew I had been ambushed as surely as Pat Desmond behind the screens. The Excise achieved what Equity could never have done. The remnants of any godlike imaginings were hurled aside as my criminal activity was ransacked.

Within seconds, the Excise man seemed to be teetering with triumph at my discovered perfidy. The sounds of his conquest scarcely disturbed the other ticket holders as the curtains trickled apart for my entrance. His hysteria became reassuring, perhaps because of its familiarity. I wasn't able to make out a balance sheet but I thought I could smoke out a bully without looking up. He thought of himself as a personal servant of the King and accused me in the same terms as an Enemy of the King, which was flattering but was a clear sign of overheated impotence even to my unpreparedness. I pleaded the Nuremberg principle of obedience to orders from above. I had taken the instruction of my absent partner, David Payne, who had failed to supply me with the necessary stamps I had meticulously requested.

In fact, Dotty David had disappeared weeks before, on his way to Oberammergau. He had said something about being engaged, but Anthony and I decided that he had gone into some Retreat or a kind of Catholic holiday camp. The Excise man began to be protective, in the way of policemen and gaolers. I said something idly about his interest in the theatre and was rewarded by confession. His daughter was a pupil at the Hayling Island School of Dancing. I said immediately that we would be wanting to cast the star role of the Good Fairy in our Christmas pantomime, *Aladdin*. His gratitude was as startling as his rage. The following day he brought her round for an audition. Anthony and I conferred, as if we, too, were servants of His Majesty, and told His Majesty's man that his daughter had been graciously given the job. For a while, I hoped, I had bought a blind eye.

On 12 December 1950, I spent my twenty-first birthday in Havant Magistrate's Court. Mr Cherry, the local grocer, had taken out a summons against us for a bill for fourteen pounds. We had begged him not to proceed, trying to persuade his never-festive spirit that the pantomime would bring in the locals where all else had failed. But he was eager for litigation as a career woman for alimony. We later based the character of Percy Elliot in *George Dillon* on him. Percy's lifetime ambition was to get the park gates closed long before dark so that no one could have any illicit pleasure. I denied any responsibility for these bills, saying that Dotty David was answerable for all company expenses. I believed this, thinking that just as I had provided work for actors, I had realized his own off-hand theatrical ambitions and my obligations were discharged. My own effort must be surely evident and my small reward undetectable. Convinced that no one would challenge me, except possibly Equity, I was disabused. Dotty David appeared in court, and was called into the witness box with his bank statements improbably to hand, which showed the sums of money he had paid out to us since the original £1,000. The magistrate was impressed by his vague but authoritative upper-class manner and his attitude changed at once. 'You are the company manager?' 'Yes,' I replied. 'I take it that you do keep properly audited books?' I hesitated. 'Yes.' Dotty David was dismissed from the case and Anthony and I were ordered to pay Mr Cherry's fourteen pounds as well as his legal costs.

The first and last night of *Aladdin*, was a cloud of unknowing nightmare. Through the innocent support of H.M. Customs, we had enlisted some volunteers to play small parts, a pianist and a dozen or so pupils of the Hayling Island School of Dancing. I had written the script and doubled as Abanaza and Dame. Anthony played Wishee Washee, ad-libbing enthusiastically and incomprehensibly throughout. We both sang 'J'attendrai' in the style of Flanagan and Allan, and attempted a comic lyric which I had written to the tune of 'Sabre Dance', which was then in Hayling Island's Top Ten. Barely rehearsed and unremembered by Anthony, it was a lot put by me into very little. I had a frontcloth act without front cloth, wearing my hat from *Springtime for Henry*, and I told all the cleaner Max Miller jokes I had ever heard. Most disastrous of all, we improvised what I could remember and Anthony had forgotten of Sid Field's golfing and painting sketches. Those who have never appeared on the stage will never know the living presence of silence. But that is familiar ground testified by more hardened pilgrims.

For someone who had scorned the sanctimonious conformity of Pat and Stella, I was fiercely derivative and plagiarist by now. The evening actually began to rouse feeling. Anthony's balding head was streaked with perspiration as I bullied and shouted at him through our halting charade. Our only hope of forgiveness from the audience lay in the girl playing Aladdin. She had quite beautiful legs and sang in an uncajoling, unpantomime, thin, apologetic way. She even persevered after our act which only the most true believers could have followed. She stood alone with a song-sheet lowered behind her trying to coax a few scattered rows of pensioners and parents to sing 'Hey, Little Hen' and 'Rudolph, the Red-Nosed Reindeer'. There was no doubt about their refusal or ill-feeling. I wished that she would kindly leave the stage, for my sake at least. It was magnificent or war even.

The opening of the second act was the Dancing School's big number, led by the Good Fairy. In the interval, His Majesty's man came round in the frenzy of the man moved only by the mole of his bureaucracy. The outrage he had suffered in watching his daughter taking part in such a disgraceful spectacle matched the perfidy of the King's unstamped tickets. 'I have never seen anything like it,' he screamed. 'You shan't have her.' He grabbed the Good Fairy and took her off like a snatched bride from the theatre. A dozen other angry parents followed, with their howling, protesting offspring. The Big Spectacular number of the show was cancelled. I took an uncaring look out front and saw that the audience had disappeared with the exception of the old man who had compared me to Benson. I explained to him that the performance was cancelled and he returned understandingly to the hotel's television room.

Anthony's flat was now available. Mr Cherry kept coming round at all hours to make sure that we were still there to be harried. H.M. Customs and Excise must surely pounce. We ordered a van from a friend of Clive's and a few days later, with our scenery, our belongings and Aladdin herself, we did a one a.m. scarper to the Big Smoke. When we got to London in the early hours of the morning, Anthony's flat proved to be occupied after all and we had to point the van towards Stoneleigh, where a triumphant Black Look greeted us.

I wrote immediately to the manager from Minehead and received a telegram by return telling me to go to his company which was now at Bridgwater in Somerset. My embarrassing performance in Ilfracombe had paid off. I was sorry to leave Anthony to Nellie Beatrice but enthusiastic about the prospect of an actual salary again. Any instant escape must be better than tunnelling out from under that wooden horse in the suburbs. For the moment, she affected to like Anthony. She would not have been so welcoming to dear, brave little Aladdin.

17. 'Great Hatred Little Room'

The Bridgwater company was run by a couple called Diplock. They were a smugly uxorious pair who had cast themselves as civic figures of theatrical respectability. They were keen on crèches, children and actors who were clean-living and time-servers of the community. Diplock was thirtyish, like a costive slug, wore a grubby beret and an open-necked shirt as worn by the Outward Bound of the time. On holiday he might have relaxed in the healthy mufti of an aertex shirt and knee-length shorts. As he ran the company like a Scout troop trained to rub plays together to make community bonfires it was an appropriate uniform. His wife was similarly open-necked, eager and odious. The company was mostly inexperienced, stupid or corrupt enough to accept Diplock's theatrical scouting ethic. Ivor, the leading man, an amiable lecher, was protected from paying much lip-service to the Diplocks' bob-a-job thespianism by his proven box-office pull with the Mendip maidens. Bob, the character man, like Mr Wood Palmer had been a major in the army, which impressed Diplock, who had spent the war in a reserved occupation. He was the kind of man for whom reserved occupations were created. Partly because of his wartime rank and fulsome eccentricity, Bob's pre-war clowning camp was tolerated, along with his mocking adoration of Maisie Gay, Jessie Matthews, Naomi Jacobs and Mary Ellis. He was almost forty, did the work of three men for six pounds a week and shone like a naughty deed in an unctuous world. Within days he had declared his hopeless love for me. It was a discouraging beginning.

Bargaining with my instinct, I decided I could cope with scouting actors, matinée queens and hostile yokels. Bridgwater was a small market town and I had no idea of the kind of scrutiny the Diplocks' troops aroused among the locals. I had inherited the previous juvenile's digs. Apart from Ivor, he alone seemed to have won Bridgwater's flinty heart. My landlady said he was a lovely boy, which also meant that he must have been a pretty good Scout to the Diplocks. A bustling bundle of non-theatrical motherliness, she told me that I reminded her of her son, which took me back to the fox terrier in Grimsby. Fortunately this son was alive and working in London. Less fortunately, he had spurned his mother's advice, upset all the plans she had made for him and got married to a girl. The wording might have been Nellie Beatrice's own. The tautology was an exact one. Married—he was—to a girl. I had the impression that I too might develop into a fairly lovely boy, though not as lovely as the last one. For a start, I wouldn't get so many badges from the troop. The costive slug would see to that.

I was made welcome to the camp fire. It was evident that I was considered an acquisition to the troupe. It was puzzling. The first play I had to rehearse was a family comedy called *My Wife's Family*. I had naturally been cast as the lovely boy who opens the play being discovered with his arms round the housemaid and kissing her. This actress turned out to be a local girl who had been to RADA and returned to become one of the two ASMs in the company. Her home town was suspicious of her and resolute that she must only prove herself in Bridgwater under the fire of local ill-will. I was aware that I had left behind the sophistication and tolerance of the true provinces. Sprung from Fulham and Stoneleigh, where feelings rarely rose higher than a black look, the power of place, family and generation in small towns was new to me. In the suburbs, allegiances are lost or discarded on dutifully paid visits. The present kept itself to itself. In such a life there was no common graveyard for memory or future. The suburb has no graveyard.

Bridgwater's undoubted feelings about this one actress were muddled but obviously strong. My landlady hinted that she was wilful, even the kind of girl mother's sons went off and married. Renee's misery or future would never have aroused interest or speculation on the 8.17. In Stoneleigh you could be jilted in daylight and no one would come to your assistance. In Bridgwater it would still be discussed in your dotage. Local feeling was complicated. As professional players, even the Diplock company were interlopers living off the parish. Pamela Lane, even as a housemaid, had to be seen to excel over outsiders. Cravenly aware of the town's combined expectation and suspicion, the costive slug was cautious about giving her opportunities. There was a focus upon her that almost excluded the rest of us.

I was reminded of this by a story about Richard Burton. Wales is the well-guarded reserve of its natural and principal species, the amateur. Someone suggested that Burton be invited to lead a National Welsh Theatre. A distinguished leader of the principality asked what were Burton's qualifications. It was explained that he had played Henry V at Stratford and a Hamlet at the Old Vic applauded by Churchill. The reply, which evoked no surprise, was, 'Yes, I see that. But what has he done in Wales?'

Pamela's refusal to be drawn was the power of her sphynx's paw. I had not than realized it. She had just recently shorn her hair down to a defiant auburn stubble and I was impressed by the hostility she had created by this self-isolating act. I was unable to take my eyes from her hair, her huge green eyes which must mock or plead affection, preferably both, at least. I was sure of it, whether or not it was directed at me. She startled and confused me. The herd casting her out, as I saw it, drew me to her. There was no calculation in my instant obsession, no assessment, thought of present, future comfort or discomfort. I knew that I was in love as if the White Plague had claimed me earlier than I had calculated. I resigned myself to it, certain that indifference, including Pamela's own, would put out any smouldering excess of nature I might have thought my flesh or imagination heir to.

I waited for the curtain to go up, holding in my arms this powerful, drawn-up creature, dressed in a green maid's uniform of all things. Life was unimaginable without her matching green eyes. Pamela's emotional equivocation seemed so unstudied that I interpreted it as ineffable passion. It was as if she had once known a secret divinity that, in time, would reveal itself and her. With both of us rehearsing every morning and Pamela collecting props or furniture during the afternoon, we had little opportunity to be alone together. Rampant mystery would show itself like a blessed virgin to be taken into unfailing voluptuary. I began waiting for her to clear up the prop room before going back with her to the Lane Family Drapers. She made no excuses about my being uninvited beyond the door and I asked none. I had seen her parents and rugby-playing West Country brothers. I expected no gestures and looked for no quarter. What did surprise me was the tide of dislike that I had been able to attract and sustain so soon. The Diplocks, who could see pillars of salt in the desert of a Dorothy Perkins display window, became visibly cold. They put on disapproval like balaclavas, and with homely wartime style.

JIMMY: There is no limit to what the middle-aged mummy will do in the holy crusade against ruffians like me. Mummy and I took one quick look at each other, and, from then on, the age of chivalry was dead. I knew that, to protect her innocent young, she wouldn't hesitate to cheat, lie, bully and blackmail. Threatened with me, a young man without money, background or even looks, she'd bellow like a rhinoceros in labour—enough to make every male rhino for miles turn white, and pledge himself to celibacy. But even I under-estimated her strength. Mummy may look over-fed and a bit flabby on the outside, but don't let that well-bred guzzler fool you. Underneath all that, she's armour plated—(*He clutches wildly for something to shock* HELENA *with.*) She's as rough as a night in a Bombay brothel, and as tough as a matelot's arm. She's probably in that bloody cistern, taking down every word we say. (*Kicks cistern.*) Can you 'ear me, mother. (*Sits on it, beats like bongo drums.*) Just about get her in there.

Look Back in Anger, 1956

Pamela had her twenty-first birthday party in April and prevailed upon herself to prevail upon her parents to invite me. I am certain I said very little. Pamela especially said little to me. I had been asked for provocation and offered none. I was not to be tricked into kicking against the heavy scrum of heavy Somerset pricks. Pamela had said almost nothing to me about her parents or brothers and I still assumed her support if I should be tackled. Still, I had an aptitude for charging down the ball while avoiding it altogether. It meant I need rely on no one, least of all the love of the one I meant to rely on most.

JIMMY: Let me give you an example of this lady's tactics. You may have noticed that I happen to wear my hair rather long. Now, if my wife is honest, or concerned enough to explain, she could tell you that this is not due to any dark, unnatural instincts I possess, but because (a) I can usually think of better things than a haircut to spend two bob on, and (b) I prefer long hair. But that obvious, innocent explanation didn't appeal to Mummy at all. So she hires detectives to watch me, to see if she can't somehow get me into the *News of the World*. All so that I shan't carry off her daughter on that poor old charger of mine, all tricked out and caparisoned in discredited passions and ideals! The old grey mare that actually once led the charge against the old order—well, she certainly ain't what she used to be. It was all she could do to carry me, but your weight (*to* ALISON) was too much for her. She just dropped dead on the way.

Look Back in Anger, 1956

The Lanes hired a private detective to follow my movements after it had been reported that they had seen Bob fumbling with my knee under the table in a teashop. I don't know where the detectives might have come from. Minehead now seems likely. But the report was true. The more I insisted on my passion for Pamela, the more he insisted upon his own for me and, like

240

Gerald in Ilfracombe, tried to persuade me that at my age, 'I didn't know what I wanted'. Mr and Mrs Lane were much coarser characters than Alison's mother and father, but their tactics were similar. They were certainly farther down in the class scale, firmly entrenched in trade for generations, and all the family had Wurzel-Somerset accents. Pamela herself still retained traces of a thick burr which RADA had not completely erased.

I began to feel surrounded and outflanked by hostility. I might have told myself that it emanated from Pamela's parents or even the Costive Slug but I had set off a crest of anger that had not been much more than drowsy before my arrival. Plainly I would not be able or allowed to stay in Bridgwater much longer. The Diplocks were touting for the merest grievance within the company to allow them to dismiss me as non-scouting material. This proved difficult. In spite of my general unpopularity, my coarse acting style had a perverted minority-following. Each actor had their band of admirers who helped to fill the theatre every week and even I had mine. The Diplocks couldn't discount or explain it. It surprised everyone, myself especially. It was scarcely important. Pamela was the battlement I was determined on.

HELENA: Oh for heaven's sake, don't be such a bully! You've no right to talk about her mother like that!

JIMMY: (*Capable of anything now*) I've got every right. That old bitch should be dead! (*To* ALISON.) Well? Aren't I right?
(CLIFF *and* HELENA *look at* ALISON *tensely, but she just gazes at her plate.*)
I said she's an old bitch, and should be dead! What's the matter with you? Why don't you leap to her defence!
(CLIFF *gets up quickly, and takes his arm.*)

CLIFF: Jimmy, don't!
(JIMMY *pushes him back savagely, and he sits down helplessly, turning his head away on to his hand.*)

JIMMY: If someone said something like that about me, she'd react soon enough—she'd spring into her well-known lethargy, and say nothing! I say she ought to be dead. (*He breaks for a fresh spurt later. He's saving his strength for the knock-out.*) My God, those worms will need a good dose of salts the day they get through her! Alison's mother is on the way! (*In what he intends to be a comic declamatory voice.*) She will pass away my friends, leaving a trail of worms gasping for laxatives behind her—from purgatives to purgatory.
(*He smiles down at* ALISON, *but still she hasn't broken.* CLIFF *won't look at*

them. Only HELENA *looks at him. Denied the other two, he addresses her.*)
Is anything the matter?

HELENA: I feel rather sick, that's all. Sick with contempt and loathing.
(*He can feel her struggling on the end of his line, and he looks at her rather absently.*)

JIMMY: One day, when I'm no longer spending my days running a sweet-stall, I may write a book about us all. It's all here. (*Slapping his forehead.*) Written in flames a mile high. And it won't be recollected in tranquillity either, picking daffodils with Auntie Wordsworth. It'll be recollected in fire, and blood. My blood.

Look Back in Anger, 1956

Early in June I asked Pamela to marry me. She accepted at once, warmly and casually. The problem was a plain one: to get married in secret. The local registrar was a personal friend of Pamela's father, so the Registry Office would be barred to us. I was in a vengeful mood but not one reckless enough to risk horse whips and rioting in the streets of Bridgwater. I knew nothing about the mechanics of getting married, so I went to the Public Library and looked up *Whitaker's Almanack.* Pamela and I got on the train to Wells and bought a special licence to get married within three days. It cost four pounds, half a week's salary. Holding this, we then went to a local vicar who scarcely knew Mr Lane and explained the situation. He was cautiously sympathetic and agreed to marry us on Saturday morning at eight o'clock, the earliest possible hour, before rehearsal at ten o'clock.

After the Friday evening performance, I broke the news to Bob, asking him if he would be a witness. He fell to the floor, grasped me by the knees weeping, and begged me not to do it. My landlady would have had second thoughts about her lovely boy if she had brought in his supper at that moment. Earlier I had approached Ivor, the leading man, to be my best man. He seemed the most appropriate choice and agreed to it almost as Pamela had done, as an absent-minded conspiracy.

JIMMY: The last time she was in church was when she was married to me. I expect that surprises you, doesn't it? It was expediency, pure and simple. We were in a hurry, you see. (*The comedy of this strikes him at once, and he laughs.*) Yes, we were actually in a hurry! Lusting for the slaughter! Well, the local registrar was a particular pal of Daddy's, and we knew he'd spill the beans to the Colonel like a shot. So we had to seek out some local vicar who didn't know him quite so well. But it was no use. When my best man—a chap I'd met in the pub that morning—

242

and I turned up, Mummy and Daddy were in the church already. They'd found out at the last moment, and had to come to watch the execution carried out. How I remember looking down at them, full of beer for breakfast, and feeling a bit buzzed. Mummy was slumped over her pew in a heap—the noble, female rhino, pole-axed at last! And Daddy sat beside her, upright and unafraid, dreaming of his days among the Indian Princes, and unable to believe he'd left his horsewhip at home. Just the two of them in that empty church—them and me. (*Coming out of his remembrance suddenly.*) I'm not sure what happened after that. We must have been married, I suppose. I think I remember being sick in the vestry. (*To* ALISON.) Was I?

Look Back in Anger, 1956

Apart from the references to Daddy and the Indian Princes, it is a fairly accurate description of our wedding. The vicar had lost his nerve at the last moment and rung the Lanes. When we left the church and got to rehearsal the whole of Bridgwater seemed to know what had taken place. The Saturday morning run-through in the theatre went on without interruption. Our marriage seemed to have settled the cast's lines and moves wonderfully. The Costive Slug looked more than ever as if he had been left to drown in a slow drizzle, and was reported to be stalking the theatre, telling staff and passers-by that he was about to get his service rifle (reserved, like his occupation, to harass the likes of me) and shoot me. In the event, he shook my hands and mumbled some congratulations, saying that of course he couldn't quite approve. I had my rehearsed answer lugubriously ready, which was that my wife and I were giving him a week's notice. 'So stick your job up your scoutmaster's arse.' I hope I did say it.

Mr Lane came to the theatre, more weary than angry, insisting that Pamela and I should have lunch with them at whatever hostelry catered for the town's Masons and Rotarians. We had pilchard salad and light ale in almost complete silence apart from an occasional wracking sob from the mottle-necked Mrs Lane. In the afternoon, we had a matinée and after the evening performance I saw Pamela back home. To my relief, I was not invited in. I was overcome with fatigue and the prospect of never-to-be-consummated excess. When I returned to my digs, the landlady was in the most motherly tears and told me what a wicked boy I was to have done such a thing. Pamela and I played the week out. Gratifyingly and, by Saturday, triumphantly, hardly a word was addressed to us. Well, not to me. The following Sunday Mr Lane saw us off on the train to Paddington. We spent our first night alone in a small hotel in the Cromwell Road, patronized by polite impoverished Indian students. We had £20 between us. I was in some kind of excess even if it was not shared.

The good fortune of friendship and the comfort of love

BILL: I am almost forty years old, and I know I have never made a decision which I didn't either regret, or suspect was just plain commonplace or shifty or scamped and indulgent or mildly stupid or undistinguished. As you must see. As for why I am here, I have to confess this: I have to confess that: that I have depended almost entirely on other people's efforts. Anything else would have been impossible for me, and I always knew in my own heart that only that it was that kept me alive and functioning at all, let alone making decisions or being quick minded and all that nonsense about me . . . That I have never really been able to tell the difference between a friend and an enemy, and I have always made what seemed to me at the time to make the most exhausting efforts to find out. The difference. But is has never been clear to me, and there it is, the distinction, and as I have got older, and as I have worked my way up—up—to my present position. I find it even more, quite impossible. And out of the question. And then, then I have always been afraid of being found out.

. . .

I never hoped or wished for anything more than to have the good fortune of friendship and the excitement and comfort of love and the love of women in particular. I made a set at both of them in my own way. With the first with friendship, I hardly succeeded at all. Not really. No. Not at all. With the second, with love, I succeeded, I succeeded in inflicting, quite certainly inflicting, more pain than pleasure. I am not equal to any of it. But I can't escape it, I can't forget it. And I can't begin again. You see?

Inadmissible Evidence, 1964

I felt I had acquitted myself in spite of Pamela's connivance. I was unable to take my eyes off her. I watched her eating, walking, bathing, making-up, dressing, undressing, my curiosity was insatiable. Seeing her clothes lying around the floor (she was hopelessly untidy, in contrast to my own spinsterish habits), I was captive, even to the contents of her open handbag

244

and the few possessions she had brought with her, including her twenty-first birthday present from her parents, a portable typewriter on which I was to type *Look Back in Anger*.

There was little doubt in my otherwise apprehensive spirit that I had carried off a unique prize. It certainly never occurred to me that it might slip away from me. Perhaps I interpreted what might have been bland complacency for the complaisance of a generous and loving heart. Perhaps there is no question to ask. It may be a dull mind which poses unanswerable questions.

We had nowhere to live and little left of the twenty pounds. There was no question of my going to Stoneleigh and none at all of telling my mother that I had married a girl. She had turned Anthony Creighton out of the house after I had written to him in reply to his complaint about the way she was treating him. The landlady of Black Look on Sea had made him stay out during the daytime when he had nowhere to go, and so on. The alternative was her forcible feeding and feigned concern marked down by voracious caprice. In my letter I had made clear, possibly for the first time, my detailed feelings about Nellie Beatrice. Going through his pockets one day, in the way of motherly women, she discovered the letter and read it. Later, she insisted that I had, in fact, written the letter to her. 'When I think of that terrible letter you wrote to me.' 'I didn't write a letter to you. I wrote a letter to Anthony which you opened.' 'I shall remember it as long as I live, that terrible letter. I don't know what your father would have said if he'd read it. He wouldn't have let you say all those terrible things about me.'

After a few days of looking through newspaper advertisements and newsagents' windows ('No Blacks, No Irish' was not yet a preference accountable to tribunals), we decided on one room in a block of flats next to Richmond Bridge. It was a tired, necessary decision. Pamela's opinion was elusive. Mutual indecision might have expressed it all. The occupant was no landlady but a colonial cast-off who agreed to rent us a room for £6 a week, on the condition that we played mah-jong with her in the evenings. The rent was three times what I had intended to pay, but the Cromwell Road hotel was out of the question for a longer stay. I did something which I had vowed never to do, like asking for unfancy salaries with other unqueer folk: I wrote to a manager called Harry Hanson who was a by-word for tatty, ill-paid, tyrannical, joyless work. He ran about half a dozen companies with queenly ruthlessness and he had a legendary wardrobe of various coloured wigs which he was said to change according to any bout of ill-humour he was indulging.

I had a swift reply and was summoned to the Palace Theatre,

Camberwell, where I was interviewed, rather as I had been for *No Room at the Inn*, by a doomed, distracted queen who was later arrested for offences against young men on the train to Deptford and committed suicide before being brought to trial. I was further surprised to find myself hired. Hanson's companies were dreaded as the last funk-hole for any actor, but they were not easy to penetrate. If there was a Hanson kind of theatre, there was a Hanson kind of actor, unpersonable, defeated from the outset and grateful to have any sort of job at all. They were apologetic about themselves, if not among themselves. Equity representatives were unknown to speak, fluffs and dries were entered into a book by the stage director and other misdemeanours, if committed enough times, ensured the sack, administered literally according to the Hanson Book. He was the theatre's Gradgrind and his theatres were administered like workhouses of despair. Binkie would have seemed all Samuel Smiles in comparison. I had to accept and Pamela must cope with mah-jong. Besides, I was convinced that her prospects must be better than mine. To understudy in the West End was the goal, an ambition open to her if not to me.

Working in Camberwell was as unpleasant as I had anticipated and the company were docile, like prisoners without heart or spirit. The repertory of plays was vintage Hanson, consisting of pre-1920s' melodramas, learnt from 'Sides', *Coming through the Rye*, hack adaptations of *Dr Jekyll and Mr Hyde*, *Gaslight*, *Dracula*, *Frankenstein*, *Charley's Aunt* and low, forgotten farces. The audience was noisy and inattentive. Rehearsals were conducted in a guilty kind of haste and the actors were only given moves where not indicated in the script. We committed our lines as if we were sewing mailbags. No one dared fudge them or forget a move.

The journey across London from Richmond to Camberwell involved several changes, including a slow-moving tram from the Embankment to the theatre. The second house ended about eleven o'clock. I had little time for sleep and less for my wife. When my rehearsal finished at one o'clock I would get on the tram across the river to Charing Cross Station and we would sit in the Embankment gardens with a packet of sandwiches she had prepared and a flask of tea. After a couple of hours I made my way back across the river knowing that when I got home to Richmond almost a dozen hours later she must be asleep. In spite of the tram rattle from Camberwell to Richmond, Pamela soon declared herself pregnant. No, she didn't declare it, she mentioned it like a passing comment. Mention seemed all we could offer each other. Anthony's mother sent us a packet of something called Penny Royal pills, with instructions to take these together with gin and a hot bath. Country girl that she was, Pamela followed Mrs Creighton's bucolic wisdom and was rewarded. If she was relieved, she never expressed it, nor I my disappointment.

Dull and boring

'I do believe intensely in the creative value of struggle.' George Devine

I had less time to find work than I had for sex. Three months later the tardy Camberwell trams came to my rescue and I was sacked for being late twice. It probably had little to do with the trams. The Hanson companies operated a policy of spot sacking and I was no doubt selected by the director, in idle depression on the last train to Deptford, as being the most replaceable, and to encourage the others.

Camberwell had been a bleak period but it was over. I thought I knew that green eyes were smiling on me. For one thing, we had left Richmond. Our colonial landlady had decided that she didn't like having lodgers and particularly those who made tea in the kitchen and were unable to play mah-jong. Anthony had recovered his downstairs flat in Hammersmith and we moved into one of his two rooms at Number 14 Caithness Road, just off Brook Green where Holst had taught the girls of St Pauls. Our room was dark but friendly. We shared Anthony's comfortable chintzy sitting-room and paid him thirty shillings. It seemed a fine arrangement. For no clear reason, the Labour Exchange abandoned its punitive attitude and urged me to draw the unemployment benefit they had contested for so long. We all talked about work. I dreaded and tried to avoid the journey from Hammersmith to the Charing Cross Road and the agents' offices, but Pamela and Anthony seldom accompanied me, keeping house in Caithness Road in case the telephone should ring.

Noel Coward, who could shoot a cliché between the eyes of a gnat and make it burst into flower about the potency of cheap music, also got it right about certain kinds of love for all kinds of people. 'We were so ridiculously over in love.' It was I who was ridiculously over in love. The melodrama of Bridgwater and the overlapping drudgery of Camberwell were gone. I tried to conceal, I think, I am afraid, successfully, the panic loneliness that gripped me in our pleasant room from day to day. I had never known anything like it and I could think of no way of discovering if she were as untroubled as she seemed.

In the New Year Pamela got herself what seemed, in view of her inexperience, a good job. She went to see an actor-manager, Philip Barrett, who offered her the leading role, Joanna, in a tour of *Present Laughter*. He was well known for having made a small living from touring narcissism, and marrying his leading lady, Eileen Herlie. He was still some improvement on Pat Desmond, and I found myself explaining why she should take the job, which she did. The tour was a short one, I would go on trying to get myself something and we would both save ourselves a little money. In the meantime, I had, so I said, decided to write another play. I had already spent most of my time between the Labour Exchange and the public library where, because of handy radiators, I would sit, write and try to take in the theology of Dante, 'with large sploshes of Eliot', as Jimmy Porter had it. The finished manuscript was written in longhand in three exercise books, which I gave to Pamela. She read it conscientiously and her verdict was characteristically bland, and possibly affectionate. 'Dull and boring'. The three words became a humourless bitter joke between us. If things weren't good, they were 'D and B'. Her own honesty, like so much else, possibly escaped her. My play was indeed Dull and Boring. The two words haunted me.

JIMMY: Thought of the title for a new song today. It's called 'You can quit hanging round my counter Mildred 'cos you'll find my position is closed.' (*Turning to* ALISON *suddenly*.) Good?

ALISON: Oh, very good.

JIMMY: Thought you'd like it. If I can slip in a religious angle, it should be a big hit. (*To* HELENA.) Don't you think so? I was thinking you might help me there. (*She doesn't reply*.) It might help you if I recite the lyrics. Let's see now, it's something like this:

> I'm so tired of necking,
> of pecking, home wrecking,
> of empty bed blues—
> just pass me the booze.
> I'm tired of being hetero
> Rather ride on the metero
> Just pass me the booze.
> This perpetual whoring
> Gets quite dull and boring
> So avoid that old python coil
> And pass me the celibate oil.
> You can quit etc.

No?

CLIFF: Very good, boyo.

JIMMY: Oh, yes, and I know what I meant to tell you—I wrote a poem

248

while I was at the market yesterday. If you're interested, which you obviously are. (*To* HELENA.) It should appeal to you, in particular. It's soaked in the theology of Dante, with a good slosh of Eliot as well. It starts off 'There are no dry cleaners in Cambodia!'

CLIFF: What do you call it?

JIMMY: 'The Cess Pool'. Myself being a stone dropped in it, you see—

CLIFF: You should be dropped in it, all right.

HELENA: (*To* JIMMY) Why do you try so hard to be unpleasant? (*He turns very deliberately, delighted that she should rise to the bait so soon—he's scarcely in his stride yet.*)

JIMMY: What's that?

HELENA: Do you have to be so offensive?

JIMMY: You mean now? You think I'm being offensive? You under-estimate me. (*Turning to* ALISON.) Doesn't she?

HELENA: I think you're a very tiresome young man.

Look Back in Anger, 1956

She played a date near London and I went to see her. She had a playmaker's tailored effective scene in the second act with Philip Barrett who was taking himself more seriously than those servants of the Master himself. She wore a purple taffeta dress, and her hair and eyes seemed redder and greener than ever. I could think of nothing like her. She seemed also to have become a rather good actress, certainly better, more stylish and more beautiful than Stella had made seem possible to me. Later, I might have described the impact as her habitual, frenzied torpor. But when the tour was over she seemed relaxed, reassured and happy. I was delighted to have her back and, for a while, we achieved some sort of drifting mutual purpose and made no effort to look for work. Being a leading lady, even to Philip Barrett, instead of a despised assistant stage manager humping furniture and props through the streets of her own small town, had exhilarated her, and I told myself and Anthony that she had acquired a quickening sparkle, or something speakably like it.

I managed to get an odd week's work here or there around London, places like Hayes and Dartford. On Coronation Day, 2 June 1952, I was performing in a play in Dartford about the Festival of Britain. I came back every night by train with an actress in the company, committing what President Carter and others unknown were to call Adultery in my Heart. On the eve of Coronation night, after the performance, we arrived at Charing Cross Station which was like the London Underground during the war, covered with slumbering bodies. It was pouring with rain and I had to walk most of the way back to Hammersmith, cursing Her Majesty's loyal lemmings. When I got back to Caithness Road at about four in the morning, Pamela was waiting—was it over-patiently?—for me and gave me my supper tray in bed. She looked agreeably sardonic, unchastening and secure in the belief that I had been committing adultery somewhere between Deptford and Hammersmith, and not only in my rheumaticky heart. If it implied reproof, it might just as well have implied love. I was too tired and depressed to accept either explanation.

My next job was working for the Under Thirty Theatre group at Frinton-on-Sea. Frinton, nearly thirty years ago, was about as untheatrical a town as one could imagine and I don't suppose it has changed. Its immovable feature was its middle-class characterlessness, rather like visiting the reproductions department in a large store. It was full of villas, bungalows and 1930s' concrete bunkers where the *Radio Times* was contained in an embossed leather cover. Nannies went there for the summer with their charges, group captains and admirals retired there and nuns recuperated from vespers. The theatre, which was a small hall, reflected some of this in its own company which seemed to have been selected deliberately by class. Bridgwater, Leicester and Camberwell, especially, had all been made up from lower middle- and working-class actors. If Camberwell never reflected Camberwell, Frinton seemed consciously to reflect Frinton.

I had been in the theatre for less than four years, suddenly I had unknowingly joined a golf club and I knew that I could expect a short stay by that kind of seaside, admitted by a careless secretary. Old ladies arrived in chauffeur-driven Rolls Royces to performances of more or less chauffeur-driven plays. I lasted about three weeks. No reason was given and it would have been bad form and obvious to ask. Like Camberwell, relief set in immediately. The sack was becoming my only feasible work satisfaction. I was replaced by a juvenile straight from RADA and the Wellington called James Villiers, who seemed an absolutely Frinton-type of actor, which indeed is what he has successfully become. The last production in rehearsal was *The Deep Blue Sea* and a young actor came down to play the judge, a part for which he was far too young. He was definitely not Frinton, more of a gypsy, I thought. His name was Peter Nichols.

Pamela worked on and off for Philip Barrett, who seemed to respect her as a useful and cheap leading lady for his tours. Pat Desmond sent for me, offering me a part as a sailor and ASM in a tour of *Rain*, with Stella as Sadie. I was hesitant and defensive. I felt wary of Stella. Tenderness is a self-abusing word, implying lesser emotions of gratitude and nostalgia, which is what I more or less felt for her. I was liberated from her but had no wish to demonstrate it. I would have preferred her to think of me as affectionate, as I was, and dependent, which I wasn't, rather than a forgetful little ingrate.

I didn't tell Pamela about Stella 'leading' the company as it was then described. Being a Desmond production, I assumed that there would be no details about it in the *Stage* for Equity to look into. Stella made clear her lack of interest in me but without much pleasure. Similarly, I noted that she was not very good and assuredly never had been. She wore a blonde wig as Sadie, which helped to make a caricature of my remembrance. It was a dull production for all the sounding brassiness of her performance and Pat's billing 'For Adults Only'. Business was poor, morale was low and after a few weeks the tour came to an end.

Stella was impatient to go and I was the least reason. When I got back to Caithness Road, Pat rang me. As ever, he was transparently offhand, a little proud and sadistic as he told me that Stella had had to pack her trunks in a hurry and leave for America. The Inland Revenue men were closing in around the screens and Holloway was no date for someone of Stella's class. When I next saw her in Los Angeles ten years later we hardly recognized each other. She had become an American and, worse, an American blonde. There was no trace of the middle-class English gypsy, if there had ever been any. She regarded me as foreign in the way that only Americans assume, without doubt or suspicion. She might almost have talked about Brighton, England. As it was, she talked about a television programme involving puppets for which she wanted money. I made a pretence of interest which could scarcely have deceived even a foreigner. I couldn't quite bring myself to pretend enthusiasm for puppets, on television or off. As I saw her out, she walked towards a man some twenty years younger than herself, got into her car, an old MG, and drove off. The MG was the only English thing left about her. I am sure we would have both been relieved if I had after all slipped her the few hundred dollars I had ready in my pocket.

I spent the summer of 1953 as Juv. Char. at Kidderminster. The director was a red-veined, boozy poof called Gaston, the men all queer save the character man. I shared an underground dressing-room with the leading man who, like my own family, talked and never listened—in his case, about afternoon tennis and night-time guardsmen, and his prowess at both. The girls were dull on the whole, but better than your average brick walls. Pamela's absence was a sore aphrodisiac. Most companies resisted employing married couples, but I was hopeful. I still thought Pamela was my awarded prize to myself. The unknowing clouds of unwanted detachment faded when we were not together. I was certain that it would not be long before I would get myself into a company like Birmingham or the Bristol Old Vic. Kidderminster courted producers, directors and journalists from Birmingham to come and see us. The leading man in Birmingham was Paul Daneman, who was hailed weekly by the local press as the next Laurence Olivier. Somewhere like Birmingham would pay off, just as Simpson's had paid off in Llandudno.

Kidderminster was sleepily agreeable, quite unlike Bridgwater or Camberwell, but I was incautious enough to think I was worth more than eight pounds a week. The leading man went off to find his guardsmen elsewhere and was unreplaced, leaving me as an accepted but inadequate fill-in. I demanded a rise of £1 which was refused without thought by the management, cheered on by the chairman of the local amateur dramatic society which paid our salary and hated us heartily for it. Pamela went in the autumn to Derby as leading lady. These titles were absurd but contractually definable. The Kidderminster Amateurs made their point easily and I left. Pamela seemed to be doing well at Derby. Like me, she thought that the prejudice against employing married actors could be overcome.

We had spent a little time together before she went up to Derby and a few weeks later she wrote saying that she thought she was pregnant again. Her letter, as always, was hard to interpret. She might have been displeased or dismayed. Delight would have been no less communicable. The Penny Royal pills may have been put to work again but the crisis stole away as it had come. She had scored a success, which was talked of in Derby during the following weeks, as Pamela Tanqueray. At Christmas I was working again at Blythe Road Post Office, as we had both done the Christmas before. Anthony had started work in a debt-collecting organization in Oxford Street.

My separation from Pamela had no consolation now that I was not working. There was no thought of prizes, only loss. I was absorbed in loss, unmistakable loss, inescapable loss, unacceptable to all but gamblers. It still needed the croupier's nod, the bland confirmation from Pamela herself.

She wrote to me saying that Mr Twelvetrees, the director, had agreed to employ me and that I could join her at once. The first night I went up to Derby I watched her play the leading role of Hester in *The Deep Blue Sea*. It was a popular choice in repertory at the time. The prize was there, all right, looking better than ever and I couldn't believe it possible that it might be slipping away. Afterwards, in bed, she said uncomplainingly that she found marriage and a career difficult. Sweet unreason was unanswerable, demoralizing as it did unconfident reason or passion. It was hard to believe that she had even uttered this women's magazine cliché about career and marriage or to guess at the kind of arrangement she had in mind. She had none. Not only weariness made me refrain from asking. Women's Lib was a far-off aberration like Concorde, the Common Market or the National Theatre. The absurdity was patent, but without malice. Almost soothingly, she had absent-mindedly wiped our slate out.

18. On the Pier at Morecambe

We were rehearsing *You Never Can Tell* in which I was to play the dentist. It was a tedious part and I knew I was giving a wretched performance. After the Monday dress rehearsal, I was unable to think about the opening night at all. I could only watch and listen to Pamela delivering her dull, unfluffed lines. In the hour or so before the performance, she listened to me berating her about Bridgwater, the calumnious testimony of her friend Lynne Reid Banks to her parents, my defeat in the face of such an immovable sense of detachment. She offered no explanation or opinion and a sickening toothache overcame me. She immediately made me an appointment with a nearby dentist, and offered to accompany me. 'I'll come with you,' are truly the words of estrangement. I was to hear them more than once. I found the dentist, unaided. He took out two of my teeth, leaning on my chest and tugging at them as they crunched like rocks in my head. 'You've got teeth like a horse,' he said chattily. Minutes later I was hovering over Shaw's dentist's chair in my white jacket, mouthing his facetious lines with a gumful of blood. When I went to sleep that night Pamela read through the play for rehearsal the next day in bed. Most of it was already in her head.

John Dexter was as well known and speculated about in Derby as Pamela in Bridgwater. He visited the theatre every week and would often come round to our digs on Sunday evenings. He seemed always to have just returned from Stratford, the latest opening in London, had read the newest book reviewed in the Sunday papers and got the latest prize hit musical LP over from America. He had no job, lived with his mother and father in a terraced house near the railway where his father had worked all his life as a railwayman. His flaunted indolence, or sponging off his father as it was interpreted, made him unpopular. There were other speculations about him and his companions, the local homosexual mafia. In those pre-Wolfenden days a discreet heavy mob provided the audience for touring theatre. The

Ram Gopal and Ballet Nègres companies, middlebrow Soldiers in Skirts, were largely sustained by it.

Unlike Blanche du Bois I had never depended upon the kindness of strangers, and I had no more reason to look for it in Derby than Bridgwater. Pamela's star rose like the weekly returns, with the management and the committee in particular. She must have longed for me to go. The committee made an issue out of insisting that the company take coffee with them after the Saturday rehearsal. Pamela, the only member of the company who might carry weight in the face of the bullying board of amateurs, pledged her support to my boycott of this time-wasting imposition. But, like the St Michael's contract, it was only observed by me. My undisguised dissatisfaction was again the reason given for the sack. Pamela was offered and accepted a renewed contract for the next season on better terms. I went alone back to the room in Caithness Road.

'She's a very cold woman, my wife, my wife. Very cold. What you might call a moron glacée. Well, I have a go lady, I do, I have a go.'

Pamela went on holiday to Switzerland with the dentist from Derby. Not only was he rich, a member of the Theatre Committee, but, before going to work on my teeth, had, it seemed, made me the town cuckold. Only sphinxes conceal such banal secrets. Dentistry was not then a profession that provoked much gratitude and the events had a logic of sorts.

It was the summer of 1954. Work was hard to come by. The McCarthy trials were at their height and I drove myself to some interest in them, thinking that Pamela must still declare herself. I spent several weeks in the American Library in Grosvenor Square, reading transcripts of the Un-American Activities Committee, taking them back home and going over them with Anthony Creighton. Out of laziness or want of companionship I agreed to write a play with him based on his own melodramatic plot. Perhaps I felt that with my writing and editing of the transcript it could be turned into a superior kind of Patrick Desmond package, specious liberalism sentimentalized like *Because I Am Black*.

We wrote the play quickly. Knowing him to be a publicized victim of the Un-American Activities Committee I sent a copy to Sam Wanamaker at the St James's Theatre, where he was playing in a successful production of *The Country Girl* with Michael Redgrave. He wrote back almost immediately, asking me to go and see him in his dressing-room. I went round to see Mr Wanamaker in his dressing-room, who told me he liked the play very much, that he would dearly like to do it but that he felt the British public was incapable at that stage of accepting something so critical of

America. Timidity will go to curious lengths to needlessly explain itself.

I had also sent a copy to Patrick Desmond, who was baffled by the material but impressed by Wanamaker's tepid endorsement. What did concern him were the homosexual inferences. The first thing to do, Pat said, was to make sure the play could get a licence before he could put it on the road as For Adults Only entertainment. We had a stand-up toxic lunch at the Salisbury and proceeded to St James's Palace where we had an appointment to meet the Assistant Comptroller. I was convinced nothing could come of it, knowing I could make out no case for the play, in which I had little belief or enthusiasm. Pat was brimming over with draught Bass and blew Panatella smoke all over the Palace telephonists, who invited defilement like the full page photograph of the week's forthcoming bride in *Country Life*. These girls, faced with consummation from one shire to dubious county, tried to send us off but Pat persisted and we got as far as the amiable Guards Officer who had heard of *someone* reading the play. 'Bloody funny, old boy. We all thought it quite clear: been rodgering her *all* night! I mean, *no* question! Can't do that, I'm afraid.'

In October I went for an audition for the part of Freddy Eynsford Hill in an Arts Council tour of Wales with *Pygmalion*. Before I went in, the stage director told me that the part had been cast already. The director was a Welshman, which discouraged me further, but I read well. He told me immediately that he had already cast the part but was I prepared to stage manage as well? He was a director of the Bristol Old Vic, persuasive, and I was so fired by my own reading that even stage managing again seemed a tolerable alternative to my room in Hammersmith.

The Arts Council took *Pygmalion* through South Wales and the Rhondda. I thought of my father and Pamela. The work was gruelling and soothing, setting up daily in tiny halls and miners' institutes, and the audiences indeed kept a welcome still in the valleys, long after the war and memories of Thorndikes or Greeks. Apart from the St George saturation tour, I had never done one-night stands before but I enjoyed the concert-party idea of it. The Arts Council were hardly the Dinky Doos and the company was dull. Anew McMaster would surely never have employed such actors, who completed the *Daily Telegraph* crossword during rehearsals and would have been always ahead of the queue in the BBC canteen. The actress who played Eliza looked as if she might be anxious to discuss gynaecological mysteries with someone, especially me, but I was able to avoid her even when she invaded my room in Llangollen complaining of ghosts. I had one day off a week from stage management and I enjoyed walking in the Welsh countryside on my own. Playing Freddie was more enjoyable than the snivelling cissy Marchbanks I had played in *Candida* and I achieved a round of cheap Welsh applause soon after I delivered my first line in the tea-party scene. It was a happier business than playing Shaw's dismal dentist anyway and The Man from The Arts Council seemed pleased.

The play itself was enjoyable to perform and to watch from within. There was an almost cosy feel about it which is scarcely a word one would apply to Shaw, who usually sounds like a giddy spinster or a eunuch who has slipped into something unsuitable when he strives after emotion. Shaw avoided passion almost as prudently as Coward. Frigidity and caution demand an evasive style and they both perfected one. Possibly, the slipper scene in *Pygmalion* is touching in spite of Shaw, but I watched it almost every night. Thrown slippers seem the exactly right comeuppance for a cold pedantic heart. The tour ended, promises about the Bristol Old Vic came to nothing and I found myself working again at Christmas for the GPO.

Anthony had left the debt collectors in Oxford Street and was working as a night-time operator at the telephone exchange, something of a sinecure for unemployed homosexuals. He had told me about two middle-aged women employed at the debt collectors who had both taken a kind of appalling fancy to him and of the crude plot he had worked on around this sickly theme. I supplied the title, *Epitaph for George Dillon*, without much enthusiasm. Collaboration with Anthony was less attractive to contemplate than it had been with Stella but it had the advantage of being undisturbed by sexual emotions, at least on my own part. I left the more tedious playmaking passages (what Stella probably called exposition) which Anthony was eager to do and concentrated on those scenes and aspects which interested me, like the entire Ruth–George scene in the second act and Barney Evans himself. It was cobbled together haphazardly in this way in less than three weeks.

Anthony seemed fired by a Damascus vision of wealth and fame coming from his dalliance with spinsters in Hendon and mums in Croydon. I had thought of him as a dedicated dabbler and his sudden faith and unlikely energy were infectious. We worked together like a pair of weekend decorators, sloshing away happily and separately, intent on getting the job done as quickly and cheaply as possible. The paint ran and the joins showed but it was exhilarating to find oneself doing it all without help from outside playmakers. Besides, I had nothing else to occupy me, and Anthony took my instruction and could never strive to be the kind of man that Stella could become. I could enjoy the rare control of a circumscribed involvement.

Critics were to point out that someone called Anthony Creighton had imposed a discipline on me which I had been unable to exercise on myself in

257

the writing of *Look Back in Anger*. The typing was indisputably all mine and we sent copies to the leading agents, managements and Patrick Desmond. I thought he might have enjoyed Barney Evans as an effective third-act scene-stealer if not as a simple joke against himself. It seemed tolerable playmaking to me, but his response was irritable and dismissive. 'I just don't know what you think you're getting at.' The principal tenet of playmaking being that no one in the world must fail to know what you were getting at, he was losing the patience Stella had abandoned to him. It was discouraging to Anthony's reveries of sausage, mash and diamond tie pins. Few who returned the scripts bothered to point out our mistakes to us, even the odious Henry Sherek, who had made some bizarre cultural reputation by presenting *The Family Reunion*. Stella would never have countenanced my title. Later, Donald Albery, no mean sawbones of the drama, insisted on it being changed before agreeing to transfer it to the Comedy Theatre. The word 'epitaph' was bad box office, he explained. Having little feeling about it, I agreed. Most Americans tell me that it is my best play. They are a trusting race.

One agent who did express insistently cautious interest was Emmanuel Wax. He was forming what he called the Haymarket Group, a collection of would-be playwrights who could meet once every month to discuss their problems. The belief that the mere fatuity of discussion in itself would eliminate or ease problems was not then orthodox as it is now. I went twice to these meetings when we were addressed by two of his clients, Denis Cannan and Christopher Fry, on our craft. The only comfort I can remember is that the audience was left as despondent as myself. Jimmy Wax, who subsequently became Harold Pinter's agent, was as morose as the playwrights he discouraged. He practised as a solicitor in the Haymarket and his office was directly opposite Frith Banbury's who seemed to be his only theatrical contact. When I gave him both *Epitaph for George Dillon* and *Look Back in Anger* he said despairingly, 'Well I gave it to Frith and he didn't like it.'

Caithness Road,
W.14.

The Dancing Bear: 'Why does the bear dance?' asks the Jew. 'Because he has no wife.'

More than neutrality, and less than enthusiasm.

Christianity makes the most noise. Does it?

Living in the waste we call time, the feeling of inevitable change, even destruction. This is tragic, noble even, this is time—not eternity which is neither.

The disease of mistaking words for things.

He is continually to be seen attending divine lip-service.

He put him in his place all right—but was it the right place?

I commanded the Maharajah's army. How could I fail to be moved as our special train pulled out for the last time, taking us away from the army, the palaces and gardens, and back to the country I had not seen for thirty years.

The present state of WHORECRAFT.

You know ever since I went into the bank as a clerk, I had just one ambition. I made up my mind that as soon as I could afford to, I was going to travel to and from work in a first class carriage every day—and by the time I could afford to, they'd done away with first class carriages on that line. That's your damned Socialism for you.

I could have slept with a score of women and never lost faith with her. She could betray me twice in an hour with a twist of the shoulder or simply a silence.

Her technique is prodigious: when you consider that she is drawing off an account that doesn't even exist. Without deposit, and, in spite of those bent, mean gestures and those insensitive, cautious hands—bingo—she produces the goods. Her acting is not even art; simply a game of bingo. It must be bingo—otherwise one's whole attitude to art collapses. After all, there are Big Bingos and Little Bingos. Eh? One day, she may be in the Big Richard Burton Bingo class, and critics will talk about the tragic mystery behind her eyes.

It convinces because it is detailed *and* outrageous.

Discussing sex as if it were the Art of Fugue.

Humour is a kind of disappointment.

Hanging things up on a wall where there's no hook.

'I must take particular care not to acquire any followers'. *Kyd.*

'The greatest enjoyment of existence is to live in danger.' *Nietzsche.*

259

'Don't bury me in this vest,' she said. 'You have it.' Lovely drawers she had. Real Wolsey.

'If you die with bedsores, mother, I'll get into trouble if they find bedsores on your body. I'm responsible for your *body*!'

'Don't like those glasses she wears.'

'What glasses?'

'Those glasses she wears.'

'Well, they're all the fashion, mother, whether you like them or not.'

'Blondie I've always called her.'

'If you mean her hair's dyed, you're all wrong, mother. It's been like that for years. I've known her for twenty years.'

'You can always tell—the roots.'

'What do you mean—roots.'

'The roots of the hair—they're dark. That's how you can tell.'

'Well, I don't care if she does dye her hair—she's a damn nice girl.'

'Girl—look she's no girl.' Pause. 'She hasn't been a girl for a long time.'

'Well, *I* call her a girl. What do you want me to say—woman?'

You may think I'm a lost cause, but I thought that if you loved me, it wouldn't matter.

I grieve deeply, not that he is dead, but that I cannot feel his loss.

Trivial people suffer trivially.

Pamela: Phoney phrases like: Know that I shall always have a 'loving need for you'. Loving balls! And, of course, 'Deep, polished wood.'

Letter to Pamela, 1 January

My dear,

Thank you very much for the two pounds. A sudden inexplicable fortune out of the blue—I am very grateful indeed.

I say 'inexplicable' because there was no note with the money, and I cannot understand what moved you to send it to me. It's difficult to believe concern for me to be your nature. On the other hand, expensive gestures of contempt are hardly in your line either. However, I suppose I should give up trying to work out your weird emotional processes and content myself with the fact that you were good and kind enough to send me this money.

Perhaps you were irritated because, although I was not too proud to accept your money, I wasn't able to return your rather cosy expression of fraternity in your last letter. Make no mistake—for the money I am sincerely grateful. But your setting up as a kind of emotional soup kitchen to your grubby husband is something else. If you had any understanding or real—and not simulated—feelings at all, you must know what a bitter taste this kind of watery gruel must have. What you may put in a registered envelope and send to me, I accept but spare me the cheesey charity of your feelings. Again, thank you for the money.

She's always so *regal*.

I suspect him of being anxious to avoid giving offence. It is an awful thing to say of anyone, and I hope I am not being unjust.

He is one of those people who answers that the truth must necessarily be unpleasant.

Every time that telephone rings something dies.

Very Important Prig.

The last thing he will give up is his suffering.

Throwing in suffering, to make up for deficiency in emotion.

There are no dry cleaners in Cambodia.

Spineless, cliquish, spinsterly, Pharaisaical and intellectually immodest— [Who could that have been?]

That point at which extreme sensibility becomes vulgarity.

There's a Smoke Screen In My Pubic Hair.

Our imperial preference for each other.

She thinks like a man—a particularly stupid oaf of a man.

Her touch is like a gelding iron.

Her life is the great unsaid. What she dreads most is the terrible, enforced necessity of being articulate.

What makes it pornographic is its lack of either intimacy or passion.

Some people marry for revenge. He's one of them. They both are.

'My dear,
    I must get away. I don't suppose you will understand, but please try. I need peace so desperately, and, at the moment, I am willing to sacrifice anything just for that. I don't know what's going to happen to us, I know you will be feeling wretched and bitter, but try to have patience. I shall always

have a deep, loving need of you.' *Alison.* [Pamela's own words as surely expressed as she had 'dull and boring.']

With a voice like the death of kings.

In a state of casual FUNK.

He suffers from excessive aspiration. He sweats blood too freely, the stain of endeavour underneath his armpits throws off a constant odour of ideals.

Wet and (plumper), when she's angry, she seems to come down in buckets.

Sex conscious, clothes conscious, music conscious—even radiation conscious. If ever it were possible to be obsessively self-conscious and unconscious at the same time, now is the time all right.

What are they doing to women? The model ideal of superb meanness, a long slink of classical contempt. It begs for defilement.

We are no longer their equals.

The pedantry of indifference.

It is impossible to escape failure.

We cover ourselves by not bothering.

If you haven't bothered, you can't be humiliated.

A worm who has managed to convince everyone that he's got a bird's eye view of what's going on.

Her expression cold; like the school lavatory seat in December.

In playwriting there's some small philosophy.

They criticize me because I don't assume virtues I haven't got.

You can have it, but you're not welcome to it.

We may live in the age of the Common Man, but, my God, how we hate him in ourselves.

The urge to *please* above all. I don't have it and can't achieve it. A small thing but more or less mine own.

The Welfare State: everyone moping about having to bear the burden of everyone else.

Irresponsible (wage) claims.

Wage restraint.

There are indications that the situation is in hand.

The credit squeeze.

'The nation needs a stronger bit. I did not know the horse was quite so fiery until it saw the oats of freedom.'

'We need to prune our roses to get better blossoms.'

'... review ... and bring into line with present day ...'

'regain the pioneering spirit with which our ancestors turned barbarous wastes into cultivated land.'

'vigorous imperial patriotism.'

'If I can help somebody ...'

'We will walk together through the years to come ...'

'Industrial disputes.'

'Co-partnership schemes.'

'Peace and prosperity.'

'His trying and difficult task.'

'An interesting alternative.'

'He urged that no decision should be taken.'

'A matter for more concern.'

'Would disrupt the agreements between them.'

'Doing our best to sell our jet-bombers in Germany.'

'However great the ideological differences.'

'We must try to live together.'

'The atomic stalemate.'

'I don't seek to deny that at all.'

'You will recall yourself.'

'Solidarity is essential.'

'In a sober mood.'

'Resumption within the framework of.'

'Freedom to sell arms to Germany.'

'Mutual inspection and control.'

'A means of creating contacts between East and West.'

'There's a military and strategic answer to everything.'

'A "get tough" policy'.

'Negotiation.'

'A Climate.'

'Very well received.'

'An atmosphere of freedom.'
'A nuclear and electronic age.'
'Talking point.'
'Ah, *training* for later life.'
'Broad issues.'
'The most important aspect.'
'A grave and growing public resentment.'
'It has been generally recognised.'
'The organisers of planned foolery: the experts.'
'BOOM BRITAIN.'
'Let the full searchlight of opinion be allowed to shine into every dark corner.'
'The paper with a twinkle in its eye.'

The great English virtue, old age.

He prides himself on his horse sense.
It must be the horse I always back.

Happiness means not looking backwards.

Making the other chap feel dowdy and old-fashioned.

Notebook, 1954

The entry for 4 May 1955 in my pocket diary reads tersely: 'Began writing *Look Back in Anger*.'
Thursday, May 5th: Vicki [my dog] died.
Friday, May 6th: *Look Back in Anger*, Act 1 finished.
Wednesday, May 11th: Saw *The Boyfriend*.
Friday, May 13th: Went to see *Hedda Gabler*.

This production of *Hedda Gabler* was the first time I saw George Devine. I knew nothing of his reputation, only that he might have done unnecessary damage at the Young Vic to Veronica Wells, already somewhat maimed by a cloying talent. The play was presented at the Lyric, Hammersmith, with Peggy Ashcroft playing Hedda and Micheál MacLiammóir as Judge Brack. The marquee risk of Henry Gibson's name was underwritten by the name of the leading lady, explaining a possible Tennent aberration, and it was difficult to get cheap seats.

Anthony and I had taken in a lodger, a youngish Pakistani businessman. He had knocked on the door one day asking if we had any rooms. He was a desperate man: 'No Blacks or Irish', and Mr Siddiqui passed for black in Hammersmith. We gratefully offered him the room Pamela and I had shared for thirty shillings a week with cooked breakfast, and half our rent was found. He left early and returned late and shivered in unshakeable good humour in his room, never taking off his dark overcoat even in the summer evenings. Like a happy mascot who had wandered in from the street, we soon felt fond and responsive, asking him to listen to the radio with us. Sitting in his hat and overcoat he chuckled joyfully at things like *The Goons* and *Take It From Here*. A pleasure to please is how Nellie Beatrice would have described him. He seemed set to sipping Anthony's gin from Ramadan to Christmas. He had a giggling turn of phrase, full of Raj archaisms and cultural references like, 'Oh, we will be having the most jolly top-hole time, as Thomas Hardy, the author of *Far from the* Maddening *Crowd*, would have it.' He seemed to have decided that the two of us shared sybaritic tastes which differed from Anthony's. He had been occasionally boastful about his textiles. But his wife and children were shrugged off as a burdensome pride. One evening, returning earlier than usual, he clasped me round the shoulder saying, 'Well, John old boy, why do the two of us not go out together tonight? We will go out and get bleeding well drunk like two bloody sailors, and then, by the Jove, we will go up to the Hammersmith Palace of Dancing and pick up a couple of girls. Now what do you say?'

Mr Siddiqui's invitation itself was tempting but not what it promised. Remembering his reference to Hardy, I wondered if H. Gibson might ring some leftover memory implanted by the recent King-Emperor. I suggested that we go out and get somewhat drunk, though not perhaps like sailors at such an early hour, take in the Henry Gibson show, and then go on to the Palace of Dancing and pick up two most top-hole English virgins. English womanhood in Hammersmith that night was uppermost in his mind and I pointed out that one of the finest examples was playing the leading role at the theatre we would visit. He accepted this at once and we set out, dropping into the George Hotel where Veronica Wells was still working part-time with all twelve volumes of Proust still on display behind her for any Irish or Blacks to see. I bought our tickets with his money quickly, and when he settled into the front row of the Lyric Theatre, he looked a little puzzled. Disappointment was forbidden alcohol to him but, even sustained by beer and whisky, he restrained the peevish disappointment he must have been feeling. In the first interval he turned to me and said, 'There are not seeming to be many girls in this performance. When are we leaving? It is most extremely jolly boring.' I assured him that the play would not be lasting very much longer and that the most interesting girls would turn up later at the dance when we would have the time to get really and most truly drunk like bloody sailors. I got him away from the theatre bar and he went back trustingly to his seat.

On Tuesday, 17th May the diary reads: Act II, Scene 1 finished.
Friday, 20th May: Morecambe

An agent had rung me with an offer of a week's work at Morecambe to play in *Seagulls over Sorrento*. The part was so small that only one day's rehearsal was necessary. However, it did mean £12 and my train fare back to the provinces. I could work on my play, the weather was warm and sunny and the town beginning to fill up. Visiting the theatre for a few minutes in the evenings, I could go down to the end of the pier every morning and spend the day in the sunshine.

On Thursday, 26th of May there is an entry which says: 95 + 85 + 35—the number of pages I had written in each of the first two acts.
Friday, 27th reads: *Look Back in Anger*. Act II finished. Act III Scene 1 started.

I would have stayed on the following week but Hammersmith was cheaper than digs. Besides, it was Whit Monday and Morecambe was packed.

Friday, 3 June: *Look Back in Anger* finished.
Thursday, 9 June: *Look Back in Anger*, scripted.

On Monday 13th are marked the names Kitty Black and Pat Desmond. Kitty Black was principal play reader for Curtis Brown, the reputable literary agents. It was a faulty aim at the top and the bottom.
A week or two earlier Anthony Creighton's mother had died and left him a few hundred pounds. Knowing his thriftlessness, I persuaded him to buy an old Rhine barge which was tied up in the Cubitt Yacht Basin in a secluded mooring beside Chiswick Bridge. The mooring fee was only twenty-five shillings a week, calor gas was inexpensive, there was a specially cheap electricity rate and a telephone for ringing agents. Even if it meant enduring the occasional Black Monday, I could surely cadge twelve and sixpence. I had no special hopes of Black or Desmond, but I was in some

state of happy grace that the act of writing the play had oddly bestowed on me.

Fifteen years later an inspired annotator in some unreadable book pronounced that *Look Back in Anger* was not originally titled as such but was, in fact, called *On The Pier At Morecambe*. He could have asked me and found out. Perhaps it is as well that he didn't.

19. 'Let Me Know Where You're Playing Tomorrow Night and I'll Come and See You.'

ARCHIE RICE

M/Y Egret
Cubitt's Yacht Basin,
Hartington Road,
London W.4.
November 1955

NELLIE BEATRICE: So much malice directed at innocence: the yellow pyjamas—'Those things aren't much good. The narrow trousers make you look thin.' That's how she talks to me. It gets you down when you feel weary and depressed.

'Sit down! What—at eleven o'clock (almost hysterically). I go straight to bed!'

'Funny about Peter getting married. (A sidelong glance.) He was always *girl* mad.' I replied that he was twenty five years old, and that it wasn't surprising that he should be married. She ignored this and started rummaging noisily in her bag for a cigarette.

Those eyes which missed nothing and understood nothing.

'Poor Kid.' Her favourite words. 'I've had enough of down and outs.' Down and outs were two more. 'I've had enough of *him*. Down and out!' Another laugh and then, 'Poor kid.' 'That letter' which became 'the one you wrote to me.'

'It's all right for you—you've got every day off. But it takes the gilt off when you work hard every day. I shall think of this tomorrow. When I'm working. I shall think, well thank God I'm not there, waiting for the bus.'

268

There is a particular kind of cruelty which she had inherited. She would play off her victim (i.e.—me) to her gallery—of often unwilling spectators—in the bus queue, restaurant or train. When she began to sense my inner rage and the disinterest of others, her nerve fails. 'But he's a good kid though. He thinks I don't know what he's thinking, but I can read John like a book. I can read him like a book.'

Notebook, 1955

Stoneleigh

'*Dear John*, I look at it like this John—I never see or speak to a soul and no one comes to see me. So I think well I might just as well have fresh surroundings as long as there are plenty of people and shops and life about. I don't want to end my days *in this flat*. All I want is 1 Bedroom, 1 Sitting room, Kitchen and Bathroom. I don't want a Dining Room. Small so I can keep it clean: and not much work: I never did like Housework but don't like dirty places....

'*Dear John*, I am getting so worked up over my flat in Brighton I am already collecting boxes and washing all china all ready for packing etc. Carpets have been washed and rolled up; blankets all washed, in fact I'm all ready to go and giving a month's notice: am painting odds and ends; washing lace curtains; am enjoying my little self doing all these little things. It's such a great big thrill I am getting even if it doesn't come off; believe me I have enjoyed doing and getting things ready for departure—I hope— ...

'*Dear John*, Gosh: your beautiful red roses were *so* beautiful, tall graceful and the most lovely coloured red I have ever seen. As Jan. is so on top of Xmas it does get a bit boring getting presents after weeks of Xmas shopping....

'*Dear John*, I have not seen a soul or spoken to anyone since I last saw you and it gets a little lonesome at times. My cat Samantha acted rather savage last night which rather frightened me. I was watching the telly all of a sudden she flew for my throat and bit me. I was so surprised I threw her from one side of the room: she had really hurt me: she can be very spiteful also most lovable, now I cover my throat up. I gave her a worm tablet: she is much quieter today. I think I have made too much fuss of her and I'm cross with her: have taken no notice of her all day....

269

'*Dear John*, I am just cooking a nice point Steak, with New Potatoes Coliflower with cheese sauce: Pine apple, Ice cream: wish you were here to share it. Finishing off with a 6d Mars: shall be sick any moment now....

'*Dear John*, Queenie is very ill: she stood on a chair and fell but to save herself the poor dear put both hands on the hot boiler and burnt them *very badly* she has a nurse going in daily to attend to her. *I* of course was terribly upset. I sent her a bottle of Brandy. Sid said the dressings are so painful: she is quite helpless as she has burnt both hands and cannot even wash her face. Women do the silliest things—why get on a dam chair when one is so unsteady on those feet as she is. Well: let's hope she will make a speedy recovery: just one of her most unlucky days: the pain must have been awful....

'*Dear John*, Stoneleigh is a dead end and shall be glad to get away and make New Friends and New Surroundings....

'*Dear John*, Now Queenie *can* write a nice letter: complete with stops, long words and spelt right—but Oh Lord above: so boring and depressing: I could scream. I read them once: give the Cats to play with the pieces. I am worried about my green stamps. I must get them completed before I leave here. I *am* looking forward to my next free gift: my carpet shampoo cleaner for my new flat: how I shall treasure it....

'*Dear John*, I hurt my back spring-cleaning its pretty painful at the moment; I washed the ceiling in the sitting room: also I ask my man I usually have how much he would charge to just paint my little bedroom. Well, you know how small it is. He wants £6.10.0. so I got a 10/6 tin of white paint and *did it myself*. And honestly John—I don't suppose you will ever see it: but it looks so nice and I feel a little proud of myself. Just had another depressing letter from Queenie: her and Sid had a row—so not on speaking terms: she ask me if I would give her £2 to buy a bird cage for her Budgies: which Mother got her: she said she didn't like to ask Mother for it. I think its an imposition don't you: in view of the fact I sent her a £1 last week to get herself a drink to cheer her up. Oh dear I suppose for peace sake I will send it. Honestly I think they are under the impression I really am in the money. I am always sending her £1s and it all add up. I expect as my back is bad I did not feel very happy with her letter....

'*Dear John*, What some of your friends must think of me I don't know: I only realize how kind you have been not to have been ashamed of me. I am not a snob: but I like real nice people. . . .

'*Dear John*, I saw my Friend this morning: she has not been very well so looks like death warmed up: I gave her 2/6 to get herself a bottle of beer. In mother's last letter she said '*What do you think of all the Royal babies*. Isn't it wonderful?' I answered *What's so wonderful*: I could not care less: each one has 5 doctors for one baby: good God said I, they ought to give birth to gold mines. Dear Mother—bless her heart.

Always in my thoughts,
Mother'

'I'll say that for him—he's never been *ashamed* of me. He's always let me meet his friends—and they're all theatrical people, a good class all of them, they speak nicely.' I am ashamed of her as part of myself that can't be cast out, my own conflict, the disease which I suffer and have inherited, what I *am* and never could be whole. My disease, an invitation to my sick room.

Her letters, her phone calls, our meetings. I would speculate on them for days. What would the first encounter be like? There was no way of telling, but in the first moments, one could precast the pattern of the day—but certainly not the next.

Those hours after he died, when I was dragged back from the corpse, the hatred between us.

Public taste is *created*—never forget that.

They seem to think I'm a sort of juvenile delinquent, the result of an undesirable background. Give him a normal reliable theatrical home, and you'll find he can behave as decently as anyone else.

'His heart is in the right place anyway.'
'Yes, where everyone can see it.'
Concealed, like Rattigan's or Coward's.

'She is beautiful, aristocratic and talented, like one of those superbly mean models who stare from the pages of glossy magazines—"a long slink of classical meanness.".'

He writes like a lout and lives like a gentlewoman's companion.
'They put it on as a vehicle for the star.'
If only it were a tumbril.

'The birth of children is the death of parents.' *Hegel.*

Well, she came to see my play, and she didn't even mention it. *Goodnight.*

Don't be afraid of being emotional. You won't die of it.

It's boring living in a world without mortality.

He is generous, understanding, sympathetic and has absolutely no feeling for people.

All I can offer you is the memory of pain.

The book-keepers and chartered accountants who go to plays and tot them up.

Double entry playgoers.

'I enjoyed it. Mind you, I don't think it is one entire and perfect chrysalis.'

Each time he staggers to his feet again, and totters after the woman with glaring eyes. Finally, she is affected, and goes to comfort him. But it is too late. When she is able to give him what he wants, he is no longer able to accept it.

Women never do anything for its own sake.

'My son was killed in the war for the likes of you'.

He suffers the realization: *that there is no real communication with those we love most.*

The common belief that suffering is a form of inferiority.

Even if one is unproductive one provides energy.

He is a tent-peg. He enjoys being knocked into the ground to hold up any old liberal marquee.

'I must create a System, or be enslaved by another Man's.' *Blake.*

Sipping gin and vodka and having visions.

It is better to be a has-been than a never-was. (True then as it is now.)

If I am choleric, I am sanguine also.

'Melancholy men of all others are most witty.' *Anatomy of Melancholy.*

We need more character, instead of *fixed mechanisms*.

What few emotional successes he has, he regards as concessions.

Often neurotics are very irritable, but to prevent themselves from blazing up when provoked, they lapse into an attitude of apathy and become blasé. Alison is no more 'normal' than Jimmy.

People who complain of any character in a play being neurotic, are objecting to the theatrical method.

Critics: those who would send Hedda Gabler to the Marriage Guidance Council.

'If Dad wanted a packet of Woodbines, us kids would have to go without a loaf of bread.'

'He'd black her eyes. I've seen her eyes all swollen.'

> *Popular song:*
> 'Every day is mother's day to me
> Since I was a baby on her knee
> For what can take the place
> of that care-worn smiling face,
> a million angels in her eyes?
> Every night I say a simple prayer,
> praying she'll never know another care.
> The whole wide world will say—
> once a year is mother's day,
> but every day is mother's day to me.'

'Well, you know, half the people you're insulting, don't know you're getting at them.'

'Don't you see, Dad—they don't want you. People don't wear patent leather shoes any more.'
The old man wears: a stock, patent leather shoes, and spats.

'I belonged to the National Sporting Club, you know.'

'I was bucked to blazes'.

It's better to take the right road, and see the wrong thing.

Even a hunch can be noble.

It contains a large element of fire—incantation.

'My husband—he's had 39 operations but he's always managed to get to a vessel.'

'If I was a man, my balls would hurt.'

'Why are you here—it ain't raining?'

'Are you Jewish?'
'Not necessarily.'

All they do is worry about their balls.

He should have a licence for walking a thing like that round the park. If I see it again, I'll shoot it.

Evading Income Tax.
That isn't British.
No, but it's very Welsh.

Everyone acts in my name without bothering even to ask who I am.

How's your mother's syphilis?

Take my own case: I am governed by fear every day of my life. Sometimes it is the first sensation I have on waking. Even the thought that I have managed to escape death by waking up. Milk bottles. Air raid shelters. Boys in balaclava helmets. Fear in rooms at Kidderminster, at Derby. Money. The dentist's chair and adultery.
Try and make a note of every example of fear you manifest. It should keep you busy.

With creaking smile like a swinging gate.

She can have the top off my egg any day.

Notebook, 1955

I threw myself into painting the boat from stem to stern as if it were a pleasant collaboration in playmaking. Anthony spent most of his time making meals for us and sunbathing unwisely on deck while I splashed away with his Dulux. I received a letter from Kitty Black, which started off something like, 'I feel like the headmistress of a large school in which I have to tell its most promising pupil that he must think again.' It was a blow magisterially struck on behalf of her agency, and the West End. Miss Black said I must think again and Mr Desmond didn't even know what I was thinking about.

Shortly afterwards I had a phone call from Patrick who had arranged a production of the McCarthy play, *Personal Enemy* at Harrogate. I had long lost interest in this and wanted to know what he thought of *Look Back*. He was not simply vituperative but reproachful, as if I had betrayed the treasure of trust that he had put in my flimsy gifts and been almost physically faithless to Stella's memory. He went on for about half an hour. 'You've just got to make up your mind what you think you're going to do. I mean this simply won't do at all.' I listened unhurt. It was the shape of things to come and from the lower depths, the voice of what Sir Peter Hall at the National Theatre later described as his forecasters.

Lying on deck in August, I read in the *Stage* that a new company, the English Stage Company, had been formed with the object of producing new plays and particularly new plays by new writers. By this time I had both Pat's and Miss Black's copies, so I sent one of them to the Artistic Director, expecting a reply within months or an unreturned manuscript. I heard within days. The English Stage Company would pay me twenty-five pounds for an option on my play, and Mr Devine, the Tesman of Mr Siddiqui's disappointment, would like to arrange a meeting. Twenty-five pounds indicated the caution of Jimmy Wax on a day out, but compared to the response I had had from the Headmistress of Curtis Brown, Pat Desmond and Frith-from-just-across-the-corridor, it was acclaim.

I rang the number I had been given, hoping for the boyish, enthusiastic tones I remembered from George's Tesman. He seemed to answer the telephone reluctantly, barked for instructions on how to find me on the boat and slammed down the receiver.

On a sunny August afternoon in 1955, the time approached for George to arrive at the boat but there was no sign of him. I had tried to explain that the tides in the basin made it impossible for anyone to come aboard at certain hours of the day. Either I had not made myself clear or, in our very brief telephone conversation, he had not listened. I put on a blazer I'd bought in Derby and a pair of grey flannels and a clubbish-looking tie. The tide rose and the barge bobbed out of access. After two hours, as I was about to take off my Loamshire wardrobe, George appeared through the trees from the river, rowing himself in a small boat. Clambering aboard *M/Y Egret* enthusiastically, in an open-necked shirt and sandalled feet, he sounded just like Tesman again.

There was no question in my mind on that muggy August day that within less than a year—and on my father's birthday—*Look Back in Anger* would have opened, in what still seems like an inordinately long, sharp and glimmering summer.

275

In 1972 and twelve plays later, *A Sense of Detachment*, a play for which it might be gathered I have some affection, was to be produced in very different circumstances to the climate of wounded bafflement of 8 May. Begrudging rancour had long since been stock-piled, mobilized and had taken up its positions after the disbelief and disarray caused by George's '56 spring offensive. In the interval of that 1972 first night, I met a woman in the foyer who had frequented all my first nights for a time. I called her the Witch of Ongar, and she always said the same thing. 'You've done it this time, Osborne, you've *really done* it to yourself! You've finished it for yourself this time! You've really *done* it.' The Witch of Ongar has not approached me since then and I miss her.

Almost everyone agreed with her, including the *Financial Times*: 'This must surely be his farewell to the theatre.'

Index

Index

279

MORE ABOUT PENGUINS
AND PELICANS

For further information about books available from Penguins please write to Dept EP, Penguin Books Ltd, Harmondsworth, Middlesex UB7 0DA.

In the U.S.A.: For a complete list of books available from Penguins in the United States write to Dept CS, Penguin Books, 625 Madison Avenue, New York, New York 10022.

In Canada: For a complete list of books available from Penguins in Canada write to Penguin Books Canada Ltd, 2801 John Street, Markham, Ontario L3R 1B4.

In Australia: For a complete list of books available from Penguins in Australia write to the Marketing Department, Penguin Books Australia Ltd, P.O. Box 257, Ringwood, Victoria 3134.

In New Zealand: For a complete list of books available from Penguins in New Zealand write to the Marketing Department, Penguin Books (N.Z.) Ltd, P.O. Box 4019, Auckland 10.